TURNING TO STONE

ROMA SERIES
BOOK FOUR

GABRIEL VALJAN

This publication is a work of fiction. Names, characters, places, and incidents either are products of the author's imagination or are used fictitiously. This work is protected in full by all applicable copyright laws, as well as by misappropriation, trade secret, unfair competition, and other applicable laws. No part of this book may be reproduced or transmitted in any manner without written permission from Winter Goose Publishing, except in the case of brief quotations embodied in critical articles or reviews. All rights reserved.

Winter Goose Publishing
2701 Del Paso Road, 130-92
Sacramento, CA 95835

www.wintergoosepublishing.com
Contact Information: info@wintergoosepublishing.com

Turning To Stone

COPYRIGHT © 2015 Gabriel Valjan

First Edition, April 2015
ISBN: 978-1-941058-23-7

Cover Art by Winter Goose Publishing
Photograph by Claudio Ferrara
Fabell Medusa, Cimitero Monumentale, Milano.
Typeset by Odyssey Books

Published in the United States of America

ROMA SERIES
By Gabriel Valjan

Book 1 – Roma, Underground (2/2012)
Book 2 – Wasp's Nest (11/2012)
Book 3 – Threading the Needle (8/2013)

For Roberto Saviano

> La camorra è il solo potere reale al quale Napoli obbedisca.
> —Alexandre Dumas père
> Napoli, 14 marzo 1862

The Camorra is the only real power that Naples obeys.
—Alexander Dumas Sr
Naples, 14 March 1862

Characters

Alabaster Black aka **Bianca Nerini:** Former forensic accountant for a covert U.S. agency named Rendition, founded before laws against white-collar crimes were written. With bearer bonds from a former Rendition target, she fled to Italy. Girlfriend of Dante Allegretti.

Aldo Giurlani: A regional Commissioner in Lombardy, in northern Italy. His specialty is organized crime.

Alessandro Monotti: A junior investigator within the Guardia di Finanza (GdF), an Italian law enforcement agency that investigates illegal financial transactions, from money laundering to drug trafficking. He is an idealistic romantic with a poor track record. He is from Tuscany, educated in Salerno.

Amerigo Totaro: Head of a Camorra family clan, the Neapolitan mafia.

Claudio Ferrero: An investigative journalist with Turin newspaper, *La Stampa*.

Dante Allegretti: An investigator within the GdF. He is from Rome, and the boyfriend of Bianca Nerini.

Gennaro DiBello: A senior investigator within the GdF. He is a veteran of several landmark investigations into organized crime. He is from Naples.

Isidore Farrugia: A senior police detective, a commissario, now affiliated with the GdF. He is experienced in narcotics undercover work. He infiltrates the Totaro clan as Giuseppe. Farrugia hails from Calabria.

Loki: An unknown agent who communicates intelligence of questionable origin to Bianca.

Lorenzo Bevilacqua: The disgraced head of Amici di Roma, a cultural organization that he created as a front for smuggling and other activities, according to Bianca Nerini. He was never convicted.

Matteo Mandracchia: A rising venture capitalist with an interest in revitalizing the Neapolitan cultural scene.

Noelle: A yoga instructor from Milan, and girlfriend of Commissario Farrugia.

Pio Piersanti: Department head of the GdF in Naples.

Silvio: A former secretary, now junior investigator within the GdF and erstwhile English translator.

Special Agent McGarrity: An FBI agent with the Organized Crime Bureau, and partner of Special Agent Murphy. He has conducted special investigations with Italian authorities, often under the auspices of U.S. Attorney Farese.

Special Agent Murphy: An FBI agent with the Organized Crime Bureau, and partner of Special Agent McGarrity.

Stefano Pugliese: A mid-level Totaro leader and colleague of "Giuseppe."

Tommaso Baraldi: An intern at the GdF. He studies the sociology of criminal organizations.

U.S. Attorney Michael Farese: United States prosecutor who has collaborated with experts within the Italian legal system in operations against organized crime.

1

"We should go, Alessandro," Gennaro said.

"Just a minute, Boss. I'm waiting to see what the financial analysts have to say."

"We can listen to the news in the car."

"I know, but why wait when we can get the forecast now."

Alessandro, standing near the office's flat-screen television, clicker in hand, spiked the volume. Gennaro DiBello resigned himself to staring out of the high-rise window, overlooking the Bay of Naples. He saw a U.S. destroyer in the distance en route to Bagnoli.

Dante was putting his papers away before leaving for lunch. He put the stack into his desk drawer, locked it, and began the ritual of backing up his electronic files to a jump key and powering down his monitor. Living with Bianca was showing in his daily work habits. Silvio was at his desk, in his own world, with his own mound of paperwork, his Italian-English dictionary closed but ready.

"Here they are," Alessandro pointed the remote at the screen and stepped up the volume again. He was a defiant kid who had to get the last word, Gennaro thought.

Gennaro saw their boss, Pio Piersanti, approaching. "Incoming."

"What is it?" Alessandro said and, seeing Piersanti through the glass, shut off the television.

"What's the word, DiBello?" asked the man entering the room.

"The word is nothing."

"Monotti," Piersanti gestured toward Alessandro, "turn that back on. I want to see what they have to say."

The television screen crackled to life. A scrolling marquee on the bottom of the screen repeated Moody's judgment: Downgrade on Italian bonds.

Piersanti's face soured. "Shit. There goes the bond auction tomorrow." He turned from the screen to Gennaro and said, "Shouldn't you be on your way to meet with Giurlani, DiBello?"

"I am. We are. I'm waiting for them."

"Late lunch," Piersanti said, confirming the time on his wristwatch.

"Yes, and then we're back here to give our reports to you and Giurlani."

"Excellent. Giurlani has a lot faith in you and your group here. He pulled some serious strings to get your team transferred from Milan to Naples, including Isidore Farrugia. The Brooks murder was a PR nightmare. I don't know how he did it."

"I thought the answer was simple: Aldo Giurlani is the regional commissioner, and when Milan talks, Naples and Rome listen. If you'll excuse me, we should get going."

"I won't delay you. You and this crew of yours have healthy appetites so please don't kill me on the expense report. My boss might think I'm in bed with the System." *System* was local slang for the Camorra, the infamous Naples crime syndicate.

Pio Piersanti, Gennaro's new boss, was a decent man, with an alliterative and triplet of holy names. Unlike Pinolo, Gennaro's former boss in Rome, he wasn't a penny-pincher or a ball-breaker. Perego, their boss in Milan, was supposed to come to Naples, but was called away to another investigation.

"*Dottore?*" It was Enzo, the mail clerk.

"Something for me?"

"Yes. I have a package. You'll have to sign for it."

"What is it?"

"Books in English. All the same title and author," the young man answered.

Gennaro's name and address were typed out. No name in the sender space. All rather peculiar, Gennaro mumbled. He hadn't forgotten the heightened security measures. The postmark was days old because the Neapolitan Guardia di Finanza Security downstairs used canine units for sniffing out suspicious parcels for chemicals and explosives. Security was not victim to Italy's latest austerity measures.

Gennaro signed and handed over the clipboard. Enzo left and Alessandro, Dante, and Silvio gathered around him as he examined the contents. The enclosed books were rubber-banded together. Five copies.

"What is it, Chief? Looks like a thin volume. Poetry?"

"You're just like a kid, Sandro. You know that?"

Dante looked at the cardboard mailer and noticed the postmark. "Better for a package to be late than have someone go to pieces. Literally. Security probably dusted this for prints."

"C'mon, Boss. What is the title?" Alessandro pestered.

"*The Man of Smoke*. Aldo Palazzeschi, a dead writer," Gennaro answered.

"Why five copies, Chief? And why in English?" Alessandro asked.

"How the hell should I know?" Gennaro said, as his eyebrows lifted. "There are four of us here. One for each of us, I guess, but that leaves one extra copy."

Dante took his copy and then another. They all looked at him.

"One for Bianca since she is part of the team. Now, let's go meet the commissioner for lunch. The elevator is waiting. Shall we?"

Alessandro said to Gennaro when the bell chimed, "Palazzeschi was the pen name for Aldo Giurlani."

"I know, Sandro. He was an anti-Fascist."

Commissioner Aldo Giurlani, who had worked with them in Milan, insisted on meeting the group in the city center for lunch. A public place was best, he had said, but had kept his travel itinerary secret. All Gennaro knew was the name of the restaurant, the appointed hour, and that the commissioner was arriving by car with a modest security detail. The commissioner, who had been receiving death threats, was fast becoming a worthy successor of Paolo Borsellino and Giovanni Falcone for his innovative strategies against organized crime.

Gennaro, at the wheel, was stalled in a stagnant sea of cars on Via San Biagio. They heard them in the distance, but could not see any emergency vehicles in the side-view mirror. *Nee-nah. Nee-nah.*

"What the hell is going on?" Alessandro said in the backseat.

"No idea," Gennaro answered, peering in his side-view mirror.

People were running on foot between cars, around them, like water over rocks. The flood of flesh was fleeing like hordes of humanity in a science-fiction film. Gennaro gripped the wheel, seeking some escape with his small Fiat Punto. He had navigated the construction site near the Greek and Roman ruins, passed remnants of colonial rule, ignored the Fascist architecture of Banca di Napoli on Via Toledo. Yet there he sat, stranded, adrift, among motionless cars, surrounded by people on foot. As he surveyed the congestion as far as the eye could see, he realized he could get out of his Punto, walk over to the Banca Commerciale Italiana, visit the Caravaggio on the second floor, and light a votive before any car began to move again.

Sandro's finger tapped his shoulder. "There's a lollipop." One of the carabinieri, a blue-suited policeman with a Stop-and-Go paddle, had come out to direct traffic.

Gennaro rolled the window down. The policeman's torso neared his window. Gennaro showed his identification before he asked for an explanation. There was the intimation of smoke in the summer air: Gennaro could smell it. The policeman held up his lollipop and peered down and surveyed the group inside the car. The policeman tipped his hat.

"There's been a car bombing in the Spanish Quarter on Via San Gregorio Armeno."

"Camorra?"

The officer shrugged. "Perhaps. I can use my whistle to move you to the curb."

"We're supposed to meet someone for lunch."

"I'm afraid that you're not going anywhere, unless you can fly. I will direct you to the side of the road. Park there and call your party on your cell phone. You will be at least half an hour late. They still have to cordon off the scene."

"Damn," Gennaro said. He slapped the steering wheel hard. He decided to admit defeat. He said to the cop, "That'll do, thank you."

After several loud whistle blows and slow, painful cuts of the wheel and hostile stares from other drivers, Gennaro managed to squeeze his Punto near the curb. His parallel parking would have failed a driver's exam. Giurlani was going to be pissed off, but what could he do?

"Let's get out and see what we can make of the scene," he told his passengers. Dante exited from the passenger side, Alessandro and Silvio maneuvered out of the backseat. Once he was on the sidewalk, Gennaro flipped open the cell phone and speed-dialed Giurlani. Without saying a word they started walking uphill in the direction of the acrid stench until they saw wisps of black and grey smoke.

"No luck getting through to Giurlani?" Dante asked.

"I'm trying, but he's not picking up."

Dante's own cell phone began to ring. He fished it out of his jacket pocket. "*Pronto* . . . Isidò? Where are you?" Dante stood still and the rest waited for him to say something. Dante cupped the receiver. "Farrugia heard about the car bombing. He's at the restaurant. I'll tell him that we'll be late." A few words later Dante closed his phone.

They traversed the cobblestones together. Farrugia had been working undercover to track the Camorra's trade in steroids and recreational drugs. Narcotics work was where he had started his career until he became an anti-mafia expert. Illicit drugs in Naples were yet another hothouse of endless euros for the System.

"It smells nasty," Alessandro said, squinting his eyes and coughing.

"Burnt rubber and melting plastic are the worst," Dante said while Gennaro tried Giurlani again on his cell phone. Dante noticed but didn't say a word.

"No answer," Gennaro said, snapping the cell phone shut.

The stench and smoke worsened as they crested the hill. They saw the car and several policemen across the street. Firemen had yet to arrive. The car and its contents were nothing now but crackling flames and twisted steel. The top of the car had been sheared off at a jagged angle. A torso in what was the driver's seat was still visible, smoldering, as well as the shape of an arm and a hand faithful to the wheel. The passenger in the backseat was nothing more than a charcoal stump of charred flesh. Gennaro thought of the late Vonnegut, *Slaughterhouse Five*, and fried jumbo grasshoppers.

Alessandro, flashing his badge, called over to one of the cops, who began walking toward them. "What happened?" Alessandro asked.

"Witnesses said the car was coming down the street when three motorcyclists ambushed it. One motorcyclist came out in front to block the car. The driver jammed on his brakes. Two gunmen with Kalashnikovs on the other motorcycles sprayed the car while the one in front took out a bazooka or an RPG and fired it into the car."

The young policeman pointed to the ejected shell casings and shattered glass on the stony street.

"A bazooka, an RPG?" Alessandro asked. "I wouldn't expect witnesses to know the difference between a bazooka and a rocket-propelled grenade." Alessandro wiped his tearing eyes. "Did any of the witnesses have anything to say about the gunmen or the victims?"

"Not really. The motorcyclists wore helmets, visors down. Three men were in the car. We'll know more once we trace the plates."

"Camorristi with AK-47s. Typical," Dante said.

Gennaro, like the rest of them, looked at the license plate. Milan.

Dante said, "Maybe you should call Giurlani again, Chief?"

"That won't be necessary."

"Why not?"

"Still have that book?"

"It's in the car. Why?"

"Because the books were a message." Gennaro stared at the car wreck. His eyes seemed distant and immune to the smoke.

A confused Alessandro asked, "What is he talking about?"

"Aldo Palazzeschi was a pen name. You said so yourself, Sandro."

"For Aldo Giurlani, why?"

Gennaro nudged his chin at the wreckage. "Dante's book might be in my car, but Giurlani is in that one."

Alessandro stared at Gennaro for an explanation.

"That's the message. Our Commissioner Giurlani is now a man of smoke."

Gennaro started the descent back to his car.

Nee-nah. Nee-nah. The sirens had arrived.

2

Bianca's morning had started out differently. She had spent the night in the chair at her desk importing and scrubbing data. Dante had stumbled out of bed, yawned, showered, and eaten breakfast. "Dinner with Giurlani tonight," he had mumbled to her, before he left, giving her a peck on the cheek. He saw the Excel spreadsheets on the screen. He asked her to call him later.

She finished the data import. Like the good analyst she knew herself to be, she checked and then re-checked all the formulae and tested all links, cell by cell, row after row, tab after tab. All was in order. This packet weighed several hundred kilobytes and should enable the Guardia di Finanza to dent the Camorra's latest scam.

Bianca took a sip of her French roast coffee. Nice and smoky. She watched the files fly from folder to filing cabinet inside the dialog box. She was uploading the data to a separate server different and remote from the two Guardia di Finanza offices in Naples.

Insurance. Just in case there was some "accidental" deletion. Corruption.

With both her hands around the warm ceramic cup, she thought of bed, perhaps a nap on their Bellora linen sheets from Milan, her head resting on her soft pillow. She opened her eyes. The status bar, its squares all green, said "Complete." She was feeling lazy tired and as if she were about to doze off, when she heard a ping. IM chat.

She watched and waited. It could mean only one thing.

"How's it going, girl?"

That was a new opening. Only thing missing was the booming hip-hop bass and gangsta signs from Loki's avatar.

"Fine. I'm too tired to talk," she responded from the keyboard.

Loki's avatar was on the screen. It was odd how animation could be simultaneously erotic and artificial. Bianca sipped her coffee. She had retired her avatar and was using an empty shadowbox with the silhouette of a female head. Unoriginal and uninspired.

"Just a small convo? A little one?" the Norse trickster with cleavage said, holding up two fingers that it squeezed from wide to narrow. Small talk.

"Sure."

Knees to chest for comfort, Bianca read the status bar. Loki was typing.

"Have u read any Puig?" Bianca had not seen that coming. Loki was going literary.

"Manuel Puig? Not much. I read *Rita Hayworth* long time ago. I saw the movie *Kiss of the Spider Woman*."

Emoticon. She hated that. The avatar smiled, the eyes changed color, the gender changed, a prelude to business. Loki was serious.

"Itsy bitsy . . ."

Bianca answered: ". . . spider."

The Norse god's face leaned in, gave her a smirk, then a sexy blink of the eye before the horned head pulled back. Loki morphed back into a female and started doing a striptease on her screen with music and lights. Bianca was too tired to be annoyed. Loki was amusing.

She continued to sip her coffee and waited. They had a history, from their first contact with the Roma Underground scandal, the stolen relics, and Amici di Roma fencing them on the market, to Boston and Nasonia, where they investigated wasp genetics and Cyril Sargent's rush to change cancer research; and then most recently, Milan and the Gladioesque operation that had included two murders and had nearly cost Farrugia his career.

Rendition, Bianca's former employer, had lurked throughout it all in the background, like a fog that never quite took shape. Big Red R, as she referred to Rendition, had remained a covert U.S. organization, doing more than investigating financial crimes.

"U must be bored," Loki typed.

She put down her coffee. "U improved ur dancing. Should I be bored with that?"

"No, bored with credit or debit scam ur working on. Child's play. Ur talent is being wasted."

"Just helping DA & Co out." Bianca used Dante's initials. Dante Allegretti.

"Up 4 a real challenge?" The avatar crossed his arms. Norse OG.

She thought about the pose: Loki was posing Original Gangsta minus gold chains and urban clothes. She decided to be playful.

"U coming on 2 me?"

A question mark was the reply. This made her pause. Claudio Ferrero, the *La Stampa* journalist in Milan, had hypothesized that Loki was not an American, but an Italian. He had acknowledged Silvio as the source for that insight. She let the question mark go without an explanation.

"A project on ur mind, huh?"

"Y" for *Yes*. Loki continued typing: "Much more interesting than cataloging and tracking iPhone pictures. Card numbers in front, security codes on back. Tedious. Unexciting credit-debit card crap. Only excitement is tie-in with Yugo mafia." The avatar yawned. "B-O-R-I-N-G" appeared next in bold. She had just finished reading the text when Loki italicized "BORING."

"Whom does Big Red want this time?" She typed fast. She wanted to know what and whom Rendition was targeting this time.

The avatar tsk-tsked. "My own initiative."

First time Loki claimed ownership.

She typed her response slowly. "No R?" It was intriguing. "Loki goes alone?"

"R has interest but the angle is my own. Complete discretion & latitude."

Bianca's fingers rested mute on the keyboard. Rendition policy was that once assignments were accepted, analysts were expected to complete them, and if they were in danger they were on their own. Her fingers moved. Loki must have run into a wall and needed help.

Gabriel Valjan **11**

"What is R's interest in Naples? Camorra?"

No answer.

"Ur interest?" she rephrased her question.

Loki responded: "The System but there's a twist."

Always a twist with Rendition, she thought. Bianca's hands were tense above the keys, almost cramped, ready to act. Her eyes reread the last two lines. An American would say *mafia, organized crime*, but an Italian, specifically a Neapolitan, would say *System*. Capital *S*. She wondered about this "twist."

"I'm listening," she answered.

"Let's resume the game." Now this was typical Loki.

"Sure."

"Itsy bitsy . . ."

Bianca repeated: ". . . spider . . ."

"Y did the spider come out?" Loki asked.

Bianca sang the nursery rhyme and even did the hand motions to imitate the climbing spider and falling water before she typed, "Rain came and washed it out."

Loki's avatar gave her a pleased look. Nursery rhymes contained hidden parables, but all Bianca could think was that this chat was heading for a discourse on meteorology. She could turn on the news and get the weather. Loki was typing whatever was next about spiders. She waited for the text to appear on her screen. It came.

"Y does the spider live in the spout?"

"IDK" for *I don't know.*

Bianca silently mouthed the verse. *Down came the rain, and washed the spider out*, and then, *Out came the sun, and dried up all the rain*, and she remembered the next line, *and the itsy bitsy spider went up . . .*

She typed, "Spiders must like damp, dark places."

The striptease music kicked up and Loki was back to doing a pole dance. Wow. Loki had moves. Bianca strummed her fingers on the mouse, thinking about the rhyme and the spout.

"They like dark places." Loki repeated the answer.

Bianca typed, "But don't spiders hate water?"

"Nope. Some spiders can walk on water. Rain or shine there's a spider. You just have to get them out of the dark places. And don't forget . . ."

The ellipses infuriated Bianca, as did the background music.

"Forget what?"

The music stopped. Loki was typing. Bianca waited.

"The female spider is the dangerous one. The male spider has to be clever."

"Great. Thanks," she typed, hitting the keys with force.

The avatar switched to female. Stared at her and started typing again.

"I could joke and say that spiders fear wasps most but that would be in poor taste." Bianca referred to the Nasonia case and Cyril Sargent's wasps. It was a bad joke after what she had gone through in Boston. No answer was her answer. Bianca waited.

"Once the spider is out. You have to know which one is the smart one and which one is the dangerous one."

She read the line and thought it confusing. What is there to know? The female spider was often larger and the male, smaller, and often a post-coital meal for her and his future kids. Loki often confused gender and number. She highlighted with her mouse: "Once the spider is out." Which spider—male or female?

"What? Which?" Bianca typed. "Camorra?" she added.

"System," the female form of Loki answered and blinked nice green eyes at her, and typed, "Oh."

"Oh, what?" Bianca answered.

The avatar pointed to the side of the screen where her avatar should have been and typed, "Like 2 see what u look like these days. I miss the handcuffs." Then Loki tapped the side of the screen again.

Bianca typed, "Patience. Next time I'll have an avatar."

"No, not that," Loki answered.

Bianca was confused. "What?"

Gabriel Valjan **13**

Loki was typing.

"Got to go. Expect a phone call soon."

Their IM went dead and her cell phone near the side of her screen rang. She stared at the docking station. While the cell phone rang, she surveyed the open box of SIM cards, which were organized like microscope slides. The phone continued to ring. It was Dante.

"*Pronto.*"

"It's me."

"I know that. What is it, Dante?" she asked, running her free hand through her hair. "I didn't get any sleep. I'll be ready with your report for the commissioner this afternoon. Then we'll all go . . ."

"Forget about that, Bianca."

"You sound upset. Was there a change of plans?"

"You can say that. Giurlani is dead."

"What?!"

Bianca stood up from the chair. She felt the blood drain from her face. Her ass hurt, her hamstrings were tight, and her lower back was also sore.

"What happened?"

Dante's voice was calm. "When he got into town, his car was diverted to a side street because of flooding. A water main had broken or some other bullshit reason having to do with construction. His car took a narrow street where he was ambushed. Killed in broad daylight. It'll be on the news soon."

Bianca heard Dante's voice saying something about motorcycles and a rocket. She thought "water" and "rain" instead; she imagined a waterspout and a narrow street, and sunlight, lots and lots of warm sunlight.

"Bianca?" A pause. "Did you hear me?"

She looked at the screen, the dead IM chat, and she thought about the rhyme.

"Bianca?"

"Yes. I heard you. Giurlani is dead. Rain or shine, a spider comes out."

"A spider? What?"

She told him that she'd explain when they met at the office.

3

The air-conditioning, the clear glass, the vacuumed rug with its faint apple scent, made the conference room seem artificial. The overhead projector, intended for their presentations, sat in the middle of the polished table. They had skipped lunch. No appetite. Words were useless right now. They sat around the table waiting for Piersanti, staring off, numb and cold from the air-conditioning and Giurlani's killing.

Gennaro got up from his seat, went over to the window, and looked out at the water in search of calmness. The weather had been unseasonably hot in and around Naples, the islands included, but no thunderstorms were in the forecast. The sky remained blue, though in the evenings occasional plumes of dark clouds or some spirals of wind-stretched formations would appear. Mediterranean serenity. Postcard-perfect. The sea continued to move as it had moved since the time of Homer, swelling and surging, and from a distance, sleeping. Gennaro knew it was all a lie.

"The question now is whether the Totaro or Marra clans were behind it," Dante said.

Silence.

Gennaro was the first to speak. "Much as I'd love for it to be the Totaros I can't go fishing for an excuse to go after them for Giurlani. That would make me no better than them. That would be vendetta, their way and not mine. We need evidence, and I mean hard incontrovertible evidence, that they assassinated him."

Everyone stared at him. They knew that the Totaro clan had ordered his wife's murder; they knew that the Totaro clan was at the top of the list of powerful families in Naples. Investigating the Camorra, the Totaro and Marra feud with exactitude and decisive strategy, was exactly why Giurlani had handpicked Gennaro and let him form his own team.

The commissioner had hoped that the war between these two powerful Camorra families would weaken the System enough for the authorities to reduce it down to something manageable. Alessandro cleared his throat.

"You have something to say, Sandro?"

"We should trace the package. That was an obvious message. Both you and Dante had noticed the postmark. It had been mailed days ago."

"What package?" Bianca asked.

Dante put the book on the table and mentioned in a low whisper that five copies had been sent inside the package. She examined the book. She fanned a few of the pages. Mondadori reprint.

"Gennaro?" He glanced over at her.

"Alessandro is right. This was orchestrated and I know that you're thinking of Falcone, but that was different and—"

Nobody wanted to think about the infamous assassination of magistrate Giovanni Falcone. His last investigation was about to expose mafia connections to the Italian government.

"Yeah, it was different. Giovanni was killed with his wife Francesca and his entourage on an open highway. Aldo Giurlani was cornered like a dog on some congested street where old ladies hung up their laundry." His face was red, his anger visceral. Understandable. "Two months later Falcone's ally, Paolo Borsellino, is killed with a bomb outside his mother's house. Men of smoke, indeed!" he said and returned to his seat.

She watched him. They all did.

"I'm frustrated and I'm embarrassed. I din't see this coming. I thought it should have been me and not Aldo. Me and not Lucia. I'm here in Naples. He was in Milan."

Bianca's voice attempted a calm tone. "Falcone was in Rome and had come to Palermo when he was killed. He was demoted. You weren't. Yes, it could've been you, but we all know—everyone in this room knows—that Giurlani's murder is a sign of power. Let's make sure that in two months you're not Borsellino."

"Bianca!" Dante said. "Show some sensitivity for God's sake."

"I'm speaking the truth and you know it."

"She's right, Dante," Gennaro said. "We should be thinking about what we do next. This is a game of chess."

It was Bianca who got up from the table this time. She started to walk the room.

"It doesn't matter who makes the next move. If the Totaros make a play, the Marra clan will watch and see if the Totaros make a mistake and act on that weakness, unless, of course . . ."

"Unless, what?" Alessandro asked.

Gennaro answered, "Unless it was a concerted effort and they've formed an alliance."

Dante was stroking the spine of the book. "Great. Just what we need."

He knew that Bianca was thinking while she paced. She did it all the time in the apartment when they talked about work. Gennaro was also watching her.

"It's not unheard of. This package; doesn't this seem, even for the System, to be a little . . . uh, intellectual? I mean, from what I've seen, Camorristi seem more interested in getting laid, talking trash, and flexing their muscles, not their gray matter. This book," she pointed at the copy under Dante's caressing hand, "is an example of Futurist literature, early twentieth-century. It's an educated and intelligent reader's choice."

"They could've picked it for the title. You know, symbolic," Alessandro said.

"That could be the case," Bianca said, "but, like you said, somebody knew Giurlani's itinerary. It was mailed before he arrived and delivered the day he dies. Coincidence? This means that somebody close to him was involved. Giurlani was a careful man."

"Not careful enough," Dante interrupted.

Bianca seemed to ignore Dante's remark. "This somebody wasn't some thug who'd overheard a phone conversation or paid off the travel secretary. This had to be somebody on the inside, high up, close to Aldo, in Milan, and who had a contact in Naples, and . . ."

"And what?" Alessandro asked.

"Piersanti is coming."

Those seated looked over their shoulders. Piersanti knocked and then entered the room. He had somebody else waiting outside the conference door. Piersanti's tie was yanked down and his left ear was red from too many telephone conversations. His cuffs were peeled back and he appeared distressed. His dark stubble was coming in uneven and it made him appear haggard and sloppy. He was so dazed that he had even left the door behind him ajar.

"I know this is terrible timing but I have an announcement."

Silence.

"Do you remember me telling you about the intern?" he said, directing the question at Gennaro. Everyone turned to Gennaro, whose face crimsoned. He rose slowly from his chair, knuckles on the table like a gorilla. Shit was about to fly.

"This is bad, bad timing. I do remember, but please, not now. Send the kid back. Apologize to the university or something. You must understand what we're going through. We have a situation."

Piersanti's voice just about cracked when he answered, "I know, and I would if I could, but you have to understand, this is a special case."

"And Aldo Giurlani's murder isn't special?" Gennaro said. "C'mon Piersanti, I beg of you. Do I have to pray to both Padre Pio and Saint Peter to talk some sense into you so you might show me some compassion?"

"But this intern," Piersanti leaned forward, whispering then. "This intern . . . this particular intern, had been sent here at Giurlani's request, his personal recommendation. Here."

Gennaro grabbed at the sheet of paper Piersanti was handing him. It was the intern's CV. Gennaro read it.

"With all due respect to you and the commissioner's memory, this kid hasn't even graduated. He's a philosopher, for God's sake."

"Sociologist, actually," Piersanti said, pointing to a line on the paper.

"Fine, he's a sociologist," Gennaro snapped. "You might as well say that he's a poet. Do I look like I need someone long on ideas and short on real-world experience? At least give me a law student or a finance person so I can put a hook into these bastards." Gennaro's face was reddening. "This is the System, Piersanti. The Camorra. These are seasoned killers without scruples. Real bastards." He pointed at Bianca. "Ask her about the last young man she knew who had bright ideas and enthusiasm. Ask her how that went in Milan."

Bianca blushed this time. The air-conditioner had stopped because it was on energy-saver mode. The room was colder.

Piersanti seemed emphatic. "Giurlani sent him to us, Gennaro. He must've had a reason."

"What the hell does a twenty-two-year-old know about the Camorra?"

There was the sound of a cough and the sound of a door clicking shut. They all turned. They saw a young man in jeans, fresh loafers, no socks, in a powder-blue shirt opened at the collar, without a tie. Nice handsome northern face, clean-shaven. He had an intense, serious face. As the young man proceeded to answer, Gennaro looked away, embarrassed.

"What I know is this: the Camorra that you see today, the one out there in the slums and suburbs, it's changing and mutating. The Camorra is evolving and becoming smart. Sure, money will be made the old way, but there'll be a new face in the leadership, an unknowable, barely recognizable face. There will be no more dirty tank-tops and incomprehensible dialect. No more *Neomelodica* music and thugs thinking they are glamorous American mafiosi from the movies. No, the System is changing."

The intern walked in slow measured steps down one side of the room while he continued his presentation.

"The lower-level stuff, like drugs, the prostitution, and the gun-running—that will be delegated to ethnic immigrants. Take your pick: former Yugoslavians from either the north or south or both. The Eastern Europeans can do the work. The mid-level stuff, the more sophisticated enterprises like construction, and waste management, will also migrate into other hands. Managerial restructuring. The Chinese will still have the fake goods, illegal textile factories, and illegal immigration. What is the future, you ask the sociologist?"

He paused after "sociologist."

"I'll tell you. The new Camorristi 'weapon' won't be Kalashnikovs. He'll use cell phones and champagne cocktails. His world will not be the stench of Neapolitan garbage in August. His streets will be the financial corridors of London, Paris, Rome, Switzerland, and the United States. The new weapons are bonds, futures, and stocks. The method? Manipulation and blading economies."

The young man paused again. He had seen their eyes squint when he used the phrase "blading economies."

Alessandro scoffed: "No offense, kid, but there are two clans out there, the Totaros and the Marras, and Naples is their turf. They are at war. There will be plenty of body bags first."

The young man returned to the spot where he had entered the room. He stood between Piersanti and Gennaro. "You're right. There is a war now, but it won't last long. Whoever is left standing around will work together and run the low-level stuff with the Eastern Europeans. You might think it's unlikely, but you saw for yourself how convincing an Eastern European could be when you were in Rome. You'd met an attractive Hungarian woman while working on the Amici di Roma case. Wasn't she persuasive?"

Alessandro squirmed in his seat. Bianca touched his shoulder. This kid had done his research. He knew about the Roma Underground scandal.

"And don't count Amici di Roma out." Bianca's head turned to look at the young man. "That's right," he said. "Multinational companies want to do business with the new System. The real power that will emerge from this transformation will be the power that runs Naples; it will form mergers with the 'Ndrangheta in Calabria and then with the Sicilians and extend its way up the peninsula to Rome, the Vatican, and Milan."

"That's like saying Pepsi will absorb Coca-Cola," Dante remarked.

"They'll have no choice because the new breed of Camorristi that is consolidating now is smart. They're Bocconi-educated and they'll have their advanced degrees from Harvard and Wharton and some will even go to the London School of Economics. They learned their lessons from the American gangsters who made Cosa Nostra legitimate. They learned from the Jewish 'affiliates,' like Rothstein and Lansky, and then from Charlie Luciano, Frank Costello, and Carlo Gambino."

"And you think this new generation will be instantly accepted? It takes generations for acceptance," Dante said.

"I do. They're ready to do business with everyone, including the Americans, and they'll state their own business terms; and everyone, from Milan to the Vatican, Naples to Palermo, will listen because there is money to be made. The money they offer is in the billions and very clean, with no connection to violence."

"And you know this how?" Alessandro asked.

The youth gave them a sly smile. "I'll explain more of that later, but suffice it to say that I study groups and dynamics, Mr. Monotti."

"I see that you know my name."

"Of course I do. I did my homework. I knew about your Hungarian girlfriend in Rome, didn't I? I also know about the ballistics expert from Bergamo."

Alessandro clenched his jaw and looked out the window. The kid had called him out on his second shortcoming in Milan while Farrugia was investigated for Charlie Brooks's murder.

The young student walked over to Bianca and extended his hand to her. She instinctively accepted it and, as they shook, he said, "I especially look forward to working with you, Signora Nerini. Commissioner Giurlani spoke highly of you."

"Thank you. And what is your name?" she asked.

"Tommaso Baraldi. Now, if you will all excuse me, I need to find my desk. *Dottore* Piersanti will give you the other news."

Baraldi closed the door behind him again. There was a dead silence until the door had clicked shut.

Gennaro motioned at the door. "Some kid there. What other news is he talking about, *dottore*?"

"Old friends of yours—two of them—from the United States, are coming to visit you."

"Who and why?" Gennaro asked.

"Agents Murphy and McGarrity."

"Why?"

"They are here to study the Camorra. Ever since Falcone was assassinated the FBI and the Italian government have had a special relationship regarding organized crime. You know that U.S. Attorney Rudy Giuliani had worked with Falcone. Make the best of it. They could help us with Giurlani's assassination."

Gennaro sighed. "Great, we lose Silvio as a resource because he'll have to chaperone and translate for them."

"Actually, Silvio doesn't have to," Piersanti answered with his first smile of the day.

"Why not? They have their own translator?" Silvio asked.

Piersanti answered, "These two are recipients of some kind of FBI scholarship in Borsellino and Falcone's names. They come highly recommended with letters of recommendation."

Gennaro ran his fingers along the inside of his belt. "They do, do they?"

"Yes. The letter is from U.S. Attorney Michael Farese." Bianca now glanced over at the window.

"And, Gennaro." Piersanti said.

"What?"

"Be nice to the kid. Remember that Aldo sent him."

"How could I forget? Thank you."

Gennaro walked over to the window. Another destroyer on maneuvers was in the distance. The sea was blue, looked calm, but he felt like

Odysseus; like Odysseus, he would have to keep his eyes open with toothpicks in order to weather the storm that was coming.

4

Alessandro had chosen the restaurant. Sushi. He was sitting with Bianca, Dante, and Gennaro. They were waiting for Farrugia. Both Bianca and Gennaro were certain that Farrugia would not like sushi. Gennaro himself had balked at the idea of raw fish, but Alessandro advocated for the culinary experience. "Live life a little, Boss," he had said.

Gennaro was not convinced. He had the recurring image of sharp knives and small gourmet blowtorches. Christ may have done his miracle with fish, but would sushi do it for a meal, for Commissario Isidore Farrugia on his day off, who had spent his week north of the city with drug-selling and drug-using scum? Gennaro had thought about the sanitation crew who had to scatter sawdust at the scene to absorb the debris and oil so that it all could be swept up, the street hosed clean.

"The chef here studied with Andrea Aprea," Alessandro said, menu in hand. Gennaro said nothing as he perused the menu, trying to understand Japanese dishes phonetically transformed into ichthyic Italian. He labored with the text, avoiding the glossy pictures meant for children and illiterates.

"Isidò should be here any moment. I can't imagine what his week was like."

"I tried calling him on his cell," Alessandro said to Bianca after he had taken a sip of some iced water.

"And?" Gennaro asked as he turned the third stiff page of his menu.

"No answer."

Gennaro's eyes continued with his menu; he wondered whether there was some southern superstition he could invoke to avoid food poisoning. The fishermen of his youth used prayers to avert Neptune's wrath. Uncooked fish did seem against the natural order of human digestion.

Alessandro asked that the waiter return in five minutes. Farrugia was usually punctual. Gennaro squinted for confirmation. The waiter had a multicolored Mohawk. Bianca had noticed it too. The sculpted shark fin of hair seemed to tilt and glide away into the restaurant's dim lighting.

Just then Farrugia walked in. Alessandro half-stood up to be seen. Farrugia found them. He had to have gone to his in-town apartment first because Farrugia looked rejuvenated in his earth-tone summer suit and immaculate white shirt. He sat down after kisses and greetings. He looked lithe and lean from regular yoga practice. His girlfriend was a yoga instructor in Milan. The only unsettling aspect to Farrugia's appearance was his beard that he grew out for undercover work.

"Noelle has been trying to get me to try this place," Farrugia said.

"Really? How is she? Oh, here comes Jaws," said Gennaro.

"Fine." Farrugia accepted a menu, noticed the Mohawk before he requested still water. Jaws poured the water and recited the evening specials. He would give them a few more minutes.

Dante said, "Next time, we'll invite her. I know she's on holiday soon."

"Yoga conference," Farrugia corrected.

"Right. Sorry. I feel bad that we didn't invite Silvio, but we wanted to tell you about developments at the office."

Bianca pointed out something to Dante on the menu. Gennaro tried like a cheating student to sneak a peek.

"Haven't a clue what to order," he said.

Farrugia closed his menu. "What developments are we talking about? I can only imagine that Piersanti is up to his ears with Milan and Rome on the phone. Giurlani's assassination is going to be national news."

"It already is," Gennaro said. "Damn, how complicated can ordering fish be?"

Farrugia folded his napkin on his lap. "I know that it is news in Turin. Ferrero called me on my cell. Naturally, I couldn't divulge anything."

Gennaro looked up, concerned. "Ferrero? *La Stampa* Ferrero?"

"Do you know any other famous journalists?"

"What did you tell him?"

"I already told you. Nothing. What is there for me to tell him, Gennaro?"

"How did your inquiring-journalist-yoga-partner accept that?"

"Fine, Gennaro. Fine. He was very professional about it."

"Jaws," said Alessandro.

Pen in hand, the waiter took their orders and collected their menus. Gennaro was the last to order, the guest with the most questions. He ended the patient waiter's misery by requesting a sake martini. This surprised them.

"What? I was curious. I want to live a little. Now . . ." Gennaro said and proceeded to update Farrugia. He summarized Tommaso Baraldi's analysis of the Camorra for Farrugia, the young man's academic background also. Gennaro reiterated Baraldi's argument as to why he would be an asset to Piersanti, to them, and the Guardia di Finanza Napoli. The martini arrived and they watched Gennaro take a taste sip. He approved.

"Did you say 'sociologist'?" Farrugia asked.

"I did. No degree yet but I've got to say he's confident. When you're twenty-two, why aim low?"

"I'll say," Alessandro muttered.

Dante offered a laugh and a teasing elbow into Alessandro's ribs. "You're just annoyed because he alluded to your Hungarian girlfriend in Rome and then—"

"I know. I know . . . Paola, the ballistics expert from Bergamo. I'll never live them down."

"Learn to pick your women better," Bianca said.

"Thanks."

Bianca spoke next. "This Tommaso might be a kid, but he's done his homework. We've got to give him credit for that. He came prepared. He kept his head straight after Giurlani was hit. He knew about Alessandro's girlfriend, which means he knew about the Amici di Roma, which also means he knows all about Lorenzo Bevilacqua."

"He wasn't upset when he heard that Giurlani had been killed?" Farrugia asked.

"If he *was* upset, we didn't hear it or see it," Dante said.

Gennaro raised his martini glass. "Let Bianca finish."

"Thank you. He suggested that Lorenzo might still be in the picture. He also knew about Brooks in Milan, possibly read Isidò's file with Internal Affairs and the ballistics report. I'll assume, for the time being, that he had educated himself on all of us while he was becoming Giurlani's top choice. A law clerk I could see, but Giurlani and a future sociologist? How did Giurlani and Baraldi find each other?"

"That's a lot of mystery for a twenty-two-year-old," said Farrugia.

Gennaro's face was pink from his martini. "No doubt that Baraldi has read my jacket. He seems to have an understanding of the System and where it is headed. He mentioned 'evolution' and a new leadership. We might not know what all that means, but we will soon. But something else bothers me about our boy professor."

"What is that?" Bianca asked.

"He said that he was looking forward to working with you. Do you think he knows about Boston and your work with the little vespas?" By "vespas" Gennaro had meant Sargent and the wasp genome.

Alessandro mumbled, "Something else bothers me about him, too . . ."

"Do you have something to say?" Gennaro said.

"I do, in fact. I'm sore that this little wiseass came out of nowhere and that he knew about my indiscretions. I'll admit that those were *my* screw-ups, but this is what I don't get." He paused and looked around the table at each of them. "He knew that McGarrity and Murphy were coming before he left the room. Did you catch that? You know damn well he had to have read Farese's letter. That just makes me wonder . . ." Sandro's voice faded.

"Say it, Sandro," Bianca said.

"Do you think he knows about Bianca and Rendition? I'm just saying that we were all there and we all watched him gush on about how he was looking so forward to working with her. Not even out of school, out of nowhere, and he has the cheek to lord over Piersanti, right in the man's own office, the little bastard; and if that's not enough, he reminds him, almost as an afterthought, to tell us about McGarrity and Murphy . . . I'm just saying."

Gennaro had finished his martini. "Stop saying 'just saying.' It makes you sound like some twit on an American sitcom. Know what I mean?" Gennaro winked as he put his glass down on the table, thinking those two English-language colloquialisms really did not translate well into Italian. They did sound funny, though.

Jaws arrived with their dishes. Bianca accepted a large square of sashimi. Various colors and textures of surgically cut raw fish littered her platter on fronds of green, fretted with sprinkles of this-and-that seasoning. Alessandro received steamers in an umami broth. Simplicity. Farrugia almost leapt into his saddle of monkfish with bacon, roasted Brussels sprouts and a mushroom ragout. They waited for Gennaro's dish to arrive. He had been the most adventuresome in his choice.

Gennaro smiled down at the bright plate of spicy lobster tacos. The cilantro, lime, mango, and avocado pieces seemed hot and acidic as a summer day, yet they were creamy and crunchy as a night breeze. He requested another sake martini.

They ate in silence.

Dante announced, "I've been thinking of joining the Napoli Sotterranea." When he heard no protest that he was thinking of resuming his archaeological interests that he had abandoned in Rome, he added, "Nothing dangerous. I'd just be a guide, although what I'm really interested in doing is marine archaeology at Baia."

No response. Bianca was sampling Saba with wasabi. Dante enthused on about nymphaeum statues from the first century AD, submerged villas, Protiro, and of the failed conspirator Lucius Piso, discovered in the late eighties. Nothing.

"Aren't any of you going to say anything?" Dante asked. Farrugia chewed. Alessandro acted as if he were deaf. He was afraid to look at Bianca. Gennaro had downed his second martini before saying what he wanted to say.

"We have a murder on our hands, a Camorra war, and you want to dress up in skintight neoprene and go snorkeling in the bay to look at dead history."

"Actually, this involves SCUBA diving."

"Even better, deeper underwater with a tank on your back. Just lovely."

"What does that mean?"

"It means that there is more of a chance of your body ending up in the current between Bacoli and Pozzuoli. Make yourself a target. Make life easier for the Camorra."

Bianca said, "I have my own announcement."

They said nothing. They looked at her.

"Loki contacted me."

Dante's fork dropped. It made a loud noise as it hit the plate.

Gennaro raised his hand. The lurking shark fin rushed over. Another sake martini.

5

"Why hadn't you told me before?" he asked as he put his apartment keys into the bowl. He had turned on the lights. Her back was to him, as she walked away.

"And when was I supposed to do *that*?" she answered, as she turned around, facing him. "Let me see . . . I was working on your data import and formatting the report for you all through the night into the next morning. You slept all night, showered and shaved, put on your clothes, and went to the office." She was sharpening her sarcasm. "If you're the one with all the questions then let me ask you one: When were you going to tell me about the Palazzeschi book?"

"The package? I didn't think it was important, Bianca. I told you that Giurlani was dead when I called you. That was important, or don't you agree?"

"Of course it was important, but so was that package," she said. He watched her brush away her dark hair from her face with her hand. It had been hot and humid outside. She was thinking.

"Fine. My mistake," he said, unbuttoning his shirt. Long day. "Sandro *was* right. It was a message. I get it. The System had planned his execution."

"That and what else, Dante? Think." He hated when she did this. It was patronizing.

"There were five copies," she said. "That means somebody else knew about me. Whether it was through Giurlani's office, his notes, or his diary—it makes no difference. Somebody knows that I exist. I'm exposed. Vulnerable."

"I said I was sorry. What is it you're trying to say? It's not my fault somebody knows."

"I know," she said. He knew she was struggling.

Gabriel Valjan **33**

"Damn! I can't believe this is happening to me," she said, yanking her blouse off her shoulders, unhooking her bra, and groping for a t-shirt. He hadn't even noticed her brief nakedness. The self-absorption was getting to him. It was always about her.

"Don't you even find it ironic that Loki contacts you the very day Giurlani is gunned down in Naples? How coincidental is that? You'd think Loki was right around the corner."

"I'm just as unnerved as you are about Loki."

"You are unnerved . . . it really shows."

"What the hell does that mean?"

He had kicked off his loafers. He hung his slacks over the Kaplan chair in their bedroom. He was being lazy about hanging them up. The armoire could wait. She'd better not nag him about it. He was in no mood.

"Don't alarm bells ring in your head at the thought that Loki and Rendition contact you the day Giurlani is killed? I think you get off on the fact that they contacted you."

Her eyes bulged in disbelief. If this were a movie, this was where the woman slapped the man. She blew out some air through pursed lips. The wisp of hair floated up and landed back in the same annoying place. She let it set there as she stared at him.

"Loki contacted me. Not Rendition."

"What difference does it make? Loki or Rendition—same people. You even have icons."

"Avatars, Dante. They are called avatars."

"Right. Avatars."

Her voice settled. "What did you mean, 'excited'?"

"All I'm saying is that I detected just a little bit of excitement in you. It was like you were intrigued; almost interested in the idea that Loki might propose another project or something. It's always been some kind of a game between you and them."

She got closer and looked him in the face. "Dante, that's crazy;

paranoid, even. You're imagining things. You know that? All I said was that Loki had contacted me. That's it. I explained exactly what happened at dinner. You were there, weren't you? Gennaro drank and the rest of you listened. I told you the conversation, word for word."

He could feel her hot breath moving the hair on his chest.

"Yes, you gave us the transcript, Bianca. Thank you very much; but I can tell you're excited. You and Rendition have this chemistry or something."

"I'm not having an affair, Dante. I don't fuck Rendition."

"I mean people get obsessed with their jobs. Same thing," he said. "I saw it in Milan when I watched the two of you interact online. Remember? The night all the stuff about Gladio had come out."

"I remember."

"I sat right there in the chair next to you as the two of you exchanged riddles. You got off on Loki. You can't deny it, Bianca. It might not be an affair but the idea of a new project attracts you. Don't deny it."

She pulled down the bed sheet, gave him an angry look. They had central air-conditioning and she claimed it got hot in the evenings. He thought otherwise.

"You're out of your mind. Are you telling me you're jealous?"

She got into bed and fluffed her pillow. Dante hesitated because he didn't want to continue the argument in bed.

"I'm just saying that you thrive on constant excitement. You like the scary and weird stuff that Rendition gives you. It's like an addiction. Loki is simply your supplier."

"I'm not an adrenaline junkie, Dante. I asked, are you jealous?"

"How can I be jealous of someone I've never met? Hell, I don't know whether Loki is a man or a woman. This whole thing is like a bad Bowie song."

"*Rebel Rebel* or *Young Americans*?" she asked. It was her attempt at levity.

He got into bed. The sheets were cold.

Gabriel Valjan **35**

"Just saying."

"Gennaro was right."

"Huh?"

"It does sound like an American sitcom. 'Just saying.' Get some sleep, Dante. Night."

He wanted to pull up the sheets but that would've disturbed her. He had hoped to sleep in, cheat the alarm clock in the morning. Damn, he realized that he had forgotten to turn the alarm clock on. Work was just a few blocks away but faster if he took the subway.

Dante looked around in the dark, imagining the place as it was during the day. They had a spacious apartment, bedroom and a large living room with Henry sectionals, in black leather, a nice plasma-screen television mounted on the wall. Satellite feed. His kitchen, since he did most of the cooking, was fit for royalty. She splurged on the amenities, like central air-conditioning, since he couldn't afford them on his salary. They even had a nice walk-in where they stacked a washer and dryer. They hung a couple items on the wall, but nothing to clutter the place since Bianca liked the minimalist look: some dark colors, some less dark, grey, but kept light and airy, Zen-like.

She had her own office, with a clay-colored textured rug on the floor, and her dark chocolate desk that sat on it along with her MAC, like some sanctuary, a sacred pagan space, where she would commune with Loki.

There was not one drop of red in the entire décor. He figured she saved that for Rendition. He thought *big red R* as he closed his eyes and tried to sleep.

For all the corruption, from the garbage strikes on down to journalist Roberto Saviano's polemical précis on the Camorra, and for all the complaints other Italians, particularly the northerners, had about the *i'napulitan*, including the dropping of the *i* that marks the plural, Naples is a seductive city. Dante was slowly coming to admire it.

Once a Greek colony called *Neapolis* or *Partenope*, named for the mythical siren living in the Gulf, modern Naples has a beautiful subway system. Dante loved it. The art-stuffed metro stations brought Naples back to the splendors of the Greek colony. Naples is not aesthetically austere like Milan, nor does it have the virgin eyes as its ancient name implies. The underground is beautiful, clean, and efficient. Every subway station, thanks to the artistic vision of Achille Bonito Oliva, the "father of Metro dell'Arte," has display pieces of contemporary art. Dante's favorite underground exhibit was Joseph Kosuth's *These Visible Things*, at the Dante Alighieri station. The artist quoted the medieval poet's *Convivio* using white neon tubes. The subway fare was equal to a discounted museum admission.

This morning he walked down the Via Alcide De Gasperi. The office building, once a flashcard of Fascist architecture, was now renovated and sanitized, but still had an elevator that one would have thought was raised and lowered in the basement by two arthritic asses that PETA had not yet rescued. He pressed the elevator button and waited. He would sometimes wait as long as the herald for the Kingdom of the Two Sicilies had waited for official unification and a national language. Some day.

He pressed the button. Again.

He and Alessandro had desks opposite each other. Gennaro and Farrugia had their desks a few feet away, also facing each other. There the four desks sat like atolls on the sea of Finanza-blue carpeting, the windows and sunlight to the east and Silvio's dark pebble of a desk to the west, near the door.

Pio Piersanti had had no say in the office design or layout. He had grouped them together at Giurlani's request, allowed them carte blanche with office supplies; but that did not amount to much since Gennaro had two phones on his person; one for personal use and the office team and one that he shared with Bianca. Dante and Silvio had taken standard-issued computers and phones. Nothing more. For all his work in the field, Farrugia was almost never in the office. Alessandro had a fetish for Nava pencils so the Finanza's Finance Department, like any redundant bureaucracy, had an open purchase order that made the local stationer happy.

"Hi, Sandro."

A grunt welcomed him.

"Are you mad at me?"

"Not mad, Dante."

Said about as convincing as a teenager, Dante thought.

"I heard my name. That's promising. I understand that you're upset Bianca and Tommaso had pointed out your less than perfect choices in women. You shouldn't let it bother you, Sandro. I had my own quarrel last night with Bianca."

Alessandro was sputtering his lips, staring at his desk blotter, and twirling his latest Nava. "I told you that I'm not mad. None of that bothers me."

"Right then, so what is it?"

Alessandro nodded his head in the direction of Farrugia's desk. It was then that Dante noticed Gennaro's and Silvio's absence.

"Where is everyone?"

"Gennaro and Silvio are with Piersanti. Farrugia is back undercover."

"Oh."

Alessandro pointed at Farrugia's desk with his pencil. "Since Piersanti figures that Farrugia spends eighty-five percent of his time out of the office, he's giving Isidò's desk to Tommasso."

"To the kid? What is Farrugia supposed to do the other fifteen percent of the time?"

Alessandro shrugged. Piersanti was a good man, but he had to be out of his mind, to use Bianca's phrase.

"Does Farrugia know?" Another Monotti symphony of shoulder shrugs, but this time the Nava pencil came crashing down and rolled across the desk.

"What does Gennaro have to say about all of this? Never mind, don't answer. I'll find out myself." As he stood up, pushing his chair back, Dante saw Gennaro and Silvio through the glass door, heading toward the elevator. He fast-footed to the door for the hallway, thinking that Pio Piersoanti had to be nuts. One doesn't just give the lion's desk to a cub intern. At least order another desk. There was plenty of room. What was the man thinking?

Piersanti had a solid reputation as a reasonable man. He got results. He was competent, a fierce opponent of the Camorra, and an advanced thinker, which might have explained his long-standing friendship with Commissioner Giurlani, possibly his acceptance of this pipsqueak Tommaso Baraldi. It was Pio Piersanti who had led the assault on the fortified compound of a Casalesi clan capo and petitioned to have the thug's *Scarface*-style mansion and holdings liquidated, and the building handed over to the local cooperative to help single mothers and their children. What was his logic?

Gennaro and Silvio had entered the elevator; the doors were still open.

"Hi, Silvio," he said to Silvio, out of politeness. "Where are you off to, Chief?"

"To Capodichino with Silvio. McGarrity and Murphy's flight is arriving soon."

Gennaro looked calm and stoic. His hair was combed back, neatly cut. The Robert Mitchum forelock would fall down on his forehead by mid-day. Gennaro's tie was askew and hanging with more style than a Milanese banker's on a profitable day.

"But the intern is getting Isidò's desk."

"What do you want me to do about it, Dante?" Gennaro pressed the button again. The doors were still open.

"What about Farrugia? Does he know yet?"

"Nope," Gennaro said, upbeat, almost bouncing upward on his toes. "Silvio and I have to pick up the FBI agents. Don't worry, Dante. Farrugia is a big boy. He even takes yoga. He can always get his yoga mat and use it for a desk." Incredible. Gennaro was smiling. He said, "He'll know how to stay calm since he has found his bliss."

The steel doors were starting to close.

"But . . ."

"Namaste, Dante."

The elevator doors closed.

6

The airport floor disturbed Gennaro: it had more of a shine and polish than his shoes did. He looked over at Silvio's shoes. Same thing. Silvio must have noticed that Gennaro was looking at his feet because he lifted his shoe up and checked the sole. No dog shit. No gum.

"Sorry, Silvio. I dislike waiting in airports."

Silvio was trying to enjoy his bad coffee. "This reminds me of that scene in *When Harry Met Sally*, the part about how airports mark the beginning of a relationship. Only thing is we already know Agents McGarrity and Murphy, or at least you do."

"Not really. We worked with them in Rome and Milan and I had a fast run-in with them in Boston . . . well, actually with McGarrity since Murphy was on vacation at the time, but that is all past history and you weren't with us that time." Silvio seemed to acknowledge Gennaro's interpretation of the past. He continued to listen.

"I didn't think you watched romantic comedies. American films."

"Good way to learn English."

"I hadn't thought of that," Gennaro said.

Gennaro was fond of Silvio. None of them admitted it, but they respected the former secretary who had worked his way up the ranks to translator and now, junior-grade investigator. Silvio had accepted Gennaro's offer to join them in Naples. Silvio had turned out to be ambitious, determined and resourceful; and, in spite of his occasional blunder with the language of the Anglo-Saxons, he had insight. He was the one who had broken the Palmisano case in Milan.

They killed time in Terminal 1. There were only two terminals and both were in walking distance of each other. They saw duty-free stores, but that's all they could do, look and see, not purchase anything in them, as neither had a ticket. They passed the Q&A kiosk for the confused and lost, the Red Cross desk for the sick and injured, and watched the skycaps driving around in their carts like kids in an amusement park, with the elderly, the lazy, or over-packed travelers on board.

The cybercafé was for the plebs and the VIP lounge for executives. The Capodichino airport reminded Gennaro of what he had read of mob-owned Las Vegas: it was an oasis without the Ten Commandments. Here it was not much different.

Gennaro saw McGarrity and Murphy in the distance, like two shimmering lawmen in a western, approaching them. Typical FBI fashion: dark suits, white shirts, and dark ties. McGarrity and Murphy must have already cleared Customs because they were now walking that quarantined portion of the airport before they could join the civilian world.

They had seen each other. They waved.

They were only steps away from each other, about to shake hands, when one of the *Polizia Aeroportuale* approached McGarrity and rattled off something about an apology, misplaced paperwork, and something about luggage. Gennaro had difficulty understanding the situation. Silvio was about to intercede, say something, when McGarrity responded to the uniformed man in rapid-fire Italian, flashing a smile when he was done. Murphy finished the man off with a comment perfectly intoned and pronunced.

Stunning, thought Gennaro and Silvio.

The airport policeman went on his way. McGarrity pocketed a sheet of paper, and then turned to greet Gennaro and Silvio, in Italian. Murphy had asked about the office and said something about the weather, in standard, thoroughly colloquial Italian.

Damn, thought Gennaro again.

McGarrity, sensing the confusion, explained. "The FBI sent us both to Monterey for intensive language training. It was a fantastic experience for the both of us. We loved it." Murphy seemed to agree, as if they were a couple that had just returned from an anniversary cruise. McGarrity then said, once again in Italian to Silvio, "It really made us appreciate all the hard work you did in Rome."

"Thank you." In English.

With the bags in the trunk and the agents waiting in the backseat, Gennaro noticed that Silvio was hanging back instead of taking the passenger seat up front.

"What is it?"

"They're speaking Italian."

"And you're speaking English. I know they're speaking Italian. I heard them. Impressive."

"I'm worried, Chief," Silvio said.

This was the first time that Silvio had ever called him *Chief*. Dante called him *Chief* and Alessandro called him *Boss* and sometimes they mixed it up to annoy him.

"Why are you worried?"

"I'm worried that I'm out of a job."

"You'll be fine, Silvio. Get in the car."

They had a lot to discuss in the four miles back into the heart of Naples.

Farrugia lived life like a reversible jacket. The night at the restaurant was his day off. Most days he didn't shower or shave, as if the scruff and personal stench gave him authenticity in the nether region north of Naples, Scampia, where the Totaro clan was running narcotics in a tender agreement with the 'Ndrangheta. At night he showered and shaved, and shed the filthy chrysalis of undercover work.

The Totaro operation was not easy to understand because it was micromanaged, decentralized, and dealers were confined to small stamps of turf. It had taken Farrugia months to map it all out, learn the nicknames of all the players involved, get embedded into the organizational ebb and flow, and, most importantly, to gain credibility. He had a schedule and a salary. He had another day off. Today.

The Totaro clan had been moving product with the Calabrians

recently and somewhere along the line they were exchanging it, with a cut to the 'Ndrangheta, for guns from the Russians which explained the omnipresent Kalashnikovs. Farrugia's pitch was that he was Calabrian, knew the dialect, and that put him in good with the Totaros because when they wanted to talk with the 'Ndrangheta, having a native speaker on their payroll to represent them helped. The Totaro clan paid Farrugia 1000 euros when he "translated," otherwise he made 800 euros a week.

Farrugia thought of the American photojournalists from the sixties when he went to "work." He worked a section of the Vele, a nasty and ugly section of public housing, a slum tenement that made pictures of Newark and Watts seem like affluent neighborhoods. From here the drugs moved into Naples and the clan provided customers with safe passage when they visited the Vele. It was a brilliant marketing idea on the clan's part because they also provided multi-purpose safe houses for dealers and customers. They could store their drugs and retrieve them later when the cops came in for a raid, and killers could dump murder weapons and change and discard clothes. No extra fee required.

The Vele was a popular destination for jocks looking to score juice for their biceps and for under-aged kids in need of cash, hired by businessmen to buy the latest party drugs, the next batch of Ecstasy or Rohypnol, for the writhing flesh on Friday nights at the clubs. Gays or straights with wood problems came for poppers or Viagra.

The Vele was the public drug bazaar; and if insects outnumbered humans a hundred to one on the planet then it was no different here with the number of pushers to customers. But it all ran as orderly and as mechanically as the renaissance guild system. Farrugia watched the traffic, both chemical and human; and when he left, there was another work shift, another "colleague" ready to move product, deliver it, and count the money—so fast that it never stained the hands.

Some things had changed since Farrugia had started in law enforcement in the eighties in Reggio Calabria. He never would have imagined that the Totaro clan would provide a needle-exchange program for its junkies and steroid users. He never would have imagined that the Totaro clan would be monitoring HIV transmission through the numerous clinics in and around its vast territory. They had infested everything, including doctors' offices, the testing labs, and the medical-supply chain. Absurd as it sounds, the Camorra has a very strict moral code around sexuality. Killing is okay, but marital infidelity or being gay is not condoned. Camorra members with unapproved private behaviors may be executed. They killed any soul, gay or straight, man, woman, or child, who became HIV-positive. Sex or blood transfusion didn't matter. They died.

Everyone imagines *Serpico* when they hear "undercover." Farrugia would disagree. Undercover work was like gardening or acting. It was a matter of bullshit, being convincing and delivering the line on time and on the mark, rolling and moving manure, keeping the lies fresh and realistic.

He had his gun, and a drop-piece strapped to his ankle. He'd rather be cited for violating departmental policy than be in a body bag or not found at all, as the Camorra occasionally chose to dismember bodies.

He was grateful that he was good enough, savvy enough, that after Milan last year nobody recognized him. He had been national news for a Warhol minute, almost a hero, thanks to Giancarlo Ragonese, the reigning idiot of the Free Channel whom Giurlani had managed to get demoted. Thank God.

Farrugia did worry that he was losing his edge. He was now in his mid-forties. He was getting sentimental. Narcs are usually loners, without attachments. He had Noelle now, though. When the Camorra feuded it killed on a haphazard tit-for-tat logic, so he did not discount the anarchic impulse of some psycho wanting to make a statement, make a name for himself. That was what happened with his mother. The 'Ndrangheta did not kill women, but that didn't stop two rogue bastards from murdering her in her kitchen as part of a vendetta. At his mother's funeral, Farrugia had seen the local 'Ndrangheta capo pay his respects.

His presence was a sign that this had not been his doing. The Camorra was different. Women were leaders. They killed and were killed. It was a different world.

Farrugia had to head into town for the group meeting, after a shower. Noelle had said something about coming down from Milan for a visit. She seemed excited on the phone when they last spoke. This meeting had him curious.

Farrugia checked his watch. McGarrity and Murphy should have arrived by now. He had plenty of time. He would be seeing the agents and meeting this Tommaso Baraldi kid for the first time.

7

Bianca had gotten up early to design a new avatar, again in black-and-white. Time for a change, though she had always liked her first avatar and how it expressed a playful part of her personality. For her new avatar, Bianca had chosen to wear a spiked collar and a hood flipped up and over to obscure her face.

Bianca was annoyed with Dante, more so now because he, too, had gotten up early. Piersanti had told all of them that they could come in late. She had wanted to chat with Loki, without any interruptions.

She could hear Dante moving behind her, like Godzilla in a fog, groping for espresso before he made something American for breakfast. For him, it couldn't be instant oatmeal: it had to be steel-cut oats; and it couldn't be an ordinary omelet: it had to be an egg-white omelet; and it couldn't be simple fruits and vegetables, because they had pesticides; and if he were to have pesticides, they had to be organic and nonviolent. He had talked recently about following the Caveman Diet.

"Do you want something?" he asked, offering to make her breakfast.

"No," she said. Short, abrupt, to the point. She was being a bitch.

Dante was in the kitchen. She heard eggs crack and sizzle, while she worked on her new avatar. Her hood was pulled forward enough to hide her eyes, cast a shadow on her cheekbones. There was a suggestive smile. It was very rock star. No body shot, no hugging a Telecaster.

A few minutes later Bianca heard the water at the sink run. Dante had washed his dish. The skillet was next. There would be no peace. There was also no Loki.

"I'm off to shower," he said.

"Try not to have too much fun or hurt yourself in there."

"I'll promise not to disappoint myself," he answered.

Even now when he irritated her, Dante still made her smile in the morning. She didn't use the bathroom first because he took longer than she did to get ready for work. She worked from home and seldom went into the office. She had had Aldo Giurlani agree to that stipulation before she came to Naples. She was a consultant.

Dante had turned on the shower. She was hearing falling water. Next time, she thought, she wanted an apartment with two bathrooms.

With no sign of Loki she decided to initiate the IM.

Seconds later Loki was online. *They* were online.

"Nice avatar." Loki's avatar onscreen was female. She gave Bianca an approving wink.

"Glad you like."

"Yummy."

"Thanks. I've got Qs." Questions.

"Early AM date or something?"

"Something like that," she answered.

The Norse avatar touched its horns, rubbing them in a way that suggested Loki was sharpening them. "Time to think then."

"Itsy bitsy . . ." Bianca said.

"Spider."

"Spider or Spider**s**?" she asked, bolding the plural marker.

Onscreen Loki smiled. Answer: "Spiders."

"Spiders from Mars or Neapolitan arachnids?"

The Loki avatar laughed like a silent film star.

"Clever. Neapolitan, but remember web = extensive."

Loki had now confirmed the plural for Bianca. Next was the gender of these spiders.

"U said last time that there was difference between ♂ and ♀ spiders."

"I did?"

She typed. "Yes, u did. ♀ = 'dangerous' & ♂ = 'clever.'"

She saw that Loki was typing. She would wait.

"U r wondering whether Camorra spider is Mars or Venus, iron or copper."

"Like duh," she answered and watched Loki's avatar for a reaction. Nothing.

Loki knew that gender signs denoted not only the astrological planets, but also war and love and alchemy; but that was not what was bothering her. She had zeroed in on "spider." Number. She now focused on "is." Verb agreement. She remembered that Claudio Ferrero had suggested that Loki might be an Italian.

"Spider or spider**s**?" she typed, almost tempted to capitalize the final *s* for emphasis.

"Spider**s**. My bad." That was a copy-and-paste answer with humor. No capitalization.

She did Unicode next: "♂ or ♀?"

"Both."

Was she reading that right? She looked at Loki's avatar. Indifference. The answer was ironic. Was Loki a he or a she? American or Italian?

"Huh?" This stumped her. She wanted to type WTF on the screen. The windowpane indicated that Loki was typing.

"Both = Camorra: 1 = ♀ & other = ♂, but ♂ = different. U + 26A5."

Loki, like a mathematician, used "=" for the verb "to be." Loki was saying that both spiders were Camorristi. Good. One was female, another, male, but somehow the male was "different." She saw the ASCII code at the end of the line.

"Confused here. Transgender?"

"Not transgender spider. Ha ha. Just different as in deviation from males of his kind."

Bianca knew that Camorra women were effective, profitable, and ruthless, especially in the construction industries. Loki's avatar had a hand covering the mouth as if laughing, changing back and forth, male to female. That made Bianca angry. She had a theory.

She typed: "1 feud. 2 clans."

"Obvious fact. Public knowledge. U can do better. Disappointed."

She gave the screen the finger. She typed, "'Obvious' is often in plain sight."

"Not this time."

Interesting. "Leadership? 1 = man & 1 = woman."

Loki's cursor did not move. Bianca read "typing" on the bottom. Loki had responded. "Yes & No."

This time she said it: "Damn!" She heard Dante from the bathroom. "What happened?"

"Nothing."

She returned to the screen. That was a sphinx answer. Loki's avatar had arms crossed and eyes staring at her. She was thinking a male Totaro, a female Marra, or vice versa, and not this cryptic bullshit.

Dante was behind her. He looped his tie, formed his knot while whistling a tune. "You should get ready," he said.

"Plenty of time, Dante. Piersosanti said the meeting wasn't until ten." Her fingers were poised on the keyboard, trying to articulate a response. Dante stopped whistling and started humming.

"Must you do that?"

Dante checked his tie in the mirror. He stopped and said, "Must you do that?"

"Do what, Dante?"

"Talk to Loki." Damn, she had walked right into that. He disappeared around the corner and she heard him whistling again.

"Yes & No? Isn't it Yes *or* No?" she asked. Simple Boolean logic.

"Something like that," Loki typed, reusing her own phrase.

"BS."

The avatar made a savage face. "No, it isn't."

She chose not to answer. The ellipses indicated that Loki was sending a reply.

"Both."

Bianca typed, "Different topic . . . Tell me about TB."

"Nasty disease. Favorite of poets & other writers."

"Ha . . . Ha . . . hysterical," she keyed. "TB, the person." She watched the Norseman shrug.

"Intern," she typed.

No answer so she terminated the session with Loki. Angry, frustrated, and now annoyed because standing there was Dante who knew that she knew that he knew that she had been conversing with Loki. He walked away, shaking his head and confirming the tie-knot against his Adam's apple.

Touché, Dante.

Ten o'clock. Almost everyone had arrived early. "Everyone" also included McGarrity and Murphy, who had arrived enthusiastic and rosy as schoolchildren on the first day of class. They surprised Alessandro and Dante with their Italian.

The table was unchanged, clean and polished. They took their seats. The overhead projector was warm, its blank light intent on the white screen on the wall. The air-conditioning was on full force. Everything was normal except for the flip-chart paper that had been taped to all the surrounding glass in the conference room, one side that faced the office and the other side, facing the skyline. Alessandro joked that any birds that might fly by as spies for the Camorra were out of luck. The room had become a cold cave, with some of the paper covering the glass rattling in protest against the air-conditioning.

Gennaro confirmed the time on his watch: five minutes after the hour. Piersanti was sitting near the head of the table. He had been the one to call this status meeting. Gennaro wasn't expecting the meeting to start with German punctuality, but Piersanti often kept to a schedule strict as that of a high-speed Italo train. No sign of the intern. Everyone was waiting, expecting Pio Piersanti to rise and announce the agenda. Alessandro was chatting with Dante. Silvio and the agents were smiling and conversing. Gennaro and Bianca exchanged looks.

Tommaso Baraldi arrived and closed the door behind him. He mumbled that he had checked the room for bugs. Piersanti cleared his throat. Sandro raised his eyebrows, almost in wonder as to whether Piersanti might want them to rise for him. The boy pontiff! The intern went to the head of the table, onto which he placed an unlabeled bottle of water and a loaf of bread. Saying nothing, he inserted a metallic jumpkey into the laptop's USB port and navigated to his file, highlighted it, but did not double-click it.

Gennaro settled into his seat, hoping for a comfortable spot since he suspected that his ass would go numb. He looked over at Piersanti, who avoided him by looking away from him at the blank screen. Bianca still seemed impassive, but Gennaro suspected that her mind was hard at work, taking the measure of the young man the way a retired tailor can't help but analyze a stranger's clothes.

"Bread and water are the staples of life. They have been for millennia," he said. He paused. Some Liceo somewhere had taught Tommaso Baraldi rhetoric, Gennaro thought.

"Italians, like any other people in this world, want to know where their water comes from and who has made their bread." He tilted the water bottle as if he were selecting a wine. "We appreciate craftsmanship. We, like other Europeans, used to form relationships with those who fed us. We knew our bakers, our grocers, our butchers, and so on; but, in today's global market, we visit the supermarket instead. Those age-old relationships I mentioned have become invisible, depersonalized, as we walk down aisles in search of name brands, enjoying the convenience of having all of our shopper's desires satisfied in one place, under one roof. Gone are the days when we went shopping with our grandma, running all over town to find all those things that she needed, to all those places where she knew all the vendors by name. We are taught that convenience is progress, convenience is modern, but, as we know, convenience has an invisible cost."

He picked up the loaf of bread, looked at it; his nose sniffed down the length of the loaf and he made a funny face, as if he had discerned mold in it. Alessandro's eyebrows went up, for a second time already, though this time out of curiosity, in spite of himself. Gennaro wondered whether the agents were getting all of this poetic Italian. Dante seemed intrigued, while Bianca's face was as unreadable as a *scuola metafisica* canvas.

Tommaso held up the bread between his two hands. Gennaro was not expecting the mystery of transubstantiation. Tommaso had his hands on opposite ends of the loaf; he twisted the ends of the bread. The bread flaked. Crumbs fell.

So this is forensic rhetoric in action, Gennaro thought, and this guy was supposed to be a sociologist. Gennaro rubbed his brow and hoped that a headache would not come on.

"The Camorra is different. Traditionally, it is messy, not as structured as the Cosa Nostra in Sicily, or as closed off as the 'Ndrangheta in Calabria." He paused for effect. "But that is all changing now."

Farrugia's patience must have worn thin, for he interjected: "The bread of life is broken; society is broken and the Camorra is the antichrist of civilization. We *get* it."

Tommaso had stopped twisting the bread. Farrugia seemed to have won the bread a reprieve. The intern said, "That's where you're wrong, Commissario. Bread is what we eat. The Camorra is Neapolitan society."

Farrugia bowed his head and said, "My apologies for interrupting you. Please continue."

"Yes, we have others in the world of organized crime. We have the Columbians, the Bulgarians, and the Russians, but they are specific, specialists, if you will. The Camorra, however, is different and, like this bread, must be broken," he said, finally splitting the loaf of bread in two.

Gennaro hoped that this was the end of this theatrical production but he saw the bottle of water. Water must be the blood of Naples.

"We used to know our relationship with the Camorra. What I mean by that is we knew where to find it, where to expect them. The problem is that the Camorra is becoming transparent like this water here; they, too, are starting to peel off their label and will in time, if not stopped, become completely invisible, tasteless, a force that wears down rocks, moving around all obstacles. But how will they do it?"

Rhetorical question. Gennaro doubted that Magi would appear on camels. He did remember the water scandal in which the Camorra had mass-produced labels for bottles filled with New York tap water. Tommaso had moved on to PowerPoint on the screen behind him.

The intern clicked through several slides of wholesome and delectable images: butter, coffee, fish, fresh mozzarella, fruit, and meat. "We eat these daily."

Then he clicked through several disgusting slides of toxic dumps, discolored fish, sad-looking animals, the suffering visible in their eyes.

"We eat this too. Breathe it, in fact, because the Camorra has infiltrated the entire food chain. This is what we have come to expect of the Camorra. They've used the cheapest and the deadliest ingredients and put them into our food. All for profit. They've also poisoned us and contaminated the environment with illegal dumping for Europe's manufacturers. They've corrupted the police and the judiciary." PowerPoint slides of arrested Camorristi went across the screen in quick succession. "But we all know this, don't we?"

The face of Lorenzo Bevilacqua appeared on the next slide. "We know this face. He is Amici di Roma and—" McGarrity raised his hand.

"Yes."

In limpid, marvelous Italian, Agent McGarrity indicated that the FBI had surveillance on Bevilacqua, even though the charges against him and Amici di Roma had failed in Boston. McGarrity seemed to doubt how Bevilacqua was any threat since the FBI had already mapped out the Amici organization, tagged Lorenzo's finances and monitored all his interactions.

"Thank you, Agent McGarrity, but Amici di Roma is now Amici di Napoli. Bevilacqua's enterprises continue to thrive in the new Camorra. I'll explain." McGarrity looked crestfallen, as if he had traveled all that way to Italy to be told that he had failed his country and his few friends in life. To Gennaro it was nothing more than the hydra's heads having grown back with more venom and hissing mouths.

The air-conditioning made it too cold to doze off.

"We know *this* man, but do know *these* men . . ." Tommaso said and clicked through several slides of faces, continuing his narration, "and some of these *women*? These individuals are all from the files of the late Commissioner Aldo Giurlani."

The interruption came from Alessandro this time. Sandro stood up, looking over at Pio Piersanti, almost as if he were asking permission to be rude, to which Piersanti's hand granted him permission to ask his question.

"Yes?"

"With all due respect, Mr. Baraldi, the question that has been weighing upon all our minds here is exactly how it is that you had come to know Aldo Giurlani. I mean—and again, I intend no disrespect—but you're a university student. By your own admission your training is as a sociologist, while these investigations into the Camorra are the domain, and rightfully so, of legal experts and law enforcement."

Alessandro sat down.

Tommaso clicked back to the slide of Lorenzo Bevilacqua.

"Aldo Giurlani was my uncle. Pio Piersanti is my cousin."

Silence.

Alessandro stood up. "I'm truly sorry for your loss, but—"

Gennaro stood up, buttoning his jacket.

"Yes?"

He hated this. Gennaro studied Tommaso at the front of the room and then Piersanti at the side, searching for words. Farrugia, who also seemed stunned by the revelation, seemed curious.

"My condolences to you both, but at the same time I believe that it is my duty to express my concerns. You have both lost a family member. It is clear that *you* are passionate about your uncle, his memory, and," looking over at Piersanti, "*you* have worked all your life against the Camorra, but are we capable of doing this work with any objectivity? Will what we do stand up in court on its own legs? I lost my wife years ago. The Totaro clan had her murdered. Commissario Farrugia here can speak to the particulars of the case. They had killed her to stop me. What I am struggling to say here is that we might be construed as vigilantes or, to use their language, engaged in a vendetta, a blood feud. It has become personal."

Pio Piersanti stood up. His eyes surveyed the room. "You're right, Gennaro. It is personal, but when hasn't it been? That is why Giurlani chose you. You have a stake in the outcome. All of you do because all of you have been affected. You lost your wife, Lucia. Commissario Farrugia lost his mother. Tommaso lost an uncle. I also grieve for Aldo. Agents McGarrity and Murphy have lost colleagues in the fight against organized crime. Allegretti and Nerini have experienced Bevilacqua's Amici di Roma firsthand."

Piersanti's eyes narrowed in on Gennaro. "Giurlani chose you—and by extension," Piersanti pointed at each one of them, "he chose all of you, because he knew that you've been touched by the violence and that has made you incorruptible. So yes, Gennaro, it is personal, but it keeps you honest, focused on the work, and mindful of what we have lost and what we can lose if we don't stop them. Is it vendetta? I'd rather have you think: When have we not had to fight for our lives?"

Piersanti sat down. The taped paper behind him vibrated like a trapped fly. Piersanti fixed his attention on Tommaso Baraldi the intern.

"We return to Lorenzo Bevilacqua. He is the first architect, the inspiration, to the new Camorra. His organizational diffusion is what inspires the new Camorra. The Amici di Roma is a multinational corporation. While Bevilacqua has stepped down like any CEO these days caught in a scandal, the Amici di Roma continues to remain active, as if nothing had happened. It's a temporary black eye. His corporation is a business entity; that means it must move and find profits or it'll wither and die. The Camorra is no different. The Camorra is becoming a corporation."

Murphy spoke. "So like most criminal organizations it is multinational and structured. So what?"

Gennaro saw that Bianca's eyes had squinted when Tommaso said "organizational diffusion."

"But the Camorra has mutated, Agent McGarrity. I had mentioned this when I was here the last time, but I understand that you were not here so I'll elaborate now."

Tommaso clicked to the next slide. It was the image of a handsome young man, an ordinary-looking university kid, not unlike the ones seen at clubs looking for girls or at sidewalk cafés, enjoying an American beer as a status symbol.

"That is the face of the next-generation Camorra."

Murphy perused the face. "Looks like a college kid to me."

Tommaso stepped to the side of the screen and examined the face with Murphy. "His is not just any face. His first name is Matteo. Make no mistake about him. He is Camorra. He may look clean-cut, but he is Camorra. Matteo attended Bocconi. He and his colleagues will acquire prestigious degrees. He'll use all the legalities that corporate law and international relations afford him, but Matteo's vision is not just for a new criminal organization. If he is successful his his method will make him one of the world's most sophisticated terrorists."

"Never heard of him," said McGarrity.

"Nobody has and that is intentional," Tommaso answered. "When you read about him, you'll be reading about him in the business section of newspapers. His specialties are acquisitions, mergers, and takeovers. Unlike most Camorristi who live like Hitler in bunkers, unable to enjoy their wealth, Matteo here will be visible, always in plain sight. He's the new terrorist."

"How is he a terrorist?" McGarrity asked.

"He plans to undermine governments and use a corporation, like the Amici di Roma, to do it."

Dante interjected, "He has to file tax returns. The Guardia di Finanza can do audits. Somewhere along the line his hands have to get dirty. If new laws have to be written then they'll get written. The United States did it with white-collar crime."

Gennaro's eyes searched Bianca's reaction. She had to know that he was thinking of Rendition and the early days before laws against white-collar crime existed. That was how Rendition had come into existence. Bianca saw Gennaro watching her. Poker face.

Tommaso was still talking. "And how long did it take for the GdF, or the FBI for that matter, to understand how Amici di Roma was robbing both Saints Peter and Paul in Rome with its shell subcontractors and dummy businesses—or defrauding museums and insurance companies? That was just with antiquities, before we understood Amici's other criminal endeavors. We understand Amici di Roma better because of Bianca Nerini."

Gennaro could see Bianca was trying to avoid the eyes that acknowledged her. Tommaso was diplomatic, though. "Allegretti, DiBello, Farrugia, and Monotti did the rest."

Silvio raised his hand.

"Yes?" Tommaso asked.

"This Matteo wouldn't use the Amici import or export model since, as you pointed out, it had been exposed."

"It has, yes."

"And we know that the Camorra has been involved in the food industry, illegal dumping, construction, and the list goes on."

"That is all in the past," Tommaso said to Silvio. "The traditional activities that you mentioned will, along with blackmail, drugs, guns, and prostitution, be handed over to ethnic groups."

Silvio was undeterred. "To steal your metaphor, all of that is their bread and water, yes?" Tommaso agreed. "I guess my question is what kind of corporation? Let's call it Amici di Napoli. How does it work?"

"Venture capital. Matteo is a capitalist. A very creative one."

McGarrity laughed. "Sorry, but that isn't new. It's a nicer word for loan-sharking."

Everyone exchanged glances, which said, "That must have been some intensive language-learning course at Monterey, if he knows the word *strozzinaggio*. Wow!" Gennaro had explained the word once to Bianca when she had seen it in a newspaper. Loan shark.

Silence.

"Not the way Matteo plans to do it," Tommaso answered.

"Why not?"

"Because he learned structure from Bevilacqua and the method from the greatest terrorists on the planet."

Tommaso had turned off the overhead projector. It was just the sound of the air-conditioner and the taped paper breathing against the glass. Tommaso took some money out of his pocket. Like a magician, he stretched out a paper note, a euro, snapped it taut and then pulled out an American five-dollar bill, an Abe Lincoln, and displayed it for everyone to see. McGarrity and Murphy seemed the most interested in this magic trick.

"Money is supposedly the root of all evil, but that is inaccurate. It is the love of money that creates evil. Money should create freedom; it should create leisure, and allow someone to do other things in life. It is all a matter of perspective. The evil in money starts when one tries to make more money with it." He touched the money on the table. "The euro and the dollar are the two dominant currencies on the world market. This is why the Americans and the European Union are at odds."

Tommaso put his finger on the American dollar. "The U.S. pressed for the creation of the European Community after the Second World War, because the Americans wanted a single point of contact where they could exert pressure on all western European countries at one time. They were the new superpower. Over time, the EU evolved beyond U.S. control and the United States had to counter with strategies to thwart or slow down the process. *Strategia della tensione* and the stay-behind organizations, like Gladio."

McGarrity stared ahead as Tommaso put his finger on the euro note.

"The EU evolved, became a competitor, but not always an obedient ally. The taste of power corrupts and those who have power want to maintain it. Note that I am not saying whether that power is American or European. The countermeasures to losing power were implemented. Step one was move sovereignty from national capitals to Brussels, and put the power in the hands of non-elected officers who are closely connected to financial lobbyists. Step two, use think-tanks and sell the idea that the State is evil and the Free-Market is good. Propaganda. Step three, dismantle public healthcare, public education, and labor guarantees. That is where we are now. The result is that both people and society are at the mercy of corporations. The new Camorra seeks the same effect: fluidity of power without national identity or political boundary."

Silvio asked, "How?"

"Excuse me for interrupting, Silvio," said McGarrity. "Explain exactly where the terrorist part comes in. I'm not clear on that."

Tommaso put the euro note on top of the American dollar, but seemed to change his mind. He put the dollar on top of the euro. He looked down at the two bills and then at McGarrity.

"Matteo knows that these two currencies are at war. With a strong euro, London loses its position as the world's second most important financial marketplace. The Chinese or the Arabs could destroy the American economy tomorrow morning. The only thing that prevents them from exerting their power of choice between the euro and the dollar is your country's military power. Matteo, however, arrived at the same conclusion that the Americans did . . ."

"And what was that?" McGarrity asked.

"Instigate a controlled breakdown of the euro currency. Become an elite controller. Matteo is a student of history. He had already learned international relations before he went to business school."

McGarrity's face was neutral. "That's suicidal. If one currency falls then the other currency falls. Why destroy the euro? He's slitting his own throat," McGarrity said.

"It appears that way, but does he? After all, the Camorra dumps toxic wastes in its own backyard. I assure you that Matteo is different."

"Still talking about hoodlums and petty criminals," McGarrity seemed to hiss.

The crew was impressed again: McGarrity knew the word *teppista*. Bianca had seen that one more frequently than *strozzinaggio*. Hoodlums apparently outnumber loan sharks.

"Yes," Tommaso answered, "and Naples is known for petty crime. The Sicilians and Calabrians won't allow it where they live, but what I'm suggesting is that Matteo's vision will change all that. Petty crime occurs because the Camorra is loosely structured but its appeal is that it is the easiest organization to export and set up anywhere in the world."

Murphy answered, "I guess that explains the terrorist part, but you haven't explained how Matteo is the great mastermind that you think that he is."

"He is a blade runner." Tommaso pressed down on the two bills.

"What does that mean?" Gennaro asked.

Dante said, "It's a sci-fi term that . . ."

"I know that, Dante. I do read," Gennaro snapped.

"This is the terrorist part. Matteo's strategy is to push countries like Spain and Italy to the brink and stop just one second before they collapse. He learned from the recent banking crises how to become a financial terrorist. It's very risky. He'll count on governments and people to do anything they can to avoid bankruptcy. Austerity measures to the hilt. He'll do what the multinational banks and other rogue financial institutions tried to do in the past."

"How will he do that?" McGarrity asked.

"As I said, money can buy freedom but in our world it is associated with consumption. In the past, having money meant that you didn't work. In today's thinking, money means that you can buy more. Matteo counts on the chains of debt, both political and psychological."

McGarrity's poised Italian was cracking. "I've been trying . . . to understand, to see what . . . what it is that you mean by 'elite controller.'"

McGarrity turned to Murphy for a second. "Also, you still have not explained how. It's as if you don't want to."

"Think of international loans . . . isn't giving loans to northern countries at an interest rate of three percent as opposed to five percent for southern countries not control? As for the psychological . . . austerity measures have led to austerity riots. That is a statement of the daily reality of the people walking the street, maxed out on credit cards and in a perpetual state of anxiety, feeling betrayed by their government or hostile to foreigners. For an American it means no more retail therapy, unless there is another credit card. It means no more picket fence and two-point-two children when a family struggles to survive and finds out jobs are abroad because profit margins are wider elsewhere. Work with no secure retirement or safety net is a form of slavery. Desperate is the social reality."

McGarrity glared at the intern. It was a lot to take in. Tommaso stopped there, saying, "It might not be the same as a bomb at a train station but fear as in financial anxiety is just as corrosive. As to how—"

Tommaso saw that Silvio had his hand up.

"Yes."

"You called him a blade runner. Please explain that."

"Matteo studied what Osama bin Laden had done with the futures market, analyzed how bin Laden had profited from the falling stock prices while the World Trade Center buildings were falling. He supposedly made millions on 'shorting stocks,' which means he played the pessimist and hoped the stock would sink. Whether bin Laden's assets were frozen or not, whether al-Qaeda received the proceeds doesn't matter. The concept was compelling. When the banking scandals came along later, Matteo saw how real estate and interest rates became unstable in a global market. That was when he started thinking."

Tommaso put the overhead projector back on. The bulb heated up and the projector's cooling fan whirred, kicking up small specks of dust. He navigated his cursor on the screen to a file, a jpeg, and clicked it.

"Who is he?" Dante asked when another face appeared on the screen.

"A master forger. He is famous for counterfeiting euro currency. He's in a German prison now."

"Does he work for Matteo?" Murphy asked.

"Don't know. He teaches art appreciation in prison. Rumor is that he allegedly gave Matteo some of his masterpieces. We assume it is plates for euros."

"Counterfeiting cash has a short shelf-life," McGarrity said. "Law enforcement is always improving detection and verification. It's a really small window. The mints are also always on the move against fraud."

Tommaso didn't seem concerned. "True, but dumping false but very accurate notes on the world market would have the same effect as increasing the circulation of genuine currency and, based on the Law of Supply and Demand, the more a commodity is available, the less it is worth. More notes means less value and that leads to more inflation. The U.S. government, for example, prints money to keep inflation at bay, but combine inflation and stagnation and you get stagflation, and that creates a recession and then a depression. I think that is what Matteo has in mind."

"Dump money on the market?" Murphy asked.

"I think so. Matteo wants to blade run the European economy. In effect, a low euro is good for the dollar and good for U.S. industries because European exports become cheaper. He'll draw the dollar in."

Silvio asked, "What happens if the government doesn't print more currency?"

"He'll still dump and dilute the euro on the world market."

Alessandro said, "That means he'll have to have a money-laundering operation."

"He already has that."

"He does?" Dante asked.

"Who?" McGarrity asked.

"Amici di Roma, for one. I'm trying to prove that, though. Matteo

Gabriel Valjan **63**

has to have other allies and if he attracts American investors he'll have himself a multinational enterprise."

"And what if, like Silvio asked, a government doesn't bite and print the money?"

Tommaso grinned. "They will. Debts have to be paid. Debts have to be generated. Governments don't pay off all of their debts. It's a game. Besides . . . he is counting on greed. Theirs, not his."

Piersanti stood up just then and announced that everyone should take lunch and enjoy the rest of the day. Tommaso turned off the projector and then cleared the USB port. Everyone started to drift towards the door, except Bianca.

"Aren't you coming?" Dante said to Bianca.

"Give me a minute."

"Okay, I'll meet you in the lobby downstairs with the rest of the group. We'll find lunch."

She agreed. She sensed that Tommaso would linger. He did, taking his time to unplug the power cord to the projector and clean up the crumbs from the bread.

He smiled at her, but said nothing. The room had emptied out. She got up from her chair and walked over to the taped-down paper and looked for an edge with her fingernail. She was trying to help him.

"Please leave it alone. I'll take care of that," he said.

"You're really that worried that people outside were going to look in on the meeting?"

He didn't say a word.

"That was a good presentation. A little overwhelming, but it was very impressive."

"Thank you. I don't think Agent McGarrity cared for it," he answered.

"I have two questions, though."

"Sure, what are they?"

"You seem to think Matteo has plates."

"I do."

"Is there a connection between Matteo and the German forger?"

"There's no proof that they did business together. You said you had two questions. What was the second one?

"It was about Matteo."

"Does it bother you that I didn't say his last name?" he asked. For all his confidence, Tommaso was just a kid, a shy one at that. He kept avoiding her eyes.

"No, not at all. I'm not particular about names. You said that he studied international-relations."

"He did. He graduated last year."

"You knew him, then?"

"Not really. An acquaintance."

Bianca smiled. She was thinking. She stood there and watched him start to unpeel the paper from the glass. The sunshine came rushing in.

"One last question."

He turned around, folding the paper over his forearm to keep the sheets unwrinkled. "Sure." She felt guilty asking him questions; it seemed sloppy of her, but this last one had suddenly come to her. She had a hunch.

"Did you know Charlie Brooks?"

His strong, intense brown eyes studied her now, without a trace of timidity this time. His lips, sensuous in a way that was unintentional on his part, moved and he answered her.

"Yes."

8

The elevator's descent was formidable. Bianca was sad, thinking about Charlie Brooks. As the doors opened, the heat enveloped her and subdued whatever goose bumps she might have had from the frigid air in the conference room upstairs. Still, the warm air also gave her an unexpected chill. She saw them waiting for her in the lobby.

"Ready for lunch?" Dante asked.

"Where to?" Alessandro asked, rubbing his hands together. Gennaro did not look interested. A security alarm was going off at the front desk. Some visitor had set it off and Dante walked over to the scene.

"Where's Silvio?" Bianca asked.

Gennaro answered her. "I asked him to take McGarrity and Murphy out to lunch." Bianca knew Gennaro's way of thinking: Silvio will distract the agents with some good food, an enthusiastic conversation about the challenges of learning another language, and wrap it all up with his pointers on how to avoid pitfalls in Italian. The intent was to mellow out McGarrity.

"Is McGarrity that unsettled?"

His eyebrow arched. "What do you think? You tell a career man that his country is less than honorable, imply hypocrisy in big, bold letters, and you think he won't get offended?"

She didn't even shrug for effect. "Power is power and money is money. The intern made his point. McGarrity saw one of his own go bad so he shouldn't be surprised." There was no need to mention that agent's name. McGarrity would want to forget what happened in Boston.

"He did, didn't he?" Gennaro seemed to agree despite his orneriness. "Did you catch our intern's allusion to the Bologna train-station bombing?"

"Uh, excuse me." It was Alessandro trying to butt in, but Gennaro was ignoring him.

Bianca answered. "I did, but I doubt McGarrity could tell you that Bologna occurred in 1980. You can be certain he doesn't know about the Piazza Fontana." Alessandro seemed to be pressing in on them. Bianca continued to ignore him. She said to Gennaro, "I doubt McGarrity was even born in '69." Her double-*s* in *sessantanove* was a bit ferocious. She turned on Alessandro and said, "Why are you hovering, Sandro?"

His hands went up and he backed away with, "*Mi dispiace*," just as Dante was approaching, saying it was a new hire that set off the alarm at the front dest. Seeing Alessandro upset and departing, Dante asked, "What the hell is it with you two? What happened?"

"I'll meet you outside," she said. "Sandro?" Bianca yelled, walking after him.

"I'm sorry, Chief. She hasn't been herself lately."

"It's okay, Dante. It's my fault. I might've provoked her. But, you know what?"

"No, what?"

"Do you really want to piss her off?"

"No, of course not, Chief. Why?"

"Then don't let her hear you apologizing for her. Let's go and get those two. I'll take Sandro in my car. You and Bianca can follow me on your Vespa." Gennaro stopped, looked around, and asked, "Where's Farrugia?"

"Outside on his cell with Noelle. He did mention that he'd like to eat healthy."

Lunch was not completely healthy but deep-pan pizza was a bargain at five euros. Farrugia was examining the menu items as if he were proofreading for grammar and syntax. The dishes were quite simple at this establishment, but since Farrugia had started seeing Noelle he insisted that he had to eat clean, eat simple, and eat nothing that he couldn't pronounce.

"Isidò? Please. You won't ruin your figure," Gennaro pleaded.

"I'm reading."

Dante kept repeating in a low voice, "*Lui legge . . . lui sta leggendo . . .* he reads . . . he is reading," when he saw Gennaro glaring at him, as if he were the only one allowed to goad Farrugia.

The waiter came to their table. Gennaro ordered the Tigullio, a pizza with basil pesto and scamorza, the smoked cheese. Sandro surrendered his menu, asking for the always simple and elegant pizza margherita. Dante decided on "Mother's pizza." Bianca handed the waiter her menu and placed her order, "*Pizza con Superpomodoro e Lardo.*"

The waiter asked, "*Lardo di Colonnata o lardo di Maiale di razza casertana?*"

"*Di razza casertana, per favore.*"

Farrugia seemed stunned. "Tomato pie and farm-raised pork?"

Bianca tapped Farrugia's menu. "Bacon is good. We're hungry. I'm hungry. I didn't have breakfast. Now order!"

"Do as she says, Isidò," Gennaro said.

Farrugia ordered a vegetable side dish: *capunatina*, a smaller caponata or eggplant casserole, after he had seen that the house used caciocavallo instead of provolone cheese. He asked for *settembrini*, small figs, to end his meal. Gennaro was staring at him. The waiter took the last of the menus.

"What is it?" Farrugia asked.

"Ordering just a side for lunch? Are you vegetarian now?"

"It has cheese."

"Oh, you *are* one of those vegetarians. You won't have any meat left on your bones after Noelle's visit." Alessandro was laughing. Even Bianca couldn't help but smile.

"And you?" Gennaro had meant Bianca. "Why didn't you eat breakfast?"

"She was busy," Dante answered.

"You answer for her, too."

"No, Chief."

The waiter returned with their drinks. They waited until he had poured them and left. The place was quiet, ideal for their group meeting. Fewer than twelve tables, in a pleasant section of Naples, the Caponapoli hill and the Decumano Superiore, which kept its ancient character: pagan and then Christian architecture.

"I'm sorry, everybody" Gennaro said. "I'm a little bit off from that meeting. This intern, Tommaso, what he said hit a nerve. He upsets Agent McGarrity and then there is this whole matter of his being Giurlani's nephew. Talk about unexpected. I just feel uneasy about this whole situation."

"He's young," Bianca said. "You can't expect him to be diplomatic. That comes with age, with experience. You know that."

Alessandro, who was snacking on a plate of olives that no one else had seen the waiter set out, said, "He might not be diplomatic but he certainly was baroque with his presentation, what with the bread and water, then that bit with the money."

"Regardless . . . something doesn't feel right." Gennaro said.

"Does the nepotism upset you?" Farrugia asked.

"It's everywhere. Bureaucracy wouldn't exist without it. But I'll say this—Tommaso is intelligent and he's committed. Youth, passion, and ideals are a potent mix. They're also deadly. What do you think, Bianca?"

"No doubt he knows his history. It's very unlikely that the younger generation would know '*la strategia della tensione*,' no less Gladio."

The waiter interrupted the conversation, announcing each dish and placing the plates before each member of his party. Farrugia's two plates looked modest for the stomach but tasty. Dante's pizza had come with a leaf of basil sticking up in the center, like a knight's feather. Alessandro's dish was deceptively simple, but still looked delicious. It was Bianca's dish that was decadent and the envy of the table.

It was not mere *lardo*, but noble pork. The Casertan pig, the pride of Caserta and Benevento in Campania, is a descendant of the boar that was depicted on ancient artwork at Capua, Herculaneum, and Pompeii. The porcine is distinctive in appearance, with two wattles, called *sciuccaglie*, its slate-colored coat, its long snout, and its absence of bristles; hence the name, *pelatella*.

"You can have some, Isidò," Bianca said, ready with her knife and fork. Farrugia declined it, looking particularly regretful and tempted.

Gennaro couldn't resist laughing. "Let him eat caponata. He's doing it all for love."

"Funny."

Gennaro ignored Farrugia's repartee and asked Bianca, "So . . . do you think McGarrity will get over Tommaso's implicit criticism of U.S. policy?"

"How should I know? He should, though. I can't believe after what happened in Boston that he is so naïve as to think any government, including his FBI, is completely virtuous."

"His Italian was impressive. Murphy's, too," Alessandro added.

They continued eating. Farrugia broke down and solicited some of Bianca's pizza. Gennaro joked that they were all sworn to secrecy. Noelle was to never know.

Dante had lifted up the basil leaf and set it down on the rim of his plate. He said as he cut his pizza: "This Matteo that Tomasso talked about. He sounds like some evil genius, don't you think?"

Gennaro did not respond. Farrugia was chewing a sample of *lardo*, his eyes closed in blatant ecstasy. Alessandro seemed envious of Farrugia's gustatory pleasure. That left only Bianca. Dante heard her answer.

"Matteo is a genius, yes, but so is Tommaso."

Alessandro, returned from his reverie, felt compelled to contribute, "Well, I certainly have more respect for him now." He drank some water and then added, "At first, I thought he was obnoxious, but now that I know he's Giurlani's nephew I can empathize with his motivation. He's holding up well, I think, considering what has happened. Piersanti, on the other hand, is the one who seems hit the hardest. Much too quiet."

Gennaro, without glancing up from his dish, said: "With youth, there is resilience, Sandro. In matters of the heart it becomes more difficult to recover as you get older. You'll see."

Bianca put down her knife and fork. She handed over her dish to a grateful Farrugia, assuring him that it was all right for him to take it. Farrugia welcomed the dish like a hungry man trying to hide the fact that he was starving.

"He is a genius, simply for that level of analysis," she said.

"He could've had a good professor," was Alessandro's comment.

"Possible, but I think his analysis is the result of associative logic. That can't be taught and Matteo and Tommaso are about the same age, which means that Tommaso understands how Matteo thinks the way that he does. Of course, Tommaso doesn't agree with him, but that's irrelevant. The point is he has that logic and insight. That also makes him dangerous."

Gennaro held on to his glass of water. "You know all he talked about regarding U.S. policy, the financial stuff, does makes me wonder about your friend in the shadows, Bianca." He toyed with his glass. "It's unavoidable no matter which way we go into this. 'Matter of national interest,' as they would say." He drank more water.

"I can see Rendition doing that," Bianca said.

Gennaro nodded. "As Alessandro would say: 'Just saying.'"

"Very funny, Boss." Alessandro threw down his napkin as if he were offended. They knew that he wasn't. Alessandro was never angry for long. There was a lull. Farrugia was still enraptured.

Then Bianca looked at Gennaro, then at Dante.

"What is it, Bianca?" Gennaro asked.

"There is another reason why Rendition might be involved or become involved as we go into this."

Gennaro stared back at her, waiting, his face expressing the word *Perché*. "Why . . . Because?"

"Tommaso knew Charlie Brooks."

After the initial impact, Dante was the first to react. "What the hell?" He stood upright, his chair almost falling backwards. "You knew that from this morning, didn't you?"

"Yes," she answered, but regretted it, realizing that when he said "What the hell?" he had it all wrong. Not *that* early in the morning.

"Damn it, Bianca. Nothing good comes from talking to that cartoon character. Excuse me, avatar." He shuffled around her to leave, bumping her shoulders as he was exiting.

"Wait, Dante. You don't understand. It's not what you think."

"The hell it isn't. I'll catch up with you later. I need to go cool off," Dante said, heading for the door.

Sandro got up and said in a soft voice, like the one the heroic character uses in movies. "I'll go and talk some sense into him. I'll be right back."

Farrugia was studying her from the side. Gennaro's face was placid.

She wanted to explain. "It's not like that. Tommaso told me himself. They went to university together in Milan."

Gennaro still said nothing. There was the sound of Farrugia's fork doing a comprehensive last scrape of the dish. He put his fork down, then his napkin. He looked up and saw Alessandro returning. "That was quick." Sandro took his chair. "What did you say to him, Sandro?"

"I told him that I'm no expert on women, but it's a bad idea to walk away. You have to talk it out."

"Wisdom from our Casanova," Gennaro said.

"Thank you, Sandro," she said; her hand stroked his arm. They were friends again. She said to Gennaro, "Don't shut me out, Gennaro. Say something, please. I explained that it wasn't what Dante was thinking. I'll explain to Dante when I see him at home."

"I know you will. It's not that."

"What is it then?"

"You were talking to Loki, weren't you?"

9

The archaeology museum itself was a relic of history, an unfortunate victim of squatter's rights. The Bourbon Spanish king had used the place as a stable for the cavalry. Heritage and history came after the equine crapper, after it became a university building in the seventeenth century. The museum, however, did revert to its former glory as The University of Naples, one of the oldest public universities in the world, the alma mater of Saint Thomas Aquinas; but it was the Spanish who ransacked Naples and the Two Sicilies, storing the best artifacts of southern Italy they could find in their king's stable. Today, the tourists surrounding Dante were likely to mistake the palace's façade for something out of *Miami Vice*. Palm trees were waving in the breeze out in front. The building's pastel pink exterior didn't help.

A teacher was shepherding and cajoling his charges to take the stairs up to the second level to the Meridiana Hall. Dante overheard the patient man saying that the exhibit of items recovered from the towns Mount Vesuvius had destroyed in 79 AD would make them better appreciate their day-trip to Pompeii tomorrow. The kids weren't listening and Dante was thinking, *Se lo dici tu.* Whatever.

Those kids were probably more interested in the gory details about the thousands who died, how archeologists had done plaster casts of empty spaces to resurrect the carnage, like mummies buried without the pomp and ceremony of the Egyptians. The Campanians, Romanized Greeks, who had died then, had died of asphyxiation after the volcano had exploded.

Dante could tell that some of the boys in the group were hormonally-inclined because they kept stealing glances at the entrance to the *Gabinetto Segreto*, the Secret Room, where all the erotica was housed. It was an exhibit requiring an additional ticket. He had been that age once. Blessed, he thought, are the horny among them for they shall always remain on that Crusade for Special Admission. He wondered what Alessandro was like at their age.

Dante confined himself to the ground floor, restricted himself to the Farnese Collection, limited his appreciation for, and his eyes to, the marble statuary from Herculaneum, Stabia, and of course, Pompeii, although he did wish to visit the bronze statues later; but that could wait until the teacher, the modern Pliny the Younger, had led his litter to safety through the destruction of falling ash, pumice, and choking fumes.

Dante walked, hands behind his back, like another cultured Italian confronting the millennia of his culture. He had been to the museum before as a child and then as a young man. He had visited the Gabinetto. He had seen the demigod Pan and his lover, the goat. They hadn't changed positions since he had last seen them. Displayed under glass, the satyr was still doing the goat. The goat on bottom was laughing at its lover's pneumatic determination.

He was angry with Bianca. Gennaro was angry with him, for considering joining Napoli Sotteranea, for wanting to explore archaeological Naples, to visit the passion he had left behind in Rome. Literally. He had deferred his pleasure in Milan. He had found no camaraderie there, no teams of professionals in Milan. There had to be brothers and sisters here in Naples who shared his enthusiasm for the hidden past, whether it was beneath the city streets or out in the sea. She had some nerve, if she agreed with Gennaro.

He re-examined his memory of the two creatures in carnal embrace. They both had tufts for beards and horns on their heads. The beard reminded him of Giancarlo Ragonese, the Free Channel reporter who had covered Charlie Brooks's murder. No horns on Ragonese but he was a mindless demon of the media, whereas the terrorist group G9 was a minion, a "false flag," for the true devils: the corporation, the politicians, and others who had opposed Lele Palmisano.

He chose to bypass the room devoted to mosaics; they made him think of the riddles between Bianca and Loki; it made him think of archeologists and historians who piece together a million shards of disparate data into a coherent picture, a not-so-coherent narrative. That was the two of them, more or less. Bianca was the analytical one, the detective. Loki was the slippery one, an eel, whether it was *anguille* or *capitoni*, male or female.

"Associative logic," she had said. Logic? There was none, he thought.

Dante had come seeking distraction. He ambled around the *Punishment of Dirce*, the massive sculpture attributed to Apollonius and Tauriscus, two brothers from Rhodes. Two brothers made him think of the café, *Due Fratelli*, where he had first met Bianca. The sculpture, the largest single piece of art from the ancient world, was a frenzy of bodies, men trying to tie a combative woman to a confused bull. Dante thought of Michelangelo's comment about art being imprisoned inside the block of marble and that the artist had to free it. He walked around the sculpture, inspecting it from several angles. There were numerous perspectives, but they all added up to drama and pain released from stone.

He thought of Charlie's body in an alley, next to a restaurant dumpster, dead only seconds after meeting Bianca. Farrugia had tried to save him, but had failed. Charlie Brooks had given her some electronic files and a kiss on the lips and, for his noble and romantic gestures, two mysterious men put two bullets into him with the precision of professional assassins: one to the chest, the other to the head.

Next up was the Hellenistic sculpture of Atlas. The giant knew that he carried the weight of a celestial sphere. A world was perched on his shoulders. Charlie had had no idea what kind of secret it was that he was carrying. He had no head on his shoulders to understand the world he had accidentally discovered while working for corporate Adastra.

There it was: the one he liked most in the entire museum. *Venus Callipyge*

This is the one that made him happiest. Not quite classic contrapposto, Dante thought, but that didn't matter. Everyone else rushed to see *Il Doriforo*, the "spear-thrower," before they left the museum because that statue, with its weight on one foot, had inspired Donatello's androgynous *David* and Michelangelo's copy of Donatello. Dante preferred her instead.

She was a woman with history. She had lost her head, but it had later been restored. While *Il Doriforo* shifted his weight onto his right leg, lifting up his left heel, looking as if he was searching for something to kill with the spear no longer in his hand, *Venus* had moved her weight to her left leg, gathered up her light robe, lifted her right foot, turned ever so modestly so she could look back and down and check out her ass. *Doriforo* had no defense and *Venus* had her own ass. Nothing had changed. Dante had no interest in the carpe diem of the Epicureans so it was straight to the bronze statues.

Bianca had history. She used to work for Rendition, an organization that he liked to call "financial vigilantes," when he felt generous. He had said to her numerous times, after they ate, while they walked and talked, when they discussed politics, after they made love (always *after* they made love), when they broached investigational strategies as to how they do forensic auditing, that any organization that was covert, by its nature had to remain hidden, was not an organization with integrity. Things should be in the open and not secretive. She agreed to disagree with him. He listened to her explain how she had joined Rendition and how she had left it, but he always countered: Rendition may have its own rules; justify its existence with language, but nothing clandestine is worthwhile. He himself, for example, worked for the Guardia di Finanza, with its gray uniforms, its gray cars that any Italian in the country would recognize. True, he and the gang did not have to wear uniforms or drive the drab cars, but that was a minor discrepancy. "Out in the open," he had told her. Overt. Rendition? It had nothing but a red *R*.

Dante took the stairs now to the top floor. The bronze statues.

There were fifty of them. The Romans had a talent for emulating the Greeks, copying them, and then copying the copies, as if originality would interrupt their plagiarism. These bronzes were from the Villa dei Papiri in Herculaneum, the vacation home of Julius Caesar's father-in-law, a notable Epicurean and collector of rare documents.

There was Hermes on a rock, his legs extended, resting his heeled wings. An inebriated faun, trying to get up off the ground, was singing to himself, like most drunks do. Dante stopped. The hall of dark statues, the long hall, the bright light and all that white of the floor, the stairs, the pedestals, had suddenly seemed sinister to him. He said to himself that it was nothing, just his being poetic like Tommaso—that is, until he had confronted one bronze statue in particular.

The Athlete. It wasn't the curly hair, the open mouth, or the way the sculptor had managed to convey his youth, his firm body, for all of eternity. It was the dark skin of bronze, the intensity of the gaze, the focused and determined blue eyes. It was those painted life-like blue eyes staring at him, the blue against the blackened bronze.

A small placard stated that other museums had replicas of numerous bronze statues from this specific gallery. It was then that Dante had thought, had wondered, whether any of these imitations of imitations were the work of Lorenzo Bevilacqua, copied, moved about and around the world with dubious paperwork from the Amici di Roma, Amici di Napoli, or some version of the corporate name-game he used to avoid detection. He began to think of names: Matteo and Amici, Matteo and Tommaso, Charlie Brooks and Tommaso Baraldi, and perhaps, Charlie Brooks and Matteo with no last name yet. Then there was that timeless stare of *The Athlete* in front of him.

Dante imagined the worst storm of possibilities: the bold stare of Camorristi eyes here in Naples, organized crime elsewhere in Italy. He imagined the distant stare of foreign, hostile eyes from across the ocean; imagined the cold, hardened stare of Gladio and the invisible glare of Rendition.

He had to go home. He had to talk to Bianca.

In the footrace home, Dante rehearsed his apology five times, edited it twice before trashing it and rethinking the matter through another five times, almost missing his subway stop and, while walking the few short blocks, avoided being hit by two cars, though he was cursed twice, once by a foreigner whose accent made the profanities hilarious, but he was too polite to laugh at the man, and then again in colorful dialect that gave him a unique understanding of God's design and the impossibilities of human anatomy.

As he put the key in the door, real dread overcame him, since this homecoming reminded him of one notorious schoolboy day when his parents were waiting for him; the news of his misdeed had preceded him, thanks to the phone, the authoritative voice of Padre Anselmo, Societas Iesu, whom he could still hear all these years later in his head. *Ad maiorem Dei gloriam.*

This was it. His key turned, the bolt slid. He pushed the door into the silence.

She was there. Waiting. He did not look. He put down his keys after he had closed the door.

"Hi," he said. Everything vanished into "I'm sorry."

"Me, too," she said. "I should've explained."

"You don't have to, Bianca. I should've stayed. There's no excuse for me walking off. For once, Sandro was right. I'm not going to lie and say I'm fine with Loki, because I'm not. I don't know what else to say, but I'm sorry."

Bianca stood there, absorbing his statement, like a lawyer waiting for the wrong word, the mistake. There were no crossed arms, no raised eyebrow, no hair pushed back. Her eyes were direct, observant, and respectful. Unnerving.

"You've said enough."

Damn. "I have? What do you have to say?" he asked.

"I do wish that you had stayed to hear what I meant to say. I understand why you thought Loki had told me that Tommaso and Charlie knew each other, but—"

"It wasn't Loki who had told you?"

Bianca shook her head.

"No. Tommaso told me himself," she said.

"He did? I'm confused."

"What about Matteo? Does he know him?" Dante felt somewhat stunned and stupid. The only thing missing was his braying. He sat down on the Henry sectional. She joined him, placing her hand on his knee.

"Tommaso didn't get into how he knows Matteo."

"I'm really sorry, Bianca."

"As for Loki, I'll try and—" she said, but stopped when his cell phone rang.

Dante stood up. He didn't know why. He just did out of reflex, just like he did when his physician enters the room. He blamed it on good Catholic manners, his Jesuit training, in recognizing the authority of the cell phone.

"*Pronto*," he listened.

Bianca sat back on the black leather. Dante always respected the fact that a phone call did not upset her nor prompt a thousand questions. She functioned from the premise that if it were important he would tell her.

"I understand. I'll get down there as soon as I can." Dante massaged his forehead. News made him think and thinking with the phone made him itch.

"Yes, she's right here, sitting next to me, in fact." A pause. "She's fine. All is good with us. Does Gennaro know?" Another pause. "I'd figured as much. I'm on my way. What?" Another silence. "Of course, I'll tell her and ask her whether she wants to come along." Some more noise and Dante ended the call.

"You won't believe it. Of all things."

"Who was it?" Bianca inched up on the sofa, concerned or intrigued, or both.

"Isidò."

"What happened?"

"McGarrity is in jail. He was arrested."

"For what?"

"I'll explain. Want to come?"

10

Farrugia was imitating Rodin's *Thinker* in a chair at the end of the hall. Alessandro was the one who saw them first; then Silvio did. They both walked toward Bianca and Dante. Farrugia merely lifted his head off of his chin but did not move from his seat.

"It's good to see you both," Sandro said to them.

"Was he drunk?" Bianca asked first.

"No, not really."

"What kind of answer is that?" Dante said. "Either he was drunk or he wasn't, so which one is it?"

"He might've had a drink. Maybe two, maybe more."

"Christ, was he that upset with the presentation?" Dante asked, looking at Silvio, expecting the answer to come from him, but instead Sandro did the job: "He was upset but not that upset. McGarrity had heard about this bar and said he wanted to try it out. He'd probably read about the place in a magazine on the flight. So they went: him, Silvio, and Murphy. Everything was going well until the U.S. Navy showed up and—"

"Did you just say 'the U.S. Navy'?" She was not sure she had heard correctly. His nod of the head confirmed that she had. Bianca looked around them and asked an obvious question, "Where's Murphy?"

"He's gone back to his place to sleep it off," Alessandro whispered.

"Sleep what off?" Bianca asked. She and Dante exchanged a look of confusion. There was no excuse for an agent to abandon his partner. None.

"Murphy was the one who'd gotten drunk, of course," Sandro said, embarrassed for the man. Drunkenness in Italy was frowned upon, like ordering a cappuccino after ten a.m. People knew that it happened but preferred that it did not.

Gabriel Valjan **83**

"Okay," Dante said, "so Murphy gets drunk, McGarrity gets arrested, I've got that, but you still haven't explained to me what the hell happened."

"I'm getting to that," Alessandro said, as if he were setting the stage. "McGarrity had seen a sailor from Bagnoli chatting up some attractive girl at the bar. You'd think that McGarrity was going to try out a line on her himself, but no." Sandro was having fun.

"No?"

"No. He said he'd seen this guy slip something into her drink. McGarrity went over thinking he could help this girl, but she was oblivious to what the creep had done. In fact, she told McGarrity off because she thought he was hitting on her. Meanwhile, the sailor got upset with him for moving in on his girl; but McGarrity was the shrewd one." Alessandro touched the side of his head to signify brilliance. "He tried to salvage the rescue."

"How did he do that?" Dante asked.

"Simple. He knocked over the girl's drink. No drink, no drug, no rape. Can you see what happened from there?"

"No, I can't, Sandro," Dante said, understanding why Gennaro often got upset with Sandro and his pencil. "Where is this story of yours going?"

"Isn't it obvious? That was when the fight broke out."

"*What* fight?" Dante asked, but feeling Bianca's hand on his elbow, he stopped.

"The one between McGarrity and the sailor," she said.

"Oh," Dante said. "So, what happened next?"

Gennaro, who had gone for water, approached them with a Dixie cup in his hand and said, "Navy guy hits McGarrity; but Agent McGarrity holds back from beating the crap out of the sailor, until his friends decide to join the fray and turned it into a free-for-all."

"I can see that," Dante commented. Gennaro wasn't finished, though.

"Like I was saying, McGarrity didn't want to hurt the kid. I guess he remembered what it was like to be that age. On leave—long time at sea and months without . . ." his voice trailed off as he blushed, seeing Bianca smiling. He tossed back the water, crumpled the cup, and sought a trashcan, but found none. He squeezed the paper harder. "The best is yet to come, though, as the song says."

"What might that be, Chief?" Dante asked.

"It turns out that the girl was a prostitute and the bar pays protection. When the carabinieri showed up, they hauled off McGarrity and some American squid. The girl disappeared and the bar owner doesn't want to press charges."

Bianca asked, "Did McGarrity identify himself as an agent?"

"Not quite."

Gennaro announced that he needed more water and that Alessandro should tell the rest of the story. Alessandro, for his part, was all set to continue reading from the playbill for the opera of the two suitors, the girl, the Camorra, and the spilt drink. Bianca and Dante were prepared for the second act.

"Stop," Dante said.

"What is it?"

"Why am I asking you when Silvio is standing here? He was there. *You* weren't. Silvio, you tell me what happened. Did he identify himself?"

"Yes."

"Shit," said Dante, touching his forehead, itching for a thought. No cell phone required.

"As FBI?" Bianca asked.

"What else? It doesn't matter, though," Silvio said.

"Why doesn't it matter?" Dante asked, just as Gennaro was returning with his water, smiling. "I'll answer that, Silvio."

"It doesn't matter because our Silvio is a genius. By the way, I hate these cups." Gennaro held up the cone of water for them to see. "The bottom is much too sharp and it hurts my hand. The cup doesn't even hold much water. It must be German engineering for water in hell."

"And why doesn't it matter?" Dante asked, seeking a complete explanation.

"Because he took McGarrity's wallet," Gennaro said.

"I did," Silvio confessed.

"His wallet?" Bianca said. Sandro seemed as excited as a kid waiting eagerly for a favorite scene from a movie to come onto the screen.

"He took his wallet."

"So I heard, Sandro," Dante said. "So when the cops came he couldn't produce any identification. That's another charge on top of 'drunk and disorderly conduct.' What happened when he said he was with the FBI?" Dante held up his hand in front of Sandro, palm out, and said, "Silvio answers this time."

"They didn't believe him because they thought he was drunk."

"Why would they think that? You just told me—I mean Alessandro told us—that he hadn't had much to drink."

"Because the carabinieri smelled him," Silvio answered.

"Smelled him?" Bianca asked.

"I spilled a couple of drinks on him."

"Spilled?" Dante asked while Alessandro laughed.

"Okay, I poured a couple drinks all over him. They'd smelled him before they heard him and when they'd heard him they wouldn't listen to him after they'd smelled him. What else can I say?"

"Brilliant." Gennaro was crumpling yet another paper cup.

"Thanks, Chief," Silvio answered. Dante was shocked. That had been his word.

"So you pinched his wallet?"

Silvio touched his breast pocket. "Naples is full of pickpockets."

"You stole his wallet. Was that before or after you'd poured drinks on him?"

"Before. I didn't want to get splashed and smell like a distillery." Silvio was not aromatic in the least. No drinks. No cigarette smoke. Not even cologne.

"I did not *steal* his wallet. I'm just holding it for him."

"And Murphy?" Bianca asked.

"I threw him in a cab and gave the driver directions."

"Please tell me they weren't carrying their weapons," was Bianca's question.

"Oh no, I wouldn't allow it."

"Why not?" Dante asked. Sandro excused himself to call Piersanti.

"You know the law. Italy isn't the Wild West. Besides, guns make me nervous."

"Guns make him nervous," Gennaro repeated. "Now we have Piersanti to worry about. We're in for an earful about the wild American out on the town. I can already hear what he's going to say."

"What's that, Chief?" Dante asked.

"*La sera leone, la mattina coglione.*"

They all laughed at that. "A lion by night, an asshole in the morning."

"And what's with Farrugia over there?" Dante asked in a lowered voice.

Gennaro tilted his head as a sign they should step away. Conference in the corner.

"He's worried because Noelle is upset with him."

"Why is she upset?" Bianca asked.

"She's still at the airport."

"What? Right now?" Dante said it loud. Gennaro shrugged. Both Bianca and Dante checked their watches. Unbelievable. Dante asked, "Why is she there?"

"Because he is *here*," Gennaro answered.

"Why didn't he say something when he called Dante?" Bianca asked. "I would've gone to pick her up."

Gennaro sighed. "He wanted it to be romantic. Isidò had no idea about the mess he was walking into here. It's kind of like Milan all over again, but not as bad: we've only the Camorra to deal with this time." Gennaro's attempt at humor fell flat with Bianca.

Sandro was returning. He had news. "McGarrity is coming up from Holding. Piersanti is pissed off, to put it mildly; but at least the American Embassy and the FBI don't know."

Except for Bianca, that news did seem to make everyone breathe more easily.

"What is it, Bianca?" asked Gennaro.

"Oh, I don't know. It's not *that* bad; except that the entire U.S. Navy knows."

She smiled; he didn't. Gennaro stood there, another Dixie cup in his hand, the pointed end digging into his palm.

The orders from Piersanti were strict and unambiguous: "Get here now!" Only Farrugia was granted an exemption from returning to the office, and that was because Piersanti knew that Farrugia had less time than the rest of them: less time to eat, less time to sleep, less time for personal matters, the personal referring to time with Noelle, because the commissario had his *other* day job working for the Totaros in Scampia. The rest of them were to report to the office without delay. That included Bianca, too.

Gennaro found food for the now liberated McGarrity. He shoved a pastry in a bag into one hand and a triple shot of take-away espresso in the other hand. The agent immediately opened the bag and made short work of the pastry and cocked the espresso back.

In the elevator with them, McGarrity's eyes were bloodshot and he reeked worse than a twelve-year-old girl with her first bottle of perfume and no sense of smell. They listened to each climbing chime of the elevator that would soon deliver them to Pio Piersanti.

"I smell," McGarrity said.

"That's the least of your worries. You need to talk to your partner," Gennaro said.

"How upset is Piersanti?" The question was meant for Alessandro, since he was the one who had last spoken with the man, but McGarrity didn't care who answered it.

"Upset enough," Gennaro said, eyes fixed on the light above. "My advice is that you keep your mouth shut."

The last chime. The doors opened up. Gennaro led the entourage, ignoring the stares from those working late. He could sense Pio Piersanti's rage from a distance. "There he is," Gennaro said to himself. Through the clear glass of his own office door and windows, Gennaro saw the man pacing the room. Tommaso sat at Farrugia's desk.

Piersanti wore a dark suit, the front of the jacket swept back to the hips as if his hands were ready for the gunfighter's draw; and his tie, also dark in color, was in stark contrast to the shirt, white as Ahab's whale but fitted, pressed, almost vulnerable, like the underbelly of a stalking panther ready to pounce on its prey. Piersanti saw them and stopped. He waited.

They filed in one by one. Alessandro, Dante, and Silvio sat down at their desks. Gennaro let Bianca have his chair, knowing the protocol that he, as their leader, had to represent them. McGarrity, either not seeing any chair for him or understanding the gravity of the situation, did the logical thing: he stood next to Gennaro. He straightened out his tie.

Tommaso had his head down, engrossed in some papers. The flatscreen television was on. Muted.

Pio took the slow pace that every commanding officer and experienced parent knew. Then he settled on McGarrity. "You're Italian better be good now, Agent McGarrity, because I can tell you this: Silvio is not going to be doing any interpreting." Piersanti had learned about Silvio's dismay at hearing both McGarrity and Murphy at the airport. "I've heard that Monterey is good. We're about to find out again today just how good." He took a half step back and stared at McGarrity.

"Do you have *any* idea the indigestion that you've caused me? Any idea?"

Gennaro had hoped that McGarrity took his advice. Mouth shut.

"Without ID you could've been detained until your nationality was verified. With Italian bureaucracy the way it is, that could have taken a lot of time."

"But . . ." McGarrity had sputtered. Gennaro closed his eyes. Bad mistake.

Piersanti was now the drill-sergeant he had seen in many American films. But Piersanti would not scream. This was to be a slow death by politeness.

"Go ahead, say it, McGarrity. Let me guess: 'I didn't have ID because Silvio took my wallet.'" He then shocked them with some choice English, "Well, boohoo to you!"

Gennaro had not heard *that* in years. Even Bianca had cracked a smile.

Piersanti pointed towards Silvio. "He took your wallet to save you and to save us." Piersanti waited a few more heartbeats. "I admire and appreciate your loyalty to Silvio, but it was for the best that he took your wallet."

McGarrity, who was taller than Piersanti, looked down, confused.

"Think about it, Agent McGarrity. You're being detained to sober up—"

"But I wasn't drunk!"

"Do not interrupt me," Piersanti said with calm authority. "I know you weren't drunk, but the last thing I need is for you, an American with the GdF, in a jail cell. It's not the roaches there that worry me, Agent McGarrity. It's word spreading throughout the facility among Camorra informants and lowlifes that you're there. That unwanted attention compromises this team; that screws all of us until we are double-jointed. Do you understand what I'm saying?"

"I was trying to help the girl. The sailor was going to drug her."

"I understand that. How ironic is it that one American tried to do the right thing while another was taking advantage of the situation—and even more ironic is that neither of you understood the context that you were in. Guess what? This is not foreign policy, Agent McGarrity. Allow me to let you in on a little secret in diplomacy. When somebody wants help they'll ask for it, or make it known somehow that they need it. You had presumed wrong. Case closed."

McGarrity's face had turned red. Gennaro was certain they all felt like a bunch of kids sitting in front of Mother Superior. She might've been yelling at one child but they *all* felt it.

"That girl was a prostitute, that bar pays protection money, and it gets its food and drink supplied by . . . guess?"

"The Camorra."

"Very good, Agent McGarrity. You've just learned how pervasive the problem is here. You're now an expert on foreign policy. Now, getting you out fast may have saved us grief on the Italian side of the equation, but—"

"'Italian side of the equation'? I don't understand."

Piersanti stared at McGarrity until McGarrity apologized for interrupting. Piersanti's tone had now turned avuncular and gentle under the drone of the air-conditioning.

"By that I meant I had to make some calls and pull some strings to get you the hell out of there. Let's hope everyone thought you were a drunk. There are never any guarantees. And I have another problem. *We* have another problem, that is," he said, wagging his finger between him and McGarrity, turning around to let the rest of the audience know they were included.

"We all know the equation. The System is the unknown variable. We know there are two sides to the equation and that we solve an equation on both sides with the equal sign in the middle. I got you out of that jail. That's the Italian side, but the question now is the American side."

Piersanti was standing near Farrugia's former desk. He picked up a pencil that Tommaso had laid out in a straight line next to an arrangement of papers. He rolled the pencil between his hands. After he'd turned around Gennaro noticed that Tommaso had replaced the pencil that had lain on his desk with one from his drawer.

"The American side is those sailors from Bagnoli. They are still in jail. They'll be handed over to military police soon. We have no way of knowing whether any of them heard your name, heard you say that you were FBI, or whether they talked to others. Who knows what they might say to each other while they're in jail. I'm afraid it might not matter at all."

"I don't understand," McGarrity asked. One more time he didn't understand the rooster might crow in the Garden of Gethsemane, Gennaro thought.

"As the cliché goes, 'Walls have ears.' A name can move through the prison system from prisoner to prisoner, and from prisoner to the outside world; but that's not the part that concerns me most. Those sailors could mention your name when they return to their world, the one on their base, perhaps during transport, or while they're in the Brig." Piersanti stopped and waited for McGarrity to look at him again.

"That's the American side of the equation?" McGarrity asked.

"Exactly."

"I don't understand." Gennaro heard the rooster crow.

"Bagnoli is one of the four bases around Naples, and then there is NATO. That NATO base, much more than the bases at Vicenza or Pisa, contributes to the local economy. Imagine a local, who works on the base, hears gossip one day and he brings it home with him. He tells a friend and that friend tells another friend. It's innocent, but the Camorra is like a dog in the garden: it hears things we don't, while you and I are trying to pull up the weeds."

McGarrity could smell himself. Piersanti wasn't finished.

"You might say, 'But, Pio. The base is a big place and I'm just a little insignificant man. Nobody'll notice. You worry too much,' and I'll tell you that I don't worry enough. Do you know what I see when I look at the military bases and NATO?"

"American military presence, the silverback gorilla in the living room."

Piersanti conceded a weak smile. He must have found the answer amusing. Gennaro thought it was beautifully articulated in Italian. Not bad, Monterey.

"That's the easy answer, Agent McGarrity, but I suggest that you look deeper. It isn't just bases and NATO that are around Naples. It's the fact that many entities, including the System, have made Naples their command center for all of the Mediterranean, Southwest Asia, and the Indian Ocean. That is what makes the Camorra multinational today, and Naples, the oldest new city for organized crime."

Piersanti returned the pencil down to the top of Tommaso's desk. Everyone was silent. Tommaso removed the pencil that Piersanti had placed on the desk and returned it to the desk drawer.

"I'm truly sorry," said McGarrity. He extended his hand. Piersanti accepted it.

Piersanti acknowledged that the hour was late. He told them to go home. He took McGarrity by the elbow and led him to a corner for some privacy. He spoke in a low voice. "For now, I'll find desks for you and Murphy. It's safer for the two of you. It's not a demotion or punishment for the two of you."

Just then they heard the television. Tommaso had stood up, aiming the remote to raise the volume.

"What is it?" Piersanti asked.

"I want everyone's attention for a moment. Have a look at the screen, please. It's something I recorded earlier."

"Can't it wait?" Piersanti asked.

"I'm afraid not," Tommaso answered, as he walked out from behind his desk to the center of the room. Everyone outside the office had left, so there was no need for paper on the glass. Tommaso fast-forwarded the recording and freeze-framed the footage until there was a single face taking up most of the screen.

Beneath the handsome face, beneath the lean physique in the bespoke Kiton suit, and beneath the banner that declared, "Rising Venture Capitalist Vows to Return Naples to World Prominence," was the Sicilian name "Matteo Mandracchia."

11

He was back at work.

Farrugia and Noelle had had a beautiful meal together, an even more beautiful night in bed together. It almost made him cry that she was so forgiving after the fiasco at the airport. Not even two minutes into his excuse making, telling her about the bullshit with McGarrity's arrest, she put her fingers to his lips and said, "Shut up and kiss me." His heart skipped the proverbial beat when she insisted that she cook for him. She had said that she had been taking a class on southern cooking as a surprise.

He felt like a child again with the antipasto. A plate of fresh-fried anchovies—*Alici fritte*—was to him what French fries were to American children. He was like the swordfish she cooked for the main course in that he gave her no struggle. *Pesce Spada alla Ghiotta*. He had pulled a Sicilian white wine from out of the rack to accompany the swordfish done "glutton's style," with tomato, capers, and olives. She told him there would be something special for dessert.

There was—they made love on the kitchen table. Love had made Commissario Isidore Farrugia *imbranato*: a goofy mess.

And now, in Scampia on an overcast morning, he was back in reality.

He watched the car ease into the parking lot. This was it. He was happy he had seen Noelle one last time, happy he had been able to spend some precious time with her in his real apartment and not in the dummy one he kept during the week in Scampia.

The car had slowed down, parked, and the door opened.

This was supposed to be a meet; "Important," he was told over the phone by some Totaro thug he knew by name but had never met. The voice sounded as if it belonged to a three hundred-pound brute in a stained wife-beater shirt, with a paunch, some gold chains around his neck that included a crucifix and a gold *cornicello*, the little horn used to ward off *malocchio*, the Evil Eye. The goon on the phone said that he was sending Stefano with the details.

Post-coital endorphins and paranoia did not mix well.

He had arrived earlier than the scheduled time for the appointment. He had developed enough of a rapport with Stefano that allowed Farrugia to call him "Ste," a shortened form of his name that maintained the part that carried the stress in the full name and reminded Farrugia of the English "stay" as he had heard in commands, such as "Stay put!" and "Stay here." That was the first sign that he was in, but the System, like most crime outfits, will send the friend to kill you. It was a courtesy not to have a stranger kill you, and a humble reminder that business is business and never personal.

Farrugia feigned fixing his belt. He had his gun near his tailbone. Would Stefano shoot him from a distance? Were there no chivalrous last words, no Judas kiss before Ste made his lethal move? Another mark of respect was to kill someone up close. The way the corpse was left behind explained why the person had been killed. There was enough sign and symbol in gangland killings to fuel several doctoral dissertations.

Stefano reached into his breast pocket. Farrugia's hand tightened around the stock. Stefano's hand was coming out.

Cigarette pack and lighter.

Asshole.

They exchanged pleasantries. This was looking as if it would be a genuine conversation, unless it was a prelude to an ambush. Farrugia kept surveying the area through his sunglasses. The Totaros could have set them both up, which is why Farrugia had cased the area earlier for all the possible entrances, exits, and blind spots.

Ste stopped, lit his cigarette, and took some small puffs. He was puffing like a slow locomotive as he approached. Ste was from Apulia, and his last name was predictable even for the dumbest genealogist: Pugliese. His record was what the police called "small-fry" because all of his infractions were from his teenage years. He would've made the upper rung of the Totaro clan had he not committed those youthful indiscretions.

No mistake about it: Stefano was a known man, not associated with System violence but with a record. He was smart, not flashy, and discreet as a small-town mayor having an affair. He got things done in a friendly manner. He was also an excellent PR man in the Totaro territories. He disliked violence unless it had a purpose. Stefano Pugliese was the perfect middle-management type, directing crews and reporting back to the capos who, in turn, reported to Amerigo Totaro.

"Good to see you," said Ste.

"Likewise. Do you want to stay here or drive around and talk?"

"Here is fine, unless you want to sit in the car for the AC."

"I'm good," said Farrugia.

"I'll try and make it quick. Something big is coming down."

"I'm listening." Let Ste spell it out since it could be anything, drugs from the Calabrians, guns from the Russians, fake fashion from a Chinese sweatshop.

"This is new, out of Foggia."

Foggia? The city was known for being bombed to rubble during the Second World War, known for its wheat fields and delicious watermelons and tomatoes. But he had a feeling the Totaros weren't interested in fruit.

"This could be more your moment, Pinuccio. This might make you."

"Pinuccio" was a diminutive of Giuseppe, Farrugia's undercover alias. A nickname was earned, and using the diminutive was a sign of respect, of affection. Ste was saying that this business might lead to Giuseppe's acceptance as a man with rank within the System.

"This sounds serious, Ste," Farrugia said. "Tell me more."

"Fake currency."

"Counterfeiting? Impressive and high-risk, although I know sentences are turned on appeal."

"Look at you—a lawyer before you get near a courthouse. Don't be superstitious. There's always a risk, but don't worry too much," Ste smiled. Farrugia tried to appear concerned.

"C'mon," Ste said, "this is a one-time gig. There's big money involved and plenty to go around. Besides, there's a truce with the Marra clan."

"You're shitting me, right? A truce?" Farrugia wasn't play-acting his shock. This was news. "When did that happen? No, never mind. You don't have to explain. The color of money did it all."

Ste fished out another cigarette and let it hang from his smiling lips. "The risk is low. I've been told that everything has been greased from high to low so a fish could pedal a bike across the Piazza del Plebiscito and nobody would say a word, including the priests."

"Really?" Farrugia said, playing along. "If it's that easy then go have a kid do it. You know how the courts treat kids."

"Relax, will you? We have somebody on the inside with the Anti-counterfeiting Unit, and the Marra clan is showing good faith."

"Good faith? What does that mean?"

"They handed over a sample from their presses in Giugliano, gratis. You're to pick up the rest. Giugliano meets Foggia."

"Is it any good?"

"Absolute artwork, my friend." Ste took the cigarette out of his mouth to kiss the tips of his fingers. "Five hundred-euro notes of such beauty that any of the renaissance masters would have cried had they seen them. Perfection."

"Five hundred-euro notes? Are you insane? That's much too large."

"In Italy, it'd get attention, but do you think the Bulgarians, the Colombians, and the Russians give a damn?"

He had a point. Farrugia also knew that the Africans and Middle Easterners were using fake euros to buy up real estate in their home countries. He remained quiet. He needed Ste to think that he was not convinced.

Giugliano was a hotbed for counterfeiting. Multigenerational counterfeiters there were masters, trained from childhood. These forgers picked every ingredient like a master chef. The chemicals, paper, the ink, dryers—the entire process had to be just right. Picking a bad tomato or a watermelon doesn't get you five to ten years in prison. So what was the connection to Foggia? What was coming out of Foggia?

Cigarette smoke lingered near his face.

"What do you say?" Ste asked.

"What do you want me to say? I know shit about fake euros. How will I know whether the goods are quality when I get there? You're telling me that the Marra family is behind this and the Totaros aren't sleeping with one eye open."

More smoke.

"You worry too much, you know that? I'll be there myself. Marra and Totaros meet, and you're responsible for our friends from Calabria. It's strictly an exchange and nothing more. The Marras have guaranteed it. Part of the new peace, don't you see? The Totaro clan gets free money as a one-time gesture, and everyone moves forward. The Marra see a sample of Totaro work done in Foggia."

Farrugia muttered, "A regular company meeting." Something wasn't adding up. He wanted to show some suspicion. "Tell me one good reason why I should do this and not be thinking chrysanthemums and a funeral hymn, huh? Tell me one."

The man put out the cigarette, exhaled a cloud of smoke, and crushed the butt with his heel. It was a nice touch. "I'll give you more than one reason if you like, Pinucc." You're the man between the Totaros and the Calabrians, and the Marras don't have that kind of in with the 'Ndrangheta. The Marras want to enjoy the benefits of working with your compatriots that the Totaros are enjoying. The Totaros know that, so they put you up. You're the Calabrian. You have any idea how huge that is? The Totaros will be very grateful to you, and since we're friends they'll be nice to me. Need I say more?"

"Yeah, I feel like Othello before the Venetian Senate." They both laughed. "And the Totaros think they'll get money for nothing? What happens afterwards?"

Ste shrugged his shoulders. "I'll be honest, I don't know. But I'll say this: if the Marras screw the Totaros, then they're screwing the Calabrians, and the Totaros can come back at the Marras with the 'Ndrangheta behind them. You tell me, why would the Marras do that to themselves?"

He said nothing. It seemed plausible, but nothing was that easy.

"What is it? You don't look convinced," Ste said.

"Did you ever think that the Marras might have some other plan in place?"

"This is serious money. Enemies will sit around a table if there is money to be made. I can tell you one thing, though." Farrugia waited for the next pitch. "They'll have a chair at the table for you to make things go well with the Calabrians."

"Ste? A few days ago I heard on the news that the euro bond had beaten expectations. Sounds like the Americans are at it again with their 'quantitative easing.'"

"Quantitative what?" The man's eyebrows lifted.

"The Fed floods the market with dollars. Then it buys back the bonds the government issues, which keeps the dollar artificially low against the euro and that makes the U.S. exports more competitive."

Ste had his fingers searching the cigarette pack but stopped. "What the hell do you care? Watch the news for the weather like everyone else! Are you in on this or what?" Another unlit cigarette hung from the man's lips.

"Yeah, I'm in. Call me later with the details."

Ste lit his cigarette. "Now you're talking. You won't regret this. I was worried about you there for a second."

"Why?" Farrugia asked.

"I don't know. You sounded like a financial analyst or something."

Bianca's morning ensemble when she walked into the office was a simple yin and yang of black and white—a pleated white skirt, strappy black shoes, a long-sleeved, gauzy black top, with her dark hair pulled back as if it belonged on a Greek statue.

Bianca had asked to work with Tommaso, and it was evident that Tommaso was thrilled. Since she had no desk of her own, he insisted they share his. At first the idea made her feel awkward, almost disrespectful. Farrugia was Isidò, but the desk was Commissario Isidore Farrugia. She felt as if she were accepting the invitation of a usurper.

She asked him for a pencil as they took their seats—lied that she preferred a pencil to a pen for taking notes. She really wanted something to fiddle with—Sandro was a bad influence. He gave her one of his pencils on the desk. He then replaced it with a pencil from his desk drawer. She said nothing as he closed it. They agreed to discuss his findings. He seemed excited.

Tommaso clicked the shortcut on his computer's desktop to access a portfolio of documents he had assembled on Matteo Mandracchia. It was obvious he had spent a considerable amount of time amassing the material. Excellent.

She saw the organizational schema of the file directory. She ignored the subdirectory of discrete file folders that Tommaso had segregated and divided into "MM_personal" and "MM_professional." She would have used a dash instead of an underscore.

As he parsed through his directory tree, narrating the content and theme of each file, her eyes noted the file size, the weight in bytes and megabytes, and the time stamps. Tommaso had been tracking Matteo for a long time, all the way from Milan to Naples. She thought of a line from Marvell. Through "hills and valleys, dales and fields."

Bianca listened to his voice as he was speaking, while her eyes were taking an inventory of his data. She thought of the files and folders as containers for water: they were the shapes that his liquid logic and perception took.

She was determined not to plug in her laptop. It was as private to her as her drawer of what were once called unmentionables. Worse, she worried that Loki might make an unexpected appearance in medias res, or would that be analytics interruptus? His voice droned and perked up now and then to emphasize some point that did not interest her.

His desk did. It was ultra-organized, approaching mathematical symmetry. He had two holders, one for pens; the other for pencils. He had four sharpened pencils to the right of his blotter, inches away from his wireless mouse. His keyboard was immaculate—no crumbs, no dust, no smudges. His screen was ergonomic, at the correct angle, as were the chair and his posture. The phone was exactly at arm's length, the cord untangled, its coils perfect. The few reports he had on his desk were piled up in a straight stack precisely two inches from the desk's edge. She sat to his left. He sat a respectful distance away from her.

They'd decided that they would discuss Matteo's funding resources for his venture-capital campaign, the one the man had declared would "return Naples to world prominence." Tommaso said he had a preliminary spreadsheet. No celebrity names, no big-name corporations, just hundreds, if not thousands, of line entries. She itched to take hold of the mouse and scroll down to the last row for the final number—another person at the keyboard was so exasperating.

She wished she were home. She could get so much more done there with her laptop open, her coffee press fueling her fingers' movement across the keyboard. And, if need be, she could hack into other systems and, as a last resort, pick Loki's brain. An office was so conventional, so painful, so damn slow, and so within the law.

The reason why she was contending with this drudgery walked into the office. Pio Piersanti was making rounds, handing out a single document and saying a few words to each office occupant, one by one. He started with Silvio. In due time he would arrive at their desk as the last stop in the circuit before he exited the room.

"So, what do your instincts tell you?" she asked.

Tommaso had his eyes fixed on his screen. "Instincts about what?"

"Matteo and his cultural-renovation program. Where does your nose tell you to go?"

"I don't believe in gut instincts, Ms. Nerini. All he has done is file a declaration of intent to form his philanthropy. We don't have much else to go on. I mean, we can read the mission statement, but that is, what I believe a former U.S. president called 'the vision thing.'"

So, the kid had a wry sense of humor. "Please, call me Bianca. Ms. Nerini makes me feel old."

A horrified expression undid the intern's face. "I didn't intend to imply that you—"

"Relax, Tommaso. You said you knew of him at school. Did you meet him? You must have formed some impression of the man." She resisted the urge to ask him about Charlie Brooks.

"What do I think of him? He's intelligent and ruthless as Niccolò Machiavelli. Clever and wily as Andreotti."

"Well, at least you think in poetic terms."

The young man smiled. Flattery worked. "Hardly poetic, but thank you."

"You seem to think in binary: True or False."

Tommaso had heard her but he chose to focus to the screen. "In the university system, tuition is on a sliding scale. If you have money, you get no break because you can pay. If you have only some money, you get a reduction on a sliding scale." He paused. "And if you have no money . . . free tuition."

"I'm aware of that. Go on."

"But the universities give you money if you earn good grades. It's like a rebate. A student of modest means has an incentive to do well—the rebate is found money. A destitute student, therefore, has the greatest incentive. Good lecture notes are money makers. And then along came Matteo."

Bianca had a McGarrity moment. "I don't understand."

"Matteo's family is poor. As you can see his last name is Sicilian. His parents emigrated north in 1980, as many southerners did, to find work. The north may have profited from exploiting the south, but the southern revenge was to bring organized crime north with them. Matteo seems to have a knack for organization even apart from the crime."

Intriguing. "Tell me more."

"The rumor was that he organized a tutoring service. Kids could get help for a nominal fee."

"And a small percentage."

"Of course. But the real business was the class notes he sold. He called them 'supplements.' All the best students were on his payroll."

"Interesting. He controls the source, meets a demand, and manages the quality of any product. A natural entrepreneur."

"I told you he is intelligent. I should have included 'resourceful.'"

Bianca was thinking back to a conversation with Gennaro. "1980? I know about some of the exploitation schemes. Cassa del Mezzogiorno."

"Among other kickback scandals. The list is endless, Bianca. Matteo grew up thinking that every time there was an earthquake, or someone in the north created some relief scheme, the south was getting ripped off. The resentment grows. It's a victim mentality—everything is always someone else's fault. Talk about a complete lack of self-criticism. It reminds me of the line Tomasi di Lampedusa had come out of the Prince of Salina's mouth: 'The Sicilians will never change, because they think they're already perfect.'"

Tommaso clicked open another file folder and then a spreadsheet.

"What do you have there?" she asked, trying to ignore the editorial.

"This is that earlier sheet of investors I showed you, except the investors are ranked according to their contribution."

"How did you get the financials?" she asked.

He didn't answer her. Perhaps he was distracted.

"How did you get the financials?" she asked again.

"I imported the data. I built a macro to run a query."

"From what database, Tommaso? I know all the GdF databases here and in Milan, even in Rome, and none of these names looks familiar to me. You had to have scoured other data sources."

"I did," he said in a soft voice.

"You mean you hacked companies and those individuals, then?"

He talked without looking at her. "We don't have the resources to do more than a cursory examination of backgrounds. I did it on my own. As you can see, the list is huge, and many of these names are subsidiaries of subsidiaries, around the nucleus that is Matteo. We can't get to the heart of the matter."

She smirked. He dodged her question with a mixed metaphor. Slick. "You're on the right track, Tommaso."

"I am?"

"The nucleus is made of protons and neutrons, but atomic mass also includes the electrons."

She said it without thought, but suddenly realized how much it sounded like something Loki would say. And she understood a bit more about Loki, and the value of tossing out information in riddles as a way of engaging different parts of the brain. Simple information was static, dead. A puzzle was a living thing, and there was no limit to how it could grow.

He turned his head away from the screen. "Matteo can't be both proton and neutron."

"Then we need to think about those electrons. Think in scientific terms."

"Okay," he said. "I remember that electrons fly around the nucleus."

She pointed to the list of names with her pencil, feeling like a school-teacher. "Electrons, Tomasso. Electrons form shells; they're held in place by an attraction to the nucleus. You said he has charisma and intelligence. That's the attractive force. What do atoms do when they form bonds?"

"They share electrons."

"Why?"

Tommaso's face was blank. Perhaps Loki had trained her at this better than she thought. She had to give him the answer.

"Stability. Sharing electrons provides stability for both elements. It's called the octet rule of valency." *La regola dell'ottetto di valenza*, or "rule of eight" she remembered from reading an Italian magazine's series on notable Italian scientists.

"Like what Piersanti had said to Agent McGarrity. Two sides of the equation."

"Exactly," she said. "Now, we can look at this either in terms of stability and sort this list by the amount of money on it, from high to low, because money is a form of a bond. Or we can do it another way." She waited to see whether his eyes might register any insight. "What do you think?"

Tommaso scoured the screen again, his cursor scrolled down the list. His lips moved. "Well, I can look at each of these as an electron in terms of stability and ask myself: Who would need Matteo the most? The answer would be the electron in the outermost orbit, the person with the least money, the most risk, and hoping for the greatest return."

"Or?"

"I can look for who is strongest, with the most money, and therefore closest to Matteo. That answer tells me who would be in the innermost orbit, but they might also expect the greatest return on their investment. Or?"

"Or what?" she asked.

"I can see if there are two sides of the equation: an Italian side and an American side."

She smiled.

"What?" he asked.

Bianca sat back in the chair. "You just learned how to follow your instinct."

"Sorry to interrupt you." Piersanti was in front of them, the last stop of the social circuit, holding out a piece of paper. "This sheet of paper has information about Commissioner Giurlani's memorial service tomorrow morning." They said nothing as the man walked away.

Piersanti had placed the sheet of paper on top of one of the stacks near the edge of Tommaso's desk. It formed a bridge across two of the stacks. Tommaso picked the sheet of paper up and placed it on top of one stack. He picked up the stack and straightened them so that the edges were uniform.

"Here is your pencil, Tommaso. Thanks for letting me borrow it."

She gave it to him and watched him take one pencil off of his desk, return it to the desk drawer, and then set down the one she had given back to him. He aligned the pencil next to the others. Aware that she was observing him, he turned his head.

"Are you okay?" she asked.

"I have OCD, Obsessive Compulsive Disorder. Things have to be in pairs or in multiples of two for me. I prefer my paperwork to be neat, in twos, and arranged in a straight line."

She saw the edge of the desk. Four stacks.

"I get irritable and I can't think, otherwise," he said. "My refrigerator has to . . . sorry. Too much personal information. I shouldn't have said a thing. I'm very sorry. You asked whether I was okay."

"I did, but I meant about the funeral service tomorrow?"

12

"*Un poco alla volta*," Farrugia muttered, as he gazed out his car window. It should be the corporate motto of the System. "Little-by-little, bit-by-bit, step-by-step."

He had finished his early-morning conversation with Noelle on the phone. He had made sure to use his other cell, the one he used with her, Bianca, and the office. The phone he carried with him was for the fictional Giuseppe.

Noelle understood that his work meant their time together during her visit would be rather limited. She mitigated whatever guilt he might be feeling for what he considered his neglect of her by telling him that she was using the time in Naples for professional reasons. She wished to meet other yoga instructors who envisioned a future yoga conference and a retreat center in Campania. They had chatted for a few minutes on his cell before they ended their conversation with "I love you." He had said it first.

Farrugia was behind the wheel of his car when he tucked the phone into his shirt pocket. He, too, had to plan for a future business meeting—Stefano and this good-faith package courtesy of the Marra clan. He came here to scope out the meeting spot. Stefano had given him the details. A real sewer.

Outside his window should have been a postcard paradise of green hills to match the name, Parco Verde di Caivano. But it was more like a circle of Dante's hell than *Felix Campania*. Happy Campania, his ass.

Abandoned factories in the distance were ghosts of forgotten prosperity. Asbestos, bleeding car batteries, paint chips all over the ground, exploded television sets, buckled refrigerators, dented washing machines, and other garbage littered the ancient farmland. Each night the trucks lumbered down the same road he was using, with the darkness of night as their camouflage, to disgorge more trash. Each night there would be the rustling sounds of garbage bags being hoisted and then thrown everywhere, or tossed into bonfires, tainting the air with the stench of burning black plastic.

Farrugia surveyed the landscape for possible safe spots. But that was ridiculous. This was Camorra territory, in and out, through and through. He'd need backup.

Illegal dumping defied his personal logic. Doctors and those scholars of diseases, epidemiologists, had drawn, like modern cartographers, a triangle of death in Campania. But instead of base times one-half the height, oncologists calculated the fourth horseman's gallop between Acerra, Nola, and Marigliano from the high incidence rate of numerous cancers.

Farrugia spotted two, possibly three, alcoves for an assault team. This would not be easy. This was not like some American crime show where the undercover agent was frisked for a wire and some pre-determined signal or code word had been established for the takedown. No. He'd be expected to stand there with a man behind him while business was discussed. Only a sniper would be able to prevent Farrugia from receiving nine grams of lead in the back of his head.

A column of black smoke was rising up in the distance. Trash from last night was smoldering. He had the AC on, and even that couldn't quell the faint odor of exhaust from passing cars and trucks. He imagined it was worse at night.

The Camorristi were not alone in the waste management trade. The 'Ndrangheta from his native Calabria had killed the journalist Ilaria Alpi in Mogadishu because she had traced their toxic waste dumping scheme across the Mediterranean into Africa, in Somalia, a former Italian colony. But after the civil war broke out there, illegal dumping became more and more difficult, and finally impossible when NATO had arrived. That's when the Camorra began dumping in their own backyards. Literally.

He decided to drive around. He saw orchards. Garbage bags dotted the sides of the road at intervals more frequent than the kilometer markers. He saw sheep. The System had outdone itself. Not only had the clans betrayed their countrymen to northern industrialists for thirty pieces of silver, they had done it *su un piatto d'argento*. Silver platter included. It made no sense to Farrugia: dump toxic wastes, build your villa on top of it, put millions of euros into Swiss banks, then live in hiding in a two-meter by two-meter underground bunker. That was the thin line between crime and insanity.

Farrugia turned on the radio and found the channel where he had heard the news about the Italian bonds. He knew that Radio Napoli was broadcasting Giurlani's funeral service. He could not attend it and risk being seen on television or photographed. Another service was planned for the commissioner in Milan.

He had already heard the grand statements from all the politicians, heard the university professors and criminologists expounding on the significance of Commisioner Aldo Giurlani. He half-expected to hear either the crowd or Jovanotti himself chanting *Cuore*. He was listening to the final section of the mass.

What he heard instead made him pull over to the side of the road.

Piersanti and Tommaso, after acting as pallbearers with a cadre of numerous state uniforms, were in the front row. The rest of them stood in the second-row pew in Santa Maria Assunta, a medieval cathedral dedicated to Our Lady of the Assumption. The men wore black suits, white shirts, black ties, and black sunglasses. Bianca wore black, too.

Gennaro suppressed the feeling of discomfort that had overcome him at the thought that his namesake, the patron saint of Naples, had a chapel here for the remains of that martyred saint. Beautiful frescoes and the fifteenth-century tomb of the fourth-century saint did not make that feeling lessen in intensity. Rather, his own name tied to that of the chapel reminded him of his own mortality, the sight of the empty wooden box with the Italian flag draped over it was unsettling.

The cathedral doors were open. Thousands of Neapolitans stood outside in respectful silence once the requiem mass had begun. As with all moments of grief, Gennaro did not hear the priest at first. He knew the mass by heart, even though he had buried his wife, Lucia, more than two decades ago. Every Catholic knew the mass for the dead and this was exactly why Gennaro was seething. He gripped the wood of the pew and ground his teeth.

It was not that this was happening again. Death comes to us all. It was not that this was another reiteration of senseless violence. Many innocents had died: common people and famous people. Aldo Giurlani died a good man. Giovanni Falcone, who was blown up with his wife and his escort on the highway from Palermo's airport, died a good man. Paolo Borsellino, also blown up, went to his maker after pressing his mother's intercom, his jacket slung over his shoulder, his signature cigarette between his lips, the retinue of five guards decimated with him, a woman officer among them. Gennaro understood killing.

Gennaro was angry with the priest, for not once saying words about the man, the departed and forever-disappearing one. The Protestants, he thought, at least commemorate the life of the deceased in the mass. This priest was talking on and on about the kingdom of God and how God the Father will welcome home his faithful son. Fuck that. Did God love ashes? Did he love the crematorium towers of the death camps and the millions who ascended to him not as doves of peace but as white smoke?

Aldo was a man of smoke.

Gennaro was bitter, finding the mass, like dull sex, all motion and procedure. They rose and sat, kneeled and stood again. They heard *Dies Irae* sung, they listened and responded to the other parts, the Sanctus, Agnus Dei, and many took Communion and waited for the concluding sections on Liberation and Paradise.

It was in refusing the sacrament that he felt most rebellious. He saw that Bianca abstained from the Eucharist as well. He wondered why. He wished he had another reason to refrain from taking Communion himself, but even there he found himself Catholic. He had committed a mortal sin. He had killed a man. While that death was deemed self-defense, it really hadn't been. He knew it and God knew it. Maybe he was unavoidably Catholic and Italian after all?

It was nearing the end of the service when the priest announced that the family had requested a portion of a particular piece of music to be played on the PA system that the media had installed. Gennaro could tell from the turning of the heads that Alessandro, Bianca, and Dante were thinking the same thought: Did *il padre* mean Pio, Tommaso, or both? Gennaro heard the priest say the music was a particular favorite of the late Aldo Giurlani. The assembled mourners sat and waited. They heard the faint scratching sound of a record begin to play.

Gennaro felt deceived by what he was hearing. Not Italian. Slow, but not adagio—but not faster than largo. *Adagietto?* Definitely not Italian. More like Mahler, but not quite Mahler. There was no brass, no percussion. There was the melody. He was hearing it. The crowd heard it start out low like someone who had been beaten trying to speak, struggling to get up, finding his senses, and then outraged at the injustice, the violence done to him. Gennaro could feel the chill; his muscles quivered.

He understood why Giurlani loved this piece, and Gennaro knew that the hundreds of people around him and the hundreds more outside and the thousands listening to the radio or watching the television also understood. It was then that he began to cry, as the single arc of melody devastated the air.

Shostakovich. Symphony No. 5 in D Minor. Third movement.

It was Giurlani speaking to them, reminding them of the terrors inflicted on their nation by the mafia, whether it was called Camorra or System, Cosa Nostra or Sicilian Mafia, or 'Ndrangheta, or some other ethnic name. It was Giurlani reminding them to remember their dead, although he would not have known the irony that he would be counted among them. The music played, accompanied by silence, punctuated by occasional sniffling and tears. More tears and understanding.

Shostakovich masked his rage at Stalin in his music and lied to the censors. The lies saved his life. The music indicted Stalin as a murderer. Giurlani's rage was directed at violence. At organized crime. He had had no lies to tell. He was uncensored. He had had no place to hide. He was killed.

Gennaro's eyes stung from tears. He wiped the wetness away and surveyed the crowd.

Wait. A man in the back of the church. It couldn't be. The resemblance was remarkable.

He turned to Bianca. She had seen him, too, and her face was emotionless. Gennaro turned his head to look again.

U.S. Attorney Michael Farese.

The radio was on. The car was parked.

Farrugia was recalling that scenes of death, the rubble, the conmingled smell of rubber and violated steel, the summer heat, the white veil of concrete dust—first with Giovanni Falcone and then Paolo Borsellino, and now, Aldo Giurlani. He also thought of his mother. He could not help the tears. They fell. He bowed his head and blessed himself old school.

"*In nomine Patris, et Filii, et Spiritus Sancti.* Amen."

13

With the sizzling of garlic and the odor of oregano, crushed red pepper, butter, some sage, and the added astringency of lemon fading in the air, Alessandro and Dante each devoured a dish of clams Gennaro had cooked. Bianca ate as well, but she was more interested in going online.

All of them had been in a solemn mood after the funeral service. Not one of them had uttered a word about Farese. They had eaten in relative silence. Dante had invited Piersanti and Tommaso, but they had declined. Silvio had left, having given Dante some odd excuse, but Silvio was Silvio, Bianca said and Dante agreed.

"I'm going online," she said to Dante.

Gennaro looked up the way a father suspected his child was watching too much television. He seemed to have expected Dante to say something.

Dante did. "Loki?"

"Yes," she said, and anticipating Gennaro's question or even his objection, "I'm up front about it now." Gennaro said nothing. When she glanced over at Alessandro to see whether he had an opinion or objection, he just shrugged like an apathetic teenager.

"I'll bring you a drink in a few minutes," said Dante, his voice fading behind her as she walked across the room to power up her screen. She sat in her chair, pulled out her notepad and a pencil. She picked one pencil, hesitated, and opened her desk drawer. She took out another pencil and placed it near her pad.

Her screen was up. Messenger open.

She could see that Loki's avatar was sleeping. She double-clicked on it, hoped the message was going through that she was online and wanted to chat.

Nothing.

Farese's appearance at the funeral service had startled her. And stirred suspicion. She had learned through Loki and Farrugia's friend, the journalist Claudio Ferrero, that Farese had the uncanny habit of showing up after assassinations; first Olof Palme's in 1986, and then later, Pim Fortuyn's in 2002. In her last face-to-face with him in Milan, they had reached a mutual understanding of sorts. He was keeping his word about Adastra and she was keeping hers.

Now Giurlani.

Loki was awake. The avatar was rubbing sleepers out of its eyes.

"Hi," she typed.

"Hi."

"Got Qs." More questions.

"OK." Loki seemed less playful, more demure.

"I saw A MF." Attorney Michael Farese.

"That's a bad word. Curse much?"

She read what she had typed. She answered, "No way."

"Funny. Qs pls?"

This was the most cooperative and forthcoming Loki had ever been with her. The avatar wasn't changing genders or acting sexually suggestive. Loki must've really been asleep.

"U OK?" she asked.

"Y?"

"U don't seem ur usual self."

The avatar's face puffed up, a smile taking up the screen, then shrank back to do a series of bodybuilder poses, flexing and pumping muscles. "Better now?"

"Better," she answered. "MF was @ AG service."

The Norse avatar tilted its head as if it were reading her statements like a bubble over a cartoon character's head. "Paying respects = his right. OC = specialty. AG = peer."

She couldn't disagree. Michael Farese was an expert in organized

116 Turning to Stone

crime, and a legal expert, just as Aldo Giurlani had been. Loki was typing again.

"R u thinking 86 & 02?"

"Yes." She tapped out periods and "MF & R?" Michael Farese and Rendition.

"Odin Inert."

Bianca stared at it. "Asked about red R & u typed Odin Inert," she said as she typed.

She was about to type another angry line back at Loki, when she saw "Odin Inert" loom large. It lingered on the screen until the individual letters started raining down and spelling out: R-E-N-D-I-T-I-O-N.

How could she have missed it? She had thought that Loki was talking about the Norse god of gods, Odin. It was a bleeping anagram.

"So MF & Odin not a couple."

"Let the jury decide."

"My turn. Diff subj," she typed. "Asked about TB last. Now ask, TB & CB?"

"Bicocca."

That was the University of Milan campus north of Milan in the old Pirelli complex. Bicocca was where Charlie Brooks had been studying economics. She bet that it had a sociology department, but hadn't confirmed it. Loki must have researched TB to equate the initials with Tommaso Baraldi since they had last messaged each other. She had another thought.

"Bocconi?"

"No TB. Diff subj, pls."

Loki was asking to change topics. Evasive maneuver? "Sure."

"IF there?"

"N." Loki was asking for Farrugia.

"If IF = undercover then not a cover."

Farrugia was undercover, but "not a cover" meant what? She was thinking about that enigmatic Loki statement when Dante came into

Gabriel Valjan **117**

the study with Gennaro, drinks on a tray. *Negroni sbagliato*. God bless him. Alessandro was in tow doing the slow walk with a tray of homemade sorbet.

"Our friend, I see," Dante said, placing her drink next to her mouse. "Ssh."

"What's with you?"

"I'm thinking, Dante."

Gennaro set down a dish of raspberry sorbet on her left. He saw the screen and read what he was seeing out loud, "'If Farrugia is undercover then not a cover.' Hey, I'm getting pretty good at this."

"Do you mind, Gennaro?"

"I was reading what your friend had written, Bianca. I thought I was being helpful."

"Speaking of Farrugia, I'm wondering how he is," Dante said.

"What is this, a community center?" she asked. "You want to help? Tell me what 'not a cover' means."

She heard a ping. Loki's avatar was waiting. Dante's phone started ringing.

"Aren't you going to take that?" she asked.

"Jesus, I'll take it in the kitchen. I'll be right back," Dante said, making a face at Alessandro and Gennaro.

Loki announced: "Going offline soon."

"No." Bianca typed fast. "Don't go. Qs. I'll play a game."

The avatar smiled. "Funny that you should say that. Here are ur clues."

A string of sentences ran across the screen, hard-returned as individual lines.

"ADAGIO ILL RUN knew A RAT TOO . . . then boom then IF."

"ARMADA BOOM LIST starts with EAT TOM."

"FEDORA INFORMS AS FREE . . . *bye bye*."

The avatar went offline. Dead space.

The lines were static on the screen. Bianca copied them down, as

Alessandro and Gennaro squinted, craning their heads in unison to read the screen, lips moving, drinks in hand, the Negroni in varying states of consumption.

"Damn." She had finished copying the last line in block print on her notepad. She grabbed her Negroni, appreciating the substitution of Prosecco for gin. No stupid slice of orange for garnish. She knew one Negroni would not be enough.

"Don't forget your sorbet. Gennaro made it." Alessandro picked up the notepad and started reading it.

"Thank you." She grabbed her notepad back. "Screen not good enough for you?"

"Wow. Aren't we grumpy?"

She remembered her insight with Tommaso on the power of the puzzle. Loki was leading her on to something deep, involving Farrugia. "I've got to figure this out."

"What do you think they are?" Gennaro pointed to the block of lines.

"Anagrams from Loki," she said, showing him and Sandro "ODIN INERT" on the screen for Rendition. Gennaro seemed more interested in his raspberry sorbet. His Negroni had disappeared. Alessandro, using his spoon for a pointer, went to the line "not a cover." "That's not an anagram. That's a direct statement."

Gennaro asked, "May I have your sorbet if you don't want it?"

"Sure. Any ideas, Gennaro."

"Loki said, 'If Farrugia is undercover then not a cover.' Cover is slang for an alias."

"Sandro, like the sorbet?"

Dante entered the room, half-finished drink in one hand, his cell phone closed in the other. "You're not going to believe this, but what are the odds of getting a phone call and a text?"

"Happens more than you think, Dante. What is it?" Bianca asked.

"Why are you in a bad mood?"

Gennaro, working on her sorbet, said, "She's used to thinking on her own and we've interrupted her. Who called?"

"Claudio. He's coming to Naples."

"Ferrero from *La Stampa*?" Gennaro asked. "He's coming down from Torino?"

"Actually, he's coming up from Catania. You remember him and . . . never mind."

"Let me guess, Dante," said Bianca. "He saw Farese on the television."

"We did talk about that but no, not because of Farese. He's investigating Mandracchia and the Marra clan."

They all stared at Dante. "Matteo and Marra?" asked Bianca.

"Yeah, and the text was from Isidò. He wants us to ask Piersanti to put in for an assault team. He gave me the GPS coordinates. Some place north of the city."

"Backup?" Gennaro asked.

"Something is coming down, but he didn't give details."

"Or 'not a cover' means Farrugia's cover is blown," Bianca said.

Gennaro's face looked as if an atheist had just proven to him that God did not exist.

14

"What do you mean my cover is blown?"

It was hard to hear, as Bianca had expected. Farrugia had asked her to hand the phone over to Dante who, with Gennaro at his side, listened to the effusive but justifiable profanities. Alessandro made the smart move of distracting Tommaso with some questions about some file or other. The agents McGarrity and Murphy were engrossed with something on their computer screens. Silvio was the absent one. He had not yet arrived at the office.

"I understand you're upset, Isidò," Dante said, then clamped his eyes shut and endured another aural assault of Calabrese invectives. Gennaro whistled. Farrugia was beyond upset; he was enraged.

"That's right. Her friend said that," Dante said into the receiver, voice calm.

"Friend? You mean Loki, don't you?"

Dante said nothing.

More curses before, "You're taking the word of a spirit in a box? Am I hearing you right?"

"Yes, that's correct." Dante answered and Bianca looked away while Farrugia impugned Dante's intelligence, his ancestry backwards and forwards in historical time, ending with, "Give me Gennaro, please."

Gennaro took hold of the phone. "Isidò . . . Isidò, you need to calm down." Again, quiet voice on Gennaro's part.

"Me, calm down? And you . . . how do you feel about all this?"

"I trust Bianca," Gennaro said, looking over at the agents, and then at her. Thumb up from Gennaro.

"I trust her, too," Farrugia said, his voice finding a middle register but not losing its edge. "But this is Loki we're talking about. I don't believe in elves, Gennaro, and need I remind you that we've never known for sure about Rendition and Loki. We don't even know whether Loki pees standing up or sitting down."

"I know that, but let's look at the facts—"

"What facts? My life is at risk and you're telling me to trust a phantom."

Loki wasn't Santa Claus, and Farrugia was being asked to have faith, bordering on the religious. That was asking for wings and magical thinking. She wasn't sure she could do it herself. How did Loki know about Farrugia undercover?

"Are you listening to yourself, Gennaro?" Farrugia was back to yelling. "I'm going into the pit with two of the clans, the Marras and Totaros, in a god-forsaken sewer. The Totaros! And you're telling me that my cover is blown. They'll kill me on sight. If I don't show, they'll hunt me down."

"I hear you, Isidò. I understand."

"Did you get Piersanti?"

"We're still trying."

"Try harder. These are the same people who put a contract out on you, the same scum who had Lucia murdered. I want to make sure you and I are on the same page."

"We are," Gennaro said, snapping his fingers at Dante. He could see through the glass door that Piersanti was coming down the hall. "Isidò?"

"What?"

"Piersanti is coming." Gennaro terminated the call and closed the lid on the cell phone.

Piersanti walked in. He was wound up, almost livid. The moment he walked in he canvassed the office. "Where's Silvio?"

"I don't know, but we need to talk," Gennaro said. "It's not like him to be late, but I'm sure there's a good reason. Well, a good Silvio reason. Can we talk?"

"It's not a good time. Regional just telephoned me. They're squeezing me like a wine press, and I've just been told that U.S. Attorney Michael Farese is on his way to this office. I was told he had specifically asked for Silvio, and the man is not here. Just fantastic. I have no translator."

"Screw him," Gennaro said. "It's Farrugia and he's asked for an assault team. We think his cover has been blown."

"What? Did he say that?"

"Not exactly, but he gave us a location. GPS coordinates."

Piersanti became nervous upset. He was sweating in an air-conditioned office. He reached for the phone to start making calls. "I hope I can get a team. The last thing I need is an undercover operation blown. Ever since Giurlani's death, nobody wants to give me the resources I need. They won't give me a hammer and nails, but they keep showing me the cross on the hill."

Alessandro cleared his throat and said, "Incoming."

Gennaro could see over Piersanti's shoulder that Silvio was sauntering down the hall.

"What is it?" Piersanti asked, back to the door.

"Silvio is about to come in," Gennaro said.

"If I can't get through we should get him to talk to Farese."

"Farese?" asked Gennaro.

"He can get an assault team faster. He's a U.S. Attorney. Nobody here wants to upset an American legal expert visiting Italy."

The door opened. Piersanti hung up the phone. Silvio entered, saw the crowd, and immediately cringed, as if he had missed an important meeting. He said his hellos and went to his desk. He walked with a slight limp.

Pierosanto began the executioner's walk over to the man's desk. Gennaro followed.

Piersanti surprised both Gennaro and Silvio: he spoke in English. "How's your English?"

"Fine, Boss. Why do you ask?" Silvio answered in the same language.

"Hi, Chief, how are you?"

"Fine, thanks." It was contagious now. Gennaro had answered in English.

Gabriel Valjan **123**

"Good," said Piersanti, returning to Italian. "Your old friend, U.S. Attorney Michael Farese, has requested your services. You're his translator when he arrives. I'd like for you to ask him a favor. It's urgent."

"I'd be honored to work with him again," said Silvio, taking his jacket off and putting it on the back of his chair, ignoring the Sardanapalo coat stand. Again, he moved with a slight limp.

"Are you all right, Silvio?" Gennaro asked.

"Fine, Chief," he answered as he arranged his paperwork, ready to start his day. It must have been a case of jitters because Silvio was still using English.

"Good. I couldn't help but notice that you have a limp."

"Jogging. I started running for exercise, and I think I overdid myself. My calf is tight." Alessandro translated Silvio's English for Piersanti's benefit.

"In Italian, please," Piersanti said.

"Of course, Boss."

"I used to be a detective in my day, Silvio," Piersanti said. "You have a limp, your eyes are bloodshot and you have scratches on your hand and neck. Now, I don't mean to pry, but are you sure that you're okay?"

Silvio looked over his hand and instinctively put it to his throat, either to check his collar or confirm that his throat was intact. Piersanti waited.

"If you must know, Boss. I confess."

"Confess what? What is it?"

"I've adopted a cat. I'm allergic and he scratched me." Silvio held up his hand—and, yes, the scratches had to be feline. Piersanti seemed convinced. Alessandro had started to laugh, but canned it when Piersanti turned and gave him the proverbial stare over the shoulder.

"A cat? And you're allergic to it?"

"Yes, I am allergic, but I'll get over it."

"I see. Does this cat have a name?"

Silvio hesitated. "Commish."

"As in Commissioner?" Piersanti failed to suppress a smile.

"I didn't want to name him Aldo. It seemed disrespectful."

"I guess that explains things, Silvio." Piersanti picked up the phone and handed it to Silvio.

"Why are you handing me the phone?"

"Call Farese and ask him to do whatever he can to get an assault team to this location," Piersanti said, also handing him the paper with Dante's GPS scribble.

The lunch hour had come, and there was no sign of the U.S. attorney. Silvio had sworn up and down that he talked to Farese and that he was given assurances.

Gennaro had called Farrugia again, heard more creative uses of the Italian language before Farrugia had resigned himself to the fact that he was not receiving any backup. Bianca could see that Gennaro was upset, guilty at not doing enough.

He was also hungry, and against all he knew and valued, was contemplating take-out. In a decisive move, he ripped off a sheet of paper to take requests for pizza or panino sandwiches. The two agents ordered salads. Bianca watched Gennaro try to persuade them otherwise, saying that you don't come to Italy to eat salad. Only an American would order arugula. Most Italians would point to the hills and laugh. She gave him her order.

"What about Silvio?" she asked.

"He's on the phone again."

"He's been on it for a while. You don't think he's talking to Farese, do you?"

"No, he's talking to The Commissioner."

"Wow, I'm impressed. The regional commissioner."

"What are you talking about, Bianca?"

"You just said he was talking to the commissioner."

"He is. The cat, not the human. Silvio is worried that Commish

Gabriel Valjan **125**

might get lonely in the apartment, so he talks to him through the answering machine."

It seemed Silvio could still surprise. "In English or Italian?"

"Does it matter? The cat'll be confused either way." Gennaro pocketed the sheet of paper of lunch orders. He planned to call them in on his cell phone. Silvio would have to take what Gennaro had chosen. He wasn't one to complain.

"See you, soon," she said. "Try not to think about Farrugia."

"Hard not to, Bianca. I hope the elf is wrong."

Tommaso was being quite social during the entire crisis. After Silvio had finished his fatherly message over the phone, he regaled Alessandro and Tommaso with stories of proud Papa and kitty. Dante and Bianca exchanged glances from their desks. She had flipped the top page of her notepad over and was revisiting the inserted sheet she had of the anagrams. There was no mathematical pattern to the letters. No substitution. She had thought that Loki had given her some kind of guiding principle or key with the Rendition example, but that was a false start. Each line here was unique, and unless she experienced the irrational jolt of insight, meaningless. Bianca closed her eyes and leaned back in the chair, waiting for revelation.

"Hey kid," Agent Murphy called out.

"It's Tommaso," said her desk partner on the other side of the room, leaving the cat stories and Alessandro behind him.

"Sorry about that, Tommaso. My partner and I were curious. You said your degree is in sociology."

"True," Tommaso answered, his voice hesitant and suspicious. Most students are enthusiastic to discuss their studies, their area of developing expertise. She continued listening to the play of voices.

McGarrity's voice: "What did you do your senior project on? You did have a senior project, didn't you?"

"I did. It might sound odd to you because you're Americans. It's controversial." Tommaso sounded, if anything, less confident. Hedging?

"Try us." Murphy's voice that time.

"Organized crime is thought of as an economic problem. I disagree. I think it's cultural."

"We're listening," said McGarrity, for both himself and Murphy.

"I mean, there has to be something broken inside the head when a crime boss lives underground and doesn't enjoy the wealth that he steals, or makes money from dumping poisons in the very place where he lives and raises his children."

McGarrity's voice: "Like a mental illness, except it's cultural. That's creative, but money is what makes the world go 'round. Don't forget that."

"You mean 'capitalism,' don't you, Agent McGarrity?"

"Politics and religion, kid," said Murphy.

"In the fifties, people simply said that the Mafia was a legend, that it didn't exist. Now, Sicilians wait outside the police stations and applaud the cops when they arrest a Mafioso. The mafia is part of Sicilian culture, but it involves a minority of the population, and it is not regarded with as much respect as it used to be in the past. Here in Naples, it is different. The Camorra is intrinsic to both the economy and the mentality."

"Interesting premise." McGarrity this time. "You seem to think that the Camorra will become multinational, like a corporation."

"I do."

Murphy spoke: "You're a smart kid, but you don't go from street thugs to multinational overnight. It takes time, it takes organization."

"That's where I disagree. It's the lack of organization that makes the System so successful, so difficult for law enforcement to break down and destroy. It's liquid, which makes it more violent. There is no 'bosses of the bosses,' no 'rules' to the violence. And another thing . . . in the Camorra, women are also powerful leaders."

"It's a nice theory you have there," McGarrity said, "but I have to agree with my partner. Structure is what makes a criminal organization powerful. There have to be rules. Corporations have rules. The System needs order before it becomes corporate."

Bianca listened as she flipped her page over and read the first two anagrams and underlined the words.

ADAGIO ILL RUN knew A RAT TOO . . . then <u>boom</u> then IF.

ARMADA <u>BOOM</u> LIST starts with EAT TOM.

Too much "boom."

Piersanti stuck his head through the opened door. "I just heard from Farese. Farrugia has backup.

15

Farrugia replayed the scene in his imagination. He would be found face down in the horrible dirt, with a hole in the back of his head, the front of his face gone. He'd hoped that the last image in his mind, the last word on his lips would be "Noelle." That was the romantic version.

The likely version was he'd have that hole in the back of the head, his face down in the muck, and echoes of a laughing Loki ricocheting around in his head before the bullet cleared out his skull. Then there was the Tarantino version, the one in which he would be shot in both legs, tied to a chair and tortured for hours, confusing his captors with Loki and Rendition before they shot him multiple times out of sheer frustration. They would then either throw his body into an acid pit, or chop him up like romaine lettuce so his body could fit inside black plastic bags for a midnight incineration. He wondered how many plastic bags he'd take. He estimated four, the kind advertised on television, with the pull handles.

Dental records would identify him. There would be no sexy female forensic doctor like the one he saw on RAI late-night television—a gorgeous American actress who had the damaged male partner, their sexual tension on low-simmer. She never wore a face-shield or apron or any other protective barrier from the spray of bodily fluids, bone-cutting saws, and chest-splitters. The *medico legale* he imagined for Commissario Isidore Farrugia was some slow-moving squat man in scrubs who worked in the basement of a hospital's cold room, like a mole who didn't see daylight most days out of the year. This coroner would be so ugly that his wife's fulfillment of the sacrament of marriage could be counted by the number of children they had.

Farrugia feared this second violence, the post-mortem inquest, more than death itself. It was an irrational fear, since he would be dead; but was it not comical to have two doctors removing and weighing his viscera so they could state the obvious on the final line of his death certificate? His COD would read "Camorra-related gunshot, secondary to the bullshit at the office."

That summed it up. The morticians would joke that he had atrocious toenails, argue over his charred remains as to whether he had placed it to the left or to the right, and debate whether he wore boxer briefs or trunks. That was it, thanks to Loki.

Damn Loki.

He knew he had to end this self-pity, but he couldn't resist one last bit of self-indulgence. He envisioned a memorial, a parade of starched uniforms, shiny medals, the shoulder braids, and the national flag. There would be the stoic sniffles of Noelle and Bianca. Well, maybe not Bianca, but he could picture Alessandro and Dante crying. Gennaro would brood. Silvio would be the wailer seen at southern funerals. Pinolo would deliver the eulogy. He imagined an empty coffin. Mere symbolism since he had ticked the box for cremation on his official paperwork. The Church had approved of cremation. It was environmental, the green thing to do these days. Noelle would be pleased.

His cell phone rang. The personal one. He'd been expecting Gennaro to call back.

"*Pronto*," he said, trying to maintain his pride. He was still pissed off.

"Isidò? Is that you?"

"Claudio?" Farrugia found himself smiling. "How did you get this number?"

"Gennaro gave it to me. Do you have time to talk?"

"I have a minute or two. I assume you're back in Turin. Thank you, by the way, for the postcard from Catania. I'm happy to hear that Arnaldo is doing well."

"He is. He's very fond of you. He's mentioned several times that you and Noelle should holiday in Catania, do some yoga and relax, enjoy the sun."

"One day," Farrugia heard himself saying, thinking that it would not be.

"Isidò?"

"Yes."

"I'm in Naples. Let's get together."

"Naples?" He hadn't expected this.

"I'm in town working on a story."

"I . . . I don't know, Claudio. Now is not a good time. Work, you know, and—"

"You're undercover, Gennaro told me. I might be able to help you. It's that, or I can keep Noelle busy. I could make her forget all about you."

"You're gay, Claudio. That would make it harder."

"I don't know about that, Isidò. I dress better than you. I have more charm. I know what to say and how to say it. I know the restaurants. Final offer."

"You're sweet, Claudio, and I appreciate the laugh, but I'm dealing with some serious shit here."

"I know. Gennaro told me, or rather Dante told Gennaro and he told me. Look, I'm working on something of my own. I didn't get into details with them, but I'll tell you. Just not over the phone."

"Claudio . . . I know you mean well, but this isn't politics, a banking scandal, or some dirty company. This is people who could make your body disappear easily because they've had lots of practice."

There was silence.

"Claudio?"

"Actually, it is all that—the politics and the rest. There's an international angle, a company, and it also involves your body-disposal guys in the System."

"Really? You have your hands full. You don't need me then."

"I disagree. We need each other on this one, Commissario."

"Why do you say that? Because of the System?"

"The Totaro and Marra clans are both in on this, and so is Matteo Mandracchia. Oh, one other thing . . ."

"One other thing?"

Another pause.

"Claudio? What's the other thing?"

"It involves counterfeiting."

The word lingered in Farrugia's head. The Ferrero knack for the *La Stampa* scoop made Farrugia think that journalists were half-fortune-teller and half-bloodhound.

"Are you there, Isidò?"

"I'm here. I heard 'counterfeiting.'"

"That's what it's supposed to look like, but it's much more than that."

He'd heard enough. They agreed to a time and a place. Farrugia would have to drive into the city. A new movie scene was playing in his head. Another script, and complicated angles, different possibilities all playing out within his imagination.

The bullet in the back of the head and the plastic bags seemed more and more real no matter how he screened it.

Gennaro would have made a great pilgrim. From Antica Pizzeria Port'Alba he secured four orders of *Napoletana* for himself, Silvio, and the agents who, Bianca could tell, were enjoying the thin crust, the fresh *mozzarella di bufala*, the fresh tomatoes, basil leaves, and olive oil. Boxes under one arm, Gennaro had braved the bookstalls and the reading crowds outside the numerous bookstores from Piazza Dante to Piazza Bellini to secure a *panino* for her; for Dante, a fast pasta dish; for Tommaso, an item from one of the side-street vendors.

The agents had that forlorn look of men who'd wished they could drink on the job. *Birra in bottiglia*. Bianca could tell they'd share a bottle of beer, put a straw in it if they had to, if only they could have one with their pizzas. Neapolitan thin crust had triumphed over New York pie and Chicago deep-dish.

Tommaso was dining with Silvio, Alessandro with Dante, while she and Gennaro had chosen solitude. Gennaro was munching away and probably worrying about Farrugia. She saw his eyes contemplate the cell phone on the desk. He looked and then looked away. Guilt. He wanted to call, but he was afraid.

She was worried as well, but the best thing she could do for Farrugia was figure out what the hell Loki was talking about. She wiped her hands on her napkin, enjoying the lingering sweet taste of basil as she looked at the first line:

ADAGIO ILL RUN knew A RAT TOO . . . then <u>boom</u> then IF.

The ellipses and lower-case phrase was a direct statement, as Alessandro had pointed out with his sorbet spoon with "no cover." The "then" made her think of Gennaro's *If-Then* logic comment. The direct statement concerned Isidore Farrugia, the IF at the end of the line. Even "knew" was not part of the anagram. That left "ADAGIO" and "A RAT."

She stared at the line. She wrote down:

SOMETHING knew SOMETHING then boom then NAME.

That didn't make sense. Things don't know other things. People know things. She modified the line:

SOMEBODY knew SOMEBODY, then X and then IF.

This seemed somewhat better. She had one name, Isidore Farrugia, but had no idea what "boom" meant and "ADAGIO" was a musical term and not a person. Was a rat a person?

Bianca tapped her pencil on "ADAGIO" and repeated "music . . . music . . ." "Boom" could be percussion, but that didn't make sense. She stared at the line once more and thought back to Loki's first example of "ODIN INERT" and looked at "ADAGIO ILL RUN" as her eyes moved between that phrase and "boom" as she checked each letter in the "ADAGIO" phrase. It was there. Because of the "boom," it was a horrible pun.

ALDO GIURLANI knew A RAT TOO . . . then <u>boom</u> then Farrugia.

Shit. Will what happened to Aldo happen to Farrugia? Who was this rat, and had exposing the rat, or Aldo's discovering the rat, gotten him killed? Will the rat kill Isidore if he discovers him?

She covered her notes with the top sheet of paper. She had to think.

Everyone was still eating. The world seemed civilized. A soundtrack of sweet violin music could be playing in the background, but it all could change in a moment. The rat was a person and this person was common to both the late Giurlani and the endangered commissario.

Who? Who was this plague-carrying vermin? If knowing the identity of this rat or uncovering his or her identity is what got the commissioner killed, then it was likely to get Farrugia killed. Gennaro might've been correct—If-Then logic. *What was the damn name?*

Bianca hadn't realized that she had been staring at the lines on the page for some time, because she heard repeated tapping on her desk. It was Gennaro.

"Sorry. I was deep in thought." She hated using clichés.

"I could see that." He said nothing more but he had seen her covering the page.

"What is it?"

"I just got a call from Farrugia. He said that he and Claudio Ferrero are meeting up. It seems they've been working both ends towards the middle."

"Really? I thought Ferrero was investigating Matteo and Marra. Is there a connection with Totaro?"

"Who knows? I wish I did. You know those two did yoga together in Milan, don't you?"

"Gennaro, yoga is a good thing."

Gennaro was shaking his head. "Ferrero calms Farrugia and that's wonderful, but this isn't the time for Buddhist kōans. Ferrero is not Yoda and he hardly qualifies as backup."

She had to agree with him. Ferrero was a journalist—the kind that is great for movies, posters, and postage stamps. The kind that gets killed. Farrugia needed firepower and not Piedmontese eloquence. It bothered her and she had to ask again, "Do you really think there's a connection between Mandracchia and the clans?"

"Ask Tommaso, not me. He's your partner." Gennaro leaned over to put a finger on her notepad. "I'd spend my time with Tommaso instead of deciphering the riddles from your friend."

"Very funny, Gennaro."

"Do you see me laughing?"

She said nothing. He was right again.

Gennaro turned to leave, but stood transfixed, turned around to head for his desk, saying, "Shit. Farese."

"Wait." She didn't want to look. He must've seen U.S. Attorney Michael Farese coming down the hallway. Piersanti was probably with him. Glass doors and windows had some purpose.

"What is it?"

"Who arranged this meeting for Farrugia?"

"Some ranking guy in the Totaro clan," he said, and snapped his fingers at Silvio, who, well-trained, reflexively stood up, put his jacket on, straightened his tie without knowing why.

Bianca did not dare give the opening door a thought. She could hear the hinges making their noise. She lifted up the top sheet of paper again. *Damn.* The answer was obvious.

ALDO GIURLANI knew A TOTARO . . . then <u>boom</u> then Isidore Farrugia.

16

Ferrero was unrecognizable. Farrugia couldn't believe that the man approaching his car was the same man he had met and gotten to know in Milan. While the smile gave him away, Farrugia did more than a double-take upon seeing the man in a floral-print shirt, dark slacks, no belt, hair slicked back, and retro wayfarers get into the car seat next to him. It wasn't the hand tattoo or the spiked wrist piece that threw him off. It was the beard. Claudio Ferrero of *La Stampa* from Turin had grown a beard. The rugged look and feminine shirt told anyone who questioned his authority that he'd break their face like an egg.

Farrugia put the car in gear and eased into traffic. "Is the trade that rough in Catania?"

"It's for effect. All part of being a journalist."

"Hell of an effect."

"Drive and I'll explain."

Farrugia looked at the hand tattoo. The silver watchband was another contrast. Metal against the red heart, yellow flames, and the Cross of Calvary.

"It's fake," said Claudio, showing his hand, putting his messenger bag on the floor.

"And the rest of you . . . isn't?"

"I'm supposed to be a messenger."

Farrugia had his left hand on the wheel, the right hand near his mouth as if he were preventing a sneeze, when he was actually hiding a smile. "A messenger? Your bike convinced me."

"What bike?" Claudio said.

"That's my point," Farrugia answered. "Never mind." He slapped Claudio's thigh, squeezed it, and said, "It's good to see you. Tell me what you wanted to see me about."

The street life and the car moved at a Neapolitan crawl, which meant slow enough that people close to the car occasionally touched it, using it as leverage to make their own way through the traffic on the narrow streets. The garbage was starting to gather and stain the cobblestones. People were walking around the black plastic bags, accepting their existence the way people stepped around the homeless in documentaries from America.

"I'm in with the Calabrian mafia, and they're behind the Totaros on some deal with Matteo Mandrachhia. I'm in with the 'Ndrangheta who are in negotiations with the Marra clan."

"You . . . from Turin . . . are in with the 'Ndrangheta? You're a northern boy."

Claudio started bitching about the slow traffic, the people moving like tortoises, gesturing at the old lady who should have been home counting her retirement money, at the old geezer who had the morality of a rooster and not a chance in hell with the lovely girl in the tasteless short skirt. Farrugia listened. Perfect Calabrese accent. Authentic diction. Priceless intonation.

"I'm impressed," Farrugia said.

"Not as impressed as I am with you—a Calabrian in with the *napulitan*."

"What's with the rough look?"

"I'll try and be modest, Isidò, but after covering the Palmisano and L&S scandals I thought going to Catania would make people forget my face."

Farrugia started laughing. Claudio gave him a surprised look.

"I'm sorry," Farrugia said. "You write the biggest story in recent years, then you go south to Catania with the man's lover, take in some sun, and you expect nobody to notice or remember you? Your own people ran the gossip columns." Farrugia paused. That had been uncalled for. Claudio was gay, but unfortunately it was true that the "gay mafia," as Claudio referred to it, had had a feast with Claudio as consoling "friend" to grieving partner of the assassinated Lele Palmisano who had stood up to the Americans and corporate and military interests. "You knew people were going to speculate about you and Arnaldo. C'mon, Claudio . . . other than Lombardo, who else do you know is gay and an active politician?"

He beeped the horn. Damn old ladies. He gave the man's shirt a fast look. "That's creative, though."

"You approve?" Claudio asked, pinching the shirt's material.

"I like it, and the beard does a good job of covering up that face of yours," Farrugia said before they both started laughing.

While Farrugia was laughing, Claudio said, "I've got something to show you," as he reached down and pulled up his bag and unzipped it. Nice shrink-wrapped square of euro bills. Five hundred-euro notes.

"*Mannaggia*," Farrugia said and then whistled. Counterfeit. Damn.

Claudio zipped the bag up. "The quality is exceptional. Absolute works of art. These even pass the UV-light check. I'm hearing the Marra clan wants to move counterfeit euros, but they need the Totaros."

"Because they have an insider with the Anticounterfeiting Unit?" Farrugia said.

"Could be, but with this kind of operation, this kind of money, the Marras could buy themselves an insider. In the end, they should be able to squeeze the Totaros out of that game."

"So what's your take on all this?" Farrugia asked. Ferrero had a falcon's ability to coast on the breeze high above and see the mouse, the crucial movement in the grass, before he plunged down at 160 kilometers per hour to snap up his prey.

"The Totaro clan is in bed with the Calabrian mafia. I can't quite figure out why the Sicilians are excluded. I'm hearing that Matteo Mandracchia is behind the Marra clan for now. This counterfeiting operation is his."

"The venture capitalist? I guess one Sicilian isn't excluded." Farrugia looked at Claudio. The traffic was moving at a good clip now. There was

Gabriel Valjan **139**

no set destination. It was just driving and listening to Claudio's investigative proceeds. "You said 'for now'? What do you mean by that?"

Claudio adjusted his wristband. The spikes had to feel weird. Farrugia wished that he could see Claudio's eyes behind the black sunglasses.

"My gut is telling me this is all a double-cross on Mandraccia's part, but I can't figure out how or why. There's supposed to be a meeting between the two clans. It's meant as an alliance, but I don't know. Something is not right."

Farrugia had his own concerns. He was the point man for the Calabrians for the Totaro clan. The Marra clan had their own diplomat with the 'Ndrangheta. Farrugia saw that he and Claudio had that in common, along with being undercover.

"What are you thinking?" Claudio asked.

"I think I'm going to be attending this meeting for the other side. What I'm trying to understand is why the Marra clan is handing over a package like that for free. That package is an example of their Giugliano product. At this meeting the Totaro clan will show off their Foggia work. Whatever it might be."

"Impressive face-to-face and exchange," Claudio said.

"It still bothers me. The Totaro and Marra clans are like the Montagues and Capulets without Romeo and Juliet. I don't buy into this money-for-nothing crap." He explained to Claudio his work, and the relationship he had been able to cultivate with Stefano.

Claudio shifted in the car seat to face Farrugia. "I saw Mandracchia on television. The rumor in the financial circles in Milan and Rome is that he's doing something about opera in Naples."

"Opera? That doesn't make sense. Naples has the Teatro San Carlo." Every kid in Italy knew that Naples had San Carlo and that Milan had La Scala.

"My thoughts exactly. This cultural program has to be a front—to what, I don't know. Counterfeiting euros has its limits. The stakes are too high. It becomes a technological war between artists and the cops, between the fox and the hen. The authorities will always get better at recognizing fake money, especially when it's big notes like these."

Claudio was right. Five hundred-euro notes drew attention. Counterfeiting money was a quick score, but all it took was one good bust and for someone to cave during interrogation, and the whole enterprise was gone. That Mandracchia would put himself so close to two Camorra clans, with the mafia in Calabria on both sides of the alliance made even less sense.

"So you are to deliver these counterfeit packages to the meeting?" Farrugia asked, his eyes referencing the bag on the floor.

"Yep. I've been delivering euros for the Marras to other gang leaders, foreign types, and some bank executives," Claudio said. Which made sense to Farrugia: foreigners buy real estate in their own countries, and the bank executives clean the money.

Both men fell silent for a moment.

"So this meeting with Stefano happens later?"

"Tonight."

"North of Parco Verde di Caivano?" Claudio asked.

"You'd better not be wearing a wire or have a digital camera on you, Claudio."

"I won't. Something still tells me this is more than euro notes," Claudio said, more thinking out loud. "Hey, at least it'll get recorded."

"Recorded?" Farrugia asked. "I'm not wearing a wire."

"I meant 'recorded' as in surveillance," Claudio said. The beard still took getting used to.

"There'll be no surveillance."

"What do you mean?"

"I have no backup, Claudio. There won't be any."

"Shit."

Both men fell silent again.

17

Bianca agreed with Gennaro but let him take the lead. He had experience and alleged wisdom to make the proposal. Alessandro was neutral on the subject.

Dante was less enthusiastic. "Invite him to dinner?" he said. "What about Silvio?"

"What about him?" Bianca asked. "He's with Farese. Silvio can help us later."

"How?"

"He'll tell us what Farese is up to. He's the man's translator."

"Just like that, Bianca? Use the man? 'Silvio, please tell us what U.S. Attorney Farese did today and whom he met and spoke with today. Do you have a copy of the latest agenda? Did U.S. Attorney Farese meet with the Prime Minister in secret?'"

"Why not?"

Bianca watched Dante pace. She had called this impromptu meeting while they were still in the office. Tommaso was with Piersanti, discussing something with Agents McGarrity and Murphy.

"Stop acting like a child, Dante. It's the best Silvio can do for us. Farese is here for a reason, and Silvio is right there next to him. We couldn't ask for better."

Dante stared at her. He paced some more. "That's not my point."

"Then what is it?"

"Did it ever cross your mind that Farese could have Silvio see and think what he wants *us* to see and think? You think that Farese doesn't know that Silvio is one of us, or that Silvio, for all his linguistic disasters, was the one who blew the Palmisano case apart, opening up the connection—no matter how gray it might've been—between Gladio, the government, and a certain corporation. Did you forget?"

"Governments, Dante. Plural, not singular. I haven't forgotten."

Dante slapped his forehead. "I can't believe what I'm hearing. She thinks this is like straining pasta. Silvio in Italian I can understand, but Silvio's English is one of the Five Joyful Mysteries." He stopped, almost yelled, "And I don't even remember how to say the rosary! Gennaro, please help me here. Say something."

Gennaro put his hands in his pockets and stepped forward. Bianca sat down. Exasperated. Dante was standing there. Exhausted.

Alessandro being Alessandro was ready to go with the flow. "She's right." He held up his hand to anticipate Dante's objection. "And you're also right. Farese's government, not Farese, would want revenge. His interests are advancing any political career that he might be thinking about. Silvio, for all his mishaps, as you've said, has proven himself. I say, go through with Bianca's plan to have Silvio sit and listen. It costs us nothing."

"I can't believe you," Dante said and asked Gennaro, "What do you have to say about all of this?"

"I have three questions: What is it I'm cooking this evening, and what time is Tommaso coming to dinner?"

"What's your third question?" Bianca asked.

"What are Agents McGarrity and Murphy doing for Farese?"

Bianca studied the letters in her study.

ALDO GIURLANI knew A TOTARO . . . then boom then Isidore Farrugia

ARMADA BOOM LIST starts with EAT TOM

FEDORA INFORMS AS FREE . . . *bye bye*

The first line had been the hardest because the logic was as twisted as one of Farrugia's seated yoga asanas, and Loki had punned on "IF/if" and "rat." The second line was another direct statement with a modest two-word phrase. The third line was a complete anagram because she remembered that Loki had signed off after sending those three lines. "Bye bye."

"I'll be in the kitchen helping Alessandro and Gennaro," Dante said from the doorway. "Will you be talking with the elf before Tommaso arrives?"

"No. I'm not ready yet."

"I've got to go back to the kitchen to save Gennaro."

She glanced at him for an explanation.

"Alessandro is lamenting the state of his love life or lack thereof."

The usual: return to the clues.

Alessandro was sitting at the kitchen table, his chair against the wall as Gennaro commandeered the counter space for prepping dinner. Gennaro was earnest about organization. Alessandro, forlorn, was nursing his third glass of wine.

Dante arrived in time for Gennaro to appoint him sous-chef.

"Has he sung his aria, Chief?" asked Dante.

"No. He is about to discourse on Italian women. You missed the preamble. Grab a knife."

"For the vegetables or him?" Dante asked.

"You might want to use it on yourself after you hear him." Gennaro did not have compassion. He had a dinner to prepare and a guest arriving soon.

Alessandro inaugurated his dissertation with a sip of wine. "Let me tell you about Milanese women. As you get closer to one, you're overwhelmed by a tidal wave of Cavalli perfume. You'll tap her on the shoulder, and as she pulls out the earphones and lowers her three hundred-euro Gucci sunglasses to give you a blasé assessment, she'll listen to your Italian and treat you as if you were a foreigner." He took another small sip of wine. "Suddenly, she'll become friendly because she doesn't want to seem provincial. After you walk away, she'll return to Laura Pausini on her iPod and wonder whether you'd noticed her fresh Vergottini haircut."

"What is Bianca doing?" Gennaro asked.

"Flogging away at those anagrams," Dante said.

"Any progress?"

"She wouldn't say, Chief. I think she'll tell us when she's done solving all of them."

Gennaro nodded, happy to leave Loki and her strange puzzles to Bianca. They continued cutting. The seafood was marinating. The meat was mixed, molded, and baking. Alessandro petitioned for Dante's attention. He failed.

"Roman women? You'll see one dressed in colorful Sweet Years and Essenza clothes, with flashy makeup and unnatural blonde hair, but she couldn't care less where you are from, so she says." Alessandro burped. "She'll pull out her earphones and you'll be treated to Negramaro playing full blast. She'll make strange faces while she makes an immense effort at understanding your request for directions." Alessandro paused to sip more of his wine. "Suddenly, she'll ask the bus driver *for* you, and she knows all of them in Rome, don't ask how. The drivers will discuss your predicament." Alessandro imitated the Queen of England's hand wave. "Each driver has his own opinion and they'll all offer them until they end up fighting. She'll excuse herself and disappear. You will discover from a driver that she's late for a date somewhere else. After twenty minutes, you'll manage to walk away while the drivers are still enumerating all the existing bus routes in Rome, but she'll be gone." There was the raising of the wineglass, another gulp, and a splash to refill the glass.

"He's getting drunk, Chief."

"I know. Keep him away from Tommaso."

"How?"

Gennaro looked at Alessandro. "We'll think of something, Dante."

"Now, southern girls," Alessandro said, wagging his finger as if he were warning an imaginary friend. "What does a southern girl do? She pulls her earphones out and you'll hear Neomelodico music you didn't think someone under seventy would listen to. She'll keep her fake Gucci sunglasses on. She got those in Naples, of course. You make the mistake of chatting with her. She'll suggest you'd better take a walk with her, because she's very busy." He took a big painful gulp this time. "Suddenly, she'll say I can wait, so she'll walk you to wherever you're going. On your way, you'll meet her three brothers and four sisters, three or four cousins and two uncles, and finally her mother, father, and old granny, who'll invite you to eat pasta *alla norma* at their place. You must name your first child after her grandfather."

Gennaro shook his head. "If I hear 'suddenly' one more time . . ."

"Relax, Chief. I'll take care of him." Dante went over to Alessandro and coaxed the wine glass out of his hand, replacing it with a clean glass of ice-cold water.

Bianca appeared in the doorway.

"Solve the elf's riddles?" Gennaro asked.

"Two out of three." She took one look at Alessandro. "Someone is getting in touch with his feelings?"

"And putting us in touch with ours," Dante said. "Anything good?"

She held up a fresh sheet of notebook paper with the three lines. "I'm still working on the third one." She handed the piece of paper to Dante for him and Gennaro to read together.

ALDO GIURLANI knew A TOTARO . . . then boom then Isidore Farrugia

TOMMASO BARALDI starts with MATTEO

FEDORA INFORMS AS FREE . . . *bye bye*

Gennaro held onto the piece of paper and read it once more. "What does 'starts with' mean?"

"No idea, but we'll start with Tommaso. Smells good in here. What's for dinner?"

Tommaso arrived with two bottles of wine, red and white, tucked into a small tote bag. He presented the wine to Dante and a box of pastries from Scaturchio on Piazza San Domenico Maggiore to Bianca. So he had been brought up with manners.

Gennaro had come out with his apron on, announcing that they should sit at the dining room table. When asked how soon he and Alessandro would be joining them, Gennaro said that they had decided to stay in the kitchen to plate the dishes. The theme was Surf and Turf.

"Isn't that steak and lobster in America?" asked Tommaso.

"Surf, as in Neapolitan seafood and Turf, as in northern Italian cuisine, in your honor." Gennaro excused himself, leaving Dante to uncork the wine.

"Thank you for having me," Tommaso said to his host and hostess. They gave him the customary smile. "I didn't know that he enjoyed cooking."

"Gennaro," said Dante, "is a man of many talents. We all have our unique skills. Alessandro is intelligent when he uses the head on his shoulders. Silvio is insightful and persistent. I like to think of myself as hardworking and the one who helps in a pinch. Reliable." Dante set the bottle of wine down, after having poured each of them a glass. Bianca admired Dante's opening remarks.

"What about you, Bianca? What do you see as your forte?"

"I don't know. I've been told that I'm quite analytical."

"She's being modest." Dante unfolded his napkin. "She has a shark's instinct when there's blood in the water. She wastes no time."

Gennaro had entered the room with plates for Bianca and Dante. Alessandro was behind him with the third plate for Tommaso.

"Here, I've made you my own recipe, *Polpo Affogato*. It's simple to make, but the trick is not to boil the octopus too long, otherwise it becomes rubbery. A little olive oil, some garlic, and parsley, and you have a classic dish with a poetic name. Enjoy."

Bianca asked Gennaro when he and Alessandro would be joining them. Gennaro said that they wished to eat in the kitchen, since the dinning room was small for five people. He was gone before anyone could protest.

"What do you see as your special talent?" Bianca asked.

"I don't know." Tommaso paused to select a bite-size piece of seafood. "I think of myself as logical, but my friends have always said that I have a weird sense of humor, and I'm prone to poetry."

Bianca saw her opportunity. "Your friends might be right. Your approach to Matteo Mandracchia seems poetic. May I ask what intrigued you about him?"

Tommaso took a taste of his wine. "Dante was right. You do go in for the kill." Another sip and their eyes met this time. "Matteo is a visionary. Men of genius all have a dark side to them, because they perceive reality as malleable. Shaping reality is exciting to them, an adrenaline rush."

Dante expressed his appreciation of the dish, then added, "A man or a woman of genius can do a lot to help other people while pleasing his or her ego. They can bring new technology into the world, achieve medical or scientific breakthroughs, entertain us, or do something that changes lives in other ways. All we know about Matteo is that he proposes to elevate Neapolitan culture. Those are his words, more or less."

Dante had made the first foray. Tommaso knew the game was on and held back his return volley. Alessandro returned to collect the dishes while Gennaro managed to carry in three dishes, one in each hand, one balanced on his forearm.

"Perverted *Risotto alla Milanese*," Gennaro said. "Perverted in the sense that I've added leeks, tomatoes, and bits of pancetta, topped with a cooked egg added to the classic rice dish."

After Alessandro and Gennaro had left, the three of them contemplated how they would eat the dish without disturbing the egg. It was so artistically done that it was a shame to spoil it.

Tommaso finally led the way, cutting his egg into four precise pieces. He spoke as he ate. "Matteo might have the potential to do humanitarian things, but I doubt he is a philanthropist."

"Is it simply about making money?" Dante asked.

"No. It's the challenge, I think. He went to business school. He understands corporations. He took his inspiration from how governments have given in to corporations, granting them wide latitude on their indiscretions, whether it is environmental violations or outright thievery. International relations were his area of concentration. He knows that national economies have become dependent on corporate income. He sees, as we all have, how corporations shape domestic and foreign policy."

"What do you think Matteo perceives as his current challenge?"

"Matteo is the man who wants to create the ultimate multinational corporation, where every government is not only dependent on his corporation, but any attempt to destroy it bankrupts them. This risotto is delicious."

They all agreed. Dante and Bianca exchanged looks.

Dante said, "So it is money and power. Classic ingredients. The Camorra is his vehicle. Governments tolerate a multinational corporation, their excesses, but they also establish laws to curb power and maintain the balance, however delicate."

"You could say it is power, but it's not just his idea of the Camorra as a corporation that is so threatening, Dante. Sure, he can find a way for Camorristi to become acceptable, more polished, villains dressed as gentlemen, with the best educations in the world, but no laws, local or international, will tame his version of the System."

Bianca had been soaking it in. Now she let Dante know with a look that she would ask the next question.

"Tommaso?"

"Yes."

"Laws are not always up to date, but why are you so certain that no law, present or future, could put limits on his vision of the Camorra?"

"Simple . . . his Camorra will control the world's economy."

Alessandro came to collect the dishes. Dante could see that Alessandro was sober now and enjoying his role as waiter. They were anticipating a Neapolitan dish for *secondo*, the main course. Tommaso asked for more water. Bianca was guessing Tommaso knew the conversation had turned serious, and that he wanted all of his wits.

Gennaro returned with a meatloaf, which contained pine nuts and raisins, declaring that there was plenty left over for hot or cold sandwiches. The pine nuts had been roasted and formed a handsome crust. The accompanying sauce was a simple reduction of red wine, shallots, rosemary, and garlic. Raisins, embedded in the ground beef and pork, promised sweetness.

As they were eating, they let the conversation drift back to small-talk to give the food its due; about where Tommaso was staying, how he liked Naples. But it was transparent that it was all a dance, a minuet of manners until someone decided to ask how and why Tommaso thought this way about Matteo Mandracchia or, at the very least, how they might discern the omens of his making his first move to transform the Camorra from violent thugs to corporate criminals in silk ties and custom-made shirts.

"You want to know why I'm so intent on Matteo, don't you?" Tommaso asked.

Dante fielded the question. "It's crossed our minds. The man has no criminal history, and his background is perfect for a movie, the rags-to-riches genre that makes people cry. I for one am wondering how he'll manage to overcome the System's propensity for violence. You don't build a new car without getting dirty."

Tommaso was either enjoying the delicious meatloaf or Dante's Camorra as vehicle metaphor or both. It was a moment before he answered. "Matteo will figure out a way to get the clans to destroy themselves, and he'll replace the leadership with his people. As for why I think the way I do about Matteo, I can't accept the credit because that belongs to Charlie Brooks." He paused. "Bianca knew him . . . briefly."

Bianca swallowed hard. She hadn't expected that, and it must have shown. Tommaso was looking right at her with a checkmate smile, as if he knew she understood the final move. Her voice was dry and it cracked. "Charlie?"

Dante's fork was midway to his mouth when Tommaso finished her off with the *coup de grâce*. "Rags-to-riches? That kind of story requires hard work and a little luck. Matteo doesn't believe in luck. Neither do I. Neither did Charlie."

Bianca took a good swig of the tannic red before saying, "You said you knew Brooks, but you didn't explain how. Bicocca?"

"So you do admit that you knew Charlie?"

"Hardly." That was as much ambiguity as she could pack into an admission on short notice.

"You asked me if I knew Charlie when we were first working together at the office," he said. "I figured you had to have known him by the way you reacted to my answer. I found it peculiar that you had asked me."

Bianca said nothing. She felt as if she had made a fatal mistake, betraying Charlie once more.

Tommaso was observing her. "I'll save you a few steps, Bianca. Charlie studied economics and ethics. He was a glorified intern at Adastra. He had found something while working there." Tommaso modulated the rhythm of his speech with sips of wine, as if it gave him courage for war. "He had come to me for advice."

Never had Bianca felt like an actress until that moment. She acted normal. Nobody knew she had been the last person to see Charlie Brooks alive. Nobody except her team. In terms of public perception, Adastra was like a royal family scandal about to break until it got handled, swept away, disappearing without the public ever knowing about the company's sinister testing plans in Sardinia and Vicenza. U.S. Attorney Farese had made sure of that.

"Charlie had asked you for advice?" she asked.

"I told him he should get help." Tommaso had finished the last of his meatloaf.

Dante asked, "How did Charlie's discovery inspire your thoughts on Matteo?"

Tommaso was drinking some water. "It didn't. But not too long after

Charlie was killed, the political candidate Lele Palmisano was found dead."

"And that made you think of Matteo?" Dante asked.

"No. The deaths of both Charlie and Lele together did."

"How?"

"I'm convinced that Adastra had Charlie murdered, and that Lele met his end for trying to prevent corporations like Adastra from getting away with murder. As for who killed Lele—my money is with a government at the behest of a corporation."

"Which government?" Dante asked.

"Does it matter?" Tommaso answered. "Lele's legislation equated certain corporate practices with terrorism."

"I'm not quite sure I follow that to Matteo and the Camorra," Dante said. Tommaso turned his head. "What do you think, Bianca?"

She was too busy maintaining the normal act to respond.

"It's the inverse of Lele's thinking," Tomasso said and explained: "The mafia—whether it's Russian, Sicilian, or some other ethnic group—already terrorizes people, preys on them. As a business, the mafia is already a multinational corporation; they're integral to the economy of several nations. Where Lele saw corporations as potential terrorists, I saw Matteo's idea of creating the ultimate terrorist from international, organized crime." He paused. "Look, here's dessert."

18

Farrugia was in Stefano's car, passenger's side. Stefano was outside under the conical spread of the car park's light, on his cell phone, pacing back and forth like an honor guard, talking low then cursing out loud, back to low voice, gesturing as if the person on the other side of the conversation could see him. Farrugia cracked the window open. He might lose some of the AC but gain something from eavesdropping.

Too late. Stefano had ended the call and was returning to the car. Farrugia raised the window. The car was sealed off again in hermetic coolness. Stefano slammed his car door shut.

"What the hell was that all about?" Farrugia asked.

Stefano gritted his teeth, yanked the gearshift into reverse, not saying a word. The sound of rubber. K-turn and then forward with a jerk. He was still processing whatever it was that had been put into his ear.

Farrugia asked again, "What happened?"

"The meeting place has been changed."

"Not north of Parco Verde?"

Stefano was still shaking his head, driving but not paying attention. The car almost clipped a plastic dumpster. "I don't like this, Pinucc. Not one bit."

Farrugia said nothing at first. He needed to make sure whatever he said next was in character.

"Ah, for Christ's sake, Ste. You can assume that the Calabrians will think I'm dog shit now. I lose face and look like I don't know my feet from my shoelaces. They think Verde and now you tell me this." Farrugia cited some obscure saints for good measure.

Hand still on the gearstick, Stefano said: "Calm down. Don't worry about that."

"Why not?"

"The change's been communicated to them."

"When? By whom?"

"Totaro." Stefano had said it like a soldier saying the name of the officer who sent the bonehead order down the line.

"Totaro was the one who just called you?" Farrugia asked.

"That was Totaro himself on the phone. He let me know himself that he had let everyone know the meeting place has been changed."

"Where is it then?"

"Scampia. You should feel at home. Via Fratelli Cervi." At least Ste's eyes were now on the road, his voice resigned. "It shouldn't surprise us to hear the details changed at the last minute. It prevents anyone from pulling a surprise."

"Like an ambush or a bust? No telling if there're any snitches."

Quiet air. "Totaro changed it for another reason. An unexpected development."

"I don't like the sound of that."

"Neither do I. It seems that the Sicilians want in on this deal and they're willing to put up a considerable amount of cash and other resources up front. The Sicilians have a way of twisting your arm without breaking it. You can imagine what the Calabrians will have to say when they hear about this."

"The Calabrians? What about the Marra clan? They're the ones who initiated this venture." Farrugia let that lie. "What did Amerigo Totaro have to say about all this? What about the peace with the Marra clan?"

Ste was still fuming. "What could he say? If he says *no* he pisses off both the Calabrians and the Sicilians."

"So how the hell did the Sicilians find out?" Farrugia asked.

"I'd like to know the same thing. Not a clue." Stefano cut the wheel to make a turn.

Farrugia had to ask. "And Amerigo doesn't think the Marra clan is behind this?"

Ste shot him a cold look. "What do you mean?"

"Isn't it possible that the Marra clan planted the seed with the Sicilians? It's that or there's a snitch somewhere."

"Neither here nor there. Figuring this out is the least of our troubles. The meeting is at the VFC."

Via Fratelli Cervi, or VFC as the police force knew it, was where the DiLauro clan and Camorra secessionists had had a standoff years ago. A bunch of cowboys thought they could break away from Cosimo Di Lauro's empire in Secondigliano and form their own cartel. Wrong. The irony was the police had come to arrest the secessionist group, and it led to a colossal standoff that included ground troops, aerial support, and trigger-happy fingers releasing thousands and thousands of rounds. Stefano explained that the new meeting place was not far from the high-rise where that standoff had taken place.

"Pinucc?"

"Yeah?" Farrugia watched the road unfolding ahead of them.

"There's something I forgot to mention about these Sicilians."

"You worry too much. We'll have to trust Amerigo on this."

"That's the thing, Pinucc. I don't trust Amerigo." Ste concentrated on the road, as if what he was saying could drive them into a ditch. "And it isn't just the idea of the Sicilians that bothers me."

"I'm listening."

The headlights burrowed into the darkness as they continued travelling from Secondigliano to Scampia. "These Sicilians have a woman boss."

Nothing shocked Commissario Isidore Farrugia.

The rise of godmothers or *madrine* might've been a new phenomenon within the Camorra, but to him it made absolute sense, as turning on a faucet for water. Camorristi women cut cocaine in their kitchens, facilitated bribes, acted as go-betweens, cooked and cleaned up after numerous meetings where they overheard every detail of business. They were raised to size up suitors not long after they threw away their training bras. It was natural that they'd run the shop when their husbands or brothers went to jail. Why would they accept a monthly allowance from the succeeding capo, pittance pay, when they knew more than he did about the business? Anna Mazza was the first significant Camorrista but not the last; and the lovely maternal image of an understanding Madonna, or some kinder manifestation of power, was pure mythology. Utter bullshit.

The 2002 firefight in Lauro between the Cava and Graziano family women had proven to everyone with half a brain that matriarchy was just as violent. Immacolata Capone's women were armed, bodyguards and soldiers, who practiced and trained in urban combat, and were instantly recognizable to civilians and carabinieri alike as Umas, for Uma Thurman in *Kill Bill*. They rode motorcycles and wore uranium-yellow outfits. No samurai swords, but they could shoot well and liked using grenades. It seems that the Sicilian mafia believed in equality between the sexes, in girl power.

As Stefano's car slowed down outside the compound on Via Fratelli Cervi, the biting gravel betraying their arrival, Farrugia realized that La Cosa Nostra had moved from the twelfth-century Sicilian village to the twenty-first century of steel and concrete.

"This is it, huh?" Farrugia asked.

"This is it," Stefano said.

They walked toward the entrance. Farrugia could see the sentries, the silhouettes of AK-47s, their distinctive profiles in the shadows. Farrugia was not carrying a weapon, and neither was Stefano. The terms of the meeting stated that each clan leader could bring an armed security detail, but they stayed outside the meeting area.

Stefano went through the door first. Then Farrugia. Both men were frisked for weapons and for a wire, and frisked again for any other kind of weapon, like a knife, or a taser. Cell phones were confiscated, tagged, and placed into simple plastic trays, like the ones used at airports. The only thing missing was the body scan.

The room was square, like a cellblock. There was a long, dark exit at the opposite end. The room was also quiet. Clan leaders were not expected to be social creatures, so small talk was not offered or expected. Farrugia wondered how this meeting would come to order. He saw his fellow *Calabresi* and they saw him. He nodded; they nodded. Farrugia could identify and name every clan leader in the room. He hoped none of the sentries outside were anxious.

No women. The Sicilians had not arrived.

They waited and waited. Farrugia half-expected someone to appear with canapés or an old lady to come out and tell them to relax and shut up while she prepared the coffee, that her *napoletana* was on the stove.

They waited.

"I've had enough," the clan leader from Afragola said. His impatience was like an annoying virus, the rumbling propagating itself around the room. The clan leaders from Arzano, Caserta, and far away Casal di Principe started bickering and bitching. It was then that Farrugia saw Claudio Ferrero, the confused messenger dressed like a Hells Angel biker in the crowd. They locked eyes like two men in a bad film.

A loud whistle resounded. The Marra clan leader.

"Gentlemen, we should get this meeting underway. Our host, Amerigo Totaro, called this meeting in good faith to foster the peace between the Marra and Totaro families. It's an agreement we expect all our affiliates to honor and obey. He requested that this meeting be held in full view of the other leaders so everybody would understand that business was on the table." The short man, with the impressive voice, surveyed the room, unafraid to make eye contact. "This business can benefit all of us in due time. We help each other and we make money together. But if one of us gets greedy then he ruins it for everyone."

"How much money?" a voice yelled out.

"So much money that we still have to pay *pizzo* to the Totaro clan," another man said. There was some laughter. *Pizzo* was the shakedown money the Camorra squeezed from shopkeepers.

The short man held up his hand. It reminded Farrugia of Mussolini's relaxed *saluto fascista* that the Germans stole for their *Sieg Heil* salute.

"Gentleman, please. Be patient. Amerigo has standing and we must respect his decision to not attend this meeting. We all know how he values his privacy." That was an eloquent acknowledgement of Totaro's agoraphobia. "The Marra family has no shame in admitting that it needs friends. Prosperity and peace go together."

"And what if we don't trust either of you?" another voice asked. A Calabrian.

The short man paused and answered. "I understand your doubts; but history has shown us that war also brings prosperity to the victor, but the price is death." Silence. "None of us can afford bloodshed."

The man walked over to the group of Calabrians. "The Marra clan recognizes our good friends from the south. In good faith to them and, with the blessing of the Totaros, we have let our friends here start distributing the product. Call it a pilot program." The short man motioned for Claudio Ferrero to step forward. "Show them."

Claudio set down his messenger bag. Every pair of eyes in the room watched the slow pull of the zipper and the square of plastic that Claudio pulled out of the bag and set out on the ground in front of Marra. Claudio stepped back as Marra began to speak.

"This, Gentlemen, is the product. Allow me to explain." Everyone now watched Marra walk over to the shrink-wrapped parcel and tear a section of plastic away. He grabbed a stack of euro notes and handed them out. "Take it, pass them around." Farrugia watched the men examine the five hundred-euro notes, front and back, some smiling, others reticent but on the verge of smiling. They were impressed.

"As you can see, you hold five hundred-euro notes. Smaller denominations are coming. What you have in your hand has passed every known testing procedure for authenticity. We guarantee to keep ahead of advances in detection, thanks to the Totaros."

"What about manufacturing?" asked a voice.

"We can thank a certain German. We have facilities in Apulia and Campania."

That would be Giugliano and Foggia.

"How do we know your German artist won't talk?" asked a face in the crowd.

"He won't."

Farrugia knew of the German counterfeiter. Every attempt to get him to talk, explain his techniques, his operation, had failed. Restrictions had failed. Giving him crap food had done nothing. Monitor his mail and visitors. Nothing. The man was content with his sentence and with teaching art classes in prison, enjoying the prison like a spa. Even his students had been threatened. Nothing again, and yet his masterpiece forgeries kept appearing on the world market.

"How can you be so sure?" the same voice asked again.

"He took up Buddhist meditation. Prison is a state of mind," Marra said.

There was a tremor of laughter. Marra stopped talking to let the men in the room appreciate the counterfeit notes. Some held them up to the light to see the watermarking, or the ink's consistency. Others used a lighter to see whether the paper would catch fire or burn smoothly.

"Where are the Sicilians?" someone asked.

Marra had his hands behind his back. He looked like a salesman, confident that he had made the sale. When he heard the question about the Sicilians again, he put his hand up to get everyone's attention.

"Gentlemen . . . you know that a woman is never on time."

There would have been laughter, but the distant sound of motorcycles turned their heads before they continued with small talk. They seemed unconcerned. It wasn't a police helicopter overhead. The distinctive rumbling of motorcycles was approaching. The throbbing engines were close, the kick of gravel closer, and then the headlight of one of three motorcycles appeared in the dark hallway of an entrance opposite Farrugia. The engines idled when the three bikes had come to a complete stop.

The riders were unequivocally women. They lined up facing the Marra clan leader. The rest of the men formed a semicircle behind the clan leader. Only one of the women had lifted her visor up. Farrugia could see green eyes but not much else. Joan of Arc in tight white leather. She held her hand out.

The Marra clan leader handed a five hundred-euro note to her. She examined the front of it then the back. She held the euro note out in her gloved hand and as the Marra clan leader was about to take it back she let it go. Everyone watched the five hurndred-euro note fall, tumbling and turning in the air until it landed on the floor.

"What the . . ." the Marra leader said.

The woman said, "It's shit." Distinctly Sicilian.

"Who the hell do you think you are?"

The Marra leader stepped forward. Farrugia was thinking the idiot might've had the idea of slapping her. One of the other cyclists gunned her throttle. The engine's snarl made him reconsider.

The woman in the middle, the one with her visor up, said, "I have a better proposition. It's more money for you, better business for all of us. Show them, girls."

Her companions opened up vents in their yellow jumpsuits. They pulled out papers and threw them up into the air. As they trickled down, the men in the room started grabbing them.

The Marra leader was chasing one piece of paper, unsuccessful at first but he did catch one.

"What are these?" he asked.

"Bonds," she answered.

The room quieted down for an explanation. Impressive. She had a gift for theater.

"I don't understand," the Marra leader said.

"U.S. bonds. Counterfeit. We control the production, and you can be part of the distribution. You'll make more money with us than you will with the Totaro or Marra clans. Your choice."

She sat there, her left hand on the clutch, the right hand behind her right hip. The Marra clan leader looked shocked at what this woman had said. He looked around him at the other men as if he'd expected their support. Silence.

"But we had a deal," the Marra leader said.

"This is a new deal," she said.

"To hell with you, you bitch."

With remarkable speed her hand whipped from around her hip with an automatic. She shot the Marra clan leader in the head, pulled down her visor and wheeled the motorcycle around, peeling rubber for the rear exit. Her two partners gunned their choppers for the entrance behind them after the short man's body hit the floor.

They were gone. So was the Marra/Totaro collaboration with the Calabrians and possibly the Marra/Totaro truce.

The sentries had come running when they heard the noise. As they opened fire at the dark exit, an assault team came crashing through the windows behind them. Farrugia saw the ropes, the black body armor, and the orange spit of assault rifle spray decimating the AK-47s. The assault team then rained fire down on the men. They hadn't noticed that the crowd under them was unarmed.

Farrugia dropped to the floor, buying some cover from the table. A canister hit and bounced on the floor not far from him. Smoke came next, like swirls of a white onion. Assault rifle fire went on and on. The metallic sound of spent cartridges bounced and frittered across the hard ground.

Farrugia felt the weight of Stefano on top of him, felt the twitches of the man's body receiving bullets.

On the ground in front of him tumbled and wheeled a crumpled, bloodstained bond.

A U.S. bond.

19

Gennaro cut the string on the pastry box and started transferring the items to an oversize dish. The *sfogliatella riccia* went around the outside. Tommaso had picked the kind with ricotta filling and candied citron peels. He arranged some *baba au rhum* next, trying to keep the stickiness off of his fingers. Impossible. He wedged in some individual slices of *torta caprese*, a moist chocolate cake that Pasticceria Scaturchio did with a touch of liqueur and coarsely chopped almonds. The *ricotta e pera con biscotti* were plated last.

He could hear an alert Alessandro regaling Tommaso with examples of Silvio's translations and his famous standoff with Human Resources in Milan.

"He sat there at his desk, solemn as a mortician, hands folded, and said, 'I prefer not to.'" Gennaro could hear Dante laughing, imagining that his cheeks were red and his eyes were wet. He listened to Sandro explain how Lino Perego, their boss at the time, snapped the job description forms out of the HR rep's hand and fed them into the paper shredder. Howls of laughter erupted from Alessandro and Dante. They stopped talking when he came into the room with the pastries. He felt like a pagan god. They all rose to pay homage and select their dessert.

"Where are my manners?" Dante said. "You're our guest. Please choose first."

"That's okay," Tommaso said. "It's been a fabulous meal. Go first, please."

"I'm glad you enjoyed the food," Gennaro said. "I wanted you to have some northern dishes so you didn't miss home too much." Gennaro pinched a clamshell *sfogliatella*.

"That was very thoughtful of you, but I grew up knowing many southern dishes."

Gennaro wiped powdered sugar and flaky pastry from his lips. "Really?"

Alessandro, reaching over, chose a *baba*. "Damn things are sticky as hell, but delicious. I don't get it, Tommaso."

"Get what?"

"You grew up and went to school in the north, but you know southern cuisine well. Did you have any relatives who moved north?"

Alessandro was referring to the massive internal migration of Italians as the country industrialized. Italy was the Korea of the fifties and sixties when labor was cheap and unorganized, a time when some northern and central parts of the peninsula were as backward as the south, a time when, for example, the Venetians arriving in Milan were called the "*Terroni* of the North."

"Aren't you the opposite, Alessandro? You were born in Tuscany but educated in Salerno."

"I forget that you've done your homework." Alessandro held up the stalk of his *baba* and congratulated him.

"Very impressive," said Gennaro. "You seem to know a little bit about each of us."

Tommaso had selected the hazelnut biscotti. It was a messy choice. Biting into the biscotti and poached pears would push out the ricotta and whipped cream together.

"Why is that so hard to believe? My uncle had dossiers on all of you. He believed in you, Gennaro, and he believed in this team that you had put together. Even Silvio. I had read about all of you. Except Bianca, but my uncle spoke highly of her."

Bianca gave him a wry feminine smile. She had selected the *torta caprese*. She might not be the typical woman, but she did like chocolate.

Gennaro reached for the bottle of Sambuca. "For someone who claims not to know Bianca, you sure seem to have your own ideas about her."

Dante fetched some glasses for the bottle of anise-flavored liqueur. "Would you like a glass, Tommaso?"

"No, thanks. Alcohol gives me a headache."

A cell phone started ringing. "I think that's you, Dante," Bianca said.

"Can't be; I shut mine off hours ago."

They each looked around the room as the mobile continued its incessant bleating. All eyes turned to Gennaro, who stood up from the table, frisked his pockets, back and front, saying, "I'm good. Not me."

"Your jacket, Chief?" Dante said. "It's on the back of your chair."

"Thanks, Dante. Ah, there it is." Gennaro retrieved the phone from the breast pocket of his jacket. He looked at the LED while the phone kept ringing. "That's odd—I don't recognize this number and there's no name."

"*Pronto*," Gennaro said into the receiver. "What?! When?!" Gennaro had turned pale. He listened and listened, occasionally running his hand through his graying hair. He looked at Bianca, his lip trembling. He looked away. "I see. I understand. Of course . . . of course and yes, I'll be right there. *Grazie*." He closed the lid on his phone.

"What is it, Boss?"

Gennaro was ashen. "That was Piersanti from Ospedale Cardarelli. Farrugia's been shot."

Alessandro bolted out of his chair. The glasses on the table tittered. "When?"

"About an hour ago. The DDA raided the meeting in Scampia. It turned into an insane bloodbath. The Camorra clans have taken to the streets. A war is well underway."

"The DDA?" Alessandro asked.

Direzione Distrettuale Antimafia. Not just any assault team. Bianca understood it as a tactical squad with a special District Attorney directing its operations. She thought of Farese and Rudy Giuliani, who had both run organized crime stings. It was the same concept but more militant, like a DA with his or her own SWAT team.

"What did Piersanti say?" Dante asked.

"Not much. He's more concerned that nobody finds out Farrugia was undercover. He isn't taking any chances with crooked cops."

Alessandro seemed incensed. "What the hell! They're treating him like some Camorra scum . . . like some criminal?"

"He'll get the medical attention he needs, but for now it's safer this way for Isidò. Let them think he's one of them. The sky is falling, and no one has an umbrella. Piersanti is apoplectic. He wants to know why this raid turned out to be a shoot-out. I told him we're going to meet him at the hospital."

Tommaso stood up. "I want to go."

"Of course, thank you." Gennaro walked away cursing.

Tommaso stayed behind in the dining room, as Alessandro and Dante left to retrieve their jackets. He stood there, listening to Gennaro cursing, and quietly said to Bianca, "Who is the elf?"

She didn't answer him. Tommaso had misquoted Gennaro, who moments earlier had actually said, "Damn that elf." "Later," she said.

Bianca was ready to go. The dishes could wait. She downed her shot of Sambuca and headed for the door. Gennaro held the door open. Tommaso went out first, then Dante and Alessandro. Bianca was about to exit next, jacket on, keys and cell phone in her hand, but Gennaro stopped her.

"What?"

"You're not going?"

"Why not? Farrugia is—"

"Don't 'Farrugia' me, Bianca. Remember 'not a cover'? When I come back I want answers."

"It doesn't work like that, Gennaro. Making contact isn't always—"

"I don't give a shit how it works. Weave a spell, cast magic, bang some rocks together for all I care. I want answers."

The slam of the door also slammed a thought into her head. She remembered what Tommaso had said to Dante: "Matteo will figure out a way to get the clans to destroy themselves."

She powered up her desktop. She put the water on for coffee. It would be a long evening. She doled out strong spoonfuls of French roast into the

Bodlum. She would wait for the water to boil, wait for the mix to form a dark cloud, wait for the coffee to brew in the turbid chaos. She would drive the plunger down, pressing all that confusion towards the bottom, straining all the unnecessary grit out. Her Bodlum, a mere coffee press, had become her wishing well. *Pozzo di San Patrizio*, or St Patrick's Well.

The water came to a boil. She shut off the flame and the whistling ceased. It was while the coffee was brewing that she thought to call Noelle. But what would she tell her?

Her phone vibrated with an incoming text. She reread the dark LED letters against the green backdrop.

IF will be OK.

IF. Isidore Farrugia.

She hit Reply, but that was odd. Nothing.

She saw the number and pressed Call Back, listened for the dial tone, and heard the Italian version of "We're sorry; you have reached a number that has been disconnected or is no longer in service. If you feel you have reached this recording in error, please check the number and try your call again" in a digital voice.

Shit. She toggled to Noelle's number in her Contacts, but then hesitated. There was no point in upsetting Noelle when she had no information. Also, it would endanger Farrugia if she showed up at the hospital. Best wait for word from either Dante or Gennaro. Her decision? She pressed the plunger down. No sugar, no milk. It was straight black coffee and Loki.

IF will be OK.

Bianca stared at the text as she pinged Loki from her desktop. She peeled over the top sheet of her notepad and thought it through. Loki would have written: IF = OK. She reread her guesswork from the other day:

ALDO GIURLANI knew A TOTARO . . . then boom then Isidore Farrugia

TOMMASO BARALDI starts with MATTEO

FEDORA INFORMS AS FREE . . . *bye bye*

No sign of Loki yet. She scripted a little animation for her avatar, collated the gif files and renamed them while she waited. The windowpane indicated that Loki was logging in.

Loki was on. She highlighted another script and ran it. It was an ISP locator.

A big metallic door appeared on the screen, with the doors on both sides of the screen slamming shut. Big letters in blood red said, "STOP IT." Loki's avatar pried the doors open and his head peered forward. Angry face.

Good. She hit the animation sequence. Loki watched her avatar get the finger. Then she copied and pasted in the anagrams.

She typed, "If IF = undercover then not a cover."

"WTF?" was Loki's typed response.

She responded with Loki-speak: "IF = ambushed = shot = Cardarelli. UR = *" She told Loki that Farrugia was in the hospital and that she thought Loki was an asshole.

"Go 2 ur first clue here: ADAGIO ILL RUN knew A RAT TOO." It seemed that Loki wanted to do schoolteacher review with her.

"ALDO GIURLANI knew A TOTARO," she typed and added, "I'm impatient."

"Patience," Loki responded, adding ellipses, ". . . A RAT."

"'TOTARO' is part of the anagram. Ur point?"

"A rat. A. TOTARO. Rat."

She sipped her coffee. She hoped the highly-caffeinated beverage would inspire insight. She did not understand the response. "A snitch within the Totaro organization?"

Loki typed again. "Not within."

She thought, outside the Totaro organization? "Next clue."

"Boom x 2."

She took a swig of coffee, thinking, I got this. She typed, "Boom. AG first & IF second."

"Y, but rat = common 2 both AG & IF."

"IDK." I don't know.

Out walked a cartoon rat on the screen, stopping in the center to stare at her, chocolate-brown eyes with a long snout. It sniffed at her. She saw the whiskers twittering before it walked off.

She typed. "RAT common 2 AG & IF?"

The rat stuck its head out and touched its nose, as if it had been playing the parlor game with her. Loki was telling her that there was an informant tied to both the late commissioner and Farrugia.

The question was: Who? She saw that Loki was typing. She waited, sipping coffee and reviewing the text message on her phone—yet another thing annoying her.

"Anticipated ur next?" Loki said. He had anticipated her next question.

"Wise a$$. What was it?"

The Norse avatar changed sexes. The clothing was scant. She disliked thongs, found them nasty, but she admitted that Loki had a nice butt.

"Puh-leez. I've seen better."

The avatar kept wiggling and shaking it. Not quite the pole dancing she had seen in the past. Closer to a lap dance.

"I have the answer. I have the answer," came across the screen like some taunting brat. "I have the answer. I have the answer."

"Have what answer?"

The stripperesque avatar's face took up the entire screen, blinking her eyes at her. Nice eyelashes. Loki receded to normal size.

"Answer to what?" Bianca asked again. She hated repeating herself. It felt like begging.

"We know who the rat is."

Bianca leaned forward in her chair. Wait . . . wait. What? Where did Loki tell her that? What had she missed?

She typed, "TOMMASO BARALDI starts with MATTEO. Tell me again: Rat?"

Loki's final line was: "Rat is explicit, now start with TB . . . *bye, bye.*" Loki was gone.

She reached out for more coffee, reading the transcript from top to bottom, and bottom to top, like a data stack. FIFO then LIFO. First-In-First-Out then Last-In-First Out. She read it and reread it. She went into the dialogue with Loki about Farrugia. Loki pointed her to both Giurlani and Farrugia. The anagram said both men knew the same destructive rat. Loki then moved the pointer forward to the next anagram, telling her to start with Tommaso and not Mandracchia.

It made no sense. The coffee was too strong, too smoky. It dried out her mouth. She read the chat again, thought about the earlier text. The caffeine was giving her a head rush.

She stared at: "A rat. A.TOTARO. Rat."

Her cell rang. She saw the Caller ID. She picked up the phone. "Dante."

"I'm at the hospital with Gennaro and—"

"Is Tommaso there?"

"Yes. Farrugia will be okay, thank God. He's sedated but the doctors said—"

"Dante."

"What?"

"I want you to call me from Tommaso's cell phone. He has one, doesn't he?"

"Uh, what? Yeah, I think so. What's going on? What should I tell him?"

"Tell him your phone battery is dying. Tell him you want to borrow his for a quick call."

"Why? What about Farrugia?"

"He's in the hospital, Dante. You just told me that he's okay. Call me," she said, and ended the call.

Two minutes later the phone rang again. "*Pronto.*"

"What the hell was that all about? I did what you asked."

"A rat. A.TOTARO. Rat" was taunting her on the screen.

"I'll explain later. Now tell me about Isidò."

She listened to Dante explain the man's condition, what the doctors had said and how disgusting it was that Commissario Isidore Farrugia was handcuffed to his bed, like some low-life thug. Dante also mentioned that the assault team had killed several clan leaders. She had to cut him off.

"Dante?"

"Yes."

"I think you should give Tommaso his phone. I'll talk to you later."

She heard obscenities as she hung up. Bianca looked at the number in Recents on her phone. She had Tommaso's number. It didn't match the earlier text. Damn.

She saw "A. Totaro" and realized that it was first initial and last name.

Loki had identified the rat. Her next step was to script a crawler that would target all of Giurlani's cases within the GdF digital archives. She wanted any hits within those files that contained the word "informant," the initials "AT" or "A.T.," and cross-reference the results with closed, ongoing, or sealed records on or related to the Totaro clan and the Camorra. The search might take hours, but she had to prove there was a connection between the late commissioner and the current Camorra leader.

She also needed anything and everything she could get on Tommaso Baraldi, from cradle to present day. Not efficient, definitely unwieldy, but she wanted to know everything there was to know about this young intern. She compiled the code and sent the two search spiders out into the GdF vaults.

Itsy bitsy spider.

Gabriel Valjan **173**

20

The schizoid contrast between classical columns and arches on the outside and placid lines, flat white walls, geometric patterns in the floor on the inside made Ospedale Antonio Cardarelli more creepy and disconcerting than most hospitals. Nothing about the place was authentic except for human illness, healing, and death. The outside betrayed the architectural influence of Luigi Vanvitelli, an Italianized Dutchman, responsible for the Royal Palace at Caserta, the "Versailles of Italy"; the inside, the work of Alessandro Rimini, an Italian Jew who fled the Nazis after leaving behind the Art Deco interior for Mussolini. Rimini had walked out of Auschwitz. Literally. He would later design Italy's first skyscraper in Milan.

The hospital, named "The 23 Marzo," was first used by the Germans in the Second World War, and then by the Americans, renamed for Antonio Cardarelli, the diagnostician of aortic aneurysms. Here, behind the soft pink walls, palm trees, down the hallway of Fascist rectangles, Commissario Isidore Farrugia as "Giuseppe" was the patient, chained to his bed rail as the doctor, not the police guard, was giving Piersanti and Gennaro hell. Dante and Alessandro were enjoying the show.

"The man is in and out of consciousness," the doctor said, in a voice just short of a yell. "He's been shot three times." The doctor looked about fourteen years old. His sad, erratic beard and squeak for a voice did nothing to enhance his professional stature.

"Don't you understand that he's a criminal?" Piersanti yelled. "He might have information that could save lives. We must talk to him!"

"I don't care if he is the Holy Father with the keys to the kingdom of God. The man needs his rest. Didn't you hear what I said? He's been shot three times."

"He's been shot two times."

"What? I said three times. *Uno, due, tre,*" the physician said, holding up his fingers.

"Being shot in the ass doesn't count," Piersanti said. "The other two, I'll allow."

"You're impossible. This man is lucky to be alive. At least ten others died in that horrible gunfight, and by my count here in the hospital none of the DDA suffered so much as a scratch."

"All the more reason why we need to talk to him. Fifteen minutes is all we ask. Fifteen." Piersanti clasped his hands in prayer before the modern incarnation of Asclepius.

"Ten and that is it," the doctor said. "If he starts to fall asleep or gets agitated, that's it. Do you understand me? The interrogation will be postponed. Understood?"

"Not an interrogation, doctor," Piersanti added. "It's an interview."

"Ten minutes and I'll have one of my nurses stop by."

"Ten minutes is fair enough. Thank you. Send us a male nurse."

"We don't have any male nurses."

"Hire some then."

Piersanti pushed the man aside to enter the room with the others, and when the doctor had been about to protest about the number of people, Piersanti ordered the guard to let no one into the room for the next twenty minutes and then shut the door.

"Doctors keep getting younger," he said to Gennaro. "I doubt that one has ever had a drink or a woman." Piersanti propped one of the extra chairs in the room under the doorknob.

Farrugia was groggy but he managed a smile. His eyes opened and then closed. He could hear them. He raised his hand but it collapsed back onto the bed because of the handcuffs. Alessandro, Dante, and Gennaro gathered around the bed. Piersanti came over to the bed with a key and unlocked the handcuffs.

"*Grazie,*" Farrugia said, his voice gravelly as if he hadn't drunk any water in a week. Tubes for IV antibiotics and hydration were bundled and organized, snaking from his left hand, running up the bed from under the bed sheet and draping over his shoulder to bags on a metal hook overhead. Monitors for his heart and lungs were doing their job nearby. A call button was near the previously fettered right hand, useless and out of reach.

"He's saying something, Chief." Both Gennaro and Piersanti looked over at Farrugia as he struggled to enunciate something.

"He's trying to say something."

"I can see that, Sandro," Gennaro said. "You'd be the same way if you'd been shot in the ass."

"All joking aside, Isidò is fortunate," Dante said, at the foot of the bed reading the notes left by one nurse to another nurse about emptying and measuring the Jackson-Pratt drains. "He's taken a bullet in the ass and shoulder, and one in the front." Dante flipped a page. "My guess is he got it in the ass first, the second one hit him in the shoulder and that spun him around where he got hit again in the front. None of his vitals were perforated, thank God."

"They found him with a guy on top of him," Piersanti said. "It could've been worse."

"He's trying to talk again, Boss."

Gennaro and Piersanti leaned forward and heard Farrugia say, "Noelle."

"She doesn't know yet, Isidò." Gennaro said, stroking his friend's face. "We wanted to make sure it was okay with you before we had her see you. In due time, my friend."

Farrugia closed his eyes and then opened them again. He dry-mouthed words again.

"Whisper it into my ear, Commissario," said Piersanti, leaning forward to capture Farrugia's word.

"What did he say?" asked Gennaro.

"'Stefano.' He means Stefano Pugliese."

"Who is he?" Dante asked.

"His contact within the Totaro clan." Piersanti touched Farrugia's hand. "I'm really sorry, but he's dead, Commissario. Stefano was the man they found on top of you. I believe he saved you. He was shot so many times in the back that he wouldn't have survived. I'm sorry."

Alessandro was the first to say it. "What the hell was the DDA thinking?"

"I'm asking the same thing," said Piersanti.

"He's trying to say something to you," Gennaro said.

Piersanti leaned forward again, putting his ear next to Farrugia's lips. He listened and then said to Farrugia, "Claudio? There was no Claudio."

Dante came from around the foot of the bed. "Claudio? Claudio Ferrero was there?"

Farrugia blinked. It might have been a signal. It might have been a blink.

"Who the hell is Claudio Ferrero?" Piersanti asked.

"Someone we knew in Milan," Gennaro said. "He helped us out."

Alessandro said, "He must've been doing an investigative piece. He's with *La Stampa*."

"Great. Just what we need—a journalist."

Farrugia's other hand lifted off the bed. Gennaro leaned down this time to talk into Farrugia's ear. "Conserve your energy, old friend. Blink once for us for *yes*. Was Ferrero undercover?" Farrugia blinked, a clear signal this time. "With the Totaro clan?" Farrugia struggled to shake his head.

"He's weak," Gennaro said. "Lord Doctor Fauntleroy might be right: he needs rest."

"Wait," said Piersanti, fishing out two plastic evidence bags from his jacket pockets. "Let me ask him about these." Piersanti put one of the bags in front of Farrugia's face. "Can you see this, Commissario?"

Bloodshot eyes opened. He blinked.

"Of course he can see it, Piersanti. You don't go blind from being shot in the ass."

"Sorry," Piersanti said to Gennaro. "Commissario, notes like this one were found scattered everywhere. Can you tell us anything?"

Farrugia's hand grabbed the plastic bag and then dropped it.

"He needs rest, Piersanti," Gennaro said. "Were you expecting a full report from the man? Have some compassion."

"He's saying something, Boss."

Gennaro put his ear next to Farrugia's mouth and listened. "Counterfeit." Gennaro grabbed the bag Farrugia had dropped and said, "Blink, Isidò. Is this Totaro?"

Farrugia blinked. There was a knock on the room's door.

Piersanti offered the other bag to Gennaro, explaining, "These were also found. They're U.S. bonds. Ask him about them, Gennaro."

"Are these counterfeit, Isidò?"

Farrugia blinked.

Piersanti said, "That's not good. Not at all."

"Isidò . . . a few more questions, forgive me. Is it Totaro?"

Farrugia did nothing.

"He could be tired, Boss."

"Isidò . . . Marra?"

Nothing.

"I told you that the man was tired. He's exhausted."

"Boss, he's trying to say something again." Gennaro moved in closer. He held Farrugia's hand. He listened. He came up. Farrugia had fallen asleep.

"What did he say?" Piersanti asked.

"It makes no sense," Gennaro said, flicking the second plastic bag in his hand with his other forefinger. Gennaro handed the plastic bag back to Piersanti. "I think he's too tired or the drugs are making him delirious. He mumbled nonsense. He said something about Sicilians and green eyes."

"Green eyes?" Alessandro asked.

Gennaro shrugged. "That's what the man said."

The loud knocking on the door became pounding. Piersanti walked over and removed the chair. The young doctor came in with two nurses and a flock of policemen and another unexpected guest: U.S. Attorney Michael Farese.

"I came as soon as I heard."

Silvio was behind Farese. Piersanti ordered the policemen out of the room. The nurses checked the machines and the drip rates, appearing and disappearing like ghosts.

"I gave Attorney Farese a synopsis of the injuries," the doctor said. So Farese had caught on that Farrugia was still undercover. He asked Silvio to ask the doctor to wait outside for a moment. The doctor left with assurances that they would not be long.

Silvio stopped translating long enough to ask how Farrugia was but nobody answered him.

"What the hell happened on that raid?" Piersanti said. "From what I'm hearing it was a slaughter. The men near and around Farrugia were unarmed. They didn't even have cell phones." Silvio translated, including the angry tone.

"This was a special operation and I think some of the men were overzealous," Farese said to Silvio for him to translate to Piersanti.

"Obviously," Gennaro said in English.

"What was so 'special' about it?" Dante asked, also in English. Piersanti was confused, searching for some traction in the exchanges. Silvio pointed at Gennaro and translated, pointed at Dante, translated. It was back to Farese.

"Because the DA and I are working on a case together. We believe we're onto a counterfeiting enterprise and—"

"And what?" Gennaro asked, as Silvio continued rapid-fire translation.

"I ordered the raid, and I'll take responsibility."

"What does this mean?" Piersanti asked.

Silvio translated what Gennaro said in Italian, "It means there will be a special investigation of the special operation, which means we won't know shit."

Silvio made an indescribable noise, the way an animal balks at his or her master's command. Alessandro asked Silvio if he was okay.

Gennaro said in Italian, "Go ahead, Silvio. Tell Attorney Farese what I said. There are plenty of words for bullshit in both English and Italian. I can assure you that my vocabulary in English will be colorful and festive if you need a thesaurus."

Alessandro walked towards the window, muttering, "Now is the time for 'I prefer not to.'"

Silvio said slowly to Piersanti, "U.S. Attorney Farese wants to repeat that he ordered the raid. It was his order. He'll investigate what happened at the scene."

"Does he have any idea what he has done?" Piersanti screamed.

Silvio stepped in between Farese and Piersanti. Farese was a tall man and he was lording his height over Piersanti.

Farese responded, "I understand that you're upset. Farrugia was hurt, but he'll recover. There will be a thorough investigation. I promise."

"Silvio," Piersanti said, "Make sure that the honorable U.S. Attorney Farese gets every word."

Silvio nodded and promised. It was David talking to Goliath now.

"Your crack team of hotheads just gunned down the top-ranking members of two of the most powerful clans in Campania, and their affiliates. Do you know what that means?"

"I'm sure you'll tell me," said Farese.

Piersanti didn't wait for the translation. "It means that every junior member is now vying for leadership. You've just instigated a full-fledged war. That's the half of it. The other half of it is that the newspapers will want to paint the police as vigilantes, as no better than the Camorra for gunning them down. The men killed at that meeting place were unarmed. The regional office will call for an investigation on the use of excessive force, and your head and the head of your colleague, the DA, will be on a platter like John the Baptist. But it gets better."

Silvio was near out of breath. Piersanti waited for the man to finish.

"It gets better, Attorney Farese. Do you want to know how?" Piersanti intruded into Silvio's personal space. David was pushing the giant back and sandwiching Silvio in between them. "I'll tell you how. In addition to the Totaros and Marra clans fighting each other, the 'Ndrangheta, with whom Commissario Farrugia was in, are now in the mix. Why? Because they think they've been betrayed and—"

"Oh shit! Now I get it." It was Gennaro.

"Get what?" Piersanti asked, distracted from his rant. Silvio stalled in mid-sentence.

"What Isidò said makes sense now. The Sicilians . . ." Gennaro said.

"What the hell is he talking about?" Farese asked.

Gennaro asked for the two evidence bags from Piersanti. With both of them in his hands, Gennaro said, "The Camorra is counterfeiting euro notes." He held up the one bag. "But this—" He held up the other evidence bag. "This is what the Sicilians brought to the meeting."

"What the hell is that?" Farese asked.

"Counterfeit U.S. bonds," Piersanti said.

Farese grabbed the bag and looked at it.

"The Sicilians must be counterfeiting them," Gennaro said.

"Bonds? I don't understand," Farese said.

Piersanti put his hand on Silvio's arm and pulled the man away from Farese so he could get closer to the American. "Please translate, Silvio. U.S. Attorney Farese, you have done what the Emperor Nero could not do. Only Rome burned while he fiddled. This—" Piersanti pointed to the fake bond in Farese's hand. "This means that Cosa Nostra is involved. The Sicilian mafia. Bravo, Attorney Farese. You have just set fire to the entire country. Italy will burn because of you. You must be proud. What do you have to say for yourself?"

"I'll tell you what I have to say: you're the one who asked for the backup, remember? It was your men, your assault team," Farese yelled, then left, flinging the door open while Silvio translated in calm Italian.

21

The door clicked behind Dante as Bianca came into the hallway from the study. She saw Alessandro and Gennaro. They were returning from the hospital. They all looked tired, exhausted. Hospitals are happy places only once in life, when there are screaming babies. No Tommaso with them.

"He went home," said Dante before she asked.

"Good," she said.

The men filed past her. Gennaro took a chair from the dining room table into the living room. The others followed suit. She asked for details. Dante recounted the blowout between Pio Piersanti and U.S. Attorney Michael Farese, while Alessandro did impersonations of Silvio and the doctor. Gennaro conveyed Farrugia's medical condition, the noble death of Stefano Pugliese, the appearance of the U.S. bonds, the fake euros, and concluded with Sicilians and green eyes.

"And what did Tommaso say during all of this?" she asked. The men glanced at each other, coming to unanimous agreement through silent man-speak.

Dante was spokesman. "Not a thing. He just listened. Why do you ask?"

"I'm thinking that Amerigo Totaro might be our rat. I think he's been feeding Aldo Giurlani information about the Totaro clan for years. It's Loki's first clue. ADAGIO ILL RUN knew A RAT TOO . . . then boom then IF."

None of them liked the sound of "boom" and the double tap of "then."

"So Totaro himself is a rat, huh? That might explain what happened to the commissioner." Alessandro had shifted in his chair to find the soft spot. "I hate to be the devil's advocate, but I have to ask: what evidence do we have?"

She hadn't expected Alessandro to be the Doubting Thomas. She'd anticipated that she would have had to convince Dante. Even Gennaro seemed receptive to indicting Totaro.

"Because—"

"Because Loki told her," Gennaro said.

"Is that true?" Dante asked.

"Not quite."

"That does sound like Loki," said Alessandro.

Bianca sought a chair for herself. The dishes were behind them, still on the dining room table. The desserts once so attractive had hardened. The powdered sugar looked like nasty cocaine and the *sfogliatella*, a dead clam.

She took her seat. "I would've thought Stefano would've been the link, since he was Farrugia's connection to the Totaro clan. Not that it explains the Sicilians."

Gennaro crossed his leg over. "Farese is proposing that the DDA be investigated for using excessive force. Foresnics will reveal that the men on the ground floor were shot at. They were unarmed. What weapons they had were set aside with their cell phones. I'd like to know who gave the order. Piersanti has Farese down for cultural insensitivity and interference. Farese screwed the pooch and Piersanti is left with dog crap."

They all had agreed with Piersanti about the pending fiasco with the media. The GdF higher-ups would come down hard on their office, while Farese sat meek and mild on the sidelines.

"What about the Sicilians, Boss?" asked Alessandro.

"What about them? It shouldn't surprise us, Sandro, that the Sicilian mafia would want a piece of the action. What I can't figure out is whether the meeting was about two counterfeiting operations or one?"

"I don't understand," Bianca said.

"Farese acted as if it were one operation. He knew that the System was counterfeiting euros. He knew Farrugia was undercover. He ordered in the DDA thinking that he was busting a coalition on euro counterfeiting and backing up Farrugia. Somehow it all went to hell. But his face changed when he heard about the counterfeit bonds."

"Did his face drop to the floor?" she asked.

"More like his face went into the basement. Farese was blindsided. He hadn't expected that, nor did he expect that the Sicilians were the ones behind the fake bonds. Farrugia confirmed that for us in his own way."

"And Tommaso?" she asked. "How did he respond to that news?"

Dante shook his head. "Not one word. He took it all in like a priest hearing confession."

"Wouldn't even have known the man was in the room," Alessandro said and then asked, "Boss?"

"Yes."

"This guy knows something about all of us, but we know nothing about him. He admitted that he read dossiers on all of us. All except Bianca."

"Everyone in the GdF has one," said Gennaro.

"I can accept that, but what about his connection to Matteo? How well does he know him? All we've got is twisted bread, and maybe some opera coming to Naples; that's not evidence. And . . . am I the only one here disturbed that Tommaso knew Charlie Brooks?"

Their eyes returned to Bianca. Charlie Brooks—that name haunted all of them.

Bianca got up, asked if anyone of them wanted some Sambuca. They nodded in near unison and she started pouring small rounds into tall shot glasses on the dining room table. They weren't clean glasses, still sticky, and she didn't know whose was whose, but that didn't matter. She needed a kick and she suspected that they did too.

"To Alessandro's point about the GdF dossiers," she said, "I'm working on accessing the late commissioner's files. My guess is that Tommaso read them. It doesn't prove a thing, but I'm hoping I'll understand whatever relationship Giurlani had with Totaro."

"Sounds good," Gennaro said. "What about Loki? Your thoughts there?"

"Loki is using anagrams this time. Who the hell knows why. I showed you the two that I solved." She tipped back her shot of Sambuca. "The first clue mentioned Aldo and the rat. The second clue names Tommaso and said to start with Matteo."

"Any luck with the third one?" Gennaro asked.

"None." She poured herself another shot. Alessandro and Dante requested more.

"I don't remember her solving any anagrams," Alessandro said.

"You were in the kitchen discoursing on love at the time, Sandro," Dante said.

"In with the Totaros or not, it doesn't explain the Sicilians."

Gennaro drank his Sambuca. "What did Loki say, Bianca?"

"Start with Tommaso." She held her empty shot glass, rolled it between her two hands.

"What is it, Bianca?"

"Green eyes. That bothers me, Gennaro."

"What about them?"

"What did Farrugia say exactly?"

"He said: '*I suoi occhi verdi.*' Why?"

"When Loki and I started talking, the first clue was from a nursery rhyme about spiders. Itsy bitsy spider." She recited the verse for them, translating it roughly.

"Spiders?" Dante asked.

"Loki told me that the female spider is the dangerous one. The male spider has to be clever."

Gennaro said. "Is it possible that the male spider is either Matteo or Tommaso and this Sicilian that Farrugia saw is the female spider?"

"Quite possible," Bianca answered.

"Chief?"

"What is it, Dante?"

"Someone needs to talk to Noelle."

"I'll talk to her in the morning," Gennaro said, nudging his shot glass at Bianca for more Sambuca.

"You want more?" she asked.

"One to toast Farrugia's recovery, and the other two are for—"

"Other two, Boss? You're having two more drinks after that one."

"I am, Sandro. You're not the only one with problems with women. I have to talk to Noelle and we have to deal with a Sicilian *madrina*. Our first female Mafia boss."

Gennaro had not expected to be conscripted into taking a morning yoga class.

He had found Noelle's temporary studio on Via del Parco Margherita near the Piazza Amedeo. He kept his opinion to himself that yoga was elitist, for bored housewives desperate to keep their bodies lithe and limber for the more advanced positions in the *Kama Sutra*, orgiastic coupling best believed in paintings and stone sculptures, since no human body was capable of the contortions without pain, and cracking cartilage. That the studio was situated in the hoity-toity Chiaia neighborhood didn't help his preconceived notion that yoga was Yuppie athleticism, along with fencing and triathlons. He waited in line to speak with the receptionist. He ignored the liters of bottled water tucked inside Prada bags, the customized yoga mats with their esoteric symbols, and the hemp sandals. He did his best to not admire the females around him, though he had to admit that the long, supple bodies would make a Trappist monk violate his vows of chastity and silence, in that order.

He showed his GdF identification, asked for a few brief words with Instructor Noelle. The young woman, young enough to be his granddaughter, said, "She'll speak with you after the class." He pleaded urgency. Politely. She was firm as her yogic body. "Not until after class."

So he found himself several euros lighter, inside a changing room, swimming inside rented sweatpants and a pirate shirt, resigning his civilian clothes to a locker, and emerging with his rented mat, the highly recommended bottle of water for hydration, and very self-conscious about his bare feet. In the studio, another young woman pointed out to him where in the room he could find his blanket, blocks, and straps. Gennaro dismissed any thought of yoga as an internal art, a mystical path to bliss and enlightenment. This was medieval self-flagellation transported to the modern age. The room's hot temperature confirmed that he was in hell.

"Excuse me, I thought this was hatha yoga," he said in a soft whisper to the young woman sitting in lotus position on the mat next to him. She answered that there was no second *h* in "hata yoga" and that he was about to experience vinyasa yoga. Movement yoga. She ended by saying, "Shanti." Since he had no idea what movement yoga was or what Shanti meant, he settled onto his purple mat, hoping he'd survive the hour and a half. One bottle of water might not be enough. He was already sweating. At least his tears could be mistaken for perspiration.

Noelle, with her soft, curly black hair, broad Lombard vowels, and petite body led the class in a flow of poses with Sanskrit names. The idyllic music hid his grunts and gasps. He reached for the refuge of his shinbone and slid down his slippery mortal flesh. He grabbed an ankle and tried to plant his foot to his opposite thigh in tree pose and found his tree shaking and trembling. The only pose he understood and prayed for her to say next was "child's pose." Although Noelle said anyone could revert to this pose as needed, his pride prevented him from collapsing into a ball of infantile surrender.

The poses in which she told the class they had the option to "bind and lock" left him confused. Under his own ass, head between his legs, he peered across the room to find but one example of what she was describing and found a multitude of women twisting and locking their hands with indescribable ease. He was frightened by what he saw, but he would try the asana. Upside down and twisted, he reached with one hand for the other wrist, stretching and trying, finding that he was unable, and just when he thought himself incapable of it he saw her smiling face, her expert hands joining his hand to his other wrist.

She smiled. "You must be Gennaro DiBello."

He wanted to say hello, or thank you, but he thought if he said a word his entire spinal column would snap. There were more positions, more sweating, more music, some chanting, and then the class was over.

He was the man on the floor. He rested there and understood Farrugia's holy reverence for "shavasana," or "corpse pose." Final relaxation pose. He processed what he had done to his body, the price and privilege of pain and pleasure. He thought he had died and seen a parade of beautiful smiling women passing him by, but he realized they were either saying goodbye or asking him if he was okay. He blithered numerous Shantis.

Noelle's face appeared next.

"You wished to speak with me?"

"I did."

She helped him up to a seated position.

"Thank you. It's about Isidò. Something has happened." He told her, explaining with a minimalism worthy of modern art what had happened to her boyfriend, but he reassured her that his prognosis and recovery were promising. Either Noelle was an enlightened human being or in shock, because she accepted the news without tears, panic, or hysterics.

"I'll go to hospital now," she said.

"You can't."

"I don't understand."

"He was undercover."

"I know that," Noelle said. "He was Giuseppe."

If you show up, the police will tag you as a Camorrista and start following you.

"But, I'm not one of them."

"It doesn't matter. They'll assume it, until proven otherwise." He accepted a cool towel that her assistant handed him. He sniffed it and found the scent a tranquil blend of lavender and something else.

"It's black pepper," she said. "We use a blend of essential oils."

He was impressed.

"So the police don't know that Isidò was undercover?"

"Correct."

"That explains a few things."

"Like what?" he asked, sniffing the towel again.

"Litsea cubeba is the other ingredient. Chinese evergreen. My colleagues and I have been trying to find a facility to host a yoga conference. We're also thinking of building a retreat center."

"And?"

"When we first researched locations, we were told that they were unavailable, or the prices were ridiculous. We didn't think we could afford Naples proper so we started looking outside the city. Then this morning one of my girlfriends got a phone call."

"And?"

"We're getting offers left and right, and the prices are not only reasonable, they've dropped significantly."

Gennaro got up from the floor, rolled his mat up. He could feel places in his body that he had never felt before. He needed a shower, his clothes, and to get to the office. He instructed Noelle not to call Farrugia. Definitely no visiting the hospital.

"Do you have any of that essential oil?"

"In the gift shop," she said, giving him directions. "Tell me what I'm supposed to make of these offerings. The prices are too good to be true."

"They are, Noelle," he said, tapping her on the shoulder.

"What?"

"When a respected Camorrista goes down, the others in the clan make sure that his close ones are taken care of. You had problems finding a place at a reasonable price. That has since all gone away with Giuseppe's shooting."

"So you're saying someone knows I'm Giuseppe's girlfriend? The police don't know about me, but the Camorra thinks I'm Camorra."

Gennaro tapped her shoulder again.

She said, "What?"

"Welcome to the System."

22

Piersanti called an emergency staff meeting. Bianca and Dante arrived to find Alessandro and Agents McGarrity and Murphy sitting at the far end of the table. Piersanti and Tommaso were at the front of the conference room, the younger man at the head of the table, ready to give his presentation. They waited five minutes.

"Where's DiBello?"

Flip-board paper was again taped to all the surrounding glass, the nice, smooth sheets rebelling against the central AC. Two pencils were in front of Tommaso and one small bag. The flat-screen television had been wheeled in from the group's office and stood mute behind him.

"Where's Gennaro?" Piersanti asked a second time, and again, shrugs. There was a knock at the door and Gennaro entered the room, taking his seat to the left of Bianca. Dante sat on her right.

She gave a sidewise glance. Gennaro looked completely disheveled, almost wrinkled from head to toe. No tie, his top two dress-shirt buttons unbuttoned, the collar spread almost as wide as a seventies disco shirt. His hair was messier than usual. He mumbled some incoherent apologies.

"Where have you been?" Piersanti asked.

"Where's Silvio?"

"With Farese," Tommaso answered, "but no need to worry about them for now."

"Why not?"

"I didn't invite them," Piersanti said, shortly. "Tommaso has something for us."

Bianca leaned toward him and asked, quietly, "Where were you? Farrugia?"

"Noelle. We did yoga and talked."

"How was it?"

"Yoga or the conversation?"

Piersanti glared at them. She straightened and Gennaro leaned back in his chair, squirming a bit. Any peace and tranquility he might have gained from his yoga had been short-lived. Agent McGarrity smiled and looked down at the table clean enough to perform surgery on.

"I recorded this earlier this morning," Tommaso said, turning on the television with a click of the remote control. "As we know, Matteo Mandracchia has filed formal papers for his corporation. Late last night, only hours after the DDA raid and before the newspapers hit the streets and online. Have a listen."

Onscreen, a relaxed Matteo in another tailored suit effused about bringing culture back to Naples. He declared his ambition to add a wing to the Museo del Teatro di San Carlo. The camera angle and lighting were flattering. Matteo enunciated scrubbed RAI Italian with mellifluous vowels. His poise was between aw-shucks humility and the debilitating charm of a young Cary Grant. He knew when to put his hands into his pockets, when to flash a pleasant smile, when to convey concern with his eyebrows, and when to let out a breathy laugh and play to the camera with his soft green eyes.

Tommaso froze the recording at a moment that managed to make Matteo look awkward.

"What do the corporate papers say?" Alessandro asked.

"He's starting an import and export business."

"And that makes him suspicious . . . how?" asked Dante.

"I'm not sure what it is that he's importing or exporting."

"That could be problematic," Alessandro said. "It could be a front."

"My guess is that he'll want to import American goods, although we all know the U.S. doesn't produce much. China does most of it for them."

"Yes, I forgot," said McGarrity. "America doesn't produce anything and China does and the Camorra has the Chinese faking the best of

Italian fashion and leather, though I fail to see the connection." His Italian was fast and biting.

"I'm sorry. I should have made my point better."

"It's not too late to try again."

"I believe he wants to bring in items wholesale, like low-cost retailers do in America. It's likely to be a mix of things, like American jeans, hip-hop music, California wines, American candy, Victoria's Secret, and—"

"National pride aside," McGarrity said, "Italy has everything it needs and there's no black market for American products. Next thing is you'll tell me that he'll import Halloween candy corn."

Tommaso seemed confused and Murphy attempted to explain the candy, its teeth-like appearance and the tie-dye colors. McGarrity stopped him.

Tommaso pointed at the screen with the remote. He let the recording play a few more seconds until there was a better capture of the man's face on the screen.

"I can't prove it but I wouldn't be surprised if the counterfeit euros and U.S. bonds are involved somehow. At the front of the house, Matteo is interested in theatre and culture."

McGarrity started laughing.

"Is something amusing you, Agent McGarrity?" Piersanti asked.

"You mix your metaphors."

"Do I? Back and front stage is to theatre as back of the house is to a restaurant."

"Never mind. Continue."

"Whatever Matteo is doing is a front. Traditional Camorra enterprises are going away."

"But you still don't know what his cover will be," snapped McGarrity.

"Why did you think he was going to import American items?" Dante asked.

"I'll explain." Tommaso put his hand into the bag and pulled out a potato. Gennaro pretended to fix his hair and made a face. McGarrity and Murphy attempted to suppress their laughter. Tommaso rolled the potato towards Bianca who stopped it with her hand. He put his hand back into the bag and pulled out a peach. He waited for Gennaro to notice the silence. He pushed the peach towards him.

"Edible poetry this time?" asked Gennaro, with the peach trapped under his fingertips.

Tommaso turned the television off behind him.

"Not quite," said Tommaso. "The front might all be bullshit, but his corporate model isn't." He surveyed the room to see whether he had engaged his audience before he continued. "Matteo and his investors have purchased many of the abandoned factories north of Naples. Totaro territory. He's claiming it is both business and a gentrification effort. It's perfect for public relations. His business headquarters are supposed to be in town. Marra territory."

Alessandro was intrigued. "Factories up north. That'll affect the drug trade. Farrugia is working that real estate. Like you said: 'Totaro territory.'"

"More like *was* Totaro territory, now that the raid instigated a war between the two clans."

Alessandro turned to the others to rally support. "Okay, divide and conquer, but even Gaul was in three parts for Caesar to conquer, and we don't even know who owns this third part—the Calabrians or the Sicilians."

"Sandro?"

"Yeah, Boss."

"A poet is enough. We don't need a historian."

Bianca put her head down and smiled.

"Amusing," Piersanti said. "Let Tommaso finish."

"Matteo purchased the buildings, offered to refurbish them, and he plans to have them pay rent to a holding company that will, in turn, claim the remodeling as an expense and deduct it from taxable revenue. That opens the door to Camorra construction companies and bribery for permits. Matteo's receiving company will transfer the rental money and pay it out as a dividend to another subsidiary that provided the upfront investment to rebuild the property. Not quite money laundering, but that's the scheme as outlined in the papers that he filed."

"Is that even legal?"

"I'll let Bianca can answer that, Agent McGarrity, because she has seen this before."

The two agents averted their gaze from Tommaso to her. Even Alessandro and Dante turned their heads. Gennaro stared at his peach, but then he knew the answer.

"It's tricky, but perfectly legal on paper if the subsidiaries are properly established. A well-known American retailer did it for years and avoided state taxes. Even when it was discovered the fine was a pittance compared to the money they had made."

"So you see," Tomasso said, "the model Matteo has on paper has an American precedent. Time will tell what those factories produce."

Silence.

"There is a cash-management agreement in place for Matteo's subsidiaries," Tommaso said. "And before you ask how many subsidiaries I'll tell you that there are at least eight. I expect there will be more once we start drilling down into the reporting structure. Do you agree, Bianca?"

"Sounds right."

"He said you've seen this before, Bianca. Where?" Dante asked.

"Amici di Roma," Gennaro said.

"So," Alessandro said, "we understand how Amici di Roma worked, so we'll factor in time and ingenuity. We keep an eye on him. The GdF will go over his paperwork the way the Vatican bankers do their books. We'll know if a hair is out of place."

"It's not that simple, Sandro," Bianca said.

"Am I missing something?"

Tommaso rested both hands on the table and put his face in front of Alessandro. "The reason I have papers taped to the windows is because by the time Matteo funnels payoff money to all the city councils and regional bureaucrats, it'll be only a matter of time before the people working on the other side of that glass are working for him. That's something the Camorra could never accomplish. And another thing: in addition to the paper on the windows, I sweep this room before our meetings for bugs."

Tommaso started walking. He seemed intent on stopping where Bianca sat. It was a slow schoolmaster's walk, eyes on Alessandro, who asked, "Find anything?"

Tommaso stopped behind Bianca, pulled something out of his pocket, and placed it on the table near her. A single espresso bean.

Agent McGarrity raised his hand. "Import and export. Tell me what it is that he'll export."

"I honestly don't know, but it won't be nativity scenes."

"You said he'd get people to buy American. Why?"

"Because," Bianca said, "Matteo's inspiration came from American business, from Amici di Roma. It also could be a way of opening the door for Amici business here in Naples." She put her hand over the coffee bean.

Tommaso said as he stood near Bianca, "I mentioned jeans, music. America isn't about producing a product, like a car. It's about an image. Whatever it is, he'll have people wanting to buy the image. It's like the music industry. Singers don't have to sing. They can lip-sync these days. It's all about the illusion; no substance. That's why I introduced the potato and the peach."

Agent McGarrity's hand moved in the air as he pointed from potato to peach like King Solomon. Tommaso asked Bianca then and Gennaro to return the two items. The potato rolled in first then the peach.

"Familiar with Stringberg's play, *The Father*?"

"Can't say that I am," McGarrity threw his hands up. "Do I have to be?"

Tommaso held the potato up in one hand and the peach in the other hand. He glanced at one and then at the other. He smiled.

"Theatre is all about creating belief. The thing itself, whether it's a depiction of a woman driving her husband mad or the experience of wearing American blue jeans made in China, it's all about symbol, a manufactured reality. Matteo Mandracchia is like Strindberg, because he'll present a potato and tell you it's a peach."

The taped paper buzzed in the frantic air. The room felt sepulchral.

"What's the plan then?" Dante asked.

Tommaso stared at the table, distracted, as if he had expected an answer to write itself on the surface.

"The plan?" Dante repeated.

"I want Bianca to research the factories and investors, trace the holding company and all the subsidiaries. I'm not so much interested in the overall structure of how Matteo organized his corporation. I've done a preliminary on that."

"What are you interested in then?"

But Bianca had the answer. "Whether he has any American investors. We need to be curious whether any of the Amici di Roma's shell companies are in business with Matteo. His business model is American, after all."

"The resurrection of Lorenzo Bevilacqua," said Agent Murphy.

"The man is in hiding, but he's not dead," Alessandro said.

"We shut down Amici di Roma," said Agent Murphy.

Tommaso rolled the potato across the table. Murphy's hand stopped it.

"Yes, you stopped Amici di Roma when you investigated it in Rome and then in Boston, but you didn't convict Bevilacqua for the theft of Roman antiquities, nor did you prove that he had Alan Ancona murdered or tried to kill Bianca here."

"We tried," McGarrity said.

McGarrity was correct: the Bureau had been on the trail of Bevilacqua's hired assassin, who they later found out had been freelancing.

"This isn't the traditional model of the mafia, Agent McGarrity,"

Tommaso said. "The analogy that it's a hydra is ancient history. The thought that you'd cut the head off and know where to expect the head to grow, as long as you had your foot on the body, is wishful thinking. It's more like the Medusa. You try and cut that head off without turning to stone."

"Mythology, huh? You think that Matteo is the Medusa."

"Agent McGarrity—can't you see what he has done?"

"Apparently not."

"He's managed to have the two most powerful clans meet face-to-face and destroy themselves. He has set up shop in their territories and—"

Silvio barged into the room.

Gennaro whispered into Bianca's ear, "I would like to know how he knows so much about Matteo. Only you can get information that quickly."

Piersanti rose from his chair at the sudden noise, about to protest the interruption when he realized Farese was behind Silvio. The U.S. Attorney closed the door.

Farese started talking and although all of them, except Piersanti, understood English they politely listened to Silvio's translation into Italian.

"Some of the U.S. bonds at the scene of the raid were authentic."

Gennaro whispered into Bianca's ear again, "What do you make of that?"

Bianca pinched the espresso bean and held it up for him to see while the others were talking. She turned in her chair.

Gennaro said, "He gave that to you."

"You know what it means."

Gennaro's eyes met Bianca's. "Mosca."

"Yes. Who else since our time in Rome knows that the espresso bean is our code for a surveillance bug?"

23

Bianca had her fingertips doing small circular motions on her diNovo keyboard. She didn't find it soothing as much as conducive to thinking. Tommaso had created the job ticket: research Matteo Mandracchia's band of corporate criminals before they commit any crimes and ferret out any signs of Amici di Roma in the shadows. Her other project of researching the connection between Giurlani and Totaro had to wait. Matteo's infrastructure had drawn inspiration from one American retail conglomerate, the Matryoshka of subsidiaries from Lorenzo Bevilacqua. But first, she had questions about Tommaso himself that needed attention.

She retraced the letters in FEDORA INFORMS AS FREE again and again on her notepad, almost carving them into the paper, trying to see the sense hidden in them. Not much luck. It was quite the teasing riddle that copious amounts of coffee and late-night drinks still hadn't unraveled. She started to envy Tommaso's capacity for free association, for bizarre metaphorical connections. Maybe she needed to get a potato and a peach.

She scoured the news. Online newspapers were documenting the daily carnage between the Marra and Totaro clans—low-level grunts and middle-management capos were most of the body count. One journalist was comparing the feud to Marius and Sulla, likening the ambushes and shootings to the purges before a new and legitimate Caesar would appear as dictator for life.

Neapolitan police, on almost every street corner, were like Keystone Cops, running from one murder scene to another. Every day seemed the same: the sound of church bells ringing in one part of Naples and the rattle of gunfire elsewhere. Bianca had half-expected to see the Italian version of the National Guard marching down the street, but she knew that Italians would rather have the Wild West than the sound of boots on their cobblestones. Americans may have had 9/11 etched into their memory, but the Europeans had the daily bombings, the rubble, and the endless bodies encoded in their collective DNA.

She watched online news footage. Like the aftermath of an earthquake, Naples was the epicenter and concentric circles drawn outward illustrated the aftershock of Camorristi violence. The closer the circle was to Naples, the more violent the deaths: bombings, knife attacks, and exchanges of gunfire between clan members also included collateral damage, from children, the elderly, and even pets. The farther out the circle from Naples, the more symbolic the feud. Kidnappings, torture, and corpses displayed with meanings known only to those conversant with the lexicon of organized crime. The gouged out eyes said the victim had seen something that he shouldn't have. Hands cut off indicated someone touched something that he shouldn't have.

North of Naples, outside one of Matteo's future factories, was an open field that the locals and the media had taken to naming "Goat's Field," not because animals grazed there, but rather for the fact that several bodies of Marra clan members had been found *l'incaprettato*. About twenty men had been kidnapped over the course of one day. They had been beaten, hooded, and then abandoned like litter in the field en masse. Each man was several meters away from a peer, face-down, bound with a rope from his neck to his feet. As nightfall came each man became cold and tired and as he lowered his feet he strangled himself. Goat-tied, dead, and left in a makeshift potter's field.

She wondered what had become of Claudio Ferrero.

Bianca closed out the news window, opened the messenger console, and sent out a ping to Loki while researching the name Baraldi. She allowed herself to be distracted by a web page dedicated to the mystery writer, Barbara Baraldi, who lived near Modena. She then questioned her use of time and went straight to the university records. Hacking the firewall was a cinch, but finding the matriculation records took a little time. Tommaso was indeed a sociology student at Bicocca. She confirmed that Charlie Brooks and Tommaso had taken two classes together: an introductory economics course and a history-of-ideas course. Two shared entry-level courses before each student advanced into their specialties. Charlie Brooks had gone to swim in the deep end of economics and international business ethics. Tommaso, of course, had gone into sociology, but interestingly had developed more than a minor concentration in information technology. Still, that couldn't explain how he had assembled the economic data earlier when they had first met and shared Farrugia's desk at the office. Then she saw something else: his thesis.

Tommaso Baraldi, for his future degree in sociology, had written a lengthy paper on "Italian Creolization," discussing the identity conflicts inherent in northern and southern Italy. A "creole" in Tommaso's definition was the product of a "mixed marriage": a southern father and northern mother, or the reverse. The result was both a linguistic and cultural collision where the northerners viewed southerners as backwards and provincial and the southerners saw northerners as pretentious and affected. Mix in the Protestant work ethic of the Swiss John Calvin, some Hapsburg influence (for that additional touch of arrogance), stir in an agricultural legacy, some Catholicism, and the marriage had TNT for bedrock and the family reunions made the Hatfields and McCoys look like the Brady Bunch.

Implicit in this history was the distinction that the Neapolitan Camorra and the indigenous population were symbiotic, unlike the Sicilian Cosa Nostra and Calabrian 'Ndrangheta organizations, which were parasitical. As Italy matured in the latter half of the twentieth century, like a precocious girl trying to determine her bra size, Italy had become urbanized almost overnight, and organized crime evolved to occupy a new niche in the ecosystem. As Bianca continued reading she could see that Tommaso had done his homework on the numerous exploitative schemes that kept the northern banker's wingtip on the southern farmer's back. Italy had a beautiful leg with more than a run in the old gal's nylons. As she read through the pristine prose she recalled Loki's odd clue for the male spider, the one she had called "transgender," and speculated that it was Loki's odd choice for "creole." The male spider was different, Loki had said.

As she navigated the document, about to start the chapter Tommaso had written on the southern exodus to the north, bringing organized crime with it, Loki's avatar presented itself.

"Hi."

"Hi yourself."

"I see that you found TB's dissertation," Loki said; the avatar was a woman this time, the eyelashes seeming longer than usual. A push-up bra accentuated the merchandise. No grand entrance this time.

"Yep," she replied. "U said start w/ dee rat. BTW, nice rack. I'm jealous."

Loki peeked downward at her cleavage. "They say show, not tell. Rat? Methinks u r confused. Clue sd start with Matteo."

"Wadda u mean start with MM? U sd Totaro rat."

"Informer = Totaro = rat. AG knew him & it got him killed. Same rodent . . . IF."

Oh. She had wasted valuable time. And what other mistakes had she made? She had made snafus of logic before. Robert Strand was the biggest one of them all and that had undermined her confidence. History could repeat itself.

Her keyboard clattered with typing. "Speaking of informer, I haven't solved last clue: FEDORA INFORMS AS FREE. Any hints?"

The Norse god changed into a male. He scratched a horn on the side of his head and then gave her a mischievous smile. "An Italian hat knows the Law."

Bianca wanted to punch the screen and say to Loki, "You're a jerk," but she typed instead: "Tautology ≠ a clue. Thanks."

"U r on the right track."

"Huh?"

"Research TB's background. Parallel web 2 MM."

Loki had given her a real clue with near-perfect clarity—no hidden, interconnected layers of meaning. Well, almost none. "Web" evoked their earlier ditty about the spider.

"Is TB = male spider?" she asked.

"N." No.

"Is MM = male spider?"

"What do u think?"

Sarcasm. Loki had no intention of being charitable and spelling it all out for her. Remembering the comment about the female spider, but too lazy to do the ASCII shortcut for the female gender, she answered with: "U said XX was the dangerous one, but male spider was less dangerous. U also ASCII transgender symbol. Throw me a clue on female spider?"

Loki crossed his arms and made a whistling sound. The letters came out slowly as if Loki knew Bianca was hungry for that clue. "U r very needy 2 day."

"Bite me," she hammered out on the keyboard.

"Think of it this way: Offspring receive X from mother & either X or Y from father. Father determines gender and . . ."

Bianca remembered the basic biology. At least this clue wasn't Mendelian genetics that she had had to review when she had faked her way into Nasonia Pharmaceutical. She decided to humor Loki.

"XX = girl & XY = boy. Father determines gender. Henry VIII didn't know it. Off with their heads."

"VG, so now connect that w/ TB's dissertation." VG was "very good."

"Clear as mud," she answered, and then added, "Been asked 2 research MM biz. Amici déjà vu."

Loki magnified the messenger box and did the moonwalk to a beatbox track from one end to the other. Loki then bowed and upon rising turned female and ended the session.

She tapped the keys. "Don't go, you . . ." she said and saw the IM box disappear and another one take place a moment later. It was a fresh dialog box, different background color.

What?

"Time 4 more clues. Ready?" Static Loki avatar this time and there was no pretense.

"Yes."

"Clue 1: Palindrome. Mother. Clue 2: Child."

"Roll Clue 1."

"MIASMA HER OF IT."

Bianca wrote it down and circled HER. That had to be mother.

"Roll Clue 2."

"A MIASMA TOE FIT."

Bianca wrote the second clue down beneath the first one and drew a connector between the two MIASMAs. That had to be the same word or concept.

"Ready for Clue 3. R/t MM biz."

That was unexpected: a clue related to Matteo. "Roll it."

"LEO ZORN LAB QUA VICE."

Bianca copied the last phrase down, but saw no obvious connection between it and her two previous clues. This had to be a stand-alone item. She counted with her pencil: three clues, plus the last unsolved anagram from their last session. "An Italian hat knows the Law" was another cryptic Loki-ism.

She heard the sound of a bell, like the one used to signal the end of a round in boxing. Loki's messenger stream said in italics, "*Bye bye.*" That was terse, odd, and quick.

Bianca terminated IM and put a big box around her latest set of clues to solve:

FEDORA INFORMS AS FREE

MIASMA HER OF IT

A MIASMA TOE FIT

LEO ZORN LAB QUA VICE

Bianca realized that she had been successful at one thing during this session with Loki: she had used no caffeine. To uncramp her mind and indulge in some brain candy before diving back into the verbal labyrinth, she decided to open up her browser and eyeball the news.

The *Corriere della Sera* web site was loading while she toyed with her pencil. Front and center on the page was the news item: "One man detained for questioning and another sought for confrontation between Camorra and Police." There was a picture of two bearded men.

One was the unkempt wild-looking Farrugia. She had hoped that no well-intentioned nurse shaved him—a picture of a shorn and coiffed Farrugia in the news meant instant recognition and death. Farrugia could thank Giancarlo Ragonese from the Free Channel in Milan for that unwanted celebrity.

This other man she didn't recognize. She thought Route 66, Steppenwolf, and a Harley Davidson burning down the American highway. Bianca moved her cursor under the text, reading it like a child would read with a bookmarker, eyes moving slowly and surely towards comprehension. The turn of phrase that frightened her, seemed most ominous, was "two *mandators* of a failed coup." The Italian legal system, unlike the American version, had distinct ideas about those who ordered crimes.

Bianca typed a search string "Claudio Ferrera+La Stampa," thinking she could find some intelligent commentary on the Marra-Totaro feud. An article began to load, led by a file photo of the journalist that almost looked like a mug shot. Suddenly she recognized the other man.

She recalled that the night Alessandro, Dante, and Gennaro had returned from the hospital they had told her all Farrugia had said in his limited capacity, that Claudio was there undercover. Nobody could make sense of it. Now the two of them had become "persons of interest." The two undercover agents, Farrugia and Ferrera, had managed to build both the bridge over the Strait of Messina and set off an earthquake in one night.

As the rest of the page loaded, the leading line from Turin said, "Leading journalist feared missing, presumed dead."

24

At the office, Gennaro felt as if he were an air-traffic controller reeling in all the overhead flights onto an unpaved landing strip with one telephone and no computers, screens, or staff. The phones around him had been lighting up all morning. Alessandro had gone out an hour ago to get the slowest cup of coffee in Naples. Bianca and Tommaso were entranced with something on their computers. He had whistled at Bianca, as if to say, "Where's Dante?"

"Overslept."

Piersanti then came in, surveyed the room, and came over to Gennaro's desk and put both of his hands on his hips, like one of those shoppers unhappy with a purchase, about to shoot the manager if he said the wrong thing this early in the morning. Cupping his hand over the receiver, Gennaro asked, "What is it?"

"We need to talk."

"Can it wait? I've been fielding calls about the Totaro and Marra feud. Every agency is either asking for help or for some kind of status. I've got news on Farrugia."

"That's what I came to talk to you about," Piersanti said, oblivious to Gennaro's maintaining two conversations. He was about to continue when the sound of the door behind them announced that someone else had entered the room. Silvio.

Both men watched Silvio hobble. The man averted his eyes, draped his jacket over the back of his chair, turned on his computer, pacing his infirmity and breathing before he mounted his chair. Gennaro gave up on the phone conversation and hung up, not quite slamming the receiver down, but with enough force for the phone to make a bruised sound.

"You!" he yelled from across the room.

Silvio's head lifted: concern, panic, and genuine fear all mixed and coalesced on his face. "*Dottore?*"

"Why aren't you with Farese?" Gennaro moved from around his desk, traversing the floor space between the desks with surprising speed, just as Alessandro came in with Dante trailing behind him. He yelled, "Don't you go anywhere, Alessandro!" Dante eased himself fluidly around Alessandro and headed for his own desk. "Don't think you're getting off that easily, Allegretti. Stay put, the two of you."

Gennaro said nothing more. Piersanti craned his head over the ledge of Silvio's desk and stared at the poor interpreter. "Why are you limping?"

Silvio opened his mouth to reply, but Gennaro answered. "He has a cat."

"A cat? Since when does a cat make a man limp?"

"Boss?" Alessandro asked.

"Be quiet. I'll get to you in a minute, Monotti." Gennaro, continuing his stare-down, said, "Now tell me, Silvio, why aren't you with Farese?"

"He doesn't need me today. He's with U.S. officials. He said 'State Department.'"

"And where are McGarrity and Murphy? What did Farese do with them?"

"He sent them to the naval base to investigate the counterfeiting operation."

Piersanti made a dramatic gesture. "Why didn't anyone tell me this?"

"Ssh," Gennaro said, inching closer to Silvio. "Farese sent the agents to the base without telling us. Why?"

"I don't know why." Silvio was stammering. "He just did. He explains nothing to me." Silvio's lips quivered, as if he were on the verge of confessing to some obscene crime. "What didn't I do?"

"Nothing."

"What the hell is going on, DiBello?"

"Yeah, Boss, what's going on?" Sandro asked.

210 Turning to Stone

"You!" Gennaro aimed his finger at Alessandro.

"What? What did I do?"

"Have you slept with a woman recently?"

Piersanti objected this time. "DiBello! I can't believe you'd ask the man such a personal question."

"Quiet, Piersanti. You don't know our corrupter of flesh here." Gennaro advanced on Alessandro. "When everything goes to hell for me or my team, it's because of him and his magic zipper." Gennaro's hand was using Silvio's desk as a guide in making his way over to Alessandro. "First it was in Rome and then Milan and now Naples. There are no beds that don't know our Monotti." Gennaro stepped closer while Alessandro found refuge behind Silvio. The horrified translator held on to the seat of his chair, fearing Alessandro behind him would use him as a shield. "Alessandro Monotti puts the rhythm in the rhythm method."

"I've been a monk since we got here, Boss. I swear. Honest."

"Stop it, Gennaro." It was Bianca's voice. "You need to clam down and explain yourself."

"Explain myself?" Gennaro said, diverting his intent from Alessandro to her. "Fine, I'll explain myself. It's not only that every agency from Naples to Rome has called me this morning for a status on the feud, and we're not regular police. It isn't that I have journalists and media hacks from all over the country wanting to know what we plan to do about it. But suddenly I get this unexpected news about the agents and about Farrugia and that we're supposed to have men watching him." Gennaro's angry eyes were bloodshot.

"Keep explaining," Bianca said.

"Farese sent the agents off to the base."

"So we heard. Any news on Isidò?"

"Why the hell did Farese send McGarrity and Murphy to the base and not to the hospital? They know Farrugia and he knows them."

"Chief, what's going on with Isidò?" Dante asked.

"U.S. military police are now guarding him at the hospital."

"Since when?" Piersanti asked. "Damn, nobody tells me a thing."

Gennaro zeroed in on Bianca. "Since late last night, Piersanti, since last night." He kept his eyes fixed on Bianca. "I would like to know when Farese made this decision and why none of us were told. Nobody but us knew Farrugia was undercover, but everybody will now know that the U.S. government has an interest in him, which will make the Camorra want Farrugia dead sooner than later. Why? They'll think he'll talk to the Americans, thanks to U.S. Attorney Farese."

"Military police?" Piersanti mumbled in a muffled voice, trying to discern the logic.

Gennaro glared at Alessandro. "And you . . . seeing how there has been a trend in leaks with our investigations in the past, I'm justifiably inclined towards healthy paranoia. I'm curious as to how Farese knew when to show up at the hospital."

"He ordered the raid," Piersanti said.

"But, somehow the DDA gets overly enthusiastic and Farrugia is shot. How did he know that Farrugia was shot and which hospital and what room to go to?"

Everyone was quiet after Gennaro posed the question.

"Ask his translator," Tommaso said.

"What's that supposed to mean?" Silvio asked.

"It means you were with Farese when he heard about Farrugia." Tommaso moved towards Silvio.

"I didn't say a word to Farese about Farrugia undercover. I told you the man tells me nothing. Messages come to him all the time from various people in the embassy. I mentioned the State Department. I interpret when we are out and about. The rest of the time I sit and wait."

Tommaso turned to the others. "Farese is a vulture. He shows up after the dead are laid out: Palme in 1986, Fortuyn in 1992, and now my uncle. The news sees Farrugia as a Camorrista and now, between the military police and McGarrity and Murphy gallivanting around the base, the U.S. Navy will know about Farrugia. We all know that the naval base employs Neapolitans, so there is no doubt the System will know his hospital room number." Tommaso paused to look at his wristwatch. "By this afternoon, but that leaves one disturbing question unanswered."

"And what is that?" Piersanti asked.

"Silvio just told us that Farese ordered the agents to investigate counterfeiting at the naval base. How convenient is it that the agents are reassigned? Out of harm's way, perhaps, or priorities have been changed for them?"

Eyes examined Silvio.

"When I am not translating, I am not allowed in his office. I said nothing and he told me nothing."

Bianca cleared her throat. "You didn't have to. Farese knew we were onto something when we started realizing that Matteo was replicating Amici di Roma's business organization. Farrugia is with military police and the agents are reassigned. How convenient."

"Meaning?" Gennaro asked.

Bianca pulled the espresso bean out of her pocket. "Mosca. Remember?" She handed it to him. "Ask Tommaso about it."

Silence. Gennaro placed the espresso bean on Silvio's desk.

Tommaso fished out the bug he said he had found in the conference room and placed it alongside the coffee bean. The bean looked like a rosary bead next to the crushed electronic device.

"Farrugia is chained to his bed," Gennaro said. "Why not add a few more bullet holes to him since he's easier to shoot now. What the hell was Farese thinking? We can't blame Giancarlo Ragonese or the Free Channel this time." Gennaro returned his focus to Silvio in the chair. Alessandro withdrew from behind him.

Silvio's voice cracked. "I knew nothing about military police. I swear."

"I have something to say," Dante said.

"What is it?" Piersanti asked.

"I walked to work this morning, and I think I was followed. I know I'm not crazy."

"What makes you think you were followed?" Bianca asked.

"I was nearly run over by a motorcyclist. But here's the thing: it was a woman."

"So what?" Gennaro said. They all understood Neapolitan traffic was a civil reality at best. "It could've been one of Sandro's dates."

"I'm not dating."

"Relax, Sandro. It's a joke. Anything else, Dante?"

"The strange thing is, Chief, this woman nearly clipped me and then she looked over her shoulder at me. It was deliberate."

"Maybe she wanted to see that you were okay," Alessandro said. "You know, a close call."

"No, it had been deliberate, almost theatrical. It felt like a message to me."

"Did you get a look at her?" Gennaro asked.

"She was wearing a helmet and a white jumpsuit."

Silvio stood up, the look on his face suggested that he had seen the Madonna.

"What's with you?" Piersanti asked.

"Same thing happened to me last night. I was out walking with The Commissioner since I can't run because of my leg. We went out for a light stroll, The Commissioner and I."

"The commissioner?" asked Piersanti.

"It's the cat," Gennaro said.

"Who walks a cat?" Piersanti asked.

"I do," Silvio said. "I have a small harness, so he can get exercise. We were walking to the park but we never made it. We were on the side of the street, and behind me came this motorcycle. She moved slowly and was beside me revving her engine. The noise frightened The Commissioner, so I picked him up." Silvio pulled away his collar to display the cat scratches as evidence. "I tried to walk faster to get away from the crazy woman, but I couldn't because my leg hurts from running. She kept the motorcycle next to me and she kept looking at me."

"So what did you do?" Dante asked.

"What could I do? I tried to escape with The Commissioner, but she stayed parallel to me and gunned her engine. She gave me one last look before she peeled away."

"And you know that she was a woman?" asked Bianca.

Silvio nodded. "It was obvious."

"Jumpsuit?" Gennaro asked.

"White," Silvio said.

"Anything else," Bianca asked.

"She sped off with two other motorcyclists. Yellow jumpsuits."

"Anything else," Bianca asked.

"She lifted her visor up. I saw her eyes, but not much else because of the helmet."

Bianca scratched the side of her neck. "Let me guess: she had green eyes."

One of the office phones started ringing.

Dante said, "I'll get that," and walked away.

"We really need to find Farese," Gennaro said to Piersanti.

"Why tell me? Who am I that a U.S. attorney would talk to me?"

They returned their gaze to Silvio.

"What? He treats me like a servant. I'm a translator, not a spy."

Alessandro returned to stand behind Silvio's chair. He rested his hands on the man's shoulders. "You're more than that, Silvio. Don't underestimate yourself."

The tone of Dante's voice, on the phone in the background, grew serious. It was of those grave conversations, like one of those melodramatic ones in the movies where bad news is delivered over the phone and not by telegram. Dante was listening more than he was speaking. He replied in the affirmative once more and hung up.

Dante returned long-faced. Gennaro asked, "What happened?"

"Farrugia is awake."

25

"I don't get it."

"Get what?" Agent Murphy asked.

"One minute we're in an office listening to an intern who makes his points with produce, and then we're sent into the field to investigate the Camorra on our own."

Murphy stopped on the sidewalk. "What? You miss Tommaso?"

"Very funny. Don't you find it peculiar that Farese's orders pull us away from Farrugia and the gang? I get into a barfight with seamen and Silvio goes through all that effort to keep my identity secure, but here we are investigating counterfeiting at the naval base."

"Still Camorra," said Murphy. "We're still undercover."

"What do we know about this guy?"

"Jacket says he's an old-timer. He's been the go-between for decades."

"Decades, huh?" McGarrity said, in English.

"Yeah, our guy goes back to when the Feds were working a deal with Lucky Luciano to secure the Bay of Naples."

"Just wonderful, Murph. Nothing like keeping it in the family."

They arrived at the bar, which was within walking distance of the base for the U.S. Sixth Fleet and U.S. Naval Forces, Europe. While Europe recovered under the Marshall Plan, beer served within these four walls helped servicemen stumble back to their daily grind of writing guilty declarations of love on postcards before liberty was over and the ships pulled out of the bay.

After a generous tip to the barkeep, they took seats at a modest table in the back. They were in loose civilian clothes and had spent hours asking discreetly about items that could be found under the table or fallen off of a truck. The local at the end of the bar was a Camorrista. The barkeep gave them the clichéd nod as he cleaned his glasses. This was their man. All that training at Monterey was paying off.

The man approached them. "A friend of a friend said that you gentlemen were interested in doing business."

"We are," said McGarrity, introducing himself and Murphy as "Mike and Mike."

"Michele e Michele," the man repeated, knowing it was bullshit. He sat down and asked for a drink.

"We're interested in what makes the world go 'round, and I don't mean love," said Murphy, enjoying the noir scene he had in his head for years but never could play out. He had stored it next to the dialogue of Hoover and G-men about to do in Dillinger at the Biograph Theater.

"Money."

The barkeep delivered the customary courtesy drink. They toasted and tilted back the whiskey shots.

"We heard a rumor that some good money came into town," said McGarrity.

"Money always comes into town," the man said, holding onto his glass.

"Not just any money," Murphy said, leaning in closer, "but money so good that people might think it's real."

"Oh, that kind of money."

"That kind of money," McGarrity said. "Think you can arrange it?"

The Italian across from the agents put his hand into his pocket, pulled out a Benjamin and placed it on the table. McGarrity picked it up, took a loose piece of paper nearby and rubbed the one-hundred-dollar bill against it. No green smudging. The ink was good, the plate was positive, and the transfer from plate to blanket to paper was good stuff. But American. Unexpected.

"I have more and in smaller denominations," the man said. "Jacksons and Grants. Best in Europe. My merchandise can pass the ultraviolet test and it's so good you can roll the bill and snort coke but the German shepherds would detect only the drugs."

McGarrity pushed the Quaker across the table, which surprised the man, who interpreted it as hardball negotiations. He started high on his price list and cited all the reasons why he'd give them the special discount that even the Vatican bankers couldn't get. McGarrity shook his head and smiled, called over the barkeep and asked for a full bottle of their best whiskey. When the barkeep nodded and McGarrity asked him to wait, he went into his billfold, knowing the man across from him was watching him, and handed him a fifty-euro note. The barkeep smiled, but as he was about to leave to fill the order McGarrity seized the man's hand and escorted it across the table to show his guest the euro note.

The Italian said something polite and asked to see the note. He broke the fifty and gave the barkeep two twenties and a ten, keeping the original fifty note.

"How did you come across this artwork?" the Italian asked.

"It was blowing in the wind, and we happened to catch it," Murphy said. Which was not far from the truth.

"I'm impressed, gentlemen."

"So are we," McGarrity said, "and while we admire the American 'artwork,' a clerk at the local 7-Eleven back home would know a fake one before the authorities do. We're interested in the home-grown crop."

"But you're Americans."

"We are, but we do business in Europe. We have access to others who move all around Europe who'd also be interested in having some pocket money, if you understand my meaning. While in Europe think and pay like a European."

"It's still risky," the Italian said.

"Is it a limited supply?" Murphy said. "Perhaps the artist would prefer to illustrate comic books."

The Italian gave them a wicked smile. "It's a time-consuming process and, as you know, it must evolve to keep its appeal. By the way, I think comic books are now called graphic novels."

McGarrity's turn to smile came. "All artists aspire to see their creativity evolve. If it didn't, it'd be simply a craft, a thing easy to duplicate. You have a supply. We have a demand. That's as fundamental as capitalism gets, my friend."

"I like you. I like your way of thinking," the man answered. He named a price. He had factored in polite haggling, and they did the usual dance before agreeing to the price they'd both known beforehand. A time and place was set. He asked for permission to make a phone call to get details.

McGarrity and Murphy watched the man walk into the darkness to find a phone. Whether he had a cell phone or not, this guy wanted privacy.

"What the hell are you doing?" Murphy asked.

"What do you mean?"

"You gave him evidence. You gave him the fake euro."

"Murph, I don't care about dollars. Let the Secret Service worry about it."

"What about Farese?"

"What about him?"

A few minutes later their euphoria evaporated. As their contact walked towards them, several naval servicemen entered the establishment, loud, burly, and with women on their arms. They had apparently already been barhopping. One of them spotted McGarrity. Through the shadows and the O-course of tables, he staggered and yelled out the drunkard's late-night lament, "Don't I know you?"

Denials.

Another brawl.

Bianca resumed researching with Tommaso at Farrugia's desk. Working this close to the intern, sharing a computer screen, and reviewing findings was like playing a duet on the piano. She had the bass, he had treble, and the keyboard and screen was at middle C.

She had heard her name once. "Bianca?" Twice. "Bianca?"

220 Turning to Stone

"Sorry. I was distracted, Tommaso."

"You sure were. I'm sitting right next to you. Did Gennaro upset you?"

"No, I'm used to him. Truth be told, Silvio upset me."

"Silvio?" The man's voice next to her paused as he did his typing. They had been dissecting Mandracchia's financials and going nowhere. They were suspiciously clean. Not so much as a window streak. She could tell he was waiting for her to elaborate, almost predatory about learning the way she'd process these two revelations: first Dante and then Silvio, their brush with Umas on motorcycles.

"I'm thinking . . ."

"I can tell," he said.

Bianca was anxious to seize the keyboard, and for once she realized that taking hold of the keyboard would be rude of her, as if she had become impatient with his driving. She would try a different approach.

Tommaso had returned to what analysts called cubing the data. He had modeled Matteo's figures in the forefront, and in a three-dimensional array he was configuring imported data from past filings of Amici di Roma, starting at the top of the alphabet and working his way down the chain of shell companies, looking for anything that suggested Matteo was laundering money. She watched as the visuals started to form a spider web. His script had been parsing and iterating across numerical data of declared Amici income and displaying the results to the screen's interface. There was no proof that Lorenzo Bevilacqua, at the center of the web, was funding Matteo Mandracchia. Dots were connecting on the screen, but none of them linked to Matteo Mandracchia. She heard Tommaso say that he was hoping to discover Bevilacqua in Naples and from there connect him to Matteo. Nothing. Yet.

"How rare are green eyes?"

The question stopped Tommaso's typing again. "You're thinking of what Farrugia said, aren't you?"

"It can't be a coincidence. He said 'green eyes' but made no mention of motorcycles."

"Farrugia wasn't exactly in the best of health to have a conversation, Bianca. I still don't understand how Claudio Ferrero is involved in all this."

"Claudio is a journalist."

"I know. *La Stampa*." Tommaso moved his mouse and clicked on data points. "I read some of his articles online. Good stuff. The Turin office is assuming that he's dead, but they didn't say he was investigating the Sicilian mafia or the System."

"Why should they? They don't know for certain that he's dead."

"I agree . . . but someone in Turin has reason to think he *is*." He took a closer look at the screen. Nothing. "So what is it with the green eyes? Do you want me to research the criminal archives in Sicily and look for a woman?"

"Not exactly," she said.

Tommaso returned his gaze to the screen and watched more dots populate it. He was paying attention to her. He mumbled that it was only a matter of time before there was a Sicilian godmother. The Camorra had its pantheon of women leaders. Crime was an equal opportunity adventure.

"Why wait?" he asked. "I can run a query. It shouldn't be too difficult."

Bianca leaned back in her chair, clasped her hands behind her head. "I'm thinking this woman doesn't have a record, but that doesn't mean she isn't associated with a known family. Running a query for Sicilian Mafiosi is a waste of time at the moment. We won't find her that way. Back to my question, 'How rare are green eyes?'"

Tommaso gave her a sideways glance. She waited to hear what he would do with the Loki-like clue. His fingers had slowed down and he stared at the screen. She sensed that he was thinking. He stopped. She waited to hear what he would say.

"Genetically? The genetics for human eye color is complicated. Light blue eyes are the most rare of the phenotypes; the genes are recessive, but the problem is whether she has genuinely green eyes or some shading that suggests green. For example, hazel eyes might be interpreted as green, but they're really a variation of brown."

She tilted back, stretched her spine. "I'm listening."

"The best way to calculate the genetic possibilities is to do a Punnett Square."

She smiled. "I didn't know you knew so much about genetics."

"I don't. I have a good memory of basic biology, but we're working backwards."

"How do you figure?" she asked.

Tommaso faced her. "In order to figure out our Sicilian madrina we'd have to guess her parentage. A green-eyed woman is as rare as a left-handed woman."

"Who says we need to know who her parents are?" she asked.

"You're confusing me, Bianca. I don't understand."

She asked him whether he had the news footage from his recent presentation. He said that he did, that he hadn't erased it yet. She requested he play it. Tommaso went and turned on the flat-screen television and cued the interview.

The men had come over. "Fine time to be watching soaps," Dante said.

"We're not watching soaps, Dante."

"Did you get something on Mandracchia?" asked Gennaro.

"May I?" Bianca asked. Tommaso gave her the remote. "I'm watching it again for this," she said, hitting the pause button. On the screen was Matteo Mandracchia, smile frozen.

Alessandro said, "He has a nice smile and he talks smooth as a salesman. So what?"

"What else do you notice?" she asked.

Silvio approached the screen, pointed to it, and turned around to face them. He had that same face. Revelation. "He has green eyes."

"'He has green eyes,'" Bianca repeated, handing the remote back to Tommaso.

Gabriel Valjan **223**

The men stared at the screen.

"I'll bet you our Sicilian Uma in the white jumpsuit on that motorcycle is either his sister or his mother. We've been looking at Matteo's public record and ignored his personal record."

"But we verified that he doesn't have a criminal record," Dante said.

"We did, but what family doesn't have secrets to hide?"

Tommaso started in on the keyboard like a hungry virtuoso.

26

Not only were they not allowed to see Farrugia but, to make matters worse, the hospital floor on which he was sequestered had been locked down, patients moved to other floors, and the hallway busy with U.S. military personnel and a small number of medical staff.

Pio Piersanti opened up his cell phone and sought Farese's number.

"What are you going to tell him?" asked Gennaro.

"Me? Nothing. I don't speak English well. Silvio here will talk to him."

Silvio, doing his best to appear positive since Alessandro and Dante had been complaining about how much they hated hospitals ever since they were kids, asked, "What would you like me to tell him?"

"Tell him you're on strike."

"Huh?"

"It's simple," Piersanti said, listening to the dial tone, "you tell him you're not his translator until he gives us some explanation."

"What if he objects?"

"Let him speak to me then." Piersanti smiled. Bureaucracy was a beautiful thing. "You work for the GdF, and you're a resource on loan. I'll tell him I need you to cover the feud. Courtesy works both ways, and for this marriage to work he needs to learn how to communicate. Why the hell isn't he answering his phone?"

Silvio took out his cell, suggesting that Farese might answer his call since he'd recognize the number. He started thumbing the number.

"Why don't you put the man's name in your directory?" Gennaro asked.

"This phone confuses me. I've tried and failed, Chief. Ah, it's ringing."

"Hello," Silvio said. A thumbs up indicated that he had Farese on the line. Piersanti lamented yet again that nobody talked to him. Gennaro stepped closer to Piersanti to whisper a translation in his ear.

Gabriel Valjan **225**

"Where am I? I'm at the hospital. I've been waiting to see Commissario Farrugia, but—" Silvio listened and made faces. Not good. "That's not right. What do I tell Piersanti?" Silvio listened some more. "What do you mean you'll take care of him?" Piersanti tried to grab Silvio's phone but Silvio deflected the man's hands. "You're putting me in an awkward position with my superior, sir." Silvio listened for a few seconds. "With all due respect, I understand who you are, but what you're suggesting is rather heavy-handed and disrespectful. You owe Piersanti an explanation. That's the least you can do."

Silvio's eyes flitted between Gennaro and Piersanti as he absorbed more of Farese's English. Gennaro brushed Piersanti's hand away when the man made another attempt at snatching the cell phone. Silvio turned his back this time and stepped a few paces away from them. Gennaro and Piersanti followed. Alessandro and Dante noticed and joined their bosses. The translator, who was listening to Farese, was now sandwiched between Alessandro and Dante in front of him and Gennaro and Piersanti behind him.

"No, Attorney Farese. I prefer not to."

The men crowded Silvio and heard an irate Farese yelling. No translation was necessary.

"Yes, you heard me. I prefer not to. Read *Bartleby*."

The voice on the other end came through clearly. "What the hell has gotten into you, Silvio? Screw Melville. I hated him in high school and I have no interest in him now. I need you tomorrow at a meeting. What's so important that you can't be there tomorrow? Tell me."

Silvo put his shoulders back. "Tomorrow I must take care of The Commissioner."

"What commissioner?" the voice screamed.

Gennaro took the phone from Silvio. "Farese, this is DiBello. Is my English good enough for you? Good. Silvio is unavailable until further notice. Why? The man just told you he has to take care of The Commissioner. What commissioner, you ask? The one who'll put his claws into you after he finds out what you did to Farrugia. This commissioner is interested in American interference." Gennaro terminated the call and returned to Italian. "Asshole. Here's your phone, Silvio."

"Thanks, Chief. I'm worried about Commissario Farrugia, though."

"Why, what did Farese say to you?" Piersanti asked.

"He wants to have him moved."

"Moved where?" Alessandro said first and Dante added "Can he do that?"

Silvio answered, "What's that American expression? Ah, yes. Possession is nine tenths of the law."

"Where does he want to relocate Farrugia?" Dante asked this time.

"Ospedale Marina."

"The balls," said Piersanti. "He's moving Farrugia to the U.S. Naval Hospital."

Tommaso was surfing the Sicilian version of the Bureau of Vital Records. He had found the Mandracchia family, but the unexpected materialized on the screen. Matteo's digital file of his birth record had been deleted. In fact, most of the electronic records on any Mandrachhia were artifacts.

"This is ridiculous," Tommaso said.

Bianca didn't think twice. "Hack the *Motorizzazione Civile*." The Italian equivalent of the Registry of Motor Vehicles.

"Driver's license? You think her picture will come up."

"Hell if I know, Tommaso, but we'll at least get an address and town for possible suspects, and from there we can narrow it down."

"That reminds me," he said. "He had to have paid some tuition. I can trace him and his family that way."

"What if he was on a full scholarship?" she asked.

"And Mom and Dad don't send him pocket money?"

"Good point, but how do you feel about breaking into university records?" she asked, knowing that she could do it in seconds. "Schools are aware of digital security."

Tommaso cracked his knuckles at the challenge. Good lad.

"I got Mandracchia's top contributors, didn't I?" he said.

"I know, and I know exactly how you did it, too. Just be careful."

"Would you like to lead the way," he said, offering her the keyboard.

"Youth before beauty," she said, and watched him telnet into the university's first node, lay down the pathway and proper syntax, back slashes and all, and navigate through each layer, walking deeper into the university's network structure. Tommaso was no tyro. He made some twists and turns and shortcuts that she hadn't known about. More impressive was that he had slashed through numerous protocols, using multiple ISP addresses from their own office computer. Impressive.

"You've rigged your trip to make it look as if you're making the request from within the university," she said, watching him type and hit the enter key multiple times. He had performed some fast breaches with a surgeon's dexterity. He was in deep.

"I'm hitched to another university user." Tommaso pointed to a series of letters and numbers. "I picked a user in the Registrar's office since they usually have system-wide access for records. While he or she does their job, I'm behind them making my own requests although the detailed session transcript will say that they made the requests."

It was geek speak for saying he was a phantom, a shadow, a whisper through the wires. Tommaso was moving fast, off-loading a virtual copy of everything he could on Mandracchia's financial aid history, line for line during his entire university and graduate career onto his jump key. He culled the demographics, but like any good thief he couldn't resist taking what he found along the way. He mirrored all the data without leaving a smudge on the glass.

He closed his session. He confirmed the time on his watch.

"Oh, yeah," she said. "You're fast and you're good."

"I wasn't checking for speed. I wanted to check that it was all within university working hours. It is. Perfect."

"What format's the data in?" she asked.

"Delimited text file. I can port them to a spreadsheet."

"You have your work cut out for you tonight," she said.

"It's fun. We can discuss it tomorrow."

Bianca watched Tommaso remove the jump key from the USB port and pocket the storage device in his jacket.

"Tommaso?" He glanced up. "What color are your mother's eyes?"

He smirked. "They weren't green, if that's what you're asking. Her hair was a lighter shade of brown and her eyes were brown like mine." She could tell that he knew she had heard his *was* and *were* because he added as an afterthought: "My mother died years ago." No mention of his father.

"I'm sorry," she said.

"Don't worry about it. I'll see you tomorrow, Bianca."

"See you tomorrow."

After she watched him walk out the glass door, her cell phone buzzed. A text.

"IF will be OK."

27

Nobody was answering her calls. Voicemail kicked in on Dante's line, and she wouldn't bother with Alessandro. Gennaro was probably ignoring his. After the morning fiasco he'd probably ignore her number, since she hadn't offered to help him with the deluge. She had to admit that Gennaro was comical standing there in the middle of the office space, tie pulled loose, collar spread for maximum oxygenation, with one phone to his ear, another phone to his other ear, rotating each of them, like satellite dishes to field the distressed voices.

Dinner was in the oven.

Call it age, call it wisdom, but Bianca found reflecting on the day's events gave her perspective. There had been a time when adrenaline sufficed, the go-go pace was all that had mattered, but experience now said that introspection was decisive and efficient. Elegance came with using mental and physical energy well.

Tommaso had demonstrated deft expertise at hacking and he was data-intuitive. Although combing the Bureau of Vital Records had been a dead-end street, it proved that someone was erasing Matteo's past. Tomorrow would reveal what he found. The question that gnawed at her with Spartan intensity is how Tommaso, a student of the soft sciences and prone to poetics, had mastered serious skills. Every hacker starts with a master and develops a perspective to see problems as multi-dimensional. She had seen Tommaso cube data. In watching him work she saw the dance of a creative mind. She witnessed him giving form to thought. He considered uncommon connections. That made him an artist.

A chill had passed over her when she was sitting next to him and she thought, spider web, as the data points clustered around Lorenzo Bevilacqua's name. It was as natural as a baby's second step to put the next foot forward and think that Tommaso was the male spider. But that couldn't be right, because Matteo was the male spider, and this dangerous female spider was his blood relation. Tommaso was supposed to be the rat, but somehow there was no evidence supporting that conclusion. The more she contemplated it all, the more she saw the beauty in Loki's clue: a female spider, clad in a white jumpsuit, and with green eyes. The helmet was the spider's hard shell. Metaphorical.

Then another, completely unexpected thought made her shiver. Tommaso was brilliantly artistic with data, and prone to intuitive leaps.

So was Loki.

It was both unnerving and unsettling. Was there a connection between Tommaso's OCD and anagrams? She took hold of her notepad and read them. She began thinking about the word games, began thinking that Loki and Tommaso were one and the same. Both seemed obsessed with metaphors. Both were poets.

Bianca peeled the top sheet off and looked at the anagrams, reviewed her circles and connective bridges. She numbered them.

FEDORA INFORMS AS FREE
MIASMA HER OF IT
A MIASMA TOE FIT
LEO ZORN LAB QUA VICE

Loki had said number two could be thought of as a palindrome, which meant it could be read the same way from front to back and back to front. Numbers two and three had "miasma." She consulted an online dictionary for miasma and read the definition: "a contagious power that has an independent life of its own." Another online source discussed that "contagious power" in terms of disease theory. A perfect locution for organized crime, whether it was the System, the 'Ndrangheta, or Cosa Nostra. All of them were pathologies.

Bianca wrote down "mafia," thought of green eyes. In that instant Loki's poetry became manifest.

Mother is Mafia = Mafia is Mother.

She realized that, earlier that day, the connection between Matteo and green eyes had popped into her head. She had to wonder how much of that was due to her subconscious having solved this riddle days ago.

She circled "Mother," convinced now that the woman in white on the motorcycle, the one with green eyes whom Farrugia had encountered at the raid, the one who had clipped Dante and had scared Silvio and his cat, was Matteo's mother. Rule out sister, unless his sister was one of the two other motorcyclists.

Number three, she concluded, had to, by extension, include "mafia." Her pencil pecked at number two and then number three, the graphite point like a knife diced back and forth between the numbers, knowing there had to be a logical connection between number two and number three as she examined the remaining letters after "miasma." Of course.

Matteo is Mafia.

Not "transgender" but different from other male Mafia members. Deviation from the normal model is a form of evolution. Down to the last two clues. She heard a ping. Messenger.

It was Loki calling from Valhalla. The Norse trickster's horns were drooping like a bloodhound's long ears.

"What's wrong?" she asked.

"Time = critical."

"Isn't it always?" she responded, and did the one thing she had never done: added an emoticon. Loki seemed indifferent.

"Solve those riddles?"

"All but two."

"Which 2?"

She wrote: "Fedora and last one, Leo Zorn."

"Explicit names."

"Good to know. What is the crisis?"

"IF = endangered. Needs 2 move." Loki was telling her that Farrugia was in trouble. She checked her phone and reread the text. "IF will be OK."

Gabriel Valjan **233**

"Status change?" she asked.

"Escalation."

"Suggestions? Advice?" she keyed in fast, confused by the text, alarmed by Loki. No riddles; no time for leisurely solutions. Just information fed quickly and cleanly. This was not good.

"Move him ASAP."

"Will do, but have 1 Q."

"Ur question then," Loki answered, the typing slower than usual.

She hesitated because this was her roll of the dice—a gamble. Loki's avatar turned its head left and right and then downward, seeking her message. He strummed his fingers. He was waiting.

"Seeking motivation here. MM = Mother = Mafia. TB's mother . . . COD?" She knew she was jumping into the abyss, asking Loki for Tommaso's mother's cause of death.

Loki smiled, changed gender to female. "Congratulations."

"What for? Is this ur dance of death? Ur not Shiva."

"Intuition. Daughter is to father as son is to mother. Freudian but Truth."

"Thanks, now what does the fortune cookie say?" she asked.

"Triangle cancer. Move IF where he can do yoga."

She read the last line. Triangle? The cell phone rang. She picked it up without seeing who was calling her. "*Pronto.*"

"It's Dante. Farrugia is being moved and we can't do a damn thing about it."

"Why not?"

"Farese is behind it. He's being moved to the U.S. Naval Hospital. I don't have time to explain. I wanted to call before you started worrying about me and dinner."

"I'm not worried about you, Dante, I'm worried about Isidò. He's not safe at that hospital."

"You think? We'd like to move him but we don't know how. There are more squids here than there are in the Mediterranean."

"What about McGarrity and Murphy? They're FBI. They can try and get him out of there."

Dante sighed. "We just found out that they're in jail again. Some bar fight. But Gennaro said they weren't carrying their badges with them. Any ideas?"

"Idiots. We need to take him to Noelle," she said, and could hear Dante relaying her plan to Gennaro. There was a jostling sound and some bumpy static.

"This is Gennaro. Did you say Noelle?"

"I did. Why do you—Damn it!"

"Bianca? What is it?" Gennaro asked.

"I don't believe it. I'll call you soon with a plan. I need to talk to Noelle first."

"Make it quick, before the U.S. Navy sends over the entire fleet for Isidò."

Next to "FEDORA INFORMS AS FREE" she wrote "Fedora = (Someone) INFORMS Farese."

28

Bianca removed the half-cooked dinner from the oven. It had to wait. Once ensconced into military custody, Farrugia would become a prisoner of the U.S. government, devoid of basic legal rights and subject to incarceration in any one of the concrete hotels in Europe or worse, exported to America and enrolled in Club Gitmo.

She took out a fresh SIM card and, using a trick Robert Strand had taught her, punched in Noelle's number and deceived her phone into thinking it was calling itself. Noelle would see her own name on her LED screen. It was an old telephonic trick from the ancient days when Ma Bell technicians would come to the house, crawl around wall-to-wall shag carpeting in suburban homes, leather belts slung low and butt crack showing, ready for the credit card swipe, and test out phone lines with color-coded phone receivers. It was simply telephony predicated on a recursive function.

"*Pronto,*" said a hesitant voice. Noelle.

"This is Bianca, a friend of Isidò. Please, listen and be patient, because we don't have much time." Noelle was calm and accepting of the update on Farrugia's pending change of residence. Noelle didn't ask who or why, when or where. Bianca admired that.

"Have you encountered anyone on a motorcycle?" Bianca asked.

"No." Again, Noelle processed the question without becoming defensive or panic-stricken. It must have been all those years of yoga and meditative bliss. Noelle explained that she had been receiving discreet calls related to her quest for a yoga retreat center. She provided a quick-fire summary of how the prices had suddenly dropped and the choice locations had surfaced overnight. Camorra.

"Do you have a studio of your own yet?"

"I do, but it's in dire need of work. The place is a spacious warehouse with a lot of potential. It used to be a leather factory. It's a pig sty at the moment." Noelle named the area: north of Naples, but not out in the boondocks where clientele couldn't get to it by train or a fast car. Perfect.

"We should meet." Bianca named the train stop.

"But that's not where the hospital is."

"No, it isn't. We have to do something first. Do you happen to have a blonde wig?"

For the first time, Noelle was speechless. Bianca repeated the question, checking the time on her computer screen. She moved the cursor to the upper-left corner of her screen to shut down her MAC.

"I can get a wig from one of my girls here. Anything else I should do?"

"Yes."

"I'm listening." Noelle's tone was serene, undisturbed. Again, admirable.

"I want you to dress like a Camorrista—blonde, mascara like Elizabeth Taylor's Cleopatra, ensemble not quite whorish, but tacky and tough. If you've got it, then flaunt it. Oh, don't forget expensive sunglasses."

"Okay, so I'm a *putana*. How is this helping Isidò?"

"You're his girlfriend. We need you to look the part."

Bianca confirmed the place where they'd meet. Noelle mentioned again that it was not the hospital, asking why there.

"We need to break into an apartment first," Bianca said.

Noelle said nothing, but her silence sounded a little lacking in zenlike tranquility.

"We need two wallets from that apartment."

Noelle did the Italian version of *uh-huh*. "Is that all? Then what do we do?"

"We have to break two FBI agents out of jail, and give them their identification."

"What are they in jail for?"

"The cops think that they're Camorra."

"Of course they do. And then what?"

"They'll get Farrugia out of the hospital, and from there we'll hide him at your new yoga center."

"Is that all?"

"It's enough for now."

Bianca waited near the metro stop on her Vespa, helmet on and visor down. She had chosen to wear all white for a reason. Had she had time, she would've rented out a motorcycle. Noelle emerged from the subway, a Venus born from the Neapolitan underground, but not quite as Botticelli had imagined his goddess. The blonde wig was obviously a wig, but nobody would dare question it. Noelle's sinewy body was encased in form-fitting jeans and tight shirt that made her breasts appear like delicate pears. The sunglasses, while not garish, did complete the look of mock celebrity. Noelle strutted over as soon as Bianca beeped the moped's horn.

The Vespa cruised around the piazza and cut down a typical side street that had colorful laundry hanging from lines overhead, men playing cards on makeshift tables on the sidewalk, and shop windows with Christmas decorations and that street's particular theme. This street was dedicated to red chili peppers. Noelle's firm embrace around Bianca's midsection kept her fixed on the Vespa as it flew around cars and between bodies.

The agents' apartment was a second-floor walkup. Noelle found the concierge who, what luck, was elderly, male, and amenable to feminine charm. Bianca kept her visor down and thought tough thoughts. Noelle was the System girlfriend and she, the bodyguard. Noelle recited from the libretto the angry and sad aria of the distressed woman, and then the frustrated lover in search of her man. When the man reminded her that two men lived there she launched into a diatribe of how men work all the time, hang out with their guy friends, avoiding the responsibility and love of a good woman and home. All she asked was that he let her into the apartment to fetch her boyfriend's wallet since he had forgotten it.

Bianca stood there silent as stone, and glad her helmet hid her smile.

The concierge pulled the retractable chain on his waist, fumbled through a miscellany of key rings and found the correct key. He kept repeating disclaimers that he didn't do this kind of thing every day, but she was special. He insisted that he had to accompany her inside the apartment, though. A matter of principle, he said.

Bianca stood in the doorway while Noelle went in with a rush, the older gentleman behind her. She fussed and expressed her dismay at how men lived like overgrown adolescents, while Bianca cased the place. The room was not quite a bachelor pad of dissipation, but it did have some scattered clothes and the lingering veil of mustiness and the odor of take-away food. Still, McGarrity and Murphy had been more civilized than expected.

A thin wallet was on top of the bureau on the opposite side of the room. There had to be another billfold somewhere, and Noelle had only one boyfriend. Noelle took the wallet from the bureau, allowing it to flip open for a second. Bianca caught a flash of FBI badge.

Noelle turned around and started jabbering nonsense to the concierge, his back turned to Bianca, buying time. Bianca scanned the room. She eased the closet door open and saw the holster. Neither agent had been armed. Smart. She had to scan fast before Noelle's histrionics wore the old man out.

Bianca thought, keys. Most apartments had a table near the front door for keys and necessary items when leaving for the day. Bingo.

She checked. Badge. She held up the wallet for Noelle to see. Noelle started her swan song, thanking the man, and for the finale, pulled him into her bosom for a crushing hug. The gratitude should keep the man seated for the rest of the day.

The entire police station of Inspector Salvo Montalbano could fit inside the vestibule of Naples Police Headquarters. It was a wide cavern of polished marble where a woman's heels running up the stairs would echo as if the cavalry had come. Bianca waited outside because she knew she would have to take her helmet off and she wanted to avoid the security cameras.

Alessandro was the first to spot Noelle. After the round of introductions, explaining the ruse they had foisted on the concierge, and the news that the wallets were on hand, the next step was liberating the agents. Bail is not a part of Italian due process. A person is either remanded into custody or released on good faith, depending on how the bureaucracy decreed.

Next was strategy. Alessandro expressed his reservations. He was Tuscan. Dante was Roman. That left Gennaro, the old-timer Neapolitan. Noelle would be the stand-in Camorrista girlfriend—silent, sullen, and bitchy only when necessary.

Gennaro and Noelle found the right office. All-male cast, square desks and papers everywhere, voices yelling across the room, into telephones, and just about everyone behind a desk smoking despite the numerous "No Smoking" signs on the walls. The window blinds were drawn, exposing the dead flies on the window ledge. Pencils, with their worn-down erasers and dull points protruded haphazardly from service-anniversary mugs; men ambled around in white shirts with very big guns in large holsters on hips or under their armpits. It was Neo-realism, Neapolitan style.

"Who are you?" the short man behind the desk asked.

Gennaro gave his name.

"Who is she?"

Gennaro glanced over his shoulder at Noelle. "Who'd you think she is?"

"My guess is she belongs to one of our prisoners, the fine but misunderstood citizenry of Campania."

"I belong to myself," said Noelle. The snap of chewing gum was missing; the head toss and insolent look over the shoulder, the pick at invisible lint, were not.

Gennaro tapped the man's desk and whispered, "Please, don't piss her off. I'll never hear the end of it."

"You have my sympathy."

Noelle walked over and tilted her flexible trunk into a side bend to look at the man's gun in the holster.

"What is it, Miss?"

"Big gun, big holster—feel the need to overcompensate?"

The man made a face, straightened out some papers and glanced sideways at Gennaro. "Which prisoner?"

"Actually, it's two of them. Irish last names."

"That should make it easy enough. Less vowels." He pulled a clipboard out from the snowfall of paperwork on his desk. "Here they are. Two names here; arrested this afternoon for causing a disturbance at a bar near the military base." His forefinger rested on the names and his eyes lifted to examine Noelle. "One man isn't enough for you, darling?"

"One is my boyfriend and the other is his cousin. I'm strictly a one-woman-one-man kind of girl."

"Sure you are, sweetheart." The cop clicked his pen and made two marks on the page. He mumbled something about the hospitality business and motioned to Gennaro with his finger. "You know these two have to appear before a judge, don't you? One of these men—" He read the name McGarrity off the clipboard, very nearly pronouncing it correctly, "—has already made a favorable impression. He likes bars and he likes fights. He has two visits before a judge, and I'm not so sure that he'll be easy to spring."

"I'd appreciate any help you can give me. They'll make their appearances."

The pen clicked again. "Are these two doing any official business for the department?"

"Not at all." Gennaro crooked his finger so the man knew to lean forward. "She's Amerigo Totaro's niece. Her uncle tolerates her interest in the Irishman because of business."

"Totaro business?"

"Sinn Fein is what I heard, but I personally don't understand the Irish and the British. Some of the beer is okay, but the food is terrible. You know that there's a war going on right outside our doors. The department looks at these two Irishmen as nothing but small potatoes. If it means less bloodshed for all involved we can learn to accommodate."

The man picked up the phone and called down to the tombs. "Bring up McGarrity and Murphy."

"Who the hell are you?" was the first sentence they heard from the man assigned to Farrugia at the hospital.

"Special Agents McGarrity and Murphy. FBI," said McGarrity, putting away his wallet. Murphy followed suit with his billfold. The crabbed expressions they both wore were part of the job description. "We're here for the prisoner."

"I don't care who you're here for, Agent McGarrity. I don't have a chit or any other piece of paper about transferring a prisoner into the custody of the FBI."

The chief petty officer behind the desk was the designated liaison person between U.S. military personnel and hospital staff. McGarrity had heard the man speaking decent Italian. East Coast kid, baby fat still in the cheeks, but he was old enough to know that in the military, independent thought meant "Follow the book." There was enough salt in him that he wasn't about to allow anyone to fry his bacon while he wore a uniform.

"Fine," said McGarrity. "I hope you realize it's your ass."

"That's why I've got it covered, agent. Paperwork says so."

Murphy sized up the hallway. Two guards outside Farrugia's room and likely another two inside, one sitting in a chair and one pacing, if not commandeering the television for badly dubbed American sitcoms.

"This guy has to move," Murphy said. "Is he medically stable when he does?"

The officer diverted his stare from McGarrity. "Believe so, Agent Murphy. He isn't on pain meds. He can do his own wound dressing changes. He's good to go when he goes." That last remark was intended for McGarrity, who winced for a smile.

"What about rehab? The man's been shot three times."

The CPO flipped the pages attached to his clipboard. "I don't see it listed under 'Permissible Activities.' All I've got is that he's allowed to ambulate about the room with assistance if needed, but he's supposed to be with at least one guard at all times. No visitors. Those are my orders."

"You mean the police haven't talked to him."

The officer's face twitched almost into a grin. "Are you nuts? The guy had been in and out of consciousness. The pain medications alone did nothing but make him sleep and babble incoherently. No statement he'd make would hold up in court."

Noelle chose the moment to make her entrance. She walked in like the Queen of the Nile, which prompted a flurry of sailors to rush her. She started screaming at them in Italian to take their filthy paws off of her. One of the MPs crooked her elbow and brought her over to the desk.

"Who are you?" the officer asked her in calm Italian.

Murphy interrupted. "You said 'babbling.' Babbling what?"

"The hell if I know, Agent Murphy. The man was delirious. All he kept saying was something about 'her eyes' and he kept repeating some name. I'm not sure. Ste? Now, if you'll excuse me I'd like to take care of this young lady here."

"Yeah, be my guest," Murphy said.

"Miss, this is a restricted area," the naval officer said in Italian so sonorous it could put sheep to sleep. "This man is a prisoner. Our job is to protect him and—"

"Protect him from what? I'm his wife."

Murphy could hear his partner's neck bones crack as his head turned. "You're his what?"

"I'm Stefi. My Giuseppe is calling me. I must be in his dreams. You must let me see him. You must."

McGarrity stepped closer to the officer. "Are you that heartless that you won't let the man's wife see him."

"Orders are orders, sir."

"Oh, for crying out loud," Murphy yelled. "The man is handcuffed to a bed! Standard procedure, my ass."

A long and loud wailing sound pierced the air. Thrown against the wall, hands outstretched in dramatic prayer, eyes upward to all the saints, Noelle played the part of the aggrieved wife.

"Make her stop," the officer implored McGarrity and Murphy.

"You made her cry," McGarrity said. "You make her stop."

Two guards came running out of Farrugia's room, and Noelle hadn't hit the high note yet.

In came Silvio and Gennaro, running to find their mark on the cold marble. Medical staff came running next to assess the commotion. They were turned away by the MPs. The charge nurse looked ready to rip the horns off of the first bull she could find. Somebody barked out commands, and some semblance of order started to manifest itself.

"Who are you two?" the officer asked Silvio and Gennaro.

Silvio said in firm Italian, "I'm U.S. Attorney Farese's personal translator. I'm here with my colleague, a special investigator from the GdF to make sure the prisoner, Giuseppe, goes with the FBI when they arrive."

"The FBI is here," the man pointed at the agents. "Look, I don't care if you're his personal masseuse. My orders are my orders. As for transporting this prisoner, it is my understanding that he goes to the naval hospital with a naval detail, not GdF, not FBI, and certainly no wife."

"Wife? What wife?" Silvio asked.

"Her." The officer tilted his head toward Noelle. "That's Stefi."

Gennaro screamed at the officer. "That's it! Giuseppe moves now."

"Over my dead body," said the officer, yelling this time, and obstructing Gennaro. Noelle's sobbing dissolved into wheezes and sniffles.

Gennaro got up close to the officer's face. "It may well be over your dead body, you idiot. Do you have any idea who she is?" He pointed at her as if she were Mary Magdalene. "Do you have any clue what you just created?"

"Created? She walked in here. She said she's his wife, Stefi."

Gennaro grabbed his head with both hands. "Good God in heaven, don't you understand? She's Camorra. She's Amerigo Totaro's niece. You'll need a fortress now that the Marra clan will come down here. We've got to move him before the shooting starts. I'm surrounded by dead men; I'm months from retirement, killed by a boy in a sailor's suit."

Silvio yelled at the chief petty officer, "We move Giuseppe now!"

"Thank you, thank you," said a tear-streaked Noelle. She had the role down better than a paid mourner at a southern funeral.

The officer flipped through pages of paperwork. "I have orders to move him to the naval hospital, but not with you."

"Screw your paperwork," Silvio said. "I'll make sure that U.S. Attorney Farese notifies your mother that you died in the line of duty. The Camorra kills you here, and the nurses can move your body to the morgue downstairs in the basement. It's an easy day."

Gennaro bullied his way into Farrugia's room. The chief petty officer ordered the men to stand down. Gennaro had himself handcuffed to the confused Farrugia, who didn't know what to do with the strange blonde creature hugging and kissing him. Agents McGarrity and Murphy shepherded the whole crowd down the hall, down the stairs, and out the front doors into the dying daylight into the waiting Fiat Punto, with Alessandro in the driver's seat. They piled in like it was a clown car, Silvio taking the passenger seat after Noelle had taken the back seat with Farrugia and Gennaro handcuffed together. The car pulled away. Bianca and Dante followed on the Vespa.

As Gennaro unfettered Farrugia, Noelle gave them the destination. Warehouse. North.

29

Farrugia slowly absorbed everything they had to say. He'd half-imagined that being shot in the ass had improved his thinking. When he heard Bianca discuss her findings, he knew which part was her analysis, and which part had been Loki. He understood Tommaso's last presentation as it had been told to him, and he kept his opinion to himself that this intern was far more knowledgeable than he had let on. A telepathic glance between him and Bianca confirmed that suspicion. He thanked Gennaro and Silvio for freeing him from the tyranny of the hospital bed.

Agents McGarrity and Murphy had disclosed their own undercover enterprise. They were to meet in two nights' time with the Camorra contact from the bar for a hefty chunk of counterfeit euros. They were told about Piersanti and Silvio's phone confrontation with Farese and Tommaso's discovery of the "mosca" in the conference room.

Farrugia described his own disastrous meeting, the three women motorcyclists, Claudio, Stefano, and the *when* and *how* everything had gone to hell. He was not amused to hear that he and Claudio were now "persons of interest" and viewed as the architects who had instigated the violent feud between the clans. He was less than pleased to hear that Farese had ordered the raid. "Green eyes" was the true inventor of mischief and mayhem. She was the one who had tormented Dante, the one who had threatened Silvio and Commissioner.

Dante had left but returned with toiletries. Farrugia wanted to shave, and Noelle insisted she would give him a haircut and humanize him. As Noelle sat next to him, holding his hand, he mused that he should be battling utility companies, scheduling bridge tournaments on weekends, running errands, and revolving these years of his life like a planet around responsibilities, such as a mortgage, fixing drains and overhead lights. His only stress in life should be sex in the missionary position one-point-five times a week: one for the success and the point-five for the attempt. Instead he had been shot three times and was neck-deep in a war between three criminal organizations and one Matteo Mandracchia.

Farrugia took in the faces around him as they talked to each other. Bianca and Dante were a couple living in sin, according to Catholic dogma. Alessandro was attempting to reform his libertine ways. The agents were secure, mid-career within the FBI. They knew Italian, damned well. Gennaro was nearing retirement. Even Silvio had a life and family; a cat counted as a dependent. He had Noelle: sweet, gutsy brunette Noelle with the Lombard hills in her Italian.

He never thought he'd be happy to be inside an abandoned building. The tannery was destitute, but it did work as a temporary refuge. Filter the light through a cobalt lens and the place might be a Diane Arbus photograph. The trauma of industrial use and abuse had passed. The building endured, the windows had withstood the onslaught of time and grime, neglect and disrespect. The disused warehouse would be perfect for a carnival of misfits: heroin addicts, dwarves and giants, meth freaks, or even a candy-rave party scene. The location was distal to the heart of Naples, but it exhibited a threading pulse, weak but discernible, ready to experience Noelle's resuscitating power of yoga, her choice of soothing colors and décor, her therapeutic voice and restorative energy practice.

"Isidò, did you hear me?"

Gennaro's voice. Farrugia's eyes focused. He knew he had been deconditioned from days in bed, his mind about as clear as the fog of a man who had a weekend bender and whose angry wife had hit him with a skillet. He was hungry for real food, eager to resume his life in the real world, freed of IV poles, nurses, and other strangers around his bed.

"Isidò? What do you think?"

His friends were standing around him in a semicircle, as if he were the surviving protagonist of a Greek tragedy.

"What do you think we should do?" It was McGarrity's question.

Farrugia cleared his throat. "Tommaso has the right idea."

"He does?" said a surprised Murphy. "How do you figure?

Bianca sat down next to Farrugia on his other side. She intertwined her hands in his. "Tommaso mentioned mythology."

"Yeah, and a potato and a peach," added Alessandro.

"Bianca's right," Farrugia said. "He has the right approach. His metaphors are confused and maybe a bit literal, but he is grasping in the right direction. Mythology is our solution. The job is to create belief." They looked at him the way an American reacts to seeing an Asian speaking German. Farrugia was too mellow to be impatient with them. It could have been the residual efforts of the last of his medication. "The Sicilian is the Medusa. We must turn her into stone."

"And how do you suggest we do that?" Dante asked Farrugia. His eyes included Bianca in the question.

"We need to get all the parties to confront each other," Bianca answered. "We need some kind of meeting. The Totaro and Marra clans were in a tentative alliance over the counterfeit euros. If we can convince her that she hasn't broken every part of the alliance, she'll think the two clans are regrouping. She'll want to show everyone that she's the one with the power. I suspect Totaro was thinking that the Sicilians simply wanted in on the action, but—"

"She made her own play," Farrugia said. "Successfully, I might add. She stands to take over all the counterfeiting if she can get control of the means of production. Totaro owns that. She has both clans blaming each other about the raid."

"Do you think Totaro knows she's with Mandracchia?" Dante asked.

"I think old Amerigo does," Bianca said.

"You do?" Dante asked.

"Amerigo Totaro was Giurlani's stool pigeon. It's possible that he and Mandracchia reached some sort of agreement; and part of that agreement, like any business merger, requires restructuring."

"Totaro," Dante said, "is on board with thinning out his men. Giurlani is out of the way. Whatever leverage the late commissioner had on Totaro is gone. That leaves the Marra clan."

"Same thing as layoffs, except this is lethal. Totaro is a recluse. Perfect for Matteo, since it is a guaranteed low-profile merger. In that sense, Totaro and Matteo are in agreement and it fits beautifully with Matteo corporatizing the Camorra."

"Like having a silent partner," Dante said.

"Just like Amici di Roma, but that leaves one possibility."

"That is?" Dante asked.

"A double-cross. A silent partner is the easiest kind to make disappear."

"Okay," Gennaro said. "How do we stop her then?"

Bianca turned to Farrugia. He squeezed her hand this time. "Simple. Let her show up, let her think she's taking over for her son, and that this is the last act. When she shows up, we just need to make sure she sees her reflection."

"Oh, anything else, Commissario?" asked Gennaro.

"Yes," Farrugia said. "I want a haircut and a shave, I want real food. Institutional food nearly finished me off."

Silvio was pacing. "We have one Medusa and two other Gorgons on motorcycles. How do we know whether it is enough to turn her into stone?"

McGarrity had his own question. "I'd like to know how Farese fits into all of this."

Murphy added, "I'd like to know where the hell that surveillance bug at the office came from."

Farrugia turned to Bianca. She didn't have to hear his answer.

Loki.

If a shave soothes the man, and a haircut calms him, and new clothes make him, then food civilizes him and the modern office conquers him. Hours afterwards, a cell phone call later, Commissario Isidore Farrugia found himself eating his dinner with Noelle and the team in the GdF conference room. Pio Piersanti had decided that nobody would expect to find Giuseppe at GdF headquarters.

Gennaro had the television on. Dante, relishing his role as gofer, returned like Moses, with parcels of food from a new hole-in-the-wall restaurant. The aroma preceded him and Dante proclaimed that, while pizza was the pride of Naples, he thought a man who'd managed to escape a fortified hospital deserved a nice steak. Noelle would have her vegetarian dish. Dante, while removing the contents of his numerous bags, drawing everyone into the sanctum of revelation, including Gennaro, explained that while the Japanese had kobe beef, and their countrymen had *bistecca fiorentina*, he had found an Argentinean *parrilla* that had a special two-steak combo dish of *bife de lomo* and *bife de chorizo*. Dante parceled out the huge portions of meat, delicious and succulent, done with absolute simplicity. Coarse salt and fire.

They ate and ate, but they saved some food for Tommaso. Silvio even bagged some for his Commissioner. It seemed to Farrugia that he had died a good death.

Dante's only lament was the disrespect shown to the wine. Plastic cups. Dante had managed to convince the Argentineans to loan him real steak knives. He promised he would return with his friends and showed them his GdF identification so they didn't think he was a Camorrista off to kill someone with their utensils. The affable Argentineans gave him the wine and had coaxed him into spending a few euros more and taking an empanada with him. The saltena, filled with carne suave, cheese and spices, green onions and potatoes, was divided up as a curious appetizer.

Tommaso arrived before they were finished.

The news on the television almost ruined their meal. If it had been Giancarlo Ragonese on the mirrored flat-screen television, the meal would have been ruined completely. As Tommaso caught up with them, a studio headpiece behind a cheap desk declaimed dramatic lines from the teleprompter with the enthusiasm of a dyslexic pallbearer. "Fugitive" was the repetitive word.

The first picture behind him was the bearded Farrugia; so sinister-looking that Farrugia apologized to Noelle for his appearance. She had made love with a wild man. The second picture, of Claudio, made him sad. No news. Both men, the balsa-wood head said, were now at large. The narrative recited the facts about the raid, the heroic DDA, and the eternal pledge to fight the scourge of organized crime as if it were polio or smallpox. The newscaster plugged some RAI documentary, with a panel of experts, on counterfeiting euros, but Gennaro clicked off the television in mid-warble. He said seeing-eye dogs were better qualified than so-called experts.

"I don't believe it," Alessandro said. "Not one word about the bonds at the scene."

Tommaso had stood up, tidying up his desk, wiping his mouth with a napkin. He threw it into the trashcan. "Enough to make you wonder why that is, isn't it?"

"It's more than peculiar," Gennaro said. "What are your thoughts?"

Tommaso, using his hand, deferred to Bianca.

"What I think doesn't matter," she said. "What we can prove is more important."

"Not exactly what I was hoping to hear," said Gennaro, who called over McGarrity and Murphy, Alessandro and Dante. Group meeting. It was time to strategize about this FBI meeting with the Camorra. Gennaro whistled over to Silvio. "C'mon, you're part of the team." Silvio limped over.

Noelle had said she needed to return to the yoga center to teach a session of yin yoga. Farrugia seemed shy about her leaving and embarrassed when she hugged and kissed him. She wished everyone well and came over to Tommaso to say it had been a pleasure to meet him.

When she was gone, Farrugia smiled at Tommaso. "So you stole my desk?"

"I'm sharing it with Bianca."

Farrugia acknowledged the answer with a shake of the head, about to join Gennaro and the crowd when Bianca said, "I think you and Farrugia should talk, Tommaso."

"Why's that?"

"You and Commissario Farrugia have something in common."

"We do?" both men answered in near simultaneity.

"Creoles—both of you are creoles. Am I right, Tommaso?"

The intern's face drained of all blood. Farrugia seemed shocked, either at Tommaso's blanched look or at being called a Creole. Bianca being classic Bianca. The tact of a rutting bull.

Farrugia found that he had to clear his throat. "My parents were Spanish and Calabrian. Mixed heritage. It was difficult at times."

Tommaso was looking at the floor as if he had lost pocket change. "My mother was from Campania, father from Lombardy. I always felt I walked between two worlds, between the dialect and customs."

Farrugia nodded in understanding, offered a smile for a mask. His dark eyes flashed up and then away from Bianca's face. They would speak of this later.

"We have something else in common, Commissario."

"We do?"

"Both of our mothers were murdered. 'Ndrangheta and Camorra."

Farrugia, hearing from behind him that Gennaro was calling him to join the group, said nothing. He nodded again, another tight smile, and walked away.

"So you researched me, read my dissertation," he said, eyebrows peaked as he leaned his head forward, pausing for her to answer. Bianca looked down and away.

"If you must know, my mother died of pituitary cancer. There are other types of cancers associated with the toxic dumping grounds, but that's the most common. She died an agonizing death."

Bianca swallowed hard, knew that her face had turned red. She almost choked out *I'm sorry*.

"Next time you go digging, do me the courtesy of talking to me first. You shouldn't have done that to Farrugia." He paused. "Don't use your friends to prove a hunch or to satisfy your ego."

Her neck pivoted away in shame as if she had been slapped. Tommaso was glaring at her. He said, "I'm on your side . . . Alabaster."

Her face froze and she felt the air inside her lungs burn. Her hand crawled up to her throat to confirm that nobody was strangling her.

"You're not the only one capable of research. I also know about Louie Patrone," he said.

So Tommaso had done his own excavation. She tried to remember to breathe as he walked away from her.

30

Dante felt as if he was in a foot race with one of those marathoners from ancient Greece. He was the one who would die when she stopped. On the way home on their Vespa she ripped through traffic, risked knocking over more than one pedestrian, exercising the vocabulary no phrasebook could teach a foreigner, one only a native understood. She had used the choicest curses of Campania, Lazio, and Lombardia. Dante simply held on for dear life and shouted apologies when he could from the back of the Vespa.

She parked. Silence. She bounded the few steps up to the entrance. More silence. She jammed the key into their door. Metallic sounds, otherwise brooding silence. She flung the door open. He caught it in time to prevent a bruised wall. She tossed the helmet onto the sofa. The leather absorbed it: the helmet didn't bounce. She headed to the study.

"For Chrissakes, Bianca. What the hell did you say to Isidò?"

"Nothing."

"What do you mean nothing? You said something."

"Tommaso said something to him," she snapped as he tried to block her, get her to stand still and talk, but she navigated around as if she were still on the Vespa.

"Then what did *you* say to Tommaso?"

"What the hell is wrong with you, Dante?"

"Me? What did I do?"

"You're acting as if it's my fault."

"Ah, mother of God. Don't twist my words. Just don't do that. I hate that. All I'm saying is that somebody said something to somebody." He was following her around the apartment now as she changed out of her clothes.

"I'm trying to understand what happened. I saw your faces. Isidò had this stunned look on his face."

She was sitting on the bed and wiggling out of her jeans. Dante, his hands clasped together, pointed them prayer-like as if he were about to bite the tops of his fingers off. He lowered the joined hands together as if he were going to point them at her.

"I then took one look at you and Tommaso. You were mortified. Tommaso was talking to you. When he turned around I saw his face. It was like when Gennaro used to get angry with Pinolo. I'm just trying to figure out what happened."

She brushed past him after pulling an oversize shirt over her head. No bra. "You think too much, Dante."

"I think too much! Tell me what happened, and I won't have to think at all. I don't know who said what to whom, but I saw three pissed-off people."

"You don't know shit, Dante."

"Apparently not, but you know what? I'm on your side. Sorry if I give a shit about you, about Farrugia, or even Tommaso." Dante went to sulk but changed his mind. He spun around. He said, "You know what . . . you figure it out on your own. That's all you ever do anyway."

"Stop being the damn martyr, Dante. As for figuring out things—here's a newsflash for you: I usually do, thank you."

She was walking away. He saw the bare backs of her legs.

"That's right. You're the resident genius. Go run away and use the Ouija board." He pointed to her computer. "Use it to solve all your problems, because I'm just a mere human. You want cold logic. A machine."

She stood there confrontational, hands on her hips, like she was thinking *you bastard*, but didn't say it. Her body language already said it for her.

"That's right," he said. "Let me fill in the blanks for you. Go to hell, Dante. Mind your own business, Dante. You wouldn't understand, Dante. I'm too bright, Dante, and I don't have the time to explain it all to you, Dante."

He crossed the room in long angry strides.

"What are you doing?"

"I'm turning your computer on. Your partner here needs electricity to think with you."

"You're acting childish. I didn't say all those things."

"You don't have to, Bianca. There," he said, verifying that the machine was on. "All you need to do is type in your password and you're all set." He gave the keyboard a slight push. "I'm sure that your security is triple encrypted. I'm sure that your password is strong; that it has one number, one upper case letter, and at least one special character. You'd give an I.T. geek a hard-on."

She made a face. Teenage-girl-annoyed-with-brother face.

"Shall I make you coffee and bring it out to you on a silver tray?" he asked, rubbing his hands together.

"No, you could go to hell for me, Dante."

"I'm living it when you don't talk to me," he yelled. "I'm not invisible. I have a mind, too."

"Fine," she yelled back.

"Fine," he returned at an equal volume.

"Where are you going?"

"What do you care?" he said, his voice tapering down. "Into the kitchen where I belong."

"All right! All right . . . I'll explain it to you."

He stood there, this time his hands on his hips. "You will?"

"After you make the coffee."

"Unbelievable." He couldn't resist smiling.

"I'm sorry," she said as she pushed her hair back with her hands. "The last thing I need is caffeine, so water will do."

"Yes ma'am."

"I'm not old," she said.

"No, you're not. Cold water it is."

He was halfway out the door.

"Dante?"

"Yeah."

"I'm sorry."

"I'll get the cold water."

"Dante?"

"Yeah."

"We need to talk to Loki."

"Okay." He knocked on the doorframe as either acceptance of communicating with the spirit world, or for good luck. He turned once more to depart.

"Dante?"

He said nothing this time. He stuck his head back through the door and waited.

"I love you."

Dante was stunned. "You really think Tommaso is Loki?"

"He has to be, Dante. How else can you explain it? I heard him say my name. My real name, and when Rendition recruited me, they made it a point to prove that they knew the obscure things. Few people—and I mean few people—know about Louie Patrone."

"Rape is not obscure, Bianca. There must be records."

"Louie Patrone's parents had serious pull. There were rumors that his father was mafia. I wanted him arrested, but nothing happened. I found out years later that the report was sealed." Dante didn't ask how she knew. He simply listened as she opened up. "I discovered that when the bastard had turned twenty-one, the record was mysteriously destroyed or had gone missing. I verified it."

He had heard the story before, but he let her repeat it out of respect. Her first contact with Rendition had been a meeting at a coffee shop. She had received a mysterious calling card and then a call that gave the location. Her handler did his best to prove that data was power. He knew about her last confession, her one girl-girl experience, her experimentation with pot, cheating in college, and Louie Patrone. With Patrone, he had used the euphemism that her experience was "less than satisfactory" and that "it hurt." It did, because he was an animal on hormones. She was fourteen and she liked him, which added to her own confusion; and she had thought he liked her. Their date went from flattery to fielding an octopus with five limbs and a persistent tongue to outright rape.

Dante sat there, legs crossed. Gennaro had shown him the yoga position. It felt surprisingly good to his hips. When she was sampling the water he commented, "That all proves how deep down Rendition went to draw you in. Do you regret joining them?"

"No. Rendition scares me but they seem to be the good guys, at least most of the time. And you know the work excites me."

Dante didn't need convincing. He knew when she was working Rendition. The sex was phenomenal.

"I don't get it, Bianca. How the hell does a kid like Tommaso who is so young get recruited into Rendition . . . and in Italy of all places?"

"Why not? He has serious computer skills. I've seen him hack into secure systems in front of me. It's second nature to him."

"Fine, he is an excellent hacker. The technology crap is a generational thing. You and I have seen it. Ten-year-olds have iPhones now and after a few years of thumbing their way through games, they have promising careers as laparoscopic surgeons but," Dante held up his index finger for emphasis, "Rendition is a U.S. organization. *This* is Italy!" He pointed to the ground and said, "*This* is Naples."

"I don't know how to explain it, Dante. I really don't know. Rendition is American based, but it's multinational in scope, like the very corporations that Tommaso talks about, like Amici di Roma, like Gladio. We learned that last point in Milan, didn't we?" He nodded. "Think about it, Dante?"

He shrugged both shoulders up to his ears. "I'm with you, but I don't know. Explain to me what you are thinking."

"The U.S. Navy is in Naples. It has been since forever."

Dante shrugged again.

"They hire Neapolitans."

"Doing laundry and making beds is one thing, Bianca. That's a far cry from what Rendition does. That doesn't explain Tommaso as Loki."

"I'm trying to explore the possibility that he's a friendly."

"A friendly?" He searched around the room for a word. "As in sympathetic but not belonging?"

"Exactly," she said, snapping her fingers. "He trades intel with Rendition. He gives them something and they return the favor and they give him something."

Dante sighed hard. "A data mercenary. If that's the case, he should be working with Farese."

"What did you say?"

"Nothing. I was just frustrated, Bianca, and being flippant."

"No . . . say it again."

Dante glanced up at the ceiling. "I said that he should be working with Farese."

Bianca rushed over to the desk, found her pad. "Here," she said, pointing to one of the riddles.

"What the hell is all this?"

"Anagrams. This one here is half solved." Her finger ran from left to right under "Informs Farese."

Dante studied the page as she explained how anagrams worked. In an incoherent stream of consciousness she repeated full-length her sessions with Loki. "It makes sense. Loki was hands-off when I was investigating Sargent and his wasps in Boston, but you saw it yourself, Dante. Loki was an equal partner when we were in Milan." Dante continued reviewing the anagrams. She kept babbling. "Silvio was right about *madrelingua*." She was alluding to Silvio's comment that language is innate, and a person's first language remains structurally dominant. She wasn't finished yet.

"Claudio had nailed it. He had suggested that Loki might've been an Italian with good English, but not perfect English. *Madrelingua*. Good, but not perfect, English. Remember?"

"Yeah, I remember, Bianca. I was there."

"I know you were."

"There is one problem, Bianca."

"What is it?"

"An anagram needs to use all the letters. I see the "Informs Farese" part, but there is no way these other letters make up "Tommaso" or "Baraldi.""

She snatched her notes from him. She read them like a prisoner reading a denied stay of execution. Disbelief.

"It doesn't add up. I'm sorry," he said

"What about the texts on my cell phone?" she asked.

"What texts?"

He watched her calves run out of the room. She returned with her purse, yanked out the cell phone, and flipped the cover open like one of the characters in old Star Trek reruns. At least she wasn't wearing a red shirt. He started appreciating that her shirt was relatively see-through. As she toggled through her texts he slipped his hand under her shirt.

"Stop that," she said, pushing his hand away. "Here they are. See?"

He pulled her in close and read out loud from the screen. "IF will be OK" and asked, "IF?"

"Shorthand for Farrugia," she said, pushing his inquiring hands away.

Bianca recounted the timing for both texts and how they had confused her. The first text had convinced her that Tommaso was Loki, but the second text was enigmatic because she had received it at the office after they had worked together. Dante listened and she must have discerned something troubling in his face.

"What is it, Dante?"

"You said that the first time you got the text you had been online with Loki."

"That's right," she said, cell phone still in her hands.

"Loki was telling you that Farrugia had to be moved in order to be safe, right?"

She nodded.

"The second time you got the text you were working with Tommaso, right?" She nodded again. "Was he sitting next to you when the text came in?"

She thought and thought. "No. I was at the desk and he was walking towards the elevator. He had his back to me. He could've texted without me seeing his phone. What are you getting at, Dante?"

"I could be wrong about this, but I see two possibilities here. Scenario one is that the first text you received might've been from Tommaso as Loki, but this second text couldn't have been him, because Farrugia was not okay. He was in danger. It wouldn't exactly make Loki a team player, would it?"

"Unless there's a gap in information."

He studied her face the way a sommelier hopes that the customer liked the wine selection.

"There is one other possibility," she said.

"And that is?"

"Look, I'm convinced that Tommaso was online helping me. I think back to other times where Loki helped us and—"

"Stop," he said. "What other possibility, Bianca?"

"Loki goes back to when . . . Rome, right? That was when I was drawn back into Rendition, when I chose to take the assignment in Boston. Agree?"

"That's right. What are you implying?"

"I think there are two of them. Two Lokis."

Dante sat there stunned.

"Dante? Are you listening to me?"

"I hear you. And . . . you're right, it makes sense."

"It does?"

"Rendition wanted you back, so what did they do? They appealed to your need for adrenaline, your intellectual curiosity. They had to make it interesting to you. That got you to Boston. You didn't trust them after the Strand case, and that certainly didn't change after the Sargent case in

Boston, either." He paused. She was still with him. "You freelance it, so to speak, and meet with Charlie Brooks. We know that Tommaso knew Brooks and that they were acquaintances or friends or something."

"But we can argue that Tommaso knew Matteo."

"Hear me out first, Bianca. Tommaso knew Brooks. You said they had taken classes together and he said Brooks asked him for advice."

"They did. He did. So?"

"Did Tommaso and Matteo take classes together?"

"No."

"Brooks got killed and his friend, Tommaso, wanted justice, or at the very least wanted to find out what happened to him. Exclude any conversations that the two of them may have had. Who is to say that Brooks didn't tell his friend Tommaso that he was meeting someone about his discovery at Adastra. Are you connecting the dots, Bianca?"

Her thumb rubbed the edge of the cell phone. "But Brooks didn't know me. He didn't even know he was meeting a woman. He wouldn't have known about Rendition."

"He didn't, but Brooks didn't live to ask questions. Tommaso did."

"So Brooks gets killed. Tommaso finds out that it's me. He could have discovered me intentionally or by accident, because once he started researching the murder he knew that Farrugia was being set up by professionals."

Dante rolled his hand to encourage her.

"He sees the bullshit from Ragonese—Farrugia was the hero at first, and then the forensics was leaked and—"

"By then he has a handle on Brooks and Adastra and he's done his homework and he knows that Farrugia was part of the Amici di Roma and Lorenzo Bevilacqua investigation. He backtracks and finds us. He certainly discovers U.S. Attorney Farese. He finds you: Bianca Nerini the consultant through his uncle, but that doesn't get us any closer to proving he knows about Rendition. How the hell does he find Alabaster Black?" Her eyes widened now. He asked, "What?"

"I don't believe it! Give me the notepad."

He gave it to her. She took it, tore off the top sheet and rewrote the anagrams and their solutions, but left the third and last one blank.

ADAGIO ILL RUN knew A RAT TOO . . . then boom then IF

Aldo Giurlani knew A(merigo) Totaro . . . then boom then Isidore Farrugia

ARMADA BOOM LIST starts with EAT TOM

Tommaso Baraldi starts with Matteo

FEDORA INFORMS AS FREE

. . . informs Farese

MIASMA HER OF IT

Mother is Mafia

A MIASMA TOE FIT

Matteo is Mafia

LEO ZORN LAB QUA VICE

Two of her fingers bracketed ". . . informs Farese" and the last anagram. "Some of these anagrams have interlocking puns. See 'boom' here," she pointed it out with her pencil, "and sometimes they become self-referential, as in the palindrome here," and she pointed to the "Mother is Mafia" and "Mafia is Mother." Then she circled "INFORMS." "This is part anagram and part statement.

Dante reexamined the anagrams. "Okay, you're smarter than me, because I'm falling short here. What are you driving at?"

"We made the wrong assumption. I thought Tommaso was a rat because I saw 'A RAT' and didn't see the *A* for 'Amerigo Totaro.' I had thought the rat was someone in the Totaro family, someone Aldo knew. I had wanted to search Aldo's records for an informant, but never got around to it. Loki was telling me that Tommaso had already started with Matteo. I started with Tommaso. That was my mistake. You *are* smart, Dante. I'm the one that didn't see the third clue. You did."

"The fedora?" he asked.

She said, "What 'informs Farese' is . . ." and she wrote down the full clue on the page: "FEDORA INFORMS = Friends of Rome = Amici di Roma. "That says there is a connection between Amici di Roma and Farese. 'INFORMS' is both statement and part of the anagram."

"I'll be damned. But I have a question."

"What is it?"

"These anagrams are in English," said Dante. "Couldn't it mean this Loki is American?"

"We can't assume that."

"Why can't we?"

"The Italian Loki could be using the anagrams to mask his English. They don't have to be grammatically correct."

"Give me your pencil," he said. He wrote as he spoke, "We need to talk to Loki about the Medusa."

"What are you writing, Dante?"

"The answer to the last one."

LEO ZORN LAB QUA VICE = Lorenzo Bevilacqua.

31

Dante had pulled up a chair next to Bianca's at the computer. They had plenty of water. She had sent out a missive to Loki. Now it was a waiting game.

"How do we know which Loki answers?" she asked.

"We don't," he told her. "We'll watch how the thread unfolds."

"This is really unnerving—not knowing whom I'm talking to." She raised her hand almost before she had finished her sentence. "Never mind. I know what you're going to say."

Dante chose to say nothing. He sipped some cold water from the one-liter glass bottle. He and Bianca had taken a stand against plastic bottles after they had seen the hideous pollution along the Ligurian coastline.

To pass the time while they lurked there for Loki, she discussed Tommaso's revelation that his mother had died of cancer. She suggested that they do some fact-finding on the Baraldis. It had to be relatively simple, since they had been told Aldo Giurlani was his uncle; and that fact meant the deceased magistrate-turned-commissioner had either a brother or sister who was one of Tommaso's parents. This was a much easier alternative to exploring the Pio Piersanti side of the family tree. Furthermore, a dead sister, morbid as it sounded, should be easier to locate in the death rolls. Simplicity of public records, she said, and Dante agreed.

A few keystrokes later they were viewing Giurlani's death notice. No mention of a sister, either living or dead. Bianca postulated that since the man had been assassinated, omissions might have been made to protect family members. Since Dante's guiding finger under the text onscreen verified what they had expected: no name for a brother either. Odd, they agreed.

"We could be going about this the wrong way," Dante said.

"Suggestion?"

"Baraldi is a distinctly northern name. When Tommaso spoke to you he said he was a Creole, which to restate the obvious meant that, like Farrugia, he was of mixed descent. We can't find the mother so how about we start with Tommaso?" Her eyes narrowed. Dante elaborated: "Let's find his birth record."

Bianca nodded and began to type. "Recordkeeping in the south can be rather hit-or-miss."

"That might've been the case a generation back, but Tommaso is of the younger generation."

"We'll see."

They watched as her query went out into the ether. They waited. She had cast a wide net with the first name. She knew they had to parse through all the "Tommaso B*" returns, but it was a quality measure on her database query.

"That one there," Dante said, tapping the screen. "That one is the best match. Correct age." Bianca highlighted the name and hit the enter key. They both moved closer to the screen.

"I'll be damned." Dante turned to Bianca. No father's name was on the birth certificate. Mother's name was a typical regional name. She lived in Nola, one of the three points in the Italian "triangle of death." The Italian environmental group Legambiente had done detailed reports on toxic dumping there.

Dante heard the rhythmic rattle and percussive strike of the return key. "I have an idea. It's a tangent, though. I want to see whether Tommaso's mother had sought medical treatment in northern Italy."

She had. Bianca located her name in the tumor registry at the Pascale Tumor Institute of Naples. There had been grant money for travel. "Always a money trail," she said. No receipt or documented husband or child in the travel logs, but after a certain date, she did have a child in the travel records to Milan.

"Giurlani was his uncle. Let's assume he was her brother. Let's just make that assumption for now."

"Go ahead."

"He'd have the resources and connections to access better health care. Giurlani was a promising lawyer, two years in as magistrate and was making his name in busting up the heroin cartel. Following me?"

"Go on."

"Sad to say, but the quality of treatment *does* matter where you live in Italy. A cancer patient in Calabria or Sicily is not likely to get the same attentive clinical care if the patient, let's say, lived in Lombardia. His mom goes north because of that and because she knows Aldo Giurlani."

Bianca was reading text while Dante was explaining. "Says here that she had tissue samples preserved for ongoing studies at the Sbarro Institute."

"Never heard of it."

"Cancer research institute in the United States. Philadelphia." Some more fast taps on the keyboard. "Here we go. She did make quite a few trips back and forth, but here's the odd thing."

"Odd? What is?"

Her forefinger touched the date on the screen. "This is the date of her prognosis."

Dante studied the date. "That means she had been traveling north on grant money before he was born."

"She was sick before Tommaso was born."

"Think she might've met Tommaso's father when she was up north?"

"She did put down his last name on the birth certificate. It's a northern name, but there is no proof she'd ever married. The birth certificate doesn't say that he's her husband. Think they could've been engaged?"

Dante shook his head. "Look at the dates again. It's too long of an engagement. She put down his name so there would be no stigma of illegitimacy."

"In this day and age. Really?"

"Southern Italy is very traditional, Bianca. I have an idea. Tommaso said Giurlani was an uncle, but maybe he meant 'uncle' as in close family friend and not blood relative."

Bianca stared at the screen.

"Many southerners went north for jobs," Dante said. "True, some of them brought organized crime with them, and the migration created a lot of tension, but many of them went north because they wanted a better life. This woman went north because she wanted medical care. She was very sick and then she became pregnant. That's one precarious medical condition on top of the other. She meets a northern man and—"

"That's what we've been trying to prove, Dante."

His hands were moving up and down, a patting motion. "Take it easy and listen. How about this idea? The man is originally from the south, but he's second generation. His mother . . . his mother married a northerner and that would explain the name change and—"

"Dante, we'll be here all day and all night with what-ifs. We need to focus."

"What I was going to say is that many southerners went up north and went into law enforcement. They were law enforcement down south, so it was an easy transition for them. We should be looking for one of Giurlani's associates in his career. Can you access the man's case files and do an internal search on the Baraldi name?"

Dante waited as Bianca typed her way through some pathways. While typing she said, "Giurlani was old-school, so I'm not certain all his records will be digital. Do you remember his office? He had papers everywhere and he had ledger books. Those leather-bound books could have been his memoirs or his earliest cases. This could be an absolute crap shoot."

Dante sipped water. The screen filled with results. Dante peered at the screen. She took a break and a swig of bottled water. She placed the bottle on a coaster. No water rings on her desk.

"We know Tommaso's birth date so we could start there," he said.

"No," Bianca said. "Let's start with his mother. We know when she died. That would be the time for Giurlani to take action. Tommaso would have been an orphan."

Dante thought a moment. "You're right, that's better."

"I'm not so interested in proving his father's identity as wanting to confirm Aldo Giurlani's relationship with Tommaso at this point."

Dante didn't dare interrupt. He excused himself to get more bottled water for the two of them. When he returned, bottle in each hand, he found Bianca grinning.

"What did you find?"

She did a hitchhiker's thumb to the screen behind her. "Evidence."

Dante approached. He squinted. "I can't read that from here. What does it say?"

"Move in closer," she said.

He did. He focused again. His lips moved as he read while he felt her hands on him. He read the details. Baraldi was a detective. His family was from the south. Campania. He was born in the north. Detective Baraldi's specialty was the Swiss border and investigating money laundering. KIA—Killed in the line of duty. Dante was trying to concentrate. It was getting more difficult. Tommaso's mother died. Aldo Giurlani had adopted Tommaso.

Dante felt Bianca. It wasn't her hands this time.

They needed more water.

He asked, "That noise. What is it?"

"Loki." She sat up suddenly, banging her head against the desk above her. They scrambled to the chairs. Dante hated the feel of leather sticking to his naked flesh, but Bianca was already at the helm, typing away.

"Does Loki know you're online?" he asked.

"Yep." She tipped back the last of the water, examined the screen, and handed the bottle in an outstretched arm to Dante behind her. He took the bottle and as he was walking away said, "Yes, ma'am. I shall return with more beverages, ma'am."

"I heard that. I am not old. Didn't I just prove that to you?" she said with a smile he could hear but not see, pulling her shirt on and waiting for Loki's response. She had pad and pencil ready.

"Thanks," she said as Dante returned, and put the next bottle of water on the coaster.

"What did Loki say?"

"Haven't started yet, but I told him you were here."

Dante put his bottled water on the floor next to the chair. "Honesty is the best policy when you're talking to spooks in the machine. Blah blah." He pulled up his chair next to hers.

"Funny, Dante, but like you said, we'll watch how this conversation goes."

"The avatar thing looks the same. Viking helmet and transvestite."

"Loki isn't a transvestite. He's a shape-shifter. He could turn into an animal if he wanted to."

"Are you listening to yourself, Bianca? You're defending a cartoon character on the screen."

"Loki is mythology—not a cartoon character . . . hush."

"Whatever," he said and she slapped his thigh. "Stop it and pay attention to the screen."

Loki's avatar this time was female and very flirtatious. Bianca said that the gender changed after she told Loki that "DA" was joining them. The female trickster was wearing lingerie and old-fashioned garters with black stockings. The snaps at the thighs had something embroidered on them. Characters.

"See that, Dante. The material there says '10ki.' That's an IRS form for corporate filings, and the source of Loki's name. I think this is the original Loki."

Dante strained his eyes. "I can't believe you're giving me permission to check out another woman's bits. Still, could be a trick. Should I put a euro in her g-string?"

"Very funny, but I'm pointing it out because I think this is Rendition Loki from Rome and Boston and not Italian Loki in Milan."

"You're kidding me, aren't you?" Dante scrutinized the avatar.

She shook her head. "Speak Italian to this Loki and see what she says."

"Won't work because she knows some Italian."

Dante stood up. "Let me get this straight. You think this is the American Loki, the Rendition Loki, because it knows Italian and English. Why is that?"

"Remember *madrelingua*?" She pointed to the screen. "This Loki even knows Italian textspeak. The Italian Loki is the one that has imperfect English. Remember Milan?"

Dante's hands went to the sides of his head. "I don't know whether I'm becoming Gennaro or Ricky Ricardo. I feel like I'm talking to Lucy."

Bianca made a sour face. "The other reason that I know this is the Rendition Loki is this is the first time I've seen "10ki" on her lingerie. I said it was a corporate filing."

"Yeah, yeah, but what does that mean, Bianca?"

She sighed. "I'll explain, and it's not because I think you're stupid."

"*Grazie*."

"When I started speaking to Rendition in Rome it was online. There was none of this with the avatar. I take that back; I had an avatar, but the communication was nothing like this." Bianca pointed at the Loki avatar. "The Rendition person didn't use a name; it used a call sign, 10ki, because that was his or her specialty within Rendition. That form was what they studied. I started calling the person Loki for simplicity's sake."

"Simplicity's sake?" Dante said.

Bianca wrote "10ki" on her notepad and held it up to him.

"Loki, right."

"Now sit down and let's talk to Loki."

Dante took his seat. "Do you think it is a boy or a girl?"

"No idea."

"Pretty sexy—not that your avatar isn't sexy," he said.

The vixen Loki was playful, snapping a whip. Dante looked over at Bianca.

"Don't even go there," said Bianca with a smile.

As Loki cracked her whip and flexed the leather handle Bianca typed and said to Dante, "Best approach is a direct one with this Loki. Talk shop and see where it goes. I've got to make the first move."

"You do seem to like that," Dante said. She gave him another wry smile. "What are you typing to our Viking goddess?"

Bianca mumbled, "You'll see."

"Tell me a story about bonds," she typed to Loki.

Loki had somehow exchanged the whip for a riding crop and was flexing it and playing with it as if it were a foil.

"Great, she thinks she's Errol Flynn," Dante said.

"Relax, Dante. Loki is thinking. It's all pose and all part of the game. Another difference is, this Loki is sexual and changes gender."

"Wonderful, and tell me this: how did Tommaso, or whoever might be the Italian Loki, learn how to play the game?"

"I don't know. All I've got is a hunch, Dante. If I get anagrams and metaphors, then I know it's Tommaso. If it's simply riddles, it's Rendition Loki. Ssh, now. Loki is answering." She pointed to the windowpane that said Loki was now typing.

"Fake 1934 bonds found in Zurich. Tied to Vulture-Medfese in Basilicata. Arrests made."

Dante said, "I remember that. Prosecutor's office in Potenza handled that case. Mafia."

"I have an idea. Let's try a little misdirection," she said to Dante and wrote out to Loki online, "What about Giugliano?"

Loki's nose crinkled. "Giugliano is counterfeiting. Euros. Marra family."

"I think Loki is taking the bait. Now for the false step . . . let's see whether this gives our Loki a run in her stockings. "How about Foggia?"

Loki had rested the riding crop on her bare shoulder. "Foggia is Totaro territory. Rumor = euro counterfeiting w/ German master."

Dante sat back in the chair. "Nothing we don't know."

"I'm doubting myself, Dante. Maybe I have it all wrong. I was expecting anagrams, and nothing. This Loki isn't acting like Loki. Too helpful this time."

"Maybe she is onto you and acting low-key. Is there anything you can ask this Loki about Rome or Boston that Tommaso or the Italian Loki wouldn't know? Something small but significant."

"Let me try something here," she said and typed, "DA asks what MF is doing about fake bonds. Mafia."

"That's not really a question, Bianca," Dante said.

"I know it isn't, but if this Loki is wired into Rendition, I want to know what big red *R* knows about Farese's operation. He's with the U.S. government. Italian Loki knew Farese was tied into a modern version of Gladio and controlling international relations. Farese showed up after Giurlani was assassinated. Let's see what this Loki has to tell us about that."

Loki did a knocking noise. She had answered. "MF = working Amici & bonds. Mafia."

"That's not saying a whole hell of a lot," Dante said.

"It tells us that Lorenzo is involved," she said. "Let me try this for a zinger."

"Mandracchia," she typed and hit Enter.

They waited.

"Mafia. Front. Friendly."

Bianca turned pale. Dante became enraged at the word *friendly*.

"I told you this organization was no good. This bitch is telling you that Matteo is involved with Rendition. Mother of God in Heaven, Satan exists!"

"Calm down, Dante. There has to be more to this."

"The hell with Loki and with Rendition. I need some fresh air. I'm going out on the balcony."

"Do that then," she said. "Make sure you don't jump."

"It's not high enough." He went to leave, but stopped and said, "I prefer the Italian Loki."

Bianca stared at the screen after Dante had left the room.

"Is DA around?" Loki asked.

"No. *Perché?*" Why, she asked Loki.

"Ready for some clues?"

"*Momento.* Is IF OK?"

Bianca heard the sound of spurs and the whistling soundtrack from the movie *The Good, the Bad, and the Ugly* come out of her speakers.

"Ready for some clues?"

"Like the anagrams you have shown me?"

"Sure. I can try."

Loki's avatar was now male and wearing a black cowboy outfit of white shirt, black vest, and black string tie. No badge.

"Roll clue."

"First clue = MF."

Farese. "Ready."

"AMICI."

She wrote down MF = AMICI.

"Second clue = TB."

Bianca tightened her fingers around the pencil. Rather unexpected line.

"Ready."

"KILO."

She wrote down TB = KILO.

"Anything else?" she asked. That clue seemed the easiest. Too easy.

"Y . . . Author is the father of Man."

She scribbled the line down, glanced up at the screen. Loki was gone. Dante had returned. "What did Loki say?"

"She doesn't like you."

"What did I ever do to her?" Dante said, his voice raising. He held a sweating bottle of water.

She took it. "Thanks. We have to see what McGarrity and Murphy have planned for their meeting tomorrow night."

"Anything else?" he asked.

"Yeah, Loki never said whether the bonds were counterfeit or not."

32

Farrugia and Noelle had spent another night together. This time it was at the office for his safety. This time she had left early in the morning. Farrugia rested on the floor, on the blanket and pillows that his friends had given him. She was gone. He cuddled with his pillow, closing his eyes until he heard the voice.

Another man was in the office, speaking bureaucratic Italian, recognizable by its fevered pitch of aggravation, seriousness and sarcasm. Pio Piersanti. Farrugia was in *his* office. He must have been out of it last night.

"I'm sorry to hear your disappointment, but Silvio remains unavailable."

A loud, angry voice could be heard screaming into Piersanti's ear.

"An inconvenience indeed, but I'm short on resources here. Doesn't Attorney Farese read the newspapers? I would have thought that a man of his reputation would be able to empathize with my situation."

So Piersanti was talking to a superior, one of the wall-eyed fish in the food chain above him.

Farrugia's hand came up and over the ledge of the desk. Its appearance had to have seemed like one of those heightened scenes in horror movies when the vampire's hand crept out of the coffin. Farrugia pulled himself up, eyes peering up and over the desk's edge. He looked left and then right, disoriented, groggy from sleep. He found Piersanti smiling at him, encouraging him to rise up and join the living.

Piersanti continued his oration. "I'm certain the man can make do. U.S. Attorney Farese is an international expert on organized crime. He must have access to another translator." Piersanti pushed a plastic-encased toothbrush at Farrugia, who accepted it with some hesitation. It must have come from the man's desk drawer for those notorious all-nighters or for those special ass-kissing meetings.

"But with all due respect, sir, I find it hard to believe he is bothering you about this matter." There was more noise out of the phone. "Silvio would be flattered to know that Farese holds him in such high esteem. I need Silvio. You know I'm in the middle of a Camorra war. You must've seen the reports and all the requests for overtime for non-exempt employees."

More one-way yelling ensued. Piersanti ought to be a few decibels short of hearing in that ear.

"Let's be rational about this, sir. Let U.S. Attorney Michael Farese find a competent translator. There must be thousands of sailors in the area who know Italian."

Farrugia was still on his knees like an altar boy when Piersanti's free hand nudged a tube of toothpaste at him. Again, Piersanti was encouraging him to get up and get on with the day. Farrugia saw that a self-service coffee machine awaited him on the other side of the room. He staggered in his boxer briefs, resisting the urge to scratch himself and yawn.

He listened to Piersanti agree with his superior with some grunts, acquiesce with half syllables. Farrugia made coffee. He pointed at the machine to Piersanti asking him if he wanted some. Pursed lips and an abrupt shake of the head gave him his answer.

"I'll do my best. What was that, sir? Oh, yes. I hadn't heard of that. Honest, this is the first time I'm hearing of Silvio taking care of The Commissioner. No, sir, I can't know everything that happens in my office. If I did, sir, I might actually be efficient and get something done." Piersanti winced at the dense verbiage emanating from the phone. He waved to Farrugia to sit down. "I'm sure that if Silvio is taking care of The Commissioner, not only must it be true, but he must be taking excellent care of The Commissioner."

Piersanti was doing several bows of the head, indicating that the conversation was about to end and he could hang up the phone. Farrugia took a seat.

"Yes, sir. Yes, you too. Good day. *Ciao.*" He hung up, sighed, and stared at the phone as if to confirm the conversation was dead.

"Did you sleep well?"

"Okay."

"Are you in any pain?"

"Some, but I'll manage." Most of the pain had dissipated. What remained was the stitch in his side when he breathed deep and muscle soreness when he walked. Farrugia was amazed how essential the gluteus maximus was to body mechanics. It was a large muscle group after all. He was even more amazed how he was recovering and reassembling lost time now that he was in the real world. Here and there he had recollections of his mother attending to him when he was in the hospital bed. It might've been a nurse's voice, but he had imagined his mother.

"Commissario," Piersanti said. For the second time, he realized.

"Sorry. My mind had drifted."

"Will you be okay? I need to know."

"I'm fine."

"Good. You'll be joining Agents McGarrity and Murphy tonight, if you are up to it. They meet with their contact about euro counterfeiting. Let's hope we catch a break."

"I'm up for it," Farrugia said. "We'll see whether there's any U.S. Navy involvement in the counterfeiting, since this contact of theirs works that quadrant of Camorra territory."

"Good point. I had Silvio go to your place and get you some of your clothes. Are you sure you're up for this?"

"No need to ask twice. But thanks for asking, anyway. Not much of a choice."

"Why do you feel you don't have a choice, Commissario?"

"I'm a fugitive. What else am I going to do?"

McGarrity and Murphy led the way. Farrugia followed in his own car. Silvio's choice in clothes, like a parent's, had him overdressed for an undercover operation. He killed the tie, tossed the nice jacket, and decided that an unbuttoned shirt would downplay the high-end dress pants. The ensemble made it obvious he was not wearing a wire or carrying a weapon. McGarrity and Murphy had entered *the zone*. He was supposed to arrive moments later. For now, it was *hurry up and wait* in the car, watching time on his wristwatch.

Five minutes.

The contact had selected a hideous building, complete with weeds out front, graffiti on the walls, the odd window broken or chipped, and pigeons roosting where they could rest out of reach of the rats.

Ten minutes.

He tilted his wrist. Fifteen minutes. It was time.

Farrugia closed the car door. He made sure somebody heard it. There were other cars in the lot. Crap cars surrounded the FBI agents' car. It seemed that the Camorra didn't believe in car-pooling. Farrugia was concerned because this constellation of cars was nondescript, not flashy, which might mean that the attendees to this convocation could be far more dangerous. Hawks were more deadly than peacocks.

He entered, hands raised, feet hips-width apart for the customary security frisk. The inquiring hand belonged to a bald-headed Camorrista. A gaudy mélange of saints and emblems of Christ on gold chains encircled his neck. Farrugia ignored the jacked-up muscles, the eyes too close together. Some woman had gone through nine months of hell, contractions, and episiotomy stitches for this thug. Farrugia tolerated the rough hands. He knew the man was trying to provoke him. He waited by the entrance for permission to enter the business area.

"Who is that?" said one of two unexpected Americans. This voice was nervous.

Two navy men in civilian clothes stood behind the Camorra contact from the bar. The man had a small army of smaller minds behind him.

"Pipe down and shut up," said the American next to his nervous friend. Colloquial English.

"That's our guy," McGarrity said. "He can vouch for us." The agent did his best to sound native, impatient, and outraged.

Murphy's Italian resonated next. "I have the money. Do you have the goods?"

The Camorrista waved Farrugia over. "Let him in." The cue ball on steroids had his meaty hand on Farrugia's chest. His grin was missing a tooth. He wiped the back of his hand on Farrugia's shirt for spite. Once released, Farrugia walked slowly, profiling the other Camorristi behind the head guy. Totaro clan. The young men were hard in the face, petty and vicious.

"What's you name?" the leader asked Farrugia.

"Giuseppe."

"Giuseppe what?"

"Giuseppe."

The contact smirked as if he had heard this routine. He had patience, a good sign. He glanced over his shoulder to his muscled staff standing there like statues, hands crossed over their groins, protecting their pride.

"Nice to meet you, Giuseppe Giuseppe. The price just went up."

"Couldn't care less," Farrugia answered with a shrug. "Not my money," he said with a turn of his head to McGarrity and Murphy. "I'm just here to say they're good for the business."

The man in front of Farrugia made that sucking sound minus the toothpick. "I know everybody there is to know between the Totaro and Marras and I never heard of no Giuseppe, particularly you. Who are you?"

"I'm from Calabria. I work in Scampia. Do I need to spell it out for you?"

"Ah, the 'Ndrangheta. I heard you had a recent setback."

Farrugia ignored the insult. "I managed somehow. Amerigo Totaro doesn't seem too upset seeing his men get wasted."

"Hey!" one of the Americans yelled. "Are we going to do business or what?"

"Hold your tongue," the leader barked as a backhand. Business had certain proprieties.

"I don't like this, Frank," said the American's friend.

"Shut up, you idiot. I told you not to use my name."

Farrugia started laughing. "Was the price increase a cover charge for this comedy show? Amateurs."

"What's he saying?" the younger of the two Americans asked. Even in civvies these two were blatant U.S. military. Their haircuts, their scrubbed faces, and comportment screamed *foreign*. All that was needed to complete the picture was bright sunlight and cornfields out of a glossy Ralph Lauren ad.

McGarrity feigned outrage with dramatic Italian. "Screw your price increase," and Farrugia raised his eyebrows at the man in front of him, as if to say *How about it?*

"Price hasn't changed," the man responded. He wet his lips and said to Farrugia, "You understand these two Americans, don't you?"

"I understand enough English to get the general idea. As I said: not my money."

"Whose money is it? 'Ndrangheta?"

"What business is it of yours? It could be, and it could be my own. We lie sometimes, and everyone seems to be doing their own thing these days."

"I'm with the Totaro family," the man said. "Have been for decades."

"Commendable," Farrugia said. "I'd figured you'd be doing something on the side."

"Why do you say that?"

"Why else are the Americans here? I couldn't blame you and your confederates here starting your own work since nobody knows how the war will turn out."

"I'm here because—" He pointed at McGarrity and Murphy. "—they wanted euros."

"What if you're selling shit?"

"I don't provide inferior merchandise."

"I wouldn't know. I'm here to help a friend, just like you are helping them. They're interested in buying euros. Personally," Farrugia did his I-don't-give-a-damn look for effect. "I told them nothing good comes from Giugliano even if it is a loud five hundred-euro note."

The man's jaw tensed. He spat out, "Fuck you. Giugliano is Marra territory. My product is from Foggia. Totaro territory. Multiple denominations, if you are so bitchy about five hundred-euro notes." The choir of bad boys behind the man moved their hands in a display of smug authority.

Farrugia smiled. "I see."

"You see what, Giuseppe?"

"What are they saying now?" asked one of the Americans.

Farrugia lifted his chin in the direction of the Americans and asked in English, "What's your name?"

"Yates," the young man answered. The Camorrista in front of Farrugia clenched his eyes.

"Morons," bristled Farrugia, and said to the Camorrista, "Lower your price."

"Why the hell should I?"

"I don't know. Isn't there a rebate on stupidity?" Farrugia let that one sit, then, "Euros are from Foggia?"

The man's face blossomed bright as a sunlit window, which is what Farrugia wanted so he could shatter the glass. He mumbled an old saying in Italian at the Camorrista.

"What did he say?" the angry American asked.

Farrugia said in English: "I'll repeat it in Italian and then translate to you."

"Just say it."

"*Fuggi da Foggia, non per Foggia ma per i foggiani,*" Farrugia said, staring at his countryman. "That means, Escape from Foggia, not for the city, but because of its residents."

"What the hell is that supposed to mean?"

"It means: Why should I trust you?" said Farrugia, pronouncing his English words with distinctive force and emphasis. His eyes held steady. "But business is business. So why are good ol' boys like you two involved with the likes of him? What kind of arrangement do you two have?"

"You speak pretty good," the American answered.

"I speak *well*," answered Farrugia.

The other American began pacing. The armed contingent had their fingers on their firepower. Farrugia said, "You must know Italian some to do business with the System."

"What's it to you?" the American snapped back.

"Nothing. But one question."

"What's your question?" the man asked.

"I—"

Someone pulled the warehouse door open and a new group of men joined the meeting. Farrugia recognized some of this crew. 'Ndrangheta.

"Is this your idea, Giuseppe?" the Camorrista asked, snapping his fingers so his crew got the message. Showdown.

Farrugia denied it in a quiet voice. He hadn't invited them. His eyes checked in with McGarrity and Murphy. Same thought.

Three men preceded the leader, who was trim, confident in his stride, tough looking, sunglasses on, and as he walked he wasn't reciting St. Francis's prayer or his *Canticle of Creatures*. He spoke Calabrese Italian as he approached them. Farrugia suppressed a smile.

Claudio Ferrero.

33

"What do we have here?" Claudio removed his sunglasses. The shirt was perfect on him. He was in better shape than Farrugia had thought—apparently not a scratch on him. Claudio was chewing gum. It made his temples throb. The scent of peppermint escaped the journalist with the macho get-up and the perfected Calabrese.

He stuck his face closer to the Camorrista and sniffed. "Totaro turd."

The Calabrians in tow laughed, but never took their eyes off of the wall of Neapolitans opposite of them.

"This is my meeting. Screw you!"

"What's with the Americans?"

"I said *Fuck off*. Didn't you hear me the first time?"

Claudio stopped chewing his gum. He stared at the man and said nothing to make him sweat.

"No, I didn't hear you the first time, asshole. My ears are still ringing from all the bullets the last time I tried to do business with you idiots."

The Camorrista's eyes narrowed. "You two were there. 'Ndrangheta."

Claudio let out a laugh. "I'm glad your mother didn't raise you dumb as a mozzarella in water. Yeah, we were there and, yeah, he's Giuseppe and—"

The American surged forward. The sudden movement had made both factions pull out their weapons. "Now I get it," the Camorrista said. "You two were in the news. I didn't recognize Giuseppe because he has no beard. You two are the masterminds behind the massacre."

Claudio glared at the man and said to his host's armed group, "Masterminds, my ass. The newscasters came up with that phrase between commericals. If you believe the news then you must believe in fairy tales, too. I was working with the Marras. He was working with the Totaros." Claudio lifted his accusatory finger at Farrugia. "We were the go-betweens for the two clans to Calabria. Then the Sicilians showed up and everything went to hell."

There was a murmur and then a voice, "What Sicilians?"

"The Sicilians who shot up the place. Oh, I forgot, the journalists didn't mention that, nor did anyone else. Why was that? Because everybody was dead! That's why." Claudio's tone and delivery were pitch-perfect. He would've made a method actor proud.

"I heard there was a shoot-out and the police came." This was from the gallery of thugs behind the Camorrista.

"That's about half-ass true. There was a shoot-out, but it wasn't between the two clans. It was all DDA after the Sicilians left. How convenient." Claudio got within an inch of the Camorrista's face. "It was a massacre, in that nobody was armed except for the DDA and a small security detail. Everybody else at the meeting had nothing. But what the hell are a few minor liberties with the facts."

The man swallowed hard while Claudio kept chewing peppermint gum.

"I didn't know."

Claudio pointed a finger at the Americans. "What's with these two? What's your business with them?"

Farrugia encroached upon the Camorrista's personal space, pinching the man in between himself and Claudio. The factions that circled them also contracted to squeeze an answer out of someone. Claudio and Farrugia stared down at the man like two eagles who had spied the same fish in the water.

"It's just to give them a taste," the man said.

"Taste of what?" asked Claudio.

"Business."

"What kind of business?" Farrugia asked.

"We haven't got all day," Claudio added.

"They wanted euros and—"

"Shut the hell up," one of the Americans said. "I don't have to understand what you're saying to know you're ruining it for us. Shut up!"

Claudio shoved the American away from him, far from Farrugia and the man sandwiched between them.

"What kind of business?" Farrugia said. "What was the exchange?"

"They're U.S. Navy. They wanted counterfeit euros to peddle on the base. You can understand why, can't you? Their pay is in U.S. dollars. The euro is stronger than the dollar and they'll lose in the exchange rate."

He pointed at McGarrity and Murphy. "These other Americans want euros, and they spoke good Italian, so I thought if there were any problems they could translate for me. A colleague referred them to me. He owns a bar."

"A colleague? I believe about half of that," Claudio said. "What else?"

"What do mean, what else?"

"What do they have that you want? This is more than just dollars and euros. You wouldn't need the entourage if it was." Claudio grabbed hold of the man's shirt and twisted the material. "I got shot at, and my friends are dead, and I want answers. What else!"

"I'm just following orders that come down from the top."

"Shut the hell up, old man," yelled one of the Americans.

"I'm at the bottom of the sink. The water drips from above," the man said, motioning with his hand at some imaginary height above him.

"Yeah, yeah," Claudio said, "and you're loyal to your boss to the end. You light candles for his long life and good health in church on Sundays. I'll go read Calvino's folktales. What's between these two and the Totaro clan?"

The man seemed frightened and claustrophobic between Claudio and Farrugia. And a gauntlet of armed men.

"They get a discount on euros from Foggia, and we get U.S. bonds from them."

Claudio's jaw went slack. Farrugia went pale. There was a rumble of discontent between the Calabrians and the Neapolitans

Gabriel Valjan **287**

"What did you say?" McGarrity asked in Italian from behind Farrugia.

"Ssh," said Farrugia.

The Camorrista saw the opportunity. "Do you want bonds? We can negotiate."

"Hey, that's our business," yelled the American.

"Ssh," repeated Farrugia.

"Screw you, man," the American announced, and then to his friend, "We're outta here."

"What was that . . ." Farrugia's head cocked back. Claudio noticed, too.

The man between them sensed that something was wrong. "What? What is it?"

Farrugia turned around and searched for the door. His eyes were wide and frantic. Sweat beaded on his forehead. The two crowds of men pointed their weapons, anxious to shoot but not knowing their target. Something was imminent, agitated, and tense in the air.

"Motorcycles," Farrugia said. "I hear them. They're coming."

The bald guard dragged the warehouse door open. It was the last light he saw.

Expecting three, Farrugia saw more than four horsemen on motorcycles. All but one of the roving marauders wore yellow. The queen of this angry swarm of Umas was wearing white, and she was riding in the forefront of a phalanx of Kalashnikovs. The hardware was active, spitting out flames from a short distance and threatening death as they moved in.

A sizzling sound twittered through the air. Dynamite.

Deafening sounds followed, loud enough that eyes watered and ears went dull. The cars in the parking lot became scrap metal.

The armed Neapolitans and Calabrians rushed to take cover, talking to each other in discordant Italian. A united Italy at last. Like all things idealistic, he knew it was ephemeral. Their shooting had begun with a few lone sputters but soon they advanced to a carcophanous volley of lead throughout the industrial space.

They were outgunned.

Weaponless, Claudio and Farrugia found cover, as did McGarrity and Murphy. Meters and aisles apart in the warehouse, Farrugia saw McGarrity calling for backup on his cell phone, finger in his ear, the radioman in the firefight. Farrugia hoped that Mercury was not in retrograde and there would be a viable signal.

Claudio tapped him on the shoulder and pointed.

The motorcyclist in white and a subset of her companions were circling the Americans. Rubber squealed 'round and 'round the terrified Americans. The cocky American made a show of antagonizing the riders, but for naught—the rider in white pulled out a handgun and shot the man's companion first. A quiet bullet through the side of the head. He died next. Single shot to the face.

A Camorrista broke for the door, and one of the cyclists accelerated after him and ran him down. As the man writhed on the ground, the queen in white dismounted from her bike and walked with regal immunity—bullets flew everywhere but none touched her. She stood over the man on the ground. The man begged for his life, or at least it appeared that way since Farrugia couldn't hear him with the violent sounds in the air.

Two shots. But not the double-tap to the chest and head that Farrugia saw Brooks received in Milan. No. Kneecap and groin. The first shot was to make him suffer and the second to torture him more so he would know what was coming next. His last minute was momentary agony before permanent darkness.

The shooting did not stop. Ejected casings sang and bounced, littering the ground like dead bugs. Splinters scattered, metal sparked, and the concrete sent up distress signals of white smoke. The combat that seemed like an eternity actually lasted minutes; but the horror was enough to stop clocks.

Camorra and 'Ndrangheta, the two cohorts, had been decimated. There was no heroic standoff. They were not infantrymen facing Hannibal at Cannae or Lake Trasimene. The last of them had formed a circle and exhausted their weapons. One by one they died. A few went down in fast succession. Some tried to make a run for the door. They never made it. One or two died cinematic deaths: hit once, twice, or multiple times, they clutched their wounded parts before they died where they had fallen.

Only two yellow-suited bodies lay on the killing floor. Farrugia could tell through the ripped fabric of their suits that they had been wearing thin body armor, the kind that weighed ounces but could sustain ballistic and fragmentary threats. He was not close enough to determine what had downed these assassins. It was clear from their corpses that they were women.

Farrugia could see through an open space between bags of sand in front of him that the white figure, gun drawn, was approaching. McGarrity's alarmed face confirmed it. Murphy signaled the way out behind them, but that meant she would see them and shoot some of them while her gang, when they heard the commotion, would come in, possibly cut them off from the exit and deliver the final blow. Farrugia saw only one choice: stay and fight somehow.

He watched her move with careful steps. She knew they couldn't hide from her or her posse. They were behind her confirming the dead and killing the wounded. Single shots perforated the air. She knew they were somewhere.

Farrugia knew that she knew. She was the huntress in the industrial park and they were her game. How would she flush them out from the aisles of high shelves that still held construction supplies?

She was short. For some inexplicable reason Farrugia thought in U.S. standards for height and weight—it must have been the dead sailors. She was five-four, a hundred-twenty pounds, if that. The helmet had heft, probably armored as well. She was nonetheless petite, deadly, and the white jumpsuit clung to lean curves. She lifted her visor and he could hear the scratchy sound of sand as she took each footstep. She was getting closer.

Farrugia swallowed hard. His mouth was dry. His side hurt, his shoulder throbbed and his legs were heavy.

A voice called out to her. Sirens could be heard in the distance. He held his breath. Claudio next to him was frozen, only his eyelashes trembled.

The Carabinieri in their blue cars, with their blue flashing lights, were screaming their way towards them. She turned, and in that one instant where he saw her but she couldn't see him, he saw her green eyes. She still ran like a girl.

They heard the motorcycles rev and *varoom* away.

But in that briefest of moments, just when they thought they could relax, they heard that sizzling sound again.

They ran before the explosion silenced everything.

34

Tommaso was at Farrugia's desk. His crisis was deciding the criteria with which to organize his pencils. He had decided to arrange them by height from short to tall, but then revised this schema when he saw that the tallest pencil's eraser had been worn down. He gathered them up and started over. Dante almost wished he had something as difficult to occupy his mind.

"Where's the remote?" Alessandro asked, running into the room from the hallway. Gennaro and Pio had been sharing a document together, reviewing financial figures.

"What is it?" Gennaro asked.

"Where's the clicker?" Alessandro moved like an American linebacker who had sensed there was a fumble, the ball nearby. Tommaso held it up. Alessandro snatched it, spun and turned the television on, increasing the volume before the picture spread out on the screen. While they waited for the amorphous shadows to take human form, the narrative was already playing.

"Word is just in that two fugitives were apprehended north of Naples in what appears to have been a clandestine meeting gone awry," said a female voice. The picture eased in to accompany the voice. Her flaming red hair contrasted with raccoon mascara. The inset picture behind her was of a burning building now magnified to dominate the screen. Firemen attended to crackling flames. Visible in the foreground were the carcasses of cars and in front of them, set aside like casual items from the supermarket, were body bags.

"Jesus Christ, Mary, and Joseph," said Piersanti.

"As you can see here, this abandoned warehouse is in flames," the female head said. "Police arrived at the scene after an anonymous phone call reported suspicious gunfire. Explosions came later. When the police arrived they captured four men fleeing the scene."

The burning building receded to a small box behind the newscaster's head. Two small photographs bubbled up to full magnification.

Alessandro pointed at the scene with the remote. "That's Farrugia."

"I can see that," said Pio and remarked to Gennaro *sotto voce*, "Thank God they didn't use a recent picture of him." The news station had used bearded Farrugia for the telecast. The next picture was one that made both Alessandro and Dante squint.

"Who is that?" Pio asked.

"Claudio Ferrero," said Gennaro.

Alessandro and Dante had near-whiplash when they snapped back their heads and then craned forward again. Claudio?

Rapunzel was still talking. "As you can see from these two photographs, one of these two men is the suspected Camorrista who had escaped from the hospital. "This other man," the camera zoomed in on Claudio, "is believed to be his accomplice, also at large, for starting the Camorra feud." The photograph of Claudio showed him in dark beard, wearing a leather jacket, and a raging pink shirt. The sunglasses were his signature fashion statement for defiance.

"Four men. Farrugia and Ferrero make two. No pictures of the agents?" Piersanti asked.

The other news anchor asked the expected near-rhetorical questions. The redheaded creature answered in RAI *journalese*. "Yes, these two are believed to be the architects behind the Marra and Totaro war. Both of these men are also said to have ties to the 'Ndrangheta in Calabria. The theory is that the Calabrian mafia was trying to stake out Camorra territory and formed alliances with both clans to turn them against each other. As you know, the Marra and Totaro clans have a long contentious history together."

Her television companion, a reject from the soap operas, nodded and asked about casualties.

"About twenty bodies have been found inside the warehouse. This appears to have been a business meeting that turned into summary executions."

"Ah, c'mon," Alessandro said. "Who'd believe this line of garbage? I believe that and I believe American wrestling is real."

"Quiet," Dante said.

The sideman on the screen asked, "And you said these two men had other accomplices at the scene?"

"It appears that way. They've been taken to an undisclosed hospital."

Dante asked, "Think the agents are at the naval hospital?"

"Likely," Piersanti said.

"What have police on the scene suggested?" asked the talking head on the screen.

"Somebody dynamited the cars to prevent any escape, and then attempted to blow up the warehouse."

Gennaro laughed. "How original."

"It's horseshit," Alessandro said.

"Just listen, Sandro," Dante said.

She said, "The two Calabrians are thought to have arranged this meeting and eliminated a substantial cadre of Totaro stalwarts. Feuding has already weakened the Marra clan beyond recovery. Among the dead was a long-time Totaro capo. More on him later."

The co-anchor shook his head, shuffled some papers. "Shocking. We hope this is the end of the terrible feud. Please keep us posted on this developing story."

"I shall," she answered, and batted her eyes.

"Shut that off," Gennaro said.

Piersanti was on his cellphone. He said little and listened. He closed the cover. "That was Central Administration."

Gennaro's face tensed. "Please don't tell me that something happened to them."

"Is Farrugia all right?" Alessandro asked.

Dante asked, "Ferrero? And what about McGarrity and Murphy?"

"Farrugia is fine. Ferrero is okay. The agents are at the naval hospital. No other news."

"Fantastic," Dante said, but Gennaro's face hadn't changed. He asked, "If that is news, then why do you look like someone just peed on you?"

"Excuse me," Piersanti said, offering the canned response that he had to make an important call. After the door closed, Alessandro said, "What the hell was that about?"

"That's what I'm trying to figure out," Gennaro said.

The only sound in the room was Tommaso placing his pencils down on the desk one by one, a parade of pencils from left to right. Dante stepped closer to see the organization scheme. Dullest to sharpest.

Tommaso picked up the last pencil, the sharpest one in the bunch and blew on it.

"The problem," he said, "is that Farese has them in his custody."

Lunch was dreadful. The food was excellent, but the mood was not. Dante had made the run to a local restaurant, but it seemed that nobody noticed, let alone appreciated his selections. They ate like Americans at work: at the desk, and only because the body needed food. Gennaro bit into his sardine-and-eggs-with-butter-on-browned-bread sandwhich as if he wanted to start an argument with it. Dante had tried to call Bianca to tell her the news. No answer.

After his pizza, Alessandro attempted levity. "You know what I can't figure out?"

Gennaro gave him the houndog's tired expression.

"I can't figure why it is that people smoke cigarettes after sex."

He spoke and they chewed and swallowed. Dante slurped his drink through a straw, making it squelch for the sake of filling the space with sound. Alessandro was alone in this monologue.

"I mean sex burns calories. It's healthy. It's fun. Why smoke? Yet it's in all the films. Post-coital strike the match and inhale the toxic cloud. The old films glamorize the smoke as if it were the veil of revelation.

Good sex is good for the lungs, so why smoke cigarettes and make it harder to breathe? Drinking I can see, marathon sex works up the thirst, so if you drink some good stuff it might lead to more sex, although too much drinking and too little happens for both parties involved."

Nothing.

"I've heard that you can burn up to five hundred calories and—"

Gennaro made a loud noise wrapping up the uneaten half of his sandwich. "You know Alessandro, you have sex on the brain. If it burned five hundred calories, most of the world would look like fashion models."

"I was just telling you what I read, Boss."

"Five hundred calories for thirty seconds of questionable effort sounds as reasonable as understanding a conversation between Andreotti and Berlusconi. If you believe that nonsense article I have monuments from the Coliseum to sell to you."

Tommaso found it amusing. He choked on a laugh.

"What are you laughing at?" Gennaro stood up and tossed the sandwich into the trash. "How is it that you're so smart?"

"What do you mean?"

"How did you know that Farese took them into custody?"

"It's not so difficult."

"Piersanti didn't know," Gennaro said as he walked over to Tommaso's desk. He placed both hands on the desk when he arrived. He noticed the pencils and moved one of them. Tommaso's hand reached for the pencil, but Gennaro placed his hand over the entire set. "How did you know?"

"I called Central."

"Bullshit. They tell an intern before they tell Piersanti? I don't think so. Try again, Tommaso. Give me one of your poetic metaphors. Or how about painting? Give me something from Giorgio de Chirico."

Alessandro and Dante joined Gennaro to stare down Tommaso.

"Answer the man," said Alessandro.

"No metaphor. Farese is going to say that he had to intervene because

McGarrity and Murphy are Americans. He'll spin this and say the agents were doing some special investigation. They are at the naval hospital where nobody can reach them. Isn't that suspicious? He'll hold Farrugia and Ferrero and say they're fugitives."

"But they were doing a special investigation," Dante said, "but for us, not Farese."

"Sure about that?" answered Tommaso. "And now it has come to a halt."

Gennaro straightened up. "I'm beginning to think that maybe McGarrity and Murphy are working for Farese."

"Technically, they are," said Tommaso. "Farese is a special attorney and they are FBI. You need to consider their reporting structure. This isn't dual citizenship."

Gennaro held up one of the pencils. "Know what I think? I think you're not telling us something, Tommaso. If McGarrity and Murphy are working for Farese—and I mean more than technically—then everything in this office including your elaborate presentations went back to Farese like an office memo and not because of some cute little bug you found in the conference room. The agents know their Italian. Farese understands English only, unless Silvio is at his side."

"That bug wasn't there the first time we all met. And even if that were the case, they still could have told Farese every word, unless . . ."

"Unless, what?"

"Unless, as you believe, McGarrity and Murphy are your friends." Tommaso held a hand out for his pencil.

Gennaro snapped it in two.

Tommaso opened up the desk drawer and selected another pencil.

"Suppose McGarrity and Murphy told them about this meeting because he is their superior," Dante said. "It doesn't explain how he'd learn what happened so quickly. He had to have known some other way."

"He did," Tommaso said.

"How?" Gennaro snatched another pencil. "Do you work for Farese?"

298 Turning to Stone

Dante picked up a pencil, poised it for breaking in two. Alessandro reached over and prevented Tommaso from opening up the desk drawer. "How did Farese know?"

Tommaso stood up to snatch the pencil out of Dante's hand.

"Answer the question," Gennaro said.

"The Sicilian told him."

"Green eyes?" Alessandro said.

"Maybe," Tommaso said. "He knew she would show up. I'm certain of that. What I don't know is whether he told her about Farrugia and Ferrero."

Gennaro lunged for Tommaso but the intern shot his chair back and stood up. Dante and Alessandro made a grab for Gennaro and managed to pull him back.

"You little son of a bitch! Let go of me."

They loosened their hold on him. Gennaro adjusted his shirt. Tommaso stepped closer to Gennaro. Eye-to-eye. "I'm rational and logical, just like Bianca. You asked me what I thought. I told you."

They locked eyes. Tommaso was the first to break the gaze.

Gennaro said, "I hope for your sake that you're wrong about the Sicilian."

"My sake? What about Farese? What about your old friends McGarrity and Murphy?" Tommaso's tone was terse and brittle. His eyes were stronger and brighter. "No more metaphors," he said, and examined each of their faces. "We don't know a thing until we talk to Farrugia."

"No chance of that happening if Farese has both of them," Dante mumbled.

"I expect Farese to stonewall us in talking to them," Tommaso said.

Piersanti opened the door in a curious way. He stepped in and held the door open. And in walked McGarrity and Murphy. Heads turned and none seemed more surprised than Tommaso. Dante watched the intern's reaction and the intern noticed that he observed.

"I thought you two were at the hospital," Dante said.

35

"What the hell happened?" Alessandro asked as he rushed forward. "The news said there was a shootout and there was explosives."

"Yeah, dynamite," Murphy said.

"We heard that." Gennaro walked over, twiddling one of Tommaso's pencils in his hand. "Seems like the two of you managed to emerge unscathed. Piersanti told us earlier that Farrugia and Ferrero are unharmed. Is that true?"

"They are, but Farese has them. He took them away from the carabinieri. I wouldn't say we escaped 'unscathed.'" Murphy unbuttoned his shirt and pulled the material aside.

Deep black and blue marks.

"We were wearing vests. They can stop bullets but they do leave behind a lot of bruising. McGarrity's worse. Two navy guys were killed, along with two Umas on motorcycles. Sicilians."

Dante approached McGarrity. "And you two just walked out of the hospital?"

"Sort of," Murphy said.

"We're FBI and we bullshit our way out, but we came here as fast as we could."

"Why?" Alessandro asked.

McGarrity answered. "Farese doesn't know we left."

"He doesn't?" Gennaro pulled Dante out of the way and stepped in. "Friends, just like I thought you two were, but try again, Agent Murphy."

McGarrity put his palms up. "We're friends, Gennaro. All of us." He made eye contact with each member of the small chorus surrounding him. "Farese doesn't know. God's honest truth."

Tommaso said. "You seriously think Farese doesn't know you are here? You follow people for a living, but are you that naive to think nobody follows you? He has to know that you are here. He must know you are talking to us."

"Well, I guess he doesn't need to bug this office then, does he?" Murphy said.

Piersanti got between the men. "I don't care if the microphone comes down from the ceiling for us to talk into. If you're here and Farese knows, that means he is confident that we can't get to Claudio and Isidò. I'd like to know why he is detaining them in special custody."

"On the record or off?" McGarrty asked. The question raised eyebrows.

"On," Piersanti said.

McGarrity tilted his head. Cue for Murphy to speak.

"Farese is, of course, investigating the Camorra," Murphy said. "With the feud and all, he sees reason to escalate investigations and exercise his privilege to provide advice and strategy to the *Consiglio Superiore della Magistratura* and—"

"And what is he telling the council that stands above all the magistrates?" Dante said. "He knows how to bypass everyone, doesn't he?"

"That's the point," Murphy said. "He's bypassing the judges because he's afraid that there's corruption, and he's arguing it's a safety matter since one commissioner has been assassinated. He's also pushing the international issue of investigating the euro counterfeiting."

"And off the record?" Gennaro said.

McGarrity answered. "I don't trust the guy. Farese doesn't give a damn about the euro counterfeiting, but he seems worried about what Farrugia and Ferrero saw at this meeting."

"I'm not following."

"Bonds. This meeting began as deal on obtaining counterfeit euros, but it became a transaction about bonds. If you remember back when Farrugia was shot, everything went to hell between the Marras and Totaros when the Sicilians showed up and offered bonds. Same thing here." McGarrity slowed down his speech. "Farese is concerned about the bonds because they're U.S. financial instruments. He's particularly concerned if any bonds are counterfeit."

Tommaso took the pencil out of Gennaro's hand. "That's mine. It makes sense now."

"What does?" Alessandro said.

"Farese's worried," Tommaso said.

"Of course he's worried," Dante said. "Counterfeit U.S. bonds would undermine the dollar."

Tommaso bobbed the pencil. "There's that; counterfeit bonds are economically disruptive, but that's not the only reason Attorney Farese is worried. Think about it. The Marra clan is done for, and the Totaros are on their last legs, but Amerigo Totaro is still standing."

"What's your point, kid?" Murphy asked.

"Isn't it obvious?" Tommaso touched Murphy's shirt with the eraser. "Matteo Mandracchia has an alliance with Totaro, and Totaro has a forgery operation in Foggia. Nobody expects bonds counterfeiting there. Matteo takes down the Camorra and reassembles it with Totaro as a silent partner. Totaro knows the territories and all the operations and he keeps a low profile. Perfect."

Gennaro and Piersanti turned away from Tommaso towards McGarrity. "Are you buying this?" Gennaro asked.

"It's plausible. Farrugia mentioned in passing that his contact, Stefano Pugliese, had said that Totaro had an in with the Anticounterfeiting Unit, but it also could explain why Farese is bypassing everyone, since that alone supports his theory about systemic corruption."

"But there is something that's bothering you, isn't there?" Gennaro asked.

McGarrity and Murphy looked at each other. McGarrity shook his head.

"Tell us," Alessandro said.

"Tommaso talked about blading the European economy. I do think that Totaro and Mandracchia are in on it together, but I keep circling back to the bonds and the Sicilians."

"You're wondering how the Sicilians got the bonds?" Piersanti asked.

Dante said, "Bianca thinks this mysterious madrina is Matteo's mother."

Gennaro rubbed his jaw and said to McGarrity, "And you think Farese is involved somehow?"

"I do and here's why," McGarrity said. "If you recall, when Farrugia was shot at that meeting at Via Fratelli Cervi, nothing was said in the news about bonds. Nothing was said about motorcycles in the news. I'd like to know how Farese and the DDA knew that the location for the meeting had changed."

Murphy added, "Farrugia had thought the meeting was some place north of Parco Verde."

"And?" Gennaro asked for the group.

"We heard the news on the way over. Two things weren't mentioned: two Americans were killed along with two Umas on motorcycles."

"And not a word about Sicilians. Convenient," Gennaro said.

"Two navy guys are dead. The impression we got was that we were buying euros, but then the bonds came up. They offered to sell them."

"Bonds, huh?" Gennaro asked.

Tommaso had a wry grin while he twirled his pencil.

"What are you smiling about?" Gennaro asked.

Tommaso now touched McGarrity with the eraser. "Answer me this, Agent McGarrity. Were these two men really with the U.S. Navy?"

"We haven't exactly had the time to do a thorough backgound check. What are you suggesting?"

Tommaso smiled, his eyes looked down in thought. "I think they are connected to Farese somehow. I think Totaro and Mandracchia are counterfeiting euros and U.S. bonds, but I think those two men were supplying authentic U.S. bonds. Totaro's men had to be using real bonds as a template for the forgeries. That German forger did euros only."

Silvio stepped in. "Excuse me, but are you saying that these men with Farese are supplying the Camorra with bonds? I can see supplying euros but not bonds."

"I can if someone wants to pit the euro and dollar against each other," said Dante.

"Is that what you are saying?" Gennaro asked.

Tommaso smiled again. "I'm saying that Farese wanted to break the Camorra's euro counterfeiting operations by supplying the mafia with the bonds, but he didn't expect Matteo Mandracchia to start counterfeiting them."

Gennaro chuckled. "So Matteo is double-crossing Farese?"

"Unbelievable," Piersanti said.

"How do we help Farrugia and Ferrero?" Silvio asked.

Everyone's eyes turned to McGarrity.

"We can't do a thing," McGarrity said, checking his watch for the time.

"Why not?" Gennaro asked.

"We have a flight to catch."

"You're leaving?" Dante asked.

"So much for friends," Tommaso said.

McGarrity snatched Tommaso's pencil out of his hand. "Listen to me. We are not on a plane because we want to leave. We are on a plane before Farese finds out we are not at the hospital. We've contacted our superior and we will do what we can when we get home. In short, we're deporting ourselves."

Gennaro surveyed the confused faces around him. He was just as confused. "What the hell are you talking about?"

"Farese sent us to investigate the Camorra near the base to draw us away from this office. We did, but we didn't tell him that we included Commissario Farrugia as our backup. He didn't expect us to find bonds." McGarrity touched Tommaso's shoulder once. "Friends don't leave friends out in the cold. If Murphy and I are lucky, we might still

Gabriel Valjan **305**

have our jobs when we get Stateside. We'll make damn sure that we start an investigation on Farese."

Gennaro rolled his finger along the tops of the pencils on Tommaso's desk. They were all in order. Satisfactory. "We need to talk to Farrugia, but I'm not sure how. Any ideas, Mr. Baraldi?"

"I'll give you an answer but you might not like it."

"We're listening," said Alessandro.

"Rattle Farese," Tommaso said.

"How do you suggest that we do that?" Dante asked, holding down a pencil.

"Bianca."

36

"Calm down, Dante. I can barely understand you."

"That smug bastard is Loki. I'm telling you, Bianca. Tommaso is Loki."

"How can you be certain?"

"Not now, Bianca. We need to focus on getting Farrugia and Ferrero away from Farese. If what Tommaso says is true, there is no guarantee that they're safe."

"I said calm down, Dante. Explain to me, what's happening with Farese, Farrugia, and Ferrero. Christ, they all have last names with the same letter. Please tell me what happened."

Dante paced in a quiet corner of the vestibule, animated with his cell phone. He explained the agents' visit. He was convinced they had told them everything, leaving no detail out. Bianca was quiet, absorbing every word of the verbatim transcript.

"Have you heard a word I said? Tommaso is Loki."

"Chill, Dante. Focus on Farrugia and Ferrero."

"Okay. You'd think Tommaso was cutting an ice floe into ice cubes. He was so casual about it all. It reminds me too much of Milan."

"I hear you, Dante, but you need to settle down."

"Are you listening to yourself, Bianca?" He lowered his voice and moved to a corner like a kid with the dunce cap. "It's one thing to deal with Loki and Rendition through the computer, but it's another thing to have Rendition sitting in front of me."

"Again, calm the hell down, Dante. Nobody ever said Loki was with Rendition. He or she knows about Rendition. And I'll say it again: I think there are two of them."

"Two? Are you sure?"

"Why is that so hard to believe? Gennaro believes in the Trinity."

"That's different. This is giving me a headache. I'll be honest with you, Bianca. I'm scared. I'm scared for you and for us, and for our friends."

"Listen to me, Dante. In Milan, Brooks walked into a minefield without knowing it. I believe Tommaso was either trying to help Brooks or find justice for his friend. Tommaso has the skills. When Farese showed up, he did due diligence. I say two Lokis because in Milan, Loki helped us. Loki in Boston helped, too, but it was a very different kind of help. Now, let's look at some consistencies."

"Do you mean to say that you see patterns?"

"I do. Farese is a mortician, figuratively speaking. He always shows up after someone dies. Examine the chronological order: Palme in 1986, Fortuyn in 2002, and now Giurlani."

"Okay. I'll buy that. Tommaso?"

"Tommaso went to school and knew Brooks and knew of Matteo. His uncle is assassinated, which is all the more motivation after Brooks died. Tommaso knows of Farese through his uncle or at least has heard of him. He sees Farese in Milan and then sees him again in Naples. Only natural that he gets suspicious. What I don't know is how he found me. I'm thinking it was through Brooks, but—and I can't stress this enough, even if he weren't Loki—Tommaso has now alleged that Farese has a tie with the Sicilian mafia and not as a legal antagonist. If Farese is involved with whatever Matteo has planned, then he's an accomplice."

Dante had his hand on his head, listening and processing, and pacing.

"Are you there?"

"I'm here," Dante said. "Does this mean your government is an accomplice, too?"

"I don't think we know enough to tell, yet. Ask me again down the road."

"I've got to go, Bianca. Talk later. Love you."

"Dammit, she said, and added, "Love you too."

But the one time she said it on the phone, he had hung up and not heard her.

Old gangster movies flashed through her head. Criminals were as diverse as their crimes, but the one common denominator across the decades, if not the centuries, is that no criminal ever wanted to be known or remembered as a stoolie, an informant. A rat.

Motivation was how cops caught criminals or pieced together the facts after they caught a break or apprehended the criminal in the act. Confessions made life easier, but lawyers had created an industry for getting confessions tossed. She had long ago concluded that crimes were of two fundamental types: Desire or Challenge. Murder was a consequence of the two.

Desire covered lust, power, and theft, while Challenge was what she and Rendition scrutinized. There are those who commit crimes to see whether they can get away with it.

Bianca kept the cell in her hand as a meditative aid. She padded around barefoot in her office. With each thought she squeezed the cell phone. Thought and pulse, thought and squeeze, around the room she went. So much conjecture was coursing through her mind without caffeine, and Dante's panicked phone call prompted her to revisit the anagrams.

ADAGIO ILL RUN knew A RAT TOO . . . then boom then IF

Aldo Giurlani knew A(merigo) Totaro . . . then boom then Isidore Farrugia

ARMADA BOOM LIST starts with EAT TOM

Tommaso Baraldi starts with Matteo

FEDORA INFORMS AS FREE

(Friends of Rome = Amici di Roma) informs Farese

MIASMA HER OF IT

Mother is Mafia

A MIASMA TOE FIT

Matteo is Mafia

LEO ZORN LAB QUA VICE

Lorenzo Bevilacqua

MF = AMICI

Michael Farese = ?

TB = KILO

Tommaso Baraldi = ?

Parking Lot Issue: Author is the father of Man.

Her thumbnail traveled down the left edge of her clues. She had two items unsolved and one parked for consideration. She pulled out her pencil and rested the point on "MF = AMICI." She read it as a relationship with Amici di Roma, so she drew a line from "AMICI" to "FEDORA INFORMS AS FREE." She tapped the pencil's point against the paper.

She needed to focus on Farese and Amici di Roma, which meant addressing the convoluted slime around Lorenzo Bevilacqua; and that was no simple task since Lorenzo was the Piranesi of corporate obfuscation. Bevilacqua had a magician's wrist for smoke and mirrors, bureaucratic prestidigitation. She had learned that in Rome and then witnessed it in Boston. She tried to resist syllogism.

If Farese is Amici di Roma

And Amici di Roma is Lorenzo Bevilacqua

Therefore, Farese is Bevilacqua

Metaphorically-speaking. She had seen Bevilacqua on television and knew that they were distinct individuals. Rather depressing and cynical, since Farese was a quasi ambassador in law enforcement, working with Borsellino and Falcone's successors and, as she had seen in Milan, a diplomat of sorts for the U.S. government when the Brooks family sought answers for their son's murder. If Claudio Ferrero was an embedded journalist, then Farese was essentially an embedded attorney in international circles. And if this were true then he was playing both sides to the middle: prosecuting mafia, except for the ones he was working with. Bevilacqua and Farese did not have to be one and the same person, but in essence they had both become immune; Bevilacqua by connection, including Farese, and Farese by virtue of power and position.

And where was the U.S. government? The inference now was that he was two-faced and corrupt, high up on the standard bearer's pole, sitting under the eagle's wing, if he was indeed connected to Bevilacqua, the Sicilian mafia, and Matteo Mandracchia. Bianca had been thinking she had only one male spider. Bevilacqua was certainly an architect of webs, but Farese was the spider nobody saw, hiding as he did out of sight, known only when he moved across the web to make the kill.

Loki had said that the female spider was the dangerous one. That echoed in Bianca's mind. All this time, she had been weighing the construct of deception; Rendition had been investigating Bevilacqua when they should have focused an interested eye on the right honorable U.S. Attorney Michael Farese.

Unless of course, Rendition had other motives.

She let the pencil fall and roll. She powered up the computer.

Doodling was merely an idle indulgence while she waited for Loki. She had perused her notes several times, walked around the room some more, sketched some more, and waited and waited, listening to her pages crinkle when she fanned them and to the hard drive whirr inside the monitor screen in front of her.

Ping. It was Loki.

Bianca straightened up. Loki was in male form, a little paler than his usual self. She started messaging this time.

"I don't like spiders," she wrote, and waited for Loki's reaction.

"Neither do I."

Not what she expected. Too bland. "I dislike rats more."

"Doesn't everybody?"

"How do u trap a rat? What attracts them?"

There was a delay in the connection and Bianca saw the status bar. She waited.

"U want 2 set trap? Traps r not always lures; some traps r about FEAR."

Bianca's eyes moved from left to right on that line and did a carriage return and read it twice. Lures were predicated on attraction, whereas Loki claimed that fear was also viable. She wanted to see whether she was on the right path.

"Rats are afraid of being caught."

"Yes & No."

"Oh, so helpful . . . NOT," she said to the screen. She hated when Loki went from binary to quantum.

"What are rats afraid of?" Loki typed.

She was frustrated and the question appeared again: "What are rats afraid of?"

Fine. "They're afraid of animals."

"Humans are animals."

Loki's eyes blinked at her. Serious mode. She had once read that mice will run from side to side when cornered, but corner a rat and he'll fight. He'll get on his hind legs. She typed more slowly than usual. "Not afraid of capture then?"

"Nope. Contact = vulnerability = exposure."

She decided to be bold. "So MF doesn't want to risk exposure."

Her sentence sat out there for an eternity. The underscore pulsed and throbbed; and worse, Loki's avatar was frozen. She then saw signs of typing.

Loki returned. "Who's talking about MF? Focus on the rat. Told u where 2 find him."

She typed, "ADAGIO ILL RUN knew A RAT TOO."

"Yep. *Bye bye.*"

The screen was dead calm. She had circled the first anagram repeatedly. Bianca did not want to think it meant starting over from the top. She had thought there was a rat and that the rat was Tommaso. She had started with Matteo when she should have started with Tommaso to understand that the intern's motivation was avenging his mother, who had died from a hideous form of cancer (not that any cancer is not hideous) as a result of Camorra toxic dumping. The easiest anagram was the palindrome, the two that said Matteo and his mother were both mafia. Matteo's records were what quicksilver was to alchemists. It all had come down to a spider's web with spiders, Matteo and his mother.

It was much more complicated.

No, she had been wrong about that, too. The center of the web was not the mafia, but the late Aldo Giurlani. Loki had given her the clue right there on the screen, right there on her notebook page, and it had sat there in dead ink, dormant. She had been trying to calculate the circumference rather than notice the radii of this web all pointed to the center. Aldo Giurlani. He knew a rat inside the Totaro family, and this particular rodent was not afraid of predators, but afraid of another human. Tommaso Baraldi has OCD and Amerigo Totaro is an agoraphobic.

The cell phone rang. She was too tired and considered letting it slip to voice mail. She reconsidered. It could be Dante.

"*Pronto?*"

"We need to talk."

"Uh, who is this?"

"Tommaso."

"How did you get my number?"

"I'm calling from Dante's phone. I insisted."

"What do you want, Tommaso?"

"We need to meet. Alone."

"As in one on one? No, Tommaso. I'm old-fashioned and don't like being alone with a man. If you want to meet with me then you meet with the team as well. You know who they are. It's all or nothing."

"Name the place."

"My apartment, tonight. Dinner works for me. You bring the wine."

"Okay." Tommaso was almost monosyllabic. Proof that he was a male and not a shape-shifter.

"What is this about?"

"The fins—I mean the recent financials on Matteo—are showing a huge infusion of cash that I think is coming from businesses connected to Totaro, and several steps behind that in the deep, deep bushes are shell companies owned by none other than . . ."

"Lorenzo Bevilacqua."

"Very good, and that's only the beginning."

"All right, we should talk, but can you give me a hint?" she asked, completing her earlier doodle of a rat with big feet, long tail and whiskers, and creepy eyes. She didn't hear an answer.

"Tommaso? Are you there?"

"I'm here."

"A hint, please."

"U.S. bonds," he answered.

Her pencil stopped moving.

"I'll bring wine. Bye bye."

The pencil fell once more, rolled, and stopped just short of the drawing of the rat she had made next to "Aldo Giurlani knew A(merigo) Totaro . . ."

37

"Did I hear you right?" Gennaro pulled his cell phone away from his ear, stared at it, and then returned it to his ear. "Are you serious?"

"I am," Bianca said without equivocation.

"And what does Dante have to say about this?"

"I don't know."

"You haven't told him yet?" Gennaro's eyebrows arched enough to make the muscles in his forehead ache. Did they have yoga for that?

"I need to go and do the shopping so you can do the cooking."

"What! But—"

Gennaro realized that Bianca had ended the call, and he was now hearing the empty wasteland of a dial zone. He responded with a one-finger delete of the call in the history log and folded over the cover of his cell phone, exercising the breadth and depth of his knowledge of Italian profanities to himself.

Tommaso arrived with two chilled bottles of wine.

The *antipasti* were two traditional southern starters. One plate had lettuce leaves as a green bed for black olives, two meats, and one cheese, capocollo, salamino, and caciocavallo. The second antipasto dish would be the bane of existence for vegetarians, since *affettati misti* included capocollo, mortadella, pancetta, prosciutto, and salame. Nobody at the table dared to point out the redundancy of capocollo to Gennaro, who had arrived and departed in tight apron and even tighter grimace that suggested that if anyone dared complain their head would become a fried dough ball, a *pettola*, for dessert.

For the entrée, everyone drank their wine and ate their *linguine alle acciughe*, linguini with anchovy sauce, in silence. Tommaso, suspecting pasta or seafood, had earned the right to eat in peace through his choice of a crisp white wine, Taburno Falanghina, which, with its quirky fruit profile and the tension in the room, might as well have been tears from the slopes of Vesuvius. He prolonged that peace with his choice of a second wine, this one from the Amalfi Coast, the crisp Greco di Tufo.

Gennaro gave Bianca an intense I-can't-believe-you-made-me-cook-for-you, for-*him*-especially look.

Bianca ignored him. She made her announcement. "Tommaso believes there is financial data that suggests Matteo is receiving funding from numerous Camorra businesses."

Gennaro had to be the spiteful one. "Why should that surprise you? We're in Naples, after all." He turned his shoulder and sipped some of his wine.

"I was sort of expecting you to say that." Bianca turned to others at the table. "But it's my understanding that not only are these businesses System-owned, there are companies in his data set that could be traced back to Lorenzo and Amici di Roma."

This time Alessandro responded, showing interest in Tommaso despite Gennaro's obnoxious disdain. "What did you find?"

Tommaso explained how he had culled the data from Matteo's cultural organization's funding. This new museum exhibit that Matteo had proposed to draw opera lovers to Naples opened the doors to the wealthy and waved the flag of opportunity for Amici. Dante listened, as did Alessandro and Silvio, while Gennaro sipped his chilled wine.

"That's blatantly obvious," Gennaro said, leg crossed over. Alessandro and Dante glanced at each other and then at Bianca, encouraging her with their hands to say something.

"What's obvious, Gennaro?" she asked.

"A museum and an exhibit scream Lorenzo's name. He's already shown a fondness for delivering antiquities through the front door of museums and walking off with their money out the back. It'd only be a matter of time. Pure luck."

"There's no need for the pissy attitude," she said, offering Tommaso a soft smile as a compliment on his presentation. He had done it without superfluous metaphors.

"But you don't understand, Mr. DiBello," Tommaso said.

"I've been a forensic accountant longer than you've been alive, Tommaso. Matteo has patrons and he launders money for Bevilacqua. What's so hard to decipher. Journeyman's work."

Bianca cleared her throat.

Gennaro turned in his chair, faced her. "Do you have something to say?"

"I should say that you're acting like a child, but what I really want to tell you is that your ears are long and you should suck on a sugar cube. Stop being an ass." She turned her head to her guest. "There's more to his discovery, isn't there, Tommaso?"

"Yes," Tommaso said, selecting the wine bottle, offering to pour Gennaro more. "I believe that the money flooding the bank accounts is the fraudulent euros that Farrugia and Ferrero uncovered. I suspect that Matteo might become the next Alan Ancona for Amici di Roma. Not right away, but in due time, and—"

"That's it," Alessandro said. "The System circulates their product and Matteo launders their money."

Dante said, "We just have to wait until the feud settles down."

"We might not have to." Tommaso waited for the statement to register, waited for their eyes to turn to him for an explanation. "The cash infusion wasn't what had caught my eye, interesting though it was." His eyes turned to Gennaro. "Because that would have been too obvious. What intrigued me is that Matteo put up assets to finance his enterprise."

He waited. They looked again. He waited some more.

"Do we need to ask?" Gennaro said.

"Money, but not realized money."

Gennaro sighed, "Is this one of your poetic utterances? Please, no riddles. You're Italian, not Greek."

"Ah, yes. Greeks and Italians—one face, one race. He's using U.S.

bonds. It's money that isn't money until the bonds mature. Value is lost if cashed early. That is what I meant by realized money. He has his U.S. bonds staggered with various maturity dates to finance his debts."

"But," and this time it was Silvio, "aren't they the fake bonds?"

"Could be," Tommaso said. "Is it plain enough now for you to see, Mr. DiBello?"

Everybody now turned to Gennaro. The student was calling out the teacher. Gennaro scanned the faces and then eyed Tommaso. "If those bonds are fake, then it's all a house of cards. He's defrauding everyone."

"That's true, but what else do you see?"

"Why don't you tell me since you're getting such a kick out of leading us through this maze." Gennaro swallowed his wine hard. "Is this another one of your theories?"

"Please give him a chance," Bianca said.

Gennaro found Alessandro and Dante agreeing with imploring looks.

"Do we all agree that the appearance of the Sicilians was unexpected?"

"We do," said Dante for the group. Gennaro gave him a sour expression.

"The Sicilian madrina not only started the feud but she threw down the destabilizing element."

"What destabilizing element?" Alessandro asked.

"U.S. bonds," Gennaro said, examing the wine as he swirled it in his glass.

"Mr. DiBello is correct. Farrugia said she presented the U.S. bonds at the meeting as a way to undercut the peace that the Marra and Totaro clan formed to do their euro business."

Alessandro held up his finger to make a point. "The DDA raid came next."

Tommaso nodded. "The raid undid everything. After that raid, they start killing each other off. Farese ordered the raid."

"And," Dante said, "the newscasters mentioned the euro counterfeiting, but there was never any mention of the U.S. bonds."

"Exactly," Tommaso said.

Gennaro shifted in his seat, and exhaled a long sigh, as if he were hearing the obvious. "It's not the first time the news reported half-truths. Technically, they told the truth, just not the whole truth. Who cares about a few details, right?"

"Like how Farese knew the meeting changed venue?" said Alessandro.

Tommaso now held up his index finger. "This is where we need to think back in time. What happened in the news prior to the feud?"

Silvio again. "The commissioner was assassinated."

"Besides that, Silvio. What else?" Tommaso saw blank stares around the room. "It may sound inconsequential, but the day my uncle was killed was also the day the euro bonds were downgraded. Next day the auction exceeded expectations. Now, here is my question: Who benefits and who loses?"

Gennaro's eyes squinted as he endeavored to fathom what Tommaso was trying to reveal by peeling each layer of the proverbial onion. He drank more wine, looking for clarity.

Silvio answered again in inmitable Italian, "The American institutions downgraded it. They had unintentionally intentioned for it to do badly but they did well."

"Exactly," Tommaso said.

"You understood that?" Gennaro asked.

"Made perfect sense, Chief," Dante said.

"Where are you going with this, Tommaso?" Bianca asked.

"Financial manipulation. The Americans don't want to see the euro get too strong nor too weak because the two dominant currencies have become interdependent. But . . . the Americans want to control outcomes, because he who controls the market controls the world. And what better way to do that than make sure there is an iron-fist control."

Dante asked, "But wouldn't fake U.S. bonds undermine the United States?"

Tommaso sipped some of his wine. "I said from the beginning that

Matteo wants to control the world market. I just wasn't sure how. But I think we now know the mechanism. Euro counterfeiting controls the euro, and the bonds affect the dollar. The United States can mock the euro all it wants, but it can't afford to have anyone question its currency. What I'm wondering is what Farese is going to do now that Matteo is doublecrossing him by counterfeiting the bonds. I'm curious whether the United States gave Cosa Nostra the bonds deliberately?"

Silence.

Gennaro was growing intrigued, despite himself. This intern might deserve a gold star. "The U.S. and Cosa Nostra do have a long history together," he said. "They have had their uneasy alliances over the years, from the Second World War and then with Castro. It's possible that the Sicilians and the U.S. government would work together again." He held out his glass for more wine. "They did with the Nazis and then later with the Communists. Why change what works? The next logical step is manipulating economies, but I doubt Matteo is an incarnation of Gladio."

"Gladio targeted Communists," Alessandro said. "Why would the U.S. or Farese target the Camorra?"

All eyes turned again to Tommaso.

"It goes back to sociology," he said. "The two clans were uniting over the euro counterfeiting. If that alliance were too successful, it would destabilize the currency market. Ask yourself who might not want that and why."

"The United States," said Bianca.

Tommaso said, "I've said it before: examine Cosa Nostra, examine 'Ndrangheta, and other groups, and you can easily see that they are structured organizations with specific domains of criminal enterprise. The Camorra, though, is fluid; its strength is its resilience. The Camorra can form and reform anywhere in the world. It has less infrastructure, so it can exploit anything from petty crime to fake goods, and as you can see here in Naples, it is deeply interwoven in the social fabric."

"Hold on," said Alessandro. "So what you're saying is that Matteo and the Sicilians are destroying the Camorra? If that is the case, I don't understand how the Sicilians and the bonds fit into all this."

"The bonds are a counterargument to the euro. Farese and Matteo used it to break the Camorra."

"But you're saying," Alessandro said, "Matteo double-crossed Farese and starting counterfeiting the bonds. Right?"

"Yes," Tommaso answered. "With an ally, which looks like Totaro since the Marra clan leader was killed at the meeting. The connection between organized crime and the legal economy is actually closer than people think. The Camorra thug in the wife-beater shirt is working side by side with the Wall Street shark in an Armani suit. The U.S. might allow it in London, but it won't in Italy, not without the mafia."

"That explains the scrutiny of the Vatican banks," Dante said as a joke, but nobody laughed. He leaned back in his chair, evaluating Tommaso, and said nothing more.

"So," Alessandro said, "the madrina with green eyes has the bonds, Matteo has the counterfeit euros, Amici di Roma is laundering both currencies, and Matteo controls both the euro and the dollar. What doesn't make sense to me is, if he damages one currency he hurts both currencies. Why do that?"

"He wants to insult the sun," Silvio blurted out.

Everyone looked at him.

"Matteo is Ahab and the U.S. government is his white whale. He wants to tame it, but it'll kill him in the long run."

Bianca sipped some wine. "You're reading Melville again."

There was no interest in dessert.

Gennaro confirmed that the bottle of wine was empty. "If the U.S. government and the Sicilians are working together, the U.S. government would trust Cosa Nostra before it trusted any other group to do this kind of financial speculation. The only problem is that a crafty Sicilian is now playing his own game."

Silvio coughed several times.

"Are you okay?" Bianca asked.

"I'm fine, but I have an observation."

"Please speak your mind, Silvio," Bianca said.

"The Marra clan had Giugliano and the Totaro clan had Foggia for their counterfeiting operations. Green Eyes kills Marra, so that leaves Amerigo Totaro who, as we know, is a ghost. He lives underground in a bunker, afraid of the world and afraid of other people."

As Bianca heard Silvio speaking, she recalled Loki's comment about rats: they might fear predators but they fear humans most. Amerigo Totaro lived in seclusion.

Silvio's voice penetrated again and she caught the last of what he was saying.

"There is no proof that Farese gave the Sicilians the bonds. The question is whether Farese would eliminate Farrugia and Ferrero so nobody knows about the bonds, real or fake. We have no choice but to go after Totaro or Mandracchia, but with Matteo we know we have to be careful because Amici di Roma is behind him." Silvio's hands were out like a beggar's for change. "Am I right?"

"You are," Bianca said. "We can beat Farese at his own game by pitting Totaro and Mandracchia against each other, the same way Farese put Marra and Totaro against each other."

"But Totaro went along with it," Dante said.

"He did because he's a rat," Bianca said. "He had Giurlani killed to cover his past. Farese knew that. I don't think Matteo has any illusions about Totaro."

"And what about Farese?"

"We can't do a thing about him," Bianca said. "We need to get Isidò and Claudio before Farese does away with them as loose ends."

"And Matteo?" Tommaso asked.

"Matteo doesn't realize that nobody defeats the U.S. government."

38

Silvio's comment about Amerigo Totaro the Hermit kept her up most of the night. Amerigo Totaro himself was both a cipher and a key.

Bianca was up earlier than Dante, showered, caffeinated, and at the computer rummaging through Aldo Giurlani's memoirs pertinent to his last cases, using every conceivable search string to find the rat's presence in the digital documents. Hacking the late official's office in Milan was not difficult. She half-thought that Giurlani would have kept his most secret information handwritten, locked away, or taped to the back of a picture frame in his favorite room in Milan, but she did find a lengthy and continuous reference to a mysterious "him."

The Italian variants for the pronouns "he"—*egli*, *lui*—peppered the notes, but not one instance of a name, not so much as a rat's whisker. The sole picture of Amerigo that existed was the result of a ridiculous incident. Totaro had been arrested for assaulting a teacher who had struck his son.

Dante wandered into the room. He peeked at the screen, thumbed her notepad and made a wry critique of her drawing of the rat. He caressed her hair from behind and kissed the top of her head. "You're obsessing about the rat, aren't you?"

"Amerigo Totaro is more groundhog than rat."

Dante pulled up a chair, sat, and sighed, running his hand through his Mediterranean bedhead. "We should be focusing our energy on the Farese and Mandracchia connection. Or better, on Isidò and Claudio."

Dante saw the mugshot. "So he isn't your typical-looking Camorrista? We should be casting out our net for a shark in the Armani suit, don't you think?"

Bianca smirked. The Camorra and Mandracchia had become a medieval bestiary of demonic creatures, with neon-yellow bitches on bikes instead of flying monkeys and fornicating nuns.

"Mandracchia doesn't wear Armani," she said. "He wears Kiton suits. I'm intrigued that prior to Totaro's arrest he was a complete unknown."

"So he was smart and kept a low profile," Dante said, nodding to the picture of Totaro on her screen. "He could use some sunlight. I guess that's what you get when you live underground. I'm off to drown myself in the shower. It'd be nice if you joined me. I'll share the water."

"Already took mine."

"You're no fun. I'll leave you to your work."

"Amerigo spends all those years keeping a low profile and then decides to do business with Marra. It doesn't make sense. Both clans had their own factories for counterfeiting. Why would Marra be interested in an alliance?"

Dante stretched and yawned. "Greed. When I'm finished with my shower, let's hit the café for a nice breakfast."

The café was not far from where Boccaccio had fallen in love with Fiammetta, the married daughter of King Robert of Naples or from where Petrarch had written poetry in a local convent. The poor poet, too, had fallen for a married woman, Laura di Noves, and spent a fair amount of time punning on the Italian word, *l'aura*.

In an attempt to court tourists, the café's owner had oatmeal out, but so far no takers. The cinnamon was nice and brown, the honey languid and sweet, but the mix of fat, dark and golden raisins in an aluminum cup reminded early-morning stomachs of dead flies.

After they had eaten and while they continued to enjoy the modest breeze, Dante had decided to play Devil's advocate. "Isn't it possible that the Sicilians learned how to counterfeit the U.S. bonds? If you remember, I told you Farese was shocked when he'd heard about the bonds at the hospital. How would he know whether they were fake or not?"

Her eyes squinted. "Someone verified the bonds found at the scene."

He lifted his shoulders. "Who? And where is the report?"

"I don't know," she said. Bianca saw Dante in thought. "What are you thinking?"

"What if . . ." Dante said, paused, and then continued. "What if Farese gave the mafia the bonds to undercut the Camorra's euro counterfeiting operation, but Matteo kept them, the real ones. That's theft. He counterfeits some of them and blades the economy with fake bonds, like Tommaso said. See my point?"

Bianca did. "It's like a gambler beating the house with its own money. He shows up with real bonds. He knows the U.S. would rather make good on them when the rest of the market is flooded with false ones."

"Farese is screwed either way. Perfect double-cross."

Bianca considered it. "Only thing is it doesn't explain Totaro."

"Sure it does," Dante said. "He is on top in the Camorra."

"I don't know, Dante. Something's not adding up."

They decided it was time to leave. They went together hand in hand towards their Vespa. The walk was slow because tourists stutter-stepped, or stopped abruptly every few paces to consult their guides or stare at monuments.

He put on his helmet, then handed her the other helmet. He drove, she held on. He eased into traffic that had its own clutch-and-release rhythm. When they stopped she tickled him. He resisted laughing. When they moved she held on tight. They were flowing through traffic at a good pace, the wind pressing their shirts and stretching their skin, the Vespa humming beneath them, when Dante felt his cell phone vibrating in his breast pocket.

They came to a bottleneck and he slowed the motorbike to a halt. The phone was stinging his skin, and he heard Bianca say something, but he couldn't hear because of a loud roar that was not one but two motorcycles that pulled up, one on each side.

The drivers were female, in skin-tight yellow suits, helmeted and visors down.

The vibration of the phone persisted. He felt Bianca's grip tighten around his torso. Car horns beeped, but he had no place to go. The Uma on his left revved her engine, her helmeted head faced forward. As the fumes from her pipes reached his nose, the other Uma revved her engine on his right. Their engines made both his ears hurt.

Dante turned his head. She turned her head. A visor of black ice returned his gaze. Several car horns beeped again. Time to move. He was about to accelerate forward but the bitch on his left cut him off, leaving behind gray smoke and a clearing for her companion.

Dante accelerated the Vespa and found an alley, where he pulled the bike to the side of the road. He yanked his helmet off. Bianca did the same.

"Christ. Did you see that?"

"I . . . yeah."

He stuck his hand in to retrieve his phone. Voicemail message. His hands were trembling and he had difficulty toggling the buttons to see who had called him.

"Let me." Bianca lifted the phone gently out of his hands and scrolled through Call History. "Alessandro." She listened to the message.

"What is it?"

"We need to go. Farese is at the office raising hell."

39

"That was close," Dante said as he followed her into the elevator.

"That was a warning." She pressed the button for the floor upstairs. "We must really be annoying someone." She poked the button again, knowing that no matter how many times she jabbed it the damn elevator would not ascend faster. But it felt therapeutic to punch something, and Dante didn't deserve it.

"Some warning. I hope that wasn't a Loki sense of humor."

"That isn't funny, Dante."

"See or hear me laughing? Did Alessandro say anything else on the message?"

"Piersanti has hidden Silvio," she said, watching the train of lights above them.

"Who is translating for Farese?"

"I don't know." The doors opened. "But we're about to find out."

Farese, on the other side of the glass, had his navy-suited back to them. The yelling in two languages could be heard from down the hall. Farese's English did not match Piersanti or Gennaro's screaming in Italian. The scene resembled a defensive parrot fending off rivals in a small cage.

Bianca led the way into the office and Dante followed.

"Thank God! At last, a person who understands English. Hello, Ms. Nerini."

"So nice of you to make an appearance, Attorney Farese."

"What's with the sarcasm? I've been busy."

"I know. You've been busy detaining Farrugia and Ferrero, but you've seemed to manage otherwise without an interpreter. Or did you not need one when you took them out of Italian police custody?"

"It's official business. Where's Silvio?"

Piersanti, hearing Silvio's name, launched into a diatribe that should have wilted Farese had he understood the Italian, but the lawyer maintained his ground, no doubt tempered by his years in courtrooms.

"Can you get them to speak English," he said to Bianca. "I know Piersanti doesn't speak it, but the others have no excuse."

"Italian is more satisfying to yell in," she said. "Go ahead, they'll still understand you."

Farese stood erect, ran his thumbs on the inside of his belt as if he were straightening out a wrinkled dress shirt. "Now, look. I don't want any trouble here. All I asked for is my interpreter for official business. Is that so hard to understand?"

"'Official business' sounds like pulling rank," Bianca said.

Gennaro idled up to Farese slowly, eyes challenging him. "Where are Commissario Farrugia and the journalist Claudio Ferrero?"

"It's a miracle," Farese said. "He speaks English."

Bianca joined Gennaro. "I'd can the humor, counselor. You're not exactly in good graces with the home crowd. They want to know why you've got their friends stowed away."

"I guess that means McGarrity and Murphy aren't friends."

"I didn't intend to imply that, but Farrugia and Ferrero can answer questions that McGarrity and Murphy can't, since they were undercover."

"It's for their own protection."

"Some protection," Dante said. "Farrugia has already been shot three times, by your men. I hate to imagine what you'll do to him."

"He managed that on his own, was my understanding. All you need to know is that he's safe. Same goes with the Ferrero." Seeing that none of that mollified them, he said, "Then ask me what you'd ask them, but it's within my discretion as to what I'll say."

The canned phrase might have worked for police brass back in the States or at diplomatic summit, but it purchased nothing but a handful of dead flowers here. Dante and Gennaro peppered Piersanti with creative commentary.

"Well?" asked Farese, thumbs hooked on his belt. "I said that I'd answer your questions."

Then Tommaso asked in a loud voice from his desk, "Sure you want to do that, Attorney Farese?"

"Who are you?"

"Tommaso Baraldi. I'm the late Aldo Giurlani's nephew."

"I'm sorry for your loss. Your uncle was a good man." Another formulaic response; the tone translated itself.

"Thank you."

"Now, where is Silvio?"

Bianca thought the attorney's insensitivity was on a par with a cobra's love for a mongoose. "You don't even shed crocodile tears, do you?"

"You of all people shouldn't lecture me on emotional openness. Now, where is Silvio?"

Gennaro asked, "You mean to tell me that you still couldn't find an interpreter."

"Not one that I was satisfied with."

"You have thousands of sailors to choose from."

"Like the two sailors who are dead in the warehouse that your friends Farrugia and Ferrero escaped from? People have a habit of showing up dead whenever Commissario Farrugia shows up. Make sure you translate that, Allegretti."

Dante had to stop to hold Gennaro back. "Don't."

"This is the first we heard about any dead Americans," said Bianca.

"It was kept out of the news. Like I said, there is more to this than meets the eye."

As Dante scuffled with Gennaro to restrain him, Piersanti awaited an explanation. Alessandro took over translation duties.

"Apparently, not the only item left out of the news," Bianca said.

"Get your hands off of me, Allegretti." Gennaro squared off with Farese and wagged his finger in front of Farese's face. "Same thing could be said about you, Attorney Farese, except your habit is to show up *after* people are dead. Isn't that ironic?"

"Why is that?"

"Vultures do the same thing."

Bianca, odd as it felt, thought it was time to add sugar to cut the acidity. "This isn't doing any of us any good, so please give us one good reason why you're holding Farrugia."

"Where's Silvio?" He eagle-eyed Piersanti and Gennaro in a cocky stance. "I'm waiting for an answer."

"The balls on this guy," Dante said in Italian in a low whisper.

"Say something, Allegretti?" Dante turned away and waved Farese off in disgust. Gennaro's face had turned red.

Farese asked again, enunciating each word, "Where is Silvio?"

Gennaro puffed his chest out. "I'll answer that for you, but it's within my discretion as to how much detail I'll provide."

"Fine. You want to play games."

"We're playing games?"

"Where is he?"

"Taking care of The Commissioner."

Farese flinched, and Bianca paused to admire the beauty of it. If Farese asked for a name, it meant that he didn't know everyone he should know, and if he tried out a few names that he did know, they could stall him like kids before the teacher who asked who had farted in class.

"'Taking care of The Commissioner,'" Farese repeated, and, seeing nothing but a chorus of stone faces, stormed out, flinging the glass door open without breaking the glass. The team remained around Bianca. Tommaso drifted into the cluster.

Bianca said, in English, "We need to set a trap for the rat." Gennaro sought permission to translate for Piersanti and Tommaso. She nodded.

"Which one?" Dante asked. "Attorney Farese, Amerigo Totaro, or Matteo Mandracchia?"

"Amerigo Totaro?" Bianca answered.

"What about Farese?" Gennaro asked her. "We let him get away with this?"

"Don't worry. Rats always have fleas," she said in English.

She felt her cell phone buzz. A text.

She read it and slammed her phone shut. Nobody had noticed. Dante was still talking. Tommaso was with the others, attentive to Dante's conversion of her findings into Italian. Bianca waited, watched, and for a second, her eyes met with Tommaso's.

The text said: IF will be OK.

40

Bianca saw the book that Silvio had rested on Piersanti's desk while they all waited for the man to return to his office. Gennaro plopped back into the leather sofa. Alessandro and Dante aired out the last of their ire and grievances about U.S. Attorney Farese. Tommaso had pulled up a chair and sat at the right hand of Piersanti's empty chair. The symbolism had not gone unnoticed. Bianca asked Silvio's permission with a glance, and then thumbed through the book.

Silvio, almost preempting judgment, said the novel was very good and that he had selected it because he had never been to Boston. He knew that Dante, Farrugia, and Gennaro had been there to help her on the Nasonia case.

"Maybe one day," she said, as Piersanti came in, folders in his hands.

"What are those?" Alessandro asked.

"One file has next to nothing on the two dead motorcyclists at Farrugia's warehouse. The other case file is what I could get on the two Americans."

"What about the Cammoristi?" Dante asked.

"Save those for later." Piersanti butterflied one folder. "I'd rather focus on what we don't know—the Cammoristi all have typical and predictable criminal records. So I want to put our energies into analyzing the two women, the dead Americans, and the bar contact with whom they met near the military base."

"Only two files?" Gennaro asked, pulling down his tie knot. They noticed that Tommaso sat there unaffected, so Gennaro asked him, "Have you had a chance to review the files?"

"I have. The women are from Sicily."

"I wasn't expecting you to say that they were from Vigàta and that Salvo Montalbano had written their letters of recommendation. Are they tied to, related to, any of the known families?"

Gabriel Valjan **333**

Tommaso shook his head.

"Bianca?" Dante called out.

"Just a sec. I'm reading a good part."

Piersanti folded his hands prayer-like and waited. When she had closed the book and handed it back to Silvio, he asked, "Is all this boring to you?"

"More like a waste of time, sir," she said.

"You think?"

"Why would you expect to find information on these women? We could spend hours on researching them to find what? Their last visit to the women's clinic, their school records, or how they learned to ride motorcycles, perhaps? Waste of time, in my opinion."

"Why's that?" Piersanti asked, his hand on top of a stack of pages.

"We can't even locate Matteo's birth mother's name, so that alone should tell you that this woman hand-picked an untraceable team of assassins. I guarantee you these women are from all over Sicily and it is pure speculation as to how they had even met. I'll bet they are all plain-Jane."

"What about that bar guy?" Alessandro asked.

"Don't bother," Bianca said. "Reading his background would be equivalent to a documentary on Naples after the Second World War. A film director's feast. Again, there'll be no connection to Matteo, but it'll be a who's who of Camorra clan history."

"Why are you sure?" Piersanti asked.

"Because of Tommaso."

"Me?" the intern said, hand to chest, proof that he wasn't a statue.

"You talked about how the Camorra was fluid, how it is the opposite of the Cosa Nostra and the Calabrians."

"And?"

"And the Sicilians are family-oriented, secretive, but their members can be opted in by some kind of special vote, a consensus. The 'Ndrangheta is more rigid, harder to infiltrate, and membership is along bloodlines, virtually no *pentiti*, and—" Dante had that where-is-this-going look, so she stopped. "Tommaso can explain the rest."

"I believe what she is saying is that Matteo's idea of a new Camorra is to start from scratch. He prefers the 'Ndrangheta to Cosa Nostra because the Calabrians are known primarily for drug trafficking, which is ideal for money laundering. That they have no *pentiti* is an insurance policy for him."

"I guess that leaves us with the Americans then," Dante said.

Heads turned to Piersanti. He thumbed through some paperwork. "The Americans aren't exactly forthcoming when it comes to their own investigations. As for those two dead Americans at the warehouse—nothing is on record for them, militarily or from what I could find for civilian records, not that I trust the documentation since the Americans control it. They aren't criminals. In fact, they make for very boring reading, and from the looks of it this is cut and dry. They were there to make quick money. I have nothing here. I wish Farrugia was here to tell us something."

"That's where you're wrong." Bianca saw Piersanti's eyebrows jump. "You have Farese protecting them, and that tells us a lot."

"Why wouldn't he?" Piersanti said. "This is potentially a political event. The naval base is sovereign territory. We haven't even seen or read the media response in America. Word will get out. It may not be the same as attacking Libya and then having hundreds of refugees drowning in the Straits of Sicily the following week, but all that is reason why he's protective."

As Piersoanti spoke, the sunlight broke through the blinds behind him, creating stripes of light and dark on the carpet. Piersanti surrendered the documents to Gennaro, who divvied them up with Alessandro and Dante. Gennaro mumbled preliminary assessments, Dante's finger pointed at some facts on the page. Tommaso continued to sit silent, unmoving until Gennaro asked him his opinion.

"People like money, money likes people. Much as I like to say that's the American way, supply and demand reigns in Europe as well. Italy is no exception. Two dead Americans are insignificant in the scheme of things for Farese."

Alessandro placed the files on the desk. "And Farese's hard line about holding Farrugia and Ferrero for their own safety? What do you make of that?"

"Farese doesn't want Ferrero doing an exposé that suggests American military involved in organized crime. Farrugia's undercover work would substantiate his journalism."

"Screw that," Gennaro said. "How do we break Mandracchia?"

The question lingered, glances were exchanged, and Bianca picked up Silvio's book again. She studied the cover.

An impatient Piersanti asked, "Must you read again?"

"I'm not reading. Thinking."

"Thinking what?"

Bianca turned her head to Gennaro, her eyes narrowed. "Something that Tommaso said has given me an idea."

"What did I say?"

"In talking about money and people, you reminded me of what no one will ever admit."

"What?"

"Supply and demand."

Alessandro asked, "What's your idea?"

"He has a demand, but we can give him a new and unexpected supply. This book's title gave me the idea." She held up the book so they could see the cover. *The Other Woman*. She watched their lips move as they read it. Gennaro translated the title for Piersanti.

"What are you trying to tell us?" Dante said.

"We need a trap. We know Farese is involved somehow, but we don't know how. We know Matteo is interested in manipulating currency." She handed Silvio the book. "We find a way for them to face off."

"How?" asked Dante.

"I have bearer bonds from Robert Stand."

"Hold on, Bianca. Are you sure you want to do that?" Alessandro asked.

"Wouldn't be the first time I fronted a sting."

She waited while Gennaro detailed for Piersanti how she had used the bearer bonds that Robert Strand had given her before he disappeared. The lure was that these bonds were instant cash for whoever possessed them. Of course Gennaro's explication was judicious and selective. No Rendition. But Piersanti understood how the bearer bonds enticed Alan Ancona and precipitated the downfall of Amici di Roma. Gennaro, however, emphasized that the bonds were never recovered.

Alessandro edged forward. "You do this, Bianca, and Bevilacqua will show up."

"Of course he will. You can always count on greed. Bevilacqua is in with Matteo. Tommaso's research of Matteo's contributors suggest it. Well hidden, but Lorenzo is there."

Gennaro said, "It's too risky."

Silvio finally spoke. "He's right. This is much too dangerous—if not Matteo then the *madrine*."

"I won't have you meeting with Matteo Mandracchia," Dante said.

"Who said I would be alone?"

They all looked at her.

She held up the book again. "I propose that we give them the other man. Let *him* bring the bearer bonds. We do that and we'll see what comes. We know Matteo will, and I'll bet Farese will."

"Think it'll work?" Piersanti asked.

"Lorenzo wants revenge, Matteo needs the bonds, and Farese has an interest in the outcome. He'd also be interested in the other man."

Gennaro asked and heard the same question echo. "What other man? Whom do you have in mind?"

Silvio examined his book with a smile, but that smile disappeared when she gave her answer.

"Silvio."

"Are you out of your mind?" Piersanti screamed.

"No. I'm perfectly sane," Bianca said. "Think about it. Matteo has a clean circle around him. That's crucial to his corporate image. His mother does all the dirty work and—"

"And? What are you saying?" Pio asked, seeking an explanation from the others in the room. "What is she saying? Somebody, please tell me. I understand her Italian but I don't grasp her thinking."

Tommaso stood up, buttoned his jacket, and faced him. "She has a point. If Farese is involved, he'll make it known somehow."

"Of course he will. Silvio is his translator."

"That's true," Tommaso said, "but there's another reason. Everyone in this room is tied to the GdF. Silvio was a secretary and he's new to investigations, but he's been Farese's personal translator since Farese came to know the people in this room with the Roma Underground investigation. Silvio is his eyes and ears in the GdF."

"I'm not a traitor!" Silvio yelled. "I never talk to Farese about the office."

"Not saying that you are or have," Bainca said, "but Matteo might see you that way. He sees you; he thinks GdF and Farese. You are a direct link between him and Farese." She paused for it to sink in. "If Farese is involved, Matteo won't tolerate it. It means that—"

"You don't have to do this, Silvio," Gennaro said, and then to Piersanti, "Tell him that he doesn't have to do this, Pio. The man is bait."

"You don't, Silvio. It's up to you."

Tommaso said, "It's the only way both to get Matteo and prove whether Farese is involved."

"I can't believe you two," Gennaro said. "If you're so keen on the plan, Tommaso, then why don't you be the other man?"

"I'm Giurlani's relative. It'll look as if I'm out for revenge."

Gennaro turned away. Tommaso sat back down. Silvio tapped the edge of Piersanti's desk. *Tap. Tap. Tap.*

"I'll do it," he said, "but how *do* we do it? Do I tell Farese that I have an idea to trap Matteo?"

"No," Bianca said.

"Then how?" Dante asked. Alessandro and Gennaro had the same question on their faces. Piersanti's face was unreadable. They sought Bianca's.

"I said I have the bearer bonds. Ask Tommaso."

"Me?" Tommaso said, surprised again.

"You know how, Tommaso. No need to be shy."

Dante and Gennaro both arose from the sofa. It was either out of curiosity or they were ready to throttle the modesty out of the intern. Alessandro remained seated, fingers massaging his temples, thinking.

"If all of you would take your seats, I'll explain."

"Please, no poetry or metaphors," Gennaro said. "We'd like a simple answer."

"You want a simple answer?"

"Simple," Dante said.

"Amerigo Totaro."

41

Totaro's residence was nondescript. It had one swing-gate for the mailman and a mailbox on the wall. There were no patrols of armed men with shepherds, no thousands of meters of lawn and concrete to cross to reach the front door. There was a modest wooden door, brass knocker, and protective screen. No conspicuous displays of wealth in the driveway. There was one car, which could have belonged to a university student except it appeared unused, given how black the tires were, immaculate paint, and shiny chrome. The only security device was a lone camera above the corner of the front entrance. Its black eye and red pupil swept periodically in a left-to-right arc.

Silvio had been let out of the car that Dante had borrowed from Gennaro. They changed out the plates just in case. Dante drove. Bianca sat in the passenger's seat, and Silvio relaxed in the backseat. The routine had been rehearsed and rehearsed until Silvio begged for them to stop.

That morning Bianca had gone to the bank and withdrawn one of the larger denomination bearer bonds from her safe-deposit box. Strand had given her the equivalent of a hundred million U.S. dollars. She had written off two million as a loss to fund Roma Underground. She sometimes teased Dante and Gennaro, telling them they had to work the debt off. But Lorenzo had absconded with her two million and probably used a portion of it to pay for the contracts he had awarded to the Bulgarian assassin he had sent to the United States. She wondered what price he had put on her head.

She figured a one-million-dollar bearer bond was sufficient for show-and-tell with Amerigo Totaro. After Silvio had sworn up and down the community of saints that he wanted to do this, and after a thousand more reminders that there would be no weapon, no wire, and no security cameras to rescue him, the interpreter received hugs from Alessandro and Dante. Gennaro gave him a prolonged hug and pinched his cheek. His eyes were moist.

Gennaro had wanted to be Barrabas and offer himself up. He was older. He was from the area. He knew the dialect. He and Amerigo Totaro had the matter of Lucia's death to settle.

Piersanti spoke: "Request denied."

Dante parked the car directly across the street. They watched Silvio approach Totaro's door. Dante wore sunglasses and kept his profile a phantom behind Bianca in the passenger seat. She had her shades propped up so her face was visible.

"That camera might be able to pick us up from across the street," Dante said.

"That's the idea. If Lorenzo is involved, Amerigo will get the video feed to him. If he isn't, then no problem, there's Matteo and his mother. You forget this man allowed her to liquidate Marra, his men, and purge his own clan."

Dante's hand tapped her shoulder. "Silvio's near the door. I hope to God he does exactly as we told him."

"He will. Tommaso's idea was brilliant. Only he could have come up with the coded references. Silvio will tell them everything without saying a word."

"I hope you're right, Bianca. I hope you're right. Looks like showtime."

Silvio, in sunglasses and a simple but understated suit, no tie, walked with confidence to Totaro's front door with a cereal box under one arm. He stood about a foot from the camera, bowed his head, and then held the cardboard cereal box up to the camera. Silvio paused for the camera's head to sway and focus. He put the cereal box down, and opened up the flaps.

The cereal box was a request for money laundering, a specific reference to a scheme in the UK where "Bin Ladens" or five-hundred-euro banknotes were stuffed inside cereal boxes. Each cereal box held a million euros. Silvio was declaring his request for the amount to be cleaned.

His next action was to hold up a receipt from a dry cleaner. He held up the green slip of paper so the camera could zoom in on the cell phone number and a time. Silvio held the piece of paper in the air for a few more seconds, folded it, and then placed it inside the box.

He reached into the breast pocket of his jacket and pulled out two five-hundred-euro notes. He held up one close to the camera and then the other. Each one had a Post-it. Each Post-it had a city name written on it. Giugliano and then Foggia. He put one five-hundred-euro note on top of the other. He then separated the Post-its and tore Giugliano in two and placed the pieces inside the cereal box. He held up the other Post-it, Foggia, and kissed it before he placed it in the cereal box.

Tommaso said that the cleaner's bill would repeat the request for cleaning money and tell Amerigo how and when he could contact Silvio. The act with the two banknotes was pure *dietrologia*, symbols behind the symbolic that Dante worried would be too obscure. Placing one banknote on top of the other denotes the two clans, their counterfeiting locations, and tearing apart the Giugliano Post-it symbolized Totaro's destruction of the Marra clan. The unscathed and kissed Foggia Post-it indicated Silvio's acknowledgement that Amerigo Totaro was the master, the conqueror, the artist. It was theater, but Tommaso always did have a gift for theater.

Silvio held up his index finger the way an announcer did for the main event. He retrieved Bianca's bearer note, unfolded it, and held it up to the camera. He let the artificial eye focus on it to make it unequivocal that this was a bearer bond and not an ordinary U.S. bond. He put the note back into his pocket and pulled out a small hand-held tape player. Silvio almost had to get on his toes to hold up the device to the camera's microphone and press Play.

It was twenty seconds of a recording of two famous sound bytes: a snippet of Blondie's song "Call Me" followed by Arnold Schwarzenegger's voice, "I'll be back."

Silvio stepped back, bowed and began his trek back to the car.

"Are you sure it'll work?" Dante asked as he started the car.

"We'll know if Amerigo calls tonight."

"I'm not sure, Bianca. I thought you said Amerigo Totaro was the rat."

"I did."

"Then all he'll do is run for cover."

Silvio opened up the rear car door and climbed in to the back seat. He exhaled a sigh of relief. "How did I do?"

"Fantastic, Silvio. Just fantastic," she said.

"That leaves Mandracchia and Totaro," Dante said as he left the curb.

"Farrugia said turn them to stone. That's what we're doing here."

"Hope it works. Your thoughts?" Dante said.

"We don't know whether Matteo knew that Totaro was the rat, but let's say he did. Matteo had his mother kill Giurlani. Good for Totaro—no more worries about being exposed. Matteo might've led Totaro to believe that he'll corporatize the Totaro clan because the Marras were sloppy in their business practices. Totaro ran an empire without anyone knowing what he looked like."

Dante agreed. "He had only one arrest."

"Green Eyes lights the fuse to a feud and levels the field. Totaro is free of Giurlani but now answering to Matteo. And possibly Farese. But now the rat—thanks to Silvio—has a way out. He doesn't need Matteo or Farese."

"Why not?"

"Totaro has the bearer bonds. They're instant cash, no questions asked. Mandracchia has counterfeit euros, a liability operation with a lot of overhead, and he has bonds that have to mature before he has real money in his hands. He has to sit and wait. Totaro, however, has cash in hand. He is now capable of double-crossing Matteo."

Dante's eyes were on the road ahead. "What if Matteo and Amerigo are genuinely in business together?"

"Let them be," Bianca said. "Then the Americans have a situation in Sicily."

"Either way," Dante said, "we have people facing off. It could be Totaro and Mandracchia, Totaro and Farese, or Farese and Mandracchia."

"And what about the madrina?" Silvio asked.

"She'll show up," Bianca said.

"Are you sure?" Dante asked.

"A mother's duty is to protect her child."

42

Bianca wrestled with the foil, using her fingernails to pry apart the shiny seams. No dice. She also used her teeth, to no avail. It was absolute hell, and she was envious of how guys could nonchalantly tear the foil off a condom, or how President Nixon could gnaw, with success, at the white bottle caps of his meds, according to John Dean. Here she was battling a membrane-thin wrapper around her imported Chuao chocolate and losing—different objectives, but same frustration.

"Can I help you with that?" Silvio asked, licking his lips, eager to assist her. This *guy thing* to solve problems always annoyed her. But Silvio was modest, and adept. He pushed the unearthed chocolate towards her. He said nothing.

"Thank you," she said, more for polite formality, because she was anxious to scarf down chunks of gourmet chef Michael Antonorsi's creation of chocolate-covered, sea-salted breadcrumbs, the perfect combination of sweet and salty.

"I never knew you had cravings," Silvio said.

She wanted to say that she didn't have a sweet tooth, but the evidence contradicted her. They had been waiting for the cell phone's mating call or for the vibratory text. Nothing. Amerigo Totaro was keen to show that he was not a desperate man.

"Are you nervous, Silvio?"

"Yes."

"I admire your honesty. Do you have any questions?"

"Who'll watch Commissioner?"

"You will. Don't worry."

The phone rang.

The voice on the phone briefly occupied Silvio's attention. The conversation was Hemingwayesque—direct and concise, if not limpid.

Dante and Gennaro waited for the call to end.

"What did he sound like?" Gennaro asked.

"If it was Totaro, he has a deep voice. He'd have a career in radio."

"What did he say?"

"Totaro compound in thirty minutes. Bring the bearer bond."

"We're on," Bianca said, getting up and cleaning her hands on a napkin. Nerini: two; Antonorsi: zero. Dante and Gennaro were watching her.

"You seem different," Gennaro said. "I can't quite figure it out. Don't you agree, Dante?"

"Bite me," she joked. "Dante and I are off to the car. Silvio, come with us. Gennaro, you know what to do. Once we're inside the Totaro fortress, it is wait and watch the clock."

Gennaro and Dante synchronized their watches.

"Don't call me Ma'am."

They started for the door but Silvio remained fixed. Bianca crooked his elbow, handing him caffeinated gum that she had in her pocket next to her next fix of Chuao chocolate, telling him to start chewing it. The gum was better than coffee, she told him, and he needed to be alert. As they moved, Silvio squeaked some protest, and she had to remind him that his Commissioner was in good hands with Alessandro, because Sandro had no woman in his life now and Tommaso had stolen all his Nava pencils.

"I think she's become bossier, Dante."

"Nah, she's always been that way."

"Why is it that if a woman is driven she's a bitch?" she said as she locked the apartment door behind them.

"Why so defensive? I didn't call you bitchy," Dante said.

"Good, because the only bitch we need to be concerned about tonight is on a motorcycle."

Two blocks from the Totaro fortress, Dante got out and Bianca took the wheel.

Silvio, inside the car, continued chewing gum. Everything was to plan and as expected. When they had parked the car across from the residence, two henchmen appeared. They got out of the car, submitted to the obligatory pat down, said nothing, and followed instructions.

The Totaro compound was a self-contained world. Their host's décor was neither as gaudy as Scarface's mansion nor as spacious as an ancient senator's, but it had amenities, signs of wealth and taste. As they stood in the marble-floored atrium she could see past one entrance to a private library of leather-bound volumes and hardcover books. Paperbacks and trade paperbacks were apparently not real books to Amerigo Totaro. Other than the surveillance screens on one wall, any hint of computers and the modern age was absent, and Amerigo must have commissioned a stonecutter for the wall opposite the security console: there they saw a tranquil cascade of water washing over Vesuvian stone. The two escorts manned their stations at the front of the house. They had provided no further instructions. Bianca and Silvio expected a butler to emerge and announce them to the master of the house. Silvio exercised his molars on the caffeinated gum and Bianca kept her sunglasses on. They waited.

Silvio's foot touched her foot. Somebody was coming.

A dark silhouette moved like a king entering court. Amerigo Totaro took measured steps. He was not gnome-like as former Prime Minister Giulio Andreotti on film, but his figure was indeed diminutive. It gave credence to the adage that the world's tyrants were men of short stature.

Totaro was now the monarch of the Camorra. He was adding Marra territory to his realm with each passing day, and counting Bevilacqua's Amici di Roma, Calabria's 'Ndrangheta, and Sicily's Cosa Nostra among his allies. This was the man who, for all his criminal successes, had but one trifling incident on record: the slapping of a schoolteacher.

Amerigo walked into the light. Age and the lack of sunlight had endowed the man with a vampiric pallor. Bianca was not accustomed to looking down at a man, but she found herself hesitant to take her sunglasses off, though she knew that it was rude to wear them indoors. Silvio had stopped chewing his gum.

He held out his hand; she did likewise. The man flicked her wrist over, bowed to kiss the back of her hand. When he lifted his head his eyes were blue and milky. He welcomed her, using standard Italian. Despite that time indoors the man knew how to switch linguistic registers.

"Please take off your glasses so I may see your eyes."

She did and their eyes met. Not quite fear, but obvious discomfort hit her primitive fight-or-flight center. Her brain told her that humans understood physical threat, and there was nothing mystical about it, despite how theologians and philosophers could wax eloquent about *evil*. She didn't care what her brain said. This man made her shiver.

"Thank you," he said. "I wanted to make sure they weren't green."

"As you can see they are not. But what if they were?"

"You'd still have my respect," he answered, moving like a royal to his next subject. Silvio and Amerigo shook hands.

"There is no need to discuss names. Business is easier that way, should matters go wrong," he said, offering a mortician's polite smile. "I don't like courtrooms and I don't like business going wrong." To Silvio, he said, "I saw your performance. Very impressive, as was your proposal, and I must flatter you and tell you that few things impress me."

"Thank you," Silvio said.

Amerigo took a step closer to Bianca. He faced her again. This time it was an uneasy stare, the kind that made animals in zoos psychotic. She locked eyes and endeavored not to blink. Bianca began to have doubts. They were inside this cultured bunker of a house with this cadaver, and there was no way of knowing whether the man had an army and an arsenal inside, or what defensive precautions he had installed. This creature had to know every countermeasure to a DDA team's tactics.

The man's milky blue eyes blinked. "Your bearer bonds interest me."

She didn't dare concede a reaction.

"As I said, we have no need for names, but you can imagine my pleasure when I had realized it was you, and that I had the honor to have you in my home. But mutual admiration aside, there is business at hand and unfortunately our business requires us to meet in council."

"Council? What council?" It seemed instinctual and stupid for Silvio to interrupt, but Totaro welcomed it. Bianca felt some relief to have the man's eyes distracted.

"I have partners, at least for the moment. This task you proposed requires them."

"Requires them?" She waited for the head to turn. "My colleague and I were under the impression that you alone were capable of completing the task. You alone. We wouldn't have come had we known to the contrary."

"This man here is your partner?"

"He is."

Amerigo snapped his fingers, and one of the hulks came over from the security desk. Totaro nodded to the man and the thug pulled out a Glock and leveled it at Silvio's head. Bianca could see Silvio swallow his gum.

"I'll ask again, but think twice before you answer. The bearer bonds are yours. I verified that, I won't tell you how. I glossed over the discrepancy of the name on the bonds. If they are yours then why do you need him? I'll ask again: Is this man here your associate?"

Bianca hesitated. Totaro nodded his head and the hammer was cocked. She stole a glance over at Silvio. He was pacing his breathing. She saw a small rivulet of sweat run down from his sideburn.

"He's my partner, but in a more Biblical sense."

"He's your lover then?" Totaro's voice cracked. "I don't believe you."

"Believe it then, or have one of your idiots here spend the next few hours scraping his brains off of this nice marble." She swept her foot in front of Totaro. "Looks like Carrara. Flawless squares, no cracks. Nice veins."

"The lady knows her marble."

Gabriel Valjan **351**

"I prefer granite, because marble smells like mold when it ages."

"And this man over here?" he asked.

"I told you."

"I could easily have him killed," Totaro said.

"But I'm fond of him."

"I thought women were practical."

"Allow me one second." Bianca turned to Silvio and stuck her hand into his breast pocket, seized the bearer bond, and then pulled him in for a deep kiss. She could sense Silvio's shock, but she did her best to ease him into reciprocity. Their lives depended on it. She ran her free hand down and squeezed his buttock and was relieved to find him responding. Not bad, but she had to cut him off and pull away.

The thug glanced over at his boss. Totaro nodded and the man eased the hammer.

"We go by car to meet my associates," Totaro announced and, seeing Bianca's surprise, he explained. "Acquaintances become associates, and they become colleagues after trial and error, after years of testing. They never become friends or lovers, because the latter clouds judgment." The statement included a jerk of his head in Silvio's direction.

"Associates, I see," Bianca said. "You asked to see my eyes. That means you haven't met her or seen her."

Totaro grinned as if he was tolerating her now. He whispered into her ear, "Business is like love sometimes. You don't have to see the person to make it work. We go by car."

Totaro walked over and straightened out Silvio's jacket, dusted his shirt off, and handed him a handkerchief to remove her lipstick.

"And if your associates inquire?" she said, holding up the bearer bond.

Totaro stepped towards her after Silvio had returned the handkerchief. He looked at the bond and then at her. "We go by car now."

The car ride was like freefall in darkness. They were blindfolded.

The car engine was soothing, the inside, air-conditioned, the leather smooth and comforting. She assumed that one bodyguard was driving and another was sitting on the back seat next to her by the way the seat sank. Totaro was in the front.

They had been guided into a car. Not for show this time, they held hands in the backseat like lovers, hoping that Dante and Gennaro were following them, undetected and with backup.

The drive involved some highway because there were no turns and gyrations, no sounds of street yelling, honking, smells of cooking, or the heave and go of negotiating an alley, or the tire strumming worn down cobblestones.

That mystery *somewhere*, she estimated, was thirty or forty minutes from Naples. The slowing down of the vehicle, the effortless brakes, the yawning of the car's front doors and an exchange of dialect from another security detail confirmed their arrival. Bianca sat and waited. Silvio waited. They still held hands.

She was craving chocolate.

"Get out," said one of the armed men.

The blindfolds were yanked off, the light stinging their eyes, forcing them to focus and refocus. Another set of muscular arms corralled them, without their having a chance to recognize or place the scene. They were hustled into an anonymous warehouse.

In the center of the concrete floor and in the forefront of rotting wood and rusty pipes was the conference of honored guests. Bianca was losing count of the armed support. This was a mixed crowd of Camorristi, of stalwart Totaro clan lieutenants and capos on one side, the uneasy and slow-trusting Marra converts on the other, and in another area there were other men, separated probably because few could understand them: the Calabrians.

No Sicilians.

The strong grip behind them was pushing her through the crowd of men. She wondered where Totaro went. Unless appearances were deceiving, he could not have scampered from car to warehouse that fast, if only because he'd be slowed receiving homage and oaths of fealty from this show of arms. Massive shoulders pivoted to make way, more shirts and arm-holsters than she had seen at the GdF, parting for her and Silvio. She had one foreign hand behind her, steering the way, and another friendly one at her side, keeping her anchored, Silvio.

In front of them was an effervescent prince, Matteo Mandracchia, exchanging hugs with Amerigo Totaro.

43

Matteo turned all smiles and confidence to face Bianca and Silvio. His suit was elegant; white cuffs edged out from the jacket's sleeves, where she spotted the dark glimmer of cufflinks. Mother had excellent taste dressing her boy for the working world. The only thing missing was the champagne flute in his hand.

"May I see the bearer bond?"

That roguish smile could inspire Harlequin romances. She had to admit his eyes were an intoxicating shade of jade green. Many women might find swagger their aphrodisiac, but she appreciated a nice pair of eyes.

Matteo Mandracchia was deadly because he had looks, charm, and was on the precipice of blatant wealth. What he needed along with his five-thousand-dollar suit was legitimacy.

He gave her that damn smirk again. "As a woman, what do you think?"

"About what?"

His right hand whisked his face. "I'm thinking of adding some scruff. Heard it adds character."

"Few men look good with beards or moustaches."

"You're right." He smiled. "Am I what you expected? I hear that television cameras add weight."

"I wouldn't know, but you do have nice eyes. I noticed those first." She had flicked her eyes up and down the man's frame before she answered to let him know that she had evaluated him.

"I get my eyes from my mother," he said.

Her mind was racing. There was way too much firepower in the room. Too many chances for all of this to go to hell, and there was no sign of the madrina with green eyes or her posse of yellowjackets on motorcycles.

Matteo held the bearer bond up. "This is very nice."

"It's instant cash, but you know that."

"I do, thank you. I assume there are more."

"There might be."

"There are more." He folded the paper, tucked it into his breast pocket, and smiled. "I know there are."

"How can you be certain?"

She noticed that Totaro had kept his distance from the conversation. Matteo moved in close. His cologne said citrus then wood and flint. His lips came closer. She felt the cool intake of his breath on her neck before he spoke, and the warmth as he did. "I know there are more because I've seen this particular bearer bond before. The series, I mean."

"Really," she said, doing her best to sound intrigued.

"A business associate of mine in Rome has had the pleasure of doing business with a certain Mr. and Mrs. Rossi who, he told me, owned a vineyard in the United States. Their logo, a red *R* for 'Rossi' was distinctive. You wouldn't happen to know anything about that?"

And the last piece fell in place. Totaro, Matteo, Farese (by implication), and Bevalacqua were all here. The only question now was, who was betraying whom, and how could she stay out of the crossfire. She said nothing. Bianca smelled the last note of his cologne, cedar; it almost nauseated her. She felt ill.

"That's odd that you don't," he said, and backed away. The air and space felt liberating.

"Why should I?"

"The peculiar thing is that you fit the description of Signora Rossi, but he doesn't fit. Care to explain that?"

Bianca motioned to Amerigo Totaro for him to join the conversation. The man idled over in his good time. "What is it?" he asked her, without giving Matteo much of an acknowledgment.

"I thought you said names are not mentioned."

Amerigo shrugged. "I have to respect that the younger generation cuts its own style."

Matteo addressed Totaro. "I was just telling her that her friend there doesn't seem to match what our other colleague told us."

Silvio coughed. "Excuse me. Is this the same friend in Rome who had his second-in-command murdered?" Silvio did his best to look indignant. "Because it does seem that he doesn't value his associates. And please don't apologize for the man and say that it was all a matter of disloyalty. Your colleague—excuse me, again—your associate, didn't have to have the man dragged across the ocean. He could have given the man the courtesy of dying in his own country."

Matteo's grin was sadistic this time. "It's odd that you say that; but indulge me for a moment. When you do business, you accept a partner's liabilities, without criticizing his methods. You establish ground rules. You and the lady are old business, and I'm extending my respect to a new business partner in accepting and paying his debts."

Silvio blurted, "What the hell is he saying?"

"It means that he plans to kill us to do business with Lorenzo Bevilacqua. We are necessary sacrifices for him to use Amici di Roma's corporate structure before he forms his own full-fledge enterprise. Am I wrong, Matteo?"

"The lady is often right."

"What about the bearer bond?" Silvio asked, confused, eyes uneasy.

Amerigo answered, "We can find the rest of them."

"Too bad you won't get to enjoy it," Bianca said to Amerigo, and gave him the dismissive turn of the head that she perfected in her teens.

"What's that supposed to mean?"

"Shall I explain it to him, Matteo?" she asked, and when he didn't respond, proceeded: "Amici di Roma is an established conglomerate. Lorenzo might be its disgraced CEO, but he built a multinational corporation, lined politician's pockets on both sides of the Atlantic. Matteo here either succeeds Bevilacqua or spins off his own subsidiary, which is what he's doing here in Naples with his cultural organization. He drew you and the System in because he knows that you and the rest are greedy. You, who double-crossed Marra and Aldo Giurlani, should know a thing or two about duplicity."

"Giurlani?" Amerigo yelled. "What is this?"

"Don't pretend in front of him." Bianca said. "You were Giurlani's private rat. You were the one who walked him through the entire Camorra maze. How else did you avoid prosecution?"

Totaro stepped forward to slap her, but Matteo seized the man's arm and said in a calm voice, "One doesn't hit a lady. Let her finish."

"And you shouldn't be so quick to smile, Matteo. This one here," she tilted her head to indicate that she meant Amerigo, "led you to believe that he was invincible, when he was nothing more than a protected informant. All those years, and he's arrested only for assaulting a teacher? His kid probably had deserved it."

Totaro lunged. "You bitch."

But before he reached her Silvio intercepted him and shoved Totaro back into Matteo.

"I've had enough," Matteo said.

"Don't believe me? Ask him." She pointed at Totaro. "He's the mastermind." Matteo glanced over at Totaro, and returned her angry face with a nasty grin, his nice green eyes this time appreciating her from head to toe.

"What?" she asked.

He walked over to her and again leaned over and spoke Sicilianized Italian. "I knew about Giurlani because of you in Milan, after Charlie and Lele were murdered. Bevilacqua simply pointed to the footprints and I followed them. To my surprise those footprints were nothing more than a pair of heels." He kissed her on the cheek as he withdrew.

She slapped him across the face.

"*Bravissima*. I admit I deserved that." He clapped his hands in a slow beat. He reached into his breast pocket and pulled out his cell phone. "Excuse me," he said, glancing down at the phone and pressing a button. "My mistake. I thought I had a message."

Bianca's eyes narrowed. "No, you just sent one."

"I did."

Amerigo, first irate and now confused, sought an answer. His jaw dropped and his head turned to her, and then to Matteo. "You son of a bitch. You called her, didn't you?"

Matteo nodded to one of his henchmen. "Your time has come, old man."

A man walked up fast from behind Amerigo, and as Totaro turned to face him, the gun went off, the bullet entering the front of his face and tearing out the back of his head. Blood splattered all over Bianca's front.

That was when the shooting began.

Before Bianca dove for cover, she saw men in black uniforms descending from the roofs. DDA. The crackling of gunfire surrounded her from all sides as she crawled on the ground amidst the jumping shell casings. A few of them burned her when they touched her skin.

Then, through the floor, she felt vibrations. The motorcycles had arrived.

The firefight escalated. Gunpowder, smoke, chaos enveloped her. She stood up to find refuge, and it was then that she felt the searing pain in her abdomen and felt warm blood run down between her legs. She fell down and felt her body thump against the hard floor.

She heard the distinctive sound of AK-47s. She looked up at the ceiling again and thought of Loki and spiders. There were more black figures, DDA assault team members, moving or dead, suspended on fast ropes from the ceiling. Farese had, in the end, betrayed them all. She thought of Lorenzo. The last thing she remembered was the blur of white, a helmet, a visor turned down, and streaks of yellow.

"Uma," her lips said, moving but not giving voice. Only weakness as sleep overtook her and the bullets gathered as a storm front and decimated those standing, fleeing, or trying to escape the wrath of the Sicilian mother.

44

The white light Bianca saw was not the afterlife. The voice she heard was not God's. It was Dante asking her whether she was awake. The next sound was that of the *bleep-bleep* of a cardiac monitor. She blinked. The banal ceiling tiles said that she was alive and in a hospital.

She felt incredibly weak. Not groggy but exhausted. She rolled her head to the right and saw the nurse checking the machine. She tried to focus. Her eyes closed again. Her next thought was to find Dante's voice.

Her head lolled to the left and she found him, and then behind him, Gennaro, who was wearing a nervous expression on his face. As were Alessandro, Farrugia, who was with Noelle, and next to them, Ferrero, Piersanti, and Tommaso, who was standing near the door. She swallowed. Her mind thought the thought but she was too dry-mouthed to say the word. She asked for Silvio.

Dante brushed her hair away, offering a smile. "Silvio was shot," and upon hearing the cardiac machine beep faster, he said, "Ssh, he'll be okay."

Piersanti approached the bedside. His head peered over Dante's shoulder. "He wasn't shot in the ass."

She tried to smile.

A doctor then came in and ordered everyone out. She tried to lift her hand up but failed. They left. She had wanted Dante to stay. The door clicked.

The doctor's face loomed large over her, a wide smile that spoke with a Roman accent. He introduced himself, asked how she felt, and then asked her questions about when she had had her last period and whether she had been having cravings.

"But . . . but I was shot," she said, building her sentence with slow blocks.

He unclipped his pen for notes. "No, Ms. Nerini. You were not. Thank God. I regret to inform you that you suffered a different trauma altogether. You miscarried. I'm sorry."

She squeezed her eyes tight and opened them, but the words still did not make sense.

"You will be okay. You've lost blood, but you arrived at the hospital in time." Bianca heard what the man was saying now but was still processing what he had said just before. Miscarriage? She tried to recollect the events. It was hazy, but she recalled the searing pain in her abdomen. It had seemed to her, most logically, that she had been shot.

She lifted up her left hand, and saw the IV and the clear tape. She said, "Blood," in English.

The doctor cocked his ear and squinted. He was trying to put two and two together. "Ah, I understand. You were bleeding profusely. That was the miscarriage."

"Oh," she said, and struggled to add, "Thank you," not for saving her life, but for the clinical revelation.

"Don't thank me," he said. "You should thank the woman who brought you to the hospital."

She wanted to say "huh," but it came out as a moan first, and then a throaty, "Who?"

"I don't know, Ms. Nerini. All I know from the documentation is that a woman dropped you off at the Emergency Room. We never got her name. We do have her on her film, but that's all. You are an American, right?"

Saying *Sì* was equal to moving a mountain.

"You can say she was your knight, except she had a motorcycle for a horse. She draped you over it and drove you in and left you there. She saved your life. We don't know much else beyond that, although I can tell you she was wearing all white. I should go. You need to rest."

"Don't," she struggled to say.

"Don't what?"

"Don't tell him," she said in Italian.

The doctor understood. He offered his practiced smile and reminded her that she should rest.

Bianca stared at the ceiling again, heard the man's shoes squeak across the floor. She heard a door open. She could hear the doctor explaining something to Dante and the others.

She stared at the wall opposite her. The sun was shining on it. She imagined warmth but felt cold. Insignificant. The white spot on the wall would grow larger as the day and the world continued on. She was small and nonexistent, like the baby she had lost, the baby she would never hold or share with Dante. She felt ignorant. She had not, for all her intelligence, known about the life inside her. When she had heard the word "miscarriage," it was as if she had failed as a woman.

A nurse glided in front of the bed and went to the IV. She heard the woman say in a soft voice that the doctor had ordered something to help her sleep. Bianca wanted to say no but lacked any will to bring the word out. She watched the nurse inject whatever that something was into the IV port. Bianca stared at the plastic tubing waiting for her punishment.

She thought of a little girl or little boy who would never run up to her with some inexplicable drawing that she would love anyway because it would say "Mommy."

Bianca felt both tears and sleep coming. A scene flashed through her mind, of a child in her lap, of her mumbling, "Itsy Bitsy Spider crawled up the water spout, Down . . ."

But sleep came and extinguished the thought.

45

Drinking was not among the doctor's orders, but one wouldn't do her any harm before she and Dante took off for their weekend getaway. It'd prove she was back in the world of the living. The investigation was over.

Farese was back in the United States. Agents McGarrity and Murphy had preceded him. Against their wishes. Farrugia and Ferrero were sprung without fanfare. Italian news soft-spun the deadly raid as the conclusion of a joint investigation between American and Italian law-enforcement specialists. There were authoritative and triumphant statements from a podium with flags behind it, subtitles, and proud faces. The news focused on the speculation that Matteo Mandracchia was brokering a deal with Amerigo Totaro, and they had been planning a hostile takeover of the Camorra. Authorities had identified Calabrians, Camorristi, and were now advancing their intent on a shockingly good batch of counterfeit euros from Foggia. The analytical and interpretive commentaries had begun in earnest.

Dead DDA team members were remembered with bowed heads. The surviving DDA were lauded in absentia but kept anonymous for their safety. There was no talk about U.S. bonds. No women. No Cosa Nostra. There was no mention of any dead Americans, no word about fugitives. It was the usual news, calming the unknowing masses with its selective facts, solemnity, and amnesia.

Gennaro had picked the place.

The first thing she did was to embrace Silvio. She heard a collective "ahh" behind her.

"About that kiss?" Alessandro said.

Bianca blushed.

"How come all I've ever gotten was a peck on the cheek from her," he said, "but the interpreter gets a full-blown smooch. That's it—I need to go undercover one day."

"It'll never happen, Sandro," Farrugia said.

"Why not? I'd make a good agent. If Claudio here can do it, then I can, although I admit it'd take me months to grow a beard. Ferrero is *un tosto*, a tough-guy journalist from Turin." He caressed his jaw and chin. "Myself, I prefer a smoother and suave style, the clean-shaven look."

"Half the disappointed women in Italy would give you up," Gennaro said.

"Ah, I have a brilliant idea: he could go undercover as a gay man," Claudio interjected, eliciting yet more laughter. Alessandro turned pale and wagged his finger at Claudio.

"I was just joking," Claudio said. "Still, I'm sure you'd make a fine honorary gay man. All it'll take is some work with your wardrobe and some Judy Garland."

"I doubt I could get the clearance from the higher-ups for Monotti to go gay," Piersanti said.

"Very funny, Piersanti. But you know, I'd like to know how Ferrero here managed to speak Calabrese. That was remarkable."

"I'll say." Farrugia lifted his glass to him and they toasted. "How did you do it, my friend?"

"The hard way," he said. "Linguistics major with a minor in comparative philology."

The barkeep had cranked the volume up on the football match between the home team of Napoli in powder-blue shirts and socks against the scarlet-shirted Roma team. This match was supposed to decide another Serie A. The chanting of the Genoese and Napoli ultras was reaching a crescendo.

"You know all this time," Farrugia yelled over the game, "we haven't spoken much English. Let's speak some English again. Someone can translate for Piersanti."

Behind Silvio's head, and facing Bianca, was a collection of vintage flyers thrown from U.S. planes to Italian soldiers that harangued against Italian headquarters and invited them to desert with the motto "Iron Soldiers, Cardboard Generals."

Bianca shouted to Silvio in English, "Are you back to running?"

"Yes." He raised his glass. "And my shoes are much better. They no longer cramp me."

She yelled again. "How's your calf?"

The ultras on the television were chanting, and the volume had become unnerving.

Silvio shook his head. "The Commissioner doesn't like that the vet shaved him," and when he looked at the blank, befuddled faces around him, he asked why they were looking at him and laughing, Bianca explained the reason. With all the noise, he had heard, "How's your cat?"

The television was becoming even more instrusive, so Farrugia suggested that they settle the bill and venture outside.

"Good idea, Isidò," Gennaro said. "I think we should switch back to Italian, for Pio's sake. And Silvio's."

Agreement and laughter.

Gennaro said to Pio, "I heard that you received a promotion."

"What did you expect? It's a nice way of telling me to shut up."

"Same old shit, I guess," Gennaro said with a tired voice. "What about Tommaso?"

"He left for Milan early this morning. He sends everyone his best. As for the outcome, he understands politics."

Alessandro toasted Tommaso. "You know I'll actually miss his presentations."

"Speaking of presentations," Dante said, turning to Claudio. "What about you? You must have something written up by now for *La Stampa* about your time undercover."

"I have, but my editor has the final say about when they'll run it. Pio got his promotion. I'll probably get nominated for some kind of investigative award once everything dies down, if and when they run the exposé. The editor told me that it isn't a good time to run the piece."

Gennaro grumbled. "Same old shit."

"Are you okay with that, Claudio?" Farrugia asked.

"Like Pio here, there's a time to fight and there is a time to know when to sit back and watch."

Piersanti declared his intention to drive back into Naples proper. He resisted their protestation and went around the tables shaking hands and offering Bianca a kiss on the cheek.

"Take care of yourself," Bianca said.

"I will. Thank you."

They watched Piersanti walk away and get into his car. They all waved once more before he reversed his car and pulled away.

"We have nothing but dead bodies from here to Sicily," Gennaro said as he put his hand down.

"Did you expect anything else, Gennaro?" Bianca said.

"Aren't you worried? We stalled Farese with a cat named Commissioner. As for Lorenzo . . . we know where we stand with him, but Farese is a big name in U.S. law enforcement, not a good enemy to have. And I don't know what to say about the madrina. I imagine she'll want revenge for her son's death and for her dead companions."

Bianca put her hand into her purse. She thought she had heard a text. Nothing.

"We'll know better next time with Farese," she said. "Let him run his investigation of the naval base. He'll use that as a pretense while he recovers his bonds in Foggia."

"I'm not so confident," Gennaro said. "And Bevilacqua?"

"He lost Mandracchia. He still has his corporation. What else can he do?"

"Wait for revenge, like the madrina."

"Do you think Farese will find his bonds?" Farrugia asked. "My guess is that she has all of them. I'll bet you she's back in Sicily and counting them."

Bianca smiled. "She can't do anything with them now—they're not real money yet. Farese will wait and wait. He'll show up the minute someone tries to cash them in. That was part of the reason why the bearer bonds were so attractive to her and the mafia. Fast cash and another way around Farese."

"Do you think there'll ever be a way to outdo him?" Gennaro asked.

"Farese?" She shook her head. "You can outsmart the man, but nobody escapes the U.S. government; it has as much patience as the mafia. Green Eyes will tend to her garden here in Italy while she and Farese keep a respectable distance from each other. Business is business."

"Don't underestimate Sicilian women," Alessandro said.

"On that note," Farrugia said, "I shall excuse myself. I owe Noelle my undivided time."

Alessandro laughed. "That's a euphemism if I ever heard one. I should be going, too."

"Very funny," Farrugia said. Then to Bianca, "I hope you and Dante enjoy a nice weekend. The drive up the Amalfi Coast is gorgeous."

As Farrugia pecked Bianca's cheek she asked, "What about the yoga center? In Campania?"

"Are you kidding? She's looking in Toscana. She said wealthy Americans go to the cooking schools there. Sounds ideal."

"Excellent. Wish her well for us."

They watched Farrugia fish his keys out while walking to his car. Claudio said he should go, too. After finishing his drink, Alessandro excused himself, saying he had a date that evening.

"What? Is that safe, Monotti?"

"There's no investigation. I'm allowed, aren't I?"

Gennaro then dismissed him and said to Silvio, "I guess that leaves us, Silvio. How about you introduce me to The Commissioner?"

"Sure, Chief."

"Could I have Silvio for a moment?" Bianca asked.

Gennaro nodded and went ahead. She threaded her arm through Silvio's elbow. "Thank you for everything, Silvio."

"You're welcome, Ms. Nerini."

"Please, it's Bianca. You don't have to prove yourself to anyone. You'll always be on my team, no matter where I'm working a case."

"Even if it is in Boston?"

"Even in Boston." She kissed him on the cheek. He then went on and joined Gennaro.

Costiera Amalfitana. The Amalfi Coast is a serpentine stretch of southern Italy with limestone cliffs for a wall, sandy and pebbled beaches for a yard facing the Mediterranean, and two types of trees, olives and lemons, that anchored the hills around the Saracen towers peering down from above. The area once rivaled Genoa and Venice, minting coins, producing bambagina paper, and ruling the sea. Hercules came here, as did Poseidon, and then the Lucan tribe, the Romans, the Turks. Then a freak tidal wave in 1343 destroyed everything, leaving the once great maritime power a tourist trap known for limoncello and alici, a sweet liqueur, and anchovies.

"Take the road slowly, Dante."

"Don't tell me how to drive."

"I'm not telling you how to drive, but this is the one time I have to say Italian engineers were insane."

She was referring to the nineteenth-century engineers who had been cantilever crazy. The road swerved and curved ahead of them. Monaco has the hairpin curve on the Route de La Tourbie, the UK has the A44, while Italy has not one, but two deathtrap roads: the Stelvio Pass Road in the north and this one in the south.

"Did you fold down the side-view mirrors?" she asked him.

"Yes, Ma'am." He anticipated her withering glare. "Just kidding."

The traffic had come to a standstill. Dante had commented on the geraniums everywhere. He babbled about wanting to do a short trip to see the Temple of Neptune in Paestum. She heard expletives and car horns.

"We should talk, Dante."

"I don't want to talk about the case anymore. This is our vacation."

"I know. God, it's hot." Bianca took a deep breath. "There's something that I've wanted to talk about since the hospital. Is the air-conditioner on?"

"Of course it is." He redirected the vents to blow on her. She knew he wouldn't dare crack wise about hot flashes. She turned down her visor and looked into the small square and her breath stopped.

A motorcyclist. Right behind them.

"I think you received a text, Bianca."

She hadn't even heard it. She clawed through her bag and searched for the cell. She found it and opened the cover. "You were right. It's a text," she said as she peered down at the screen.

"Who the hell can be texting you?"

She read the text. "Haven't heard from u? Solve last 2?"

She thumbed her response, "N," although she had solved one of them. She heard Dante ask, "Who is it?"

"Loki. Let's see what kind of response I get after I send this." She pressed the button.

"I shouldn't have asked," Dante said.

The cell buzzed twice more. She ignored them. The traffic wasn't moving and she peeked again in the mirror. She saw the darkened visor.

Dante pointed at the cell. "Aren't you going to tell me what the gremlin said?"

She recited from memory. "MF equals Amici."

Dante gripped the wheel and tried to glance around the car in front of him to determine the cause of the holdup. "That's easy, Farese is with Amici di Roma, in bed with Lorenzo."

"Wait. Why the hell hadn't I thought of that?" Bianca said.

"What?"

"It's an anagram. Amici is not Amici."

Dante ran his fingers through his hair. "You're talking in riddles like Loki."

"Don't you get it, Dante? Amici di Roma is Bevilacqua but Michael Farese is not Amici di Roma." He stared at her as she turned in her seat to face him. "Amici is an anagram."

"What is an anagram of Amici?"

"I'm CIA."

"Farese is CIA? You just said that the text had asked whether you solved two of them. What was the second anagram?"

"TB equals Kilo, but I had figured that one out."

The caravan of cars started moving. Some idiot fruit vendor had dared to cross the dangerous road and lost some of his produce. It seemed that he had now collected his goods.

He eased the car forward. There was more cursing, more horns blaring, and one loud aggressive growl from behind.

"What the hell is that?" Dante turned to glance over his shoulder. It was more immediate, reflexive than examining his rear-view mirror.

"Oh my God, next to you. Outside your window, Dante."

"What?" Dante turned to his other side to look outside his window. He saw what was terrifying her.

A woman on a motorcycle was outside his door. She had pulled up alongside him, looked at him, but he could see nothing through the black visor. She gunned her throttle and then cut him off and took the road.

A horn behind him honked. It was time to move.

"Are you okay?" He put his hand out while he drove. She grabbed it and squeezed it. "She's gone," she heard him say, but her heart was pounding. She had thought of how Charlie Brooks was killed, how Mino Pecorelli was shot in his car. She heard Dante's reassuring voice. "You said you wanted to talk. We have time, but tell me what 'TB equals Kilo' means."

There was a slight pause before she spoke. "Tommaso is Loki. Or at least one of them."

A Note to the Reader

The Financial Crises of 2007 and 2008 inspired *Turning to Stone*, along with my reading of Roberto Saviano's *Gomorrah*. In his book, he would reveal the extensive corruption, horrific violence, and the all-out entrepreneurial spirit of the Neapolitan Camorra. The *System* is an equal-opportunity confederation of clans, who will work with any group that can turn a profit for them, whether it is through drugs, firearms, fashion, or garbage removal.

Gomorra spares the reader no details about the drug trade, the thugs, and the feuds. Roberto Saviano softened nothing. He named names and places, dates and times. Matteo Garrone, who made Saviano's 2006 book into a film, *Gomorra*, in 2008, used authentic locations and known *Camorristi* in the film. Saviano now lives in exile, a price on his head.

What I found particularly disturbing about the *Camorristi* is that the clan leaders were as reclusive as Howard Hughes, opting for fortified underground bunkers. Saviano describes midnight truck caravans and the burning of trash in open fields. This long-term practice may explain why Campania, a region in southern Italy to which Naples belongs, has astronomical cancer rates. The World Health Organization has gathered considerable epidemiological evidence on the Triangle of Death.

For creative reasons, I took liberty with some details of Saviano's reports from the field. He devotes considerable space to the leadership role of women within the Camorra; they are just as ruthless and as violent as their male counterparts. Here, on this point, I switched criminal organizations, swapping out a female *Camorrista* for a Sicilian *madrina* because Cosa Nostra is traditionally a patriarchal organization; but this seems to be changing now with the recent arrest of Patrizia Messina Denaro, sister of Matteo Messina Denaro, considered the *capo dei capi* of Cosa Nostra. I kept faithful to Saviano's account of marauding female assassins on motorcycles, the Umas, but make them accountable to the Sicilian with green eyes.

One last note on creative license: I exaggerated the Camorra's twisted sense of morality. In *Turning to Stone*, I mention that the Camorra kills HIV-positive individuals. Saviano suggests that the System is into the medical-waste management business and it is highly likely that they do have access to medical records, but they do not kill HIV or AIDS patients. I made that leap, not Saviano. I did it to emphasize their brutality.

Corporate Citizen
By Gabriel Valjan
Roma Series Book Five

"Is this Mr. DiBello?" said a woman's voice.

"It is," Gennaro answered.

Bianca raised her eyes at hearing him speaking in English. She had just come into the room with their afternoon drinks. She was even more concerned that the call had come to Gennaro's cell phone and not the house phone. They were apartment sitting for their friend Claudio Ferrero, *La Stampa's* top investigative journalist, who was on assignment. This call also threatened their afternoon ritual of talks out on the balcony where they enjoyed the sights below San Salvario, the neighborhood near Turin's city center. Gennaro was motioning for her to come over and eavesdrop.

"What can I do for you?" he asked the caller.

"Not for me, Mr. DiBello. I'm calling on behalf of your friend, Diego Clemente. He had asked me to dial your number for him. It's not easy dialing Italy from a hospital phone."

"Hospital?" Gennaro said, alarmed. His eyes flashed his concern to Bianca.

"I'm a nurse at MGH and he's my patient. MGH is Mass General—"

Gennaro stammered, "Hospital in Boston. I know that. *Scusi*—I mean I'm sorry for interrupting you, but is Diego all right?"

"He took a fall at home and broke his hip. You speak English well, Mr. DiBello. I didn't know what to expect when he had me dial the number for him. Anyway," the woman seemed to sigh as she continued speaking, "slip rugs are dangerous, you know. He can tell you the rest himself. I'll hand over the phone to him so you two can talk. There isn't much time."

"Thank you. Much time?" Gennaro asked, confused. "I don't understand."

"He's due for surgery and I've started his IV. I'd say you have about ten minutes before he starts getting happy."

"Diego happy?" Gennaro said, not understanding. "Please give him the phone and thank you, Nurse."

"You're welcome." Gennaro heard the phone shuffle and heavy breathing. The connection was quite good.

Gennaro and Bianca heard the departing nurse pull the curtain. "Diego?"

"Hold on, Gennaro. I want privacy."

"I'll wait. You broke your hip?"

Another moment passed, and more ruffling sounds. Gennaro and Bianca huddled closer around the phone as Clemente spoke, "Slip rug, my ass. That's some hell of a story, from Mason Street to MGH and now hip-replacement surgery. Jesus Christ, I can feel the drug working its way up my arm already."

"You're making no sense, Diego."

"Gennaro, please listen to me, since I don't know how fast Nurse Ratched's cocktail will work."

"Less than ten minutes. I'm listening."

"Thanks, Gennaro. My head feels light. Damn."

"Wait—where's your wife? You shouldn't be alone in a hospital."

"My wife passed away. Look, Virgil showed me the apartment, the dead girl, and it's a real mess, a real setup, and my life is going to hell. To hell, you understand, Gennaro, in a boat, hole in the bottom, and toothpicks for oars." The voice was distinctly Diego, irritated in hyper mode.

"Slow down, Diego. You're making no sense. I'm sorry about your wife. Why the hell didn't you tell me?"

A deep, relaxed sigh. "I didn't want to trouble you. What could you have done? Send me a Mass card, or some self-help book on how to deal with grief? You know. You've been through it yourself."

Gennaro'e eyes turned downward. He remembered Lucia. "But still, Diego. I'm your friend. Friends do something."

"Help me then."

"First, I need to understand what you're telling me. Who is Virgil?"

"I wish I knew, Gennaro. I wish I knew. I think Virgil is one of Farese's people."

"Farese?" The name, as it came out of Gennaro's mouth, made Bianca's eyes widen.

U.S. Attorney Michael Farese was a chameleon of a character, changing colors when he worked for the Department of Justice, when he handled diplomatic requests for the State Department and when he worked for the CIA, as they thought he might after their last run-in with him during their investigation of the Camorra in Naples.

"Diego? Concentrate. Why do you think Farese?"

"That doesn't matter. She's dead and he's dead."

"Who? Who is she? Who is he?" Gennaro asked. His voice almost cracked.

"Norma Jean. She had such nice lingerie, too, and that son of a bitch was in such a nice bed." Clemente's voice was almost singing as he was speaking. The wonders of pharmacology.

Gennaro rubbed his eyebrows. He was frustrated. "Diego, stay with me. Who is Norma Jean? Who was in the bed?"

"Marilyn Monroe was a sad girl." Diego giggled.

"He's giggling," Gennaro said to Bianca.

"Oh, it's a party line!" Diego almost shouted. "Who else is there?"

"Bianca," Gennaro announced. "She is staying with me."

"You naughty boy," Diego said. "Put her on, please."

"Here." Gennaro handed his cell phone to Bianca. "Talk some sense into him. I think the medication has gotten into his brain."

Bianca seized the phone. "Clemente, this is Bianca," she said, hoping that using the man's last name would snap some momentary sense into his head. "Forget about Marilyn Monroe. Who is dead?"

"Marilyn, of course. Somebody murdered her," Diego answered.

"That's right, but who is 'the son of a bitch in such a nice bed'?"

"James Guild, former special agent, FBI, scourge of my loins."

Bianca put her hand over the receiver and repeated, "Guild is dead."

"Shit. What happened?" said Gennaro into the receiver.

"Hell if I know. Virgil gave me the tour of hell. I got nice slippers, though. He had a needle in his arm."

"Virgil? Who had a needle in his arm?" Bianca asked.

Clemente became belligerent. "I just told you that son of a bitch Guild had a needle in his arm. He was in that expensive bed. I saw it. No gun, too. Norma was out in the living room. He was in her bedroom. Nice bed, and what a nice view, and did I tell you what a beautiful kitchen she had?"

Gennaro asked, "I couldn't hear that last part. What did he say?"

"Never mind," she said. "He's getting delirious."

"I'm not delirious," Clemente yelled. "I'm serious! Oh, that rhymes."

"Calm down, Clemente. We know you are serious," Bianca answered.

"I saw it. I saw the computer. My life, your life . . . it all goes to hell."

Bianca, trying a soothing voice, said, "You saw the computer. What did you see, Clemente?"

"Black, black background," Diego's voice was now sputtering.

"That's good, Diego. Back to black," Bianca said.

"You can rhyme, too," he said with glee.

In a coaxing tone and hoping for more, Bianca asked, "What else did you see?"

"Big, big." More sputtering. Bianca closed her eyes.

"Big red *R*!" Diego said triumphantly. Bianca's eyes opened.

Clemente's voice lowered, "Big bad *R*."

Bianca and Gennaro understood what they had heard: black background and red *R*.

She said softly, "Fuck me."

"Lingerie?" Clemente asked. Bianca handed the phone back to Gennaro. She put her hands to her eyes and walked away. She thought of Boston, the Sargent case, Nasonia Pharmaceutical, and the body count.

"Diego, this is Gennaro again. We're coming to Boston."

"That would be nice. Somebody should feed the floor people. I feel sleepy now," Diego said, mewing.

Gennaro stared at his phone. "Get some sleep, Diego. We'll be there as soon as we can." Gennaro heard more purring and then the cacophonous drop of the receiver on the floor on the other end. He ended the call on his cell phone.

"Did he say anything else?" Bianca asked.

"He said someone should feed floor people. I think he has cats."

"How do you know he has cats?" she asked.

"Blame it on hanging around Silvio." Bianca didn't question the logic. Silvio was a translator, Farese's interpreter, their friend, member of the team, and lately, animal whisperer.

"We should go to Boston," Gennaro said.

"He saw the red *R*."

"I know. You should call Dante."

"Do I really have to?" she asked.

"Yes, and you have to tell him."

"Which part? Clemente and Guild, or that Clemente saw the red *R*."

"Doesn't matter. Tell him everything," Gennaro said. "It adds up to the same."

Red *R* meant Rendition.

Acknowledgments

My recurring gratitude and appreciation to:

Dean Hunt, who endured and edited the writing through several versions.

Editor Dave King, for his encouragement and love of Silvio.

Claudio Ferrara, my cultural editor, for his amazing knowledge of history and linguistics.

Sherry Foley, whose eyes on this manuscript saved me from myself again.

Deb Well, another critical pair of eyes and ears on continuity and proofing.

James Logan and Jessica Kristie at Winter Goose Publishing, who continue to believe in Bianca.

Rachel Anderson, publicist extraordinaire.

About *The Roma Series*

Book 1: *Roma, Underground*

Savvy forensic accountant Alabaster Black is hiding in Rome from her former employer, covert U.S. organization *Rendition*. While there under an assumed name she meets Dante, an investigator, erstwhile explorer, and member of the Roma Underground, a band of amateur archaeologists who map the city beneath Rome. With Italian artifacts disappearing at an alarming rate, Alabaster and Dante search for answers and create a trap for the thieves. Through a mysterious online contact Alabaster learns she is being followed, and with her safety at risk she is forced to rethink her chosen alliances and discover hidden truths about herself.

"A provocative thriller with a riveting and surprising plot."
—M.J. Rose, International bestseller

". . . the strong, captivating heroine and an allure of conspiracy and organized crime make this novel an undoubted success."
—*Kirkus Book Reviews*

Book 2: *Wasp's Nest*

In the highly anticipated sequel to *Roma, Underground*, Bianca returns to the U.S. for her former employer, the covert organization Rendition, to investigate Cyril Sargent and Nasonia Pharmaceutical. Although ambivalent about the assignment and uneasy about her online "friend," Loki, she is enticed into researching what Sargent is doing with insect genetics that might upset the world of cancer research and treatment. Old friends Farrugia and Gennaro uncover a twisted conspiracy from their past and join Bianca in Boston where they will experience conflicted loyalties, question allies, and confront uncertain enemies as they're drawn into the wasp's nest.

". . . the mood and pace remain consistent throughout this thrilling page-turner. Black is back and just as entertaining as ever."
—*Kirkus Book Reviews*

Book 3: *Threading the Needle*

Bianca's curiosity gets a young university student murdered, but not before he gives her a file that details a secret weapon under development with defense contractor Adastra. Guilt may drive her to find justice for the slain Charlie Brooks, but she is warned by the mysterious Loki to stay away from this case that runs deep with conspiracy. Bianca must find a way to uncover government secrets and corporate alliances without returning Italy to one of its darkest hours, the decades of daily terrorism known as the "Years of Lead."

"Valjan's characters, from Bianca to investigator Isidore Farrugia to the irascible Gennaro, are memorable and worth following, in this book and the others in the series; the international terrorism and tech investigating ring true, and the European tensions—which I double-checked for reference—are intriguing and of ongoing concern . . . Characters, plot, ideas, background: In *Threading the Needle*, Valjan weaves it all into an international crime novel worth the read."
—Kingdom Books

Book 4: *Turning to Stone*

Alabaster Black returns as an investigation into a public official's death squares Bianca and her friends against a backdrop of financial speculation, organized crime, and female assassins on motorcycles. Her tenuous collaboration with the mysterious online contact Loki takes on a new twist with the appearance of a brilliant young obsessive-compulsive man who joins her team. As new mysteries unfold, old enemies and Rendition reappear on the scene, and Bianca's group quickly discovers that Naples might just be the most dangerous city in Italy.

Book 5: *Corporate Citizen*

Bianca is back in Boston to help an old friend. She doesn't care about the dead hooker, about the drug overdose, or the other body at the scene. She does care that her former employer is implicated. Her enemy Lorenzo Bevilacqua has made startling revelations about U.S. Attorney Farese, and Loki. Confused, shocked, and with little time to think, Bianca must save lives: her own, her friends, and that of a new ally, a troubled military veteran, who may just have the key to Rendition's true purpose, and Loki's real identity.

About the Author

Ronan Bennett short-listed Gabriel Valjan for the 2010 Fish Short Story Prize for his Boston noir, *Back in the Day*. Gabriel's short stories and some of his poetry continue to appear in literary journals and online magazines. He won first prize in *ZOUCH* Magazine's inaugural Lit Bit Contest. He lives in New England but has traveled extensively, receiving his undergraduate education in California and completing graduate school in England.

CPSIA information can be obtained
at www.ICGtesting.com
Printed in the USA
FFOW02n0530100315
11591FF